son Roberts is a New Zealander, currently lucky ough to be living in the South of France. She is also cky enough to write for the Mills & Boon Medical omance line. A primary school teacher in a former life, e is now a qualified paramedic. She loves to travel d dance, drink champagne, and spend time with her ughter and her friends.

n in the UK, **Becky Wicks** has suffered interminable derlust from an early age. She's lived and worked ver the world, from London to Dubai, Sydney, Bali, C and Amsterdam. She's written for the likes of *GQ*, *llo!*, *Fabulous* and *Time Out*, a host of YA romance, s three travel memoirs—*Burqalicious*, *Balilicious* d *Latinalicious* (HarperCollins, Australia). Now she ends travel with romance for Mills & Boon and loves ery minute! Tweet her @bex_wicks and subscribe at eckywicks.com.

STOLEN NIGHTS WITH THE SINGLE DAD

ALISON ROBERTS

FLING WITH THE CHILDREN'S HEART DOCTOR

BECKY WICKS

MILLS & BOON

Published in Great Britain 2021
by Mills & Boon, an imprint of HarperCollins*Publishers* Ltd,
1 London Bridge Street, London, SE1 9GF

www.harpercollins.co.uk

HarperCollins*Publishers*
1st Floor, Watermarque Building,
Ringsend Road, Dublin 4, Ireland

Stolen Nights with the Single Dad © 2021 by Alison Roberts

Fling with the Children's Heart Doctor © 2021 by Becky Wicks

ISBN: 978-0-263-29767-6

06/21

MIX
Paper from
responsible sources
FSC™ C007454

This book is produced from independently certified FSC™ paper
to ensure responsible forest management.
For more information visit www.harpercollins.co.uk/green.

Printed and bound in Spain
by CPI, Barcelona

STOLEN NIGHTS WITH THE SINGLE DAD

ALISON ROBERTS

MILLS & BOON

CHAPTER ONE

'ALL SET FOR TOMORROW, Mitch?'

'Almost.' Dr Andrew Mitchell looked up from where he was filing a laboratory report into a set of patient notes. 'How 'bout you, Euan? I'm sorry it's such short notice to cover my list as well as yours. I wasn't really expecting them to still have a place available on this course when I rang yesterday.'

Euan McKendry added a shrug to his smile as he stepped further into this consulting room in Allensbury's medical centre. 'It's not a problem. You're covering for me through the Christmas holidays—like you always do.' His smile widened. 'This is the first chance I've had to repay that cover.' He was beside Mitch's desk now. Close enough to pick up the glossy pamphlet that had been anchored by a plastic model of a human heart.

'Don't lose that. I need it to find where I'm going tomorrow morning or I might get horribly lost.'

'At least it's on the south side of London. You must know the area around Croydon pretty well, given thatit's not too far from where you used to work.'

'I haven't had that much to do with the ambulance service there, though, and that's where the course is being held.'

Mitch closed the patient notes and put them to one side, going back to his computer screen to make sure the digital copy had also been filed. A bit like this picturesque village in Surrey, Allensbury Surgery and Dispensary's filing system was a mix of modern with the trusted, traditional way of doing things. And he was fine with that. It was one of the things that had drawn him back to his childhood home, after all.

'FRAME.' Euan was reading the pamphlet. 'Catchy name.'

'First Responder at Medical Emergencies.'

'I've heard about it. I thought it was a course to train people like nurses in remote areas so that they had the skills to bridge the gap until air rescue or ambulance services could get there.'

'It is.' Mitch nodded. 'There's a five-day course for that. But they also run a two-day initiation course specifically for GPs so that we can keep up to date with skills we might not get to use that often. Like, you know, intubation or cricothyroidotomy.'

'Should be the rest of us here doing that. It's only a few years since you were running one of London's busiest emergency departments, Mitch. If anyone's up to date with critical interventions, it's you. You could be running these sessions yourself.' He was clearly peering at the bullet points covering the course material. 'Acute pulmonary oedema, anaphylaxis, management of arrhythmias. A difficult airway…'

A difficult airway.

A succinct description often used by doctors or paramedics to label anatomy or circumstances that made it challenging and sadly sometimes impossible, to ensure that someone could continue breathing if they needed a critical intervention like intubation and ventilation. A situation that was up there with the most dramatic kind of life or death crises any medic had to face.

'Hmm...' The sound was a noncommittal grunt as Mitch clicked out of various windows to close down his computer.

He knew where his colleague was tempted to take this conversation and he needed to shut it down fast. Because, even now, more than a year since it had happened, those three words could make his breath catch in his throat and he'd have to brace himself for the flashback that could replay itself in his mind in the space of a heartbeat. A montage of emotions more than actual images, the trigger almost always a faint echo of that trickle of despair down his spine when he'd known he was fighting a battle that he wasn't going to win.

That his skills hadn't been enough to save a young mother's life...

They were three words that would also make an eye-catching title for something other than a critical care workshop—a case history report in an emergency medicine journal, perhaps. The kind of article that someone like Andrew Mitchell might well have picked up and read, years ago, as he grabbed a sandwich or a cup of coffee during a break in a relentlessly busy shift as head of an emergency department in a huge, London hospital.

He could write it himself now. He probably should, in fact, as a warning for doctors who might think that working in a big city emergency department could prepare them for coping with anything, even if they'd chosen to take a completely different direction in life to live and work in a small village less than an hour's drive from the outskirts of London.He *would* write it one of these days. Just…not yet.

Everybody had told him that nobody could have won that particular battle. The post-mortem had confirmed it but that reassurance hadn't stopped the flashbacks. Or those 'what ifs…'? that always bubbled to the surface whenever the incident was mentioned. At least he was quick enough to deflect them this time and he even stood up to signal the new direction he was taking.

'You've got a good point, though,' he told Euan briskly. 'If it's as useful as I think it might be, we'll arrange for everybody else to do the course.' This thriving small town medical centre had four doctors on staff and could easily employ another one soon. Their senior practice nurse, Meg, would probably love the challenge of attending a full course herself.

'What makes you so confident it'll be that useful?' Euan raised an eyebrow. 'What can a paramedic teach someone who was an emergency medicine consultant?'

'The woman running this course is an APP—a critical care, advanced paramedic practitioner. You know, the ones that crew those single-responder vehicles or motorbikes and get to the scene before anyone else?'

Euan nodded. 'Yeah… I guess they get more experience with serious situations than any of us see in sleepy little Allensbury.'

'Not only that…the whole initiative is the brainchild of the instructor who's running this particular course and when I rang to book in, I was told that I was super lucky because Jenna Armstrong is the best. She's the senior instructor for FRAME nationwide. She trains the trainers.'

'Sounds formidable.' Euan was grinning. 'What's the bet she's in her fifties, single and built like a battleship?'

Mitch laughed. 'I couldn't care less as long as she's good at her job.' He reached to take the pamphlet out of Euan's hands. 'I've got to get going. I promised Ollie we'd have hamburgers and chips for dinner tonight at the Riverside pub and then we both need an early night. I'll have to be on the road by seven a.m. at the latest for the next couple of mornings.'

'You could always stay in town for a night or two. Your dad's there for Ollie, isn't he? Like he is when you're on call at night?'

'Of course.' But it was Mitch's turn to shrug as he slipped the pamphlet into his laptop bag. 'But I don't want to change his routine any more than I have to. Having his grandpa look after him for a few hours here and there is a lot different to having his dad vanish for two days. He's just started school and that's enough change for a four-year-old to cope with for the next few weeks at least.'

Euan blew out a breath. 'They complicate life, don't they? Kids?'

'It's worth it.' Mitch could feel a smile tugging at the corners of his mouth. He could feel a squeeze around his heart at the same time that was sending a warmth into every cell in his body. 'You'll find out one of these days.'

'Not me.' Euan was shaking his head as he followed Mitch out of the room. 'No, thank *you*.'

How could someone be *that* sure about something as huge as turning your back on ever having a family of your own?

Mitch had to swallow a rather large lump in his throat as he looked down at the spiky black hair of the small boy who'd fallen asleep, cuddled up to him, as he listened to the story he'd been reading. It felt as though his heart could actually burst with the amount of love he had for this child and that made his movements even more gentle as he slipped his arm free from beneath Ollie, tucked the duvet securely around his son and stooped to press a kiss onto that soft hair, gently enough not to wake him, inhaling that familiar and delicious smell of baby shampoo that never seemed to fade completely between washes.

Avoiding the creaky board in front of the chest of drawers was so automatic he didn't even notice he was doing it but then everything about this small room tucked into a corner of the upper level of this rambling, old house was as familiar as the back of his own hand. Mitch had been sleeping in this room when he'd been Ollie's age. He'd never lived anywhere else, in fact, until he'd headed off to university and then medical school.

He paused by the windows to draw the curtains enough to close the gap in the middle and keep out any draughts and caught a glimpse of the garden below. His father was outside, patiently waiting for Jet, their sixteen-year-old black Labrador, to finish a slow perimeter patrol of the property and people he needed to protect.

Mitch knew as well as Jet exactly what was out there, beyond the garden gate. A narrow street filled with solid, red brick houses like this one, with its tall chimneys and the hidden garden out the back. Some of them were whitewashed and half-timbered like the old dwelling that had been converted into the medical centre and some still had thatched roofs. Allensbury was

one of the Surrey villages that always made the list of
'must see' attractions not too far from London with its
pretty streets, welcoming pubs, stone churches, a village square with a weekend market and the quiet river
with its tree-lined banks. The surrounding forest was a
little wilder but just as familiar to Mitch as this house
and his childhood bedroom had been.

That familiarity that felt like safety—like *home*—
had been the reason he'd turned his life upside down
and come back here.

No…that wasn't true, was it? His world had already
been well and truly turned upside down before he'd had
to admit defeat and give up on the lifestyle and career
that had been a dream come true. If he had known what
was coming—the brutal rollercoaster of just a few, short
days in which his son had been born but he'd lost his
wife—would he have chosen to go down that path? Or
would he have been just as emphatic as Euan in vowing
that it wasn't for him?

Maybe he would have been. Who, in their right mind,
would ever put their hand up to experience that kind
of pain? That lump was back in his throat as he took
one more glance at Ollie's face, bathed in the soft glow
from his dinosaur nightlight, dark lashes fluttering on
pale cheeks as his dreams captured him.

It was just as well Mitch had never been given that
choice, then, because he would never have known just
how much it was possible to love a small human. How,
from that first moment of holding his tiny son in his
arms, he'd discovered a new form of love that could actually change how you viewed the entire world, including the new appreciation for the love of his own parent.
Sadly, he'd lost his mum years before but his dad, Mi-

chael—along with his childhood home and even Jet the dog—had been the anchor he'd badly needed in a world that had suddenly gone so very, very wrong.

His small family had been his absolute priority in those darkest of days. The only thing that had really mattered.

It still was.

She'd noticed him the instant she'd walked into the classroom.

It wasn't simply that he was an extremely good-looking man. Jenna Armstrong had been immune to surface attraction like that for too many years to count now. No...there was something else about him. Something she couldn't quite define. Maybe it was the way he was sitting, with those long limbs relaxed enough to suggest it would be difficult to find an environment that would intimidate him but with an aura of energy that contradicted any laid-back impression. This was a man who looked as if he could take command of any situation in the space of a finger-click.

'Welcome, everybody,' she said, putting the box of handouts she'd just finished printing onto a desk in the corner of the room. 'I'm Jenna and we've got a busy couple of days ahead of us as I take you through our FRAME initiation course for doctors.'

She moved to close a window as the sound of a siren being activated just beneath them startled everybody enough to turn their heads. Everybody except the man at the back, she noticed.

'Sorry about that. This is a busy ambulance station so we'll get a bit of that kind of disruption but the resources we have here make this an ideal training space.'

She smiled at the group. 'It might also remind us of why we're here. I know that you're all doctors with your own busy practices so I want to thank you for taking the time to join this programme and become a valuable extension to emergency ambulance services. You'll leave here with a specialised kit including the latest technology we have available, for example, a video laryngoscope that can make the difference in a difficult intubation but, more importantly, you'll leave with the skills you need to use it and any rust brushed off other skills you might not use on a regular basis.'

She had the attention of every one of the dozen or so people in this room but Jenna could feel a particular intensity coming from that man at the back. It was an effort not to let her gaze get immediately drawn back to him but, for some reason, that intensity was oddly disturbing.

'Bit of housekeeping before we start,' she continued. 'Toilets are out the door to the left and you'll find the fire escape there as well. Food and drinks will be supplied for breaks and lunch and, please, if you go outside, stay within the red lines by the buildings. As you can tell by how early the sirens go on, some of our crews are very keen to get to a Code Blue priority call and it wouldn't be a good look if anyone on a FRAME course got squashed by an ambulance. Now…let's do a quick round robin, to get started. We'll introduce ourselves, say where we're from and maybe why we're here?'

Her smile widened. 'I'll start. I'm Jenna Armstrong, a critical care paramedic. I live not far from this station in south London and I'm here because I'm passionate about this course. I started developing it quite a few years ago and I've been all over the country getting it up and running. It's been going long enough now for statistics to confirm that it's one of the most effective strategies we've put in place to save lives in more remote areas. It's something I'm very proud of. And it's something that I can promise has the potential to make an important difference to you—and to the communities that you care for.'

There was a moment's silence when she finished speaking. Had she sounded a bit over the top? Too passionate? But it was hard not to, when this had been the total focus of her life for so long.

The only thing that had really mattered for so long.

It didn't take long to get around the group. Jenna ticked names off her list as they introduced themselves. Melanie, Ravi and Judith had come from as far away as rural areas near Basingstoke and Brighton. There were older doctors, like Peter and Jack, who felt they were getting rusty on emergency procedures and young GPs, like Susie and Indira, who were nervous about being so far away from major hospitals and advanced ambulance services. It wasn't deliberate, but the man at the back was the last person to introduce himself.

'I'm Mitch,' he said, quietly. 'I'm one of four GPs in the only medical centre in Allensbury, which is a small town in Surrey.'

Jenna was frowning at the sheet of paper in front of her. Mitch? The only person who wasn't ticked off was an Andrew. Then she noticed his surname and almost smiled because it fitted him so well to go by a shortened version of Mitchell.

Because it was just that bit different?

'I'm here because I think we get so caught up in the ordinary busyness of general practice that we can miss opportunities to keep up to date,' Mitch said. 'And…you never know—that one skill we got rusty in might be the one skill we absolutely need to save someone's life.'

His voice was deep enough to be a bit like his body language and how he looked. Unusually attractive. Calm and confident but…somehow contradictory? Was it Jenna's imagination or was there something he wasn't saying, here?

It had only been polite to look up from the paper that listed the expected attendees for the course and meet this man's gaze as he continued speaking but it was suddenly difficult to break that eye contact.

Because she felt like she recognised what was different about him.

He was searching for something.

Something of personal significance.

And…disturbingly enough to send a tiny chill down Jenna's spine, it felt like she might have been singled out as the only person who could help him find what it was he was searching for.

CHAPTER TWO

JENNA ARMSTRONG WASN'T someone that would stand out in a crowd.

She wasn't tall—Mitch guessed a few inches over five feet, which would mean the top of her head wouldn't even reach his shoulder. She was also slim and fine-featured, which probably made her look a lot younger than she actually was. Or maybe that was partly due to the very short hairstyle, which made him think of a curly version of Ollie's soft spikes that had a mind of their own when it came to being tamed.

Any ability to vanish into a crowd physically, however, was more than compensated for by an astonishing…what was it, exactly? Her *presence*? There was a confidence about her. He might have put that down to the crisp uniform she was wearing but, in fact, you could actually feel the passion that she had, not only for her work as a highly skilled paramedic but for sharing her knowledge and skills by teaching. She was a natural teacher, too. She had this entire class in the palm of her hand within minutes of completing the introductory hoops of learning each other's names and the overview of the course they were enrolled in.

There was a sense of drama as Jenna rolled down

the blinds on the windows and dimmed the lights in the room to show a short video on a large screen. A dramatic footage that had to be a clip from a movie. An historical setting, judging by the clothing worn, so it had little relevance to contemporary life but it still made Mitch's blood run cold. Because it had someone riding a horse. Flying through an idyllic countryside, galloping over flower-studded fields and jumping rustic wooden gates and… he knew what was coming.

He was braced for the moment the music changed to become far more sinister and the filming went into slow motion as the horse caught its leg on a fallen log and both horse and rider somersaulted through the air before the shocking collisions with the ground that made everybody watching wince. It made Mitch close his eyes and take a slow breath in. By the time he opened his eyes again, the camera was panning out from above the scene. The horse got to its feet, stood still for a moment and then took off at a gallop.

The rider remained completely motionless and there was no sign of life as the image got smaller and smaller, until that lifeless looking person was no more than a speck in an endless—and apparently deserted—rural landscape.

There was a long moment's silence before Jenna began speaking and it was then that Mitch really heard her voice for the first time. He could hear the faint accent that might be a touch of Welsh background but, more than that, he could hear the tone of someone who knew exactly what they were doing and why.

'The horse jumps another fence and gets onto a road. Someone has the sense to go looking for the rider and then calls for help as soon as they see them lying in the field. The call taker in the emergency response centre looks up the co-ordinates and pinpoints the location of the accident on a map. They look for the nearest ambulance that might be available in the area but it's miles away—being used to transport a patient to the nearest hospital big enough to have a catheter laboratory that can deal with an evolving myocardial infarction. There's no helicopter immediately available, either, but the system flags that there's is a FRAME doctor in a nearby village medical centre, so they activate that call first.'

Jenna's voice was soft but as clear as a bell and just as captivating.

'Your pager goes off,' she tells them. 'You apologise to the patients in your waiting rooms who'll have to wait a while longer, grab your backpack kit and jump into your car. You're at the scene within minutes. And—' the pause was dramatic '—right now, you're the only medically qualified person there and you've got the gear in your pack that could tip the balance between life and death. You need to identify the critical actions that are needed urgently to prevent someone's condition from deteriorating to the point of them becoming a fatality. It's up to you to do whatever you can to save this life.'

Mitch didn't have to imagine what that would be like. He knew, only too well, how huge that sense of responsibility seemed. How powerful the determination to win was and how crushing the weight of failure could be. He also knew that their instructor couldn't possibly have deliberately chosen a scenario that was so close to the bone for him that it felt like a physical blow but that didn't help. He could feel his fingers tightening into fists as he took another deep, slow breath and fought the urge to head outside for some fresh air to clear his head as the blinds on the windows were lifting again.

This was what he'd come here for, after all. A way to revisit that nightmare and find answers to some of those 'what ifs' that might stop the fear of it happening again haunting him for the rest of his life. And he was clearly in the right place.

It almost felt as if this course had been designed specifically for him.

Maybe he wasn't hiding his reaction as well as he thought he was because Jenna turned her head to catch his gaze at that moment and there was a tiny frown between her eyes.

Brown eyes, he noticed, as the light from the windows caught them. But not as dark as his own. More a golden, hazel kind of brown. Warm eyes. Empathetic. They only held his gaze for a heartbeat and, while he had the odd feeling that she could see far more than he would have chosen to show, he didn't mind.

Because it felt like he was being understood rather than judged. As if Jenna Armstrong knew what it was like to fight that kind of battle.

And lose…

Wow…

A dramatic opening to a session on critical interventions for a FRAME doctor on scene always got everybody on board but that expression on Mitch's face meant that Jenna was the one being sucked into this scenario now—as if she could see what was happening from the point of view of the injured person and Mitch was the hero who was about to do whatever it took to save her life.

And he would, wouldn't he? Even in a split second of eye contact, she could sense just how hard he would try. How important it was to him to care for others and... she had to suck in a quick breath as she broke that contact. There was a pull here that was inexplicable and too strong to feel remotely comfortable.

'Okay...' She kept her tone brisk. Urgent, even. 'What's the first thing that's going to kill someone the fastest?'

'An occluded airway,' Ravi offered.

Jenna nodded. 'Absolutely.' She tapped the keyboard in front of her and the first slide of a presentation filled the screen. 'One of our sessions tomorrow is going to cover identifying and managing risks on scene and whether a major incident activation is warranted but, for the moment, we're going to assume that our scene is safe and risks are controlled so we can focus on the immediate threats to life. And yes, it goes back to the basic ABCs that you will all be very familiar with. The occluded airway could be as simple as someone who's unconscious and unable to lift their chin off their chest.'

The picture on the screen now was of a car accident, the deeply unconscious driver still held upright by the safety belt but with his head flopped forward far enough to easily cut off any air entry. Jenna clicked again and this time the image was a more confronting illustration of a serious face and neck injury. 'It could also be as complex as this kind of blunt force or crush injury to the face and/or the neck that has distorted the anatomy and rapidly continues to deteriorate due to bleeding and swelling.'

She could feel the focus with which Mitch was listening to her speak. The way he was watching her. It could have come across as creepy but it didn't. If anything, it was giving her a strange sort of internal tingle—as if he might be interested in *her* rather than what she was saying? She shook the sensation off. 'Indicators of airway compromise?'

The responses came quickly.

'Stridor.'

'Cyanosis. Or pallor.'

'No chest wall movement to be seen. Or felt.'

Mitch was the last to contribute. 'Accessory muscle use,' he said. 'Like intercostal retractions or a tracheal tug. And agitation,' he added quietly. 'Fear, even…'

There was a collective pause. This had just become rather more significant than simply discussing the theory of a medical examination. This was about people. Possibly terrified people. Somehow, it came as no surprise that it was Mitch who had made signs and symptoms something they could all relate to on a human level rather than reciting a paragraph from a medical textbook.

Jenna spoke into that moment's silence. 'You all know the list. And you all know what we need to do. Which is?'

'Open the airway,' Judith said.

'Head tilt, chin lift.' One of the younger doctors, Indira, nodded. 'And then we can move on to reassessing the respiratory efforts.'

'You're not going to do that if there's any suspicion of a spinal injury,' Jack said. 'And, if we're using that example of the horse-riding accident, that would be top of my list.'

'In that case, of course we'd use a modified jaw thrust.' Indira shook her head. 'Basic first aid, isn't it?

And an occluded airway is going to kill someone faster than a potential spinal injury, isn't it? I believe it's only about ten percent of unconscious trauma patients that do have a C spine injury.'

Jenna intervened before the discussion could go off track.

'Basic first aid can very well be life-saving,' she said calmly. 'A lot of what this course is about is reminding us of things we might not have used in a long time. I think Mitch hit the nail on the head with what he said about why he had come to this course—that one skill that we're a bit rusty in might be the one that we need, if not to save a life, then possibly to prevent making an injury a whole lot worse. I agree with you, Indira, in that making sure there's a patent airway can take precedence over anything else depending on circumstances, but I also agree with you, Jack—in the mechanism of injury like coming off a horse at high speed, a spinal injury would be well up my list as well.' She glanced around the group. 'Out of interest, who has done a modified jaw thrust recently?'

Nobody put their hand up or nodded their head. Jenna walked a few steps to the full-body mannequin that was lying on the floor at the front of the classroom.

'Let's have a quick demo.' She looked around the room but she already knew where her glance was going to stop this time. 'Mitch? You up for it?'

'Sure.'

He was taller than she'd realised. By the time he'd joined her at the front of the room, Jenna could tell that the top of her head would barely reach his shoulder. She noticed the faded, denim jeans that clung to his long legs and the soft shirt with the top buttons casually open and the sleeves rolled up almost to his elbows to reveal well-defined muscles beneath tanned skin. It was impossible not to notice the way he moved, too—with a grace that belied his height and muscle mass. The errant thought that he was probably an excellent dancer came from nowhere and was entirely inappropriate.

Without looking directly at Jenna, Mitch knelt in front of the mannequin's head. He put his hands on each side of the face, with his thumbs on the cheekbones and his fingers hooked under the angle of the jawbone. Pressing down with his thumbs and pulling up with his fingers moved the jaw without changing the line of the head or neck.

'Perfect,' Jenna announced.

Mitch got to his feet in another fluid movement and, this time, he did catch Jenna's gaze for a moment before heading back to his seat, his lips tilting into an embryonic smile as he acknowledged her commendation. The corners of a pair of very dark brown eyes crinkled a little at the same time, which made the almost smile as genuine as a wide grin might have been.

For just another moment, Jenna watched him walk away, aware of that tingle she'd dismissed not long ago. But this time it was even stronger and she could recognise it for exactly what it was.

Attraction.

The kind of attraction she hadn't felt in for ever.

Well, not exactly for ever but certainly not since she'd lost Stefan and eight years could definitely feel like for ever. She'd never expected to feel it again, either, but there it was.

Very much alive and kicking.

Nobody could have the faintest idea what had just

flashed through her head but Jenna took a sharp inward breath and lifted her chin, anyway. This might be totally unexpected but it wasn't anything she couldn't deal with. She dealt with far more difficult things on a regular basis, after all.

'Right...' Her smile was bright. 'We've got that airway open. What are some of the adjuncts we might use to secure it?'

Jenna picked up a tray of items that included a hard, plastic oropharyngeal airway, a soft nasopharyngeal tube, a laryngeal mask airway and kits for more invasive airway management like tracheal intubation, needle cricothyroidotomy and surgical airways. She deliberately turned to the opposite side of the classroom from where Mitch had just taken his seat again and offered the tray to Jack.

'Pick one,' she invited. 'Tell us what it is, the indications for using it and whether it's something you carry in your own first response kit. Later today, we'll be using all of them in a practical session but, if you've used one recently yourself, tell us about that case.'

It was going to take some time to get to Mitch's side of the classroom and, by then, Jenna was quite confident she would be able to interact with him in exactly the same way she had interacted with hundreds and hundreds of students over the last few years. There was no real reason why Andrew Mitchell should be any different.

No reason at all.

The last session of the first day was a workshop. The large classroom had been rearranged to provide stations equipped with mannequins and all the gear needed to refresh skills that hadn't been used recently enough or to learn new ones. Jenna moved between where class members were working alone or in pairs, helping them to smooth over rough points or challenging them to try new techniques. Voices were quiet and the atmosphere one of intense concentration, despite a background weariness after a long and intense day of both academic and practical instruction.

This was the highlight of Mitch's day. He had a video laryngoscope in his hands for the first time in years and he could see an impressive improvement in the technology. There was a light source and a digital camera built into the tip of the laryngoscope blade and a small screen attached to the side of the sleek, easy-to-hold handle. This screen provided an enlarged view of the larynx and all the anatomical landmarks you were looking for in order to pass a breathing tube into the trachea and secure an airway. With his other hand, he was following the angle of the blade to slip the tip of the stylet, loaded with the endotracheal tube, through the vocal cords and into the trachea. He then needed to advance the tube and remove the stylet.

That was when the process stopped going so smoothly.

Mitch could feel the hairs on the back of his neck prickle as he felt the resistance beneath his fingers. It was all too easy to imagine that this was a real emergency situation—maybe even the last chance to secure an airway before his patient ran into the life-threatening complications that came from a prolonged lack of oxygen. He tried again but still couldn't advance the tube.

What the hell was going on? Was this a crisis in confidence because the last time he'd needed to use this skill had been such a catastrophe? Had he lost an ability that had been a strength he had relied on more times than he could ever have counted?

He felt, rather than saw, someone coming to stand by his shoulder and he knew, beyond any shadow of doubt, that it was Jenna Armstrong—not just because she was running this workshop and making a point of coaching everybody, but because he could feel that…presence she had. The calmness. Confidence. Empathy…?

Whatever. She was the last person that Mitch wanted to watch him fail. He might have even sworn softly, under his breath.

Jenna's voice was quiet. She didn't seem the least bothered by the difficulty he was in.

'Good to see you've found the downside of this new breed of stylet,' she said. 'The angle of the curve is sharper than we've used in the past. It mirrors the angle of the video laryngoscope's blade, which is good but it makes it harder to advance the tube once you've got the tip through the cords. Try popping the stylet off with your thumb, back it out a bit and then try advancing the tube.'

And, just like that, it was suddenly easy. Mitch slid the tube into place, removed the stylet completely and attached the syringe to the balloon valve, inflating it with enough air to secure it within the trachea. Then he covered the mannequin's mouth and nose with the mask and squeezed the bag. It was so much easier to watch exposed, pink plastic lungs rather than putting his stethoscope onto a real person to check correct tube positioning by watching and listening to see if the air entry was equal on both sides.

'Cool…' The praise from his instructor was matter-of-fact. 'Now…start again.'

He glanced sideways. Were there enough of the video laryngoscopes for everybody to be getting a chance to practise this much? Tomorrow afternoon would be an assessment scenario and they would all be expected to discuss and demonstrate the use of emergency procedures like this before being signed off as FRAME practitioners. He didn't want to monopolise this station.

But Jenna met his glance steadily.

As if she *knew* how important this was to him.

Silently, he removed the tube from the mannequin and set everything up to do it again. He didn't mind Jenna watching this time. Quite the opposite. Especially when he heard the tiny hum of approval she made.

'You've had a lot of experience with intubation, yes?'

'Mmm.' Mitch was focused on the screen. 'Used to work in an ED,' he told her, casually. She didn't need to know that he'd been the head of that department, did she? And it was part of a life he'd left behind so it wasn't even relevant. 'It's a lot different in general practice,' he added. 'I'm planning to seriously upgrade our emergency kits. Video laryngoscopes. Flexible endoscopes. If only…' He trailed into silence, having already said more than he'd intended.

'If only you'd had one of them on a difficult case?' Jenna's voice was quiet. 'I have to admit that I got the feeling there's a story behind why you came on this course.'

'Yeah…' Mitch could see the vocal cords on the screen now. He could push the stylet and tube through but his hand had stilled.

'We've all got "if only" cases,' Jenna said. 'I've got a few of my own.'

'But you wouldn't get the children coming into your

surgery.' Mitch swallowed hard. 'Three little kids who are growing up without their mum because it wasn't possible to give her an airway.'

'And you think having a video laryngoscope would have made the difference?'

'They said not. Post-mortem results showed a laryngeal fracture, a C3/4 fracture *and* cord damage so even if she had survived, she would have been tetraplegic.'

'Sounds like a very nasty accident. What was she doing?'

Mitch's gaze flicked up. 'Riding her horse. Jumping cross country. She was one of our local equestrian stars and she was training for last year's three-day event at Burghley.'

He saw the way Jenna's pupils dilated. Heard the sharp intake of her breath. 'Oh...' There was no need for her to say that she understand exactly what a gut-punch her introductory video must have been. 'I'm so sorry, Mitch.'

'You weren't to know. It was a good reminder of why I'd come.' Mitch turned back to his task and, this time, it was a smooth process to get the tube into place and secure it. He was reaching for the bag mask when Jenna spoke again, quietly enough for him to know that these words were only for him to hear.

'They say so much, don't they? Or hide it. Those two little words. "If only". Or "what if"?'

Mitch had two fingers under the mannequin's jawbone to help hold the mask on firmly. He inflated the bag and watched the lungs fill with air. 'They do.'

'I find they can blindside you in the most unexpected moments.' Jenna's voice wasn't much more than a murmur. Certainly none of the other people in this room would be hearing this private conversation.

'And keep you awake in the tiny hours of the night,' Mitch agreed.

'They're not necessarily a bad thing, though. As long as you don't let them take too much away from what's important in your life.'

He didn't need to inflate the lungs again but he did. Slowly. Without even thinking about what he was doing, because he was wondering what kind of things kept Jenna Armstrong awake at night or blindsided her when she least expected it. What was even more curious was how much he wanted to know. How interested he was in this woman...

'And they can be a very good thing,' Jenna added. 'When they make you grab them with both hands and shake them until an answer falls out, they can be life-changing.'

Mitch looked up again in time to see Jenna's lips curving into a smile.

'Like you coming on this course,' she told him. 'Becoming someone that'll be registered on the emergency services system and able to be responded fast to critical situations—with the best kit we can supply.'

'Jenna?' Judith was calling from the other side of the room. 'I'm having trouble with this video thingy.'

'Coming...' But Jenna didn't move for a moment. She was still holding Mitch's gaze. 'Think about that the next time you're doing the "if only" game. Think about how the changes you're making now might affect future cases. How many lives that might get saved because you're doing this.'

Mitch watched her walking over to where Judith was

working. He needed to tidy up this station and move on himself because he probably had time to practise with the cricothyroidotomy mannequin before he needed to hit the road and battle rush hour traffic to get home.

But he stayed very still for a moment longer.

Watching Jenna.

Letting it sink in that the brief, almost whispered conversation he'd just had with Jenna had done something that might have just lifted the remnants of the significant weight he'd been carrying on his shoulders for the last year.

It was such a cliché to think in terms of a silver lining to a cloud or some such rubbish but there was definitely something profound that Jenna's words had left him with and…it did feel like coming on this course might be going to mark a changing point in his life. A positive change.

'Ah…coffee…'

'Here, have this one.' Susie was already pouring a mug of coffee from the table set up at the back of their classroom. 'You look like you need it more than I do, Mitch.'

'Early start. And I got home pretty late. The traffic was appalling yesterday evening.'

'I got the train. Bit of a walk from the station to get home but I rather like that. The calm before the storm.' Susie was smiling as she handed him a steaming mug. 'Milk?'

'No, thanks. Black's good.'

'Storm?' Jenna queried as she joined them. She picked up two mugs and handed one to Susie.

'Circus might be a better description. You know—husband, kids and the dog all demanding attention?'

Jenna shook her head. 'No. I don't have to cope with any of that. Thank goodness. Good for you, fitting in this course on top of your work and home commitments like that on top. I couldn't do it.'

Mitch stepped back to one side, sipping his coffee as more people arrived and headed their way. The tone of her voice when she'd said 'Thank goodness' made it sound as if a husband and kids were the last thing she would want in her life.

Judith had heard the exchange between Susie and Jenna. 'You do far more, from what I heard. Someone told me yesterday that you've written a book? A text-book for paramedics?'

'It kind of grew from the first set of clinical guidelines I helped write when the FRAME initiative was set up.' Jenna's shrug was modest. 'And they need updating already, which is an extra project I've got on at the moment. Things change, as you'll all be well aware of—like the emergency management of heart attacks and now occlusive strokes by thrombolysis in the field.'

'You travel all around the country with your teaching, as well.' Susie's tone was admiring. Or possibly envious?

'Not so much these days. We're getting a great cohort of instructors based in various cities. In the early days, I was hardly ever at home. I couldn't have done my job if I'd had a dog, let alone a whole family, like you, Susie.'

'But you love it.' Mitch's quiet comment wasn't a question. She hadn't needed to tell them all how much she loved her job yesterday because it had been so obvious. The passion she had for her career gave her a glow that made it hard to look away from her.

Especially when she smiled like that.

'I do,' she agreed. 'I'm particularly loving the work on the new clinical guidelines—which you'll all receive in the mail as soon as they're completed, by the way. We've got a great team of experts on board, including emergency department consultants and specialists from cardiology, neurology and orthopaedics, to name just a few. It's exciting.'

'And you still find time to work on the road,' Judith said. 'I can't even get round to weeding my garden.'

'I need to keep my own skills current,' Jenna said. 'I'd feel like a complete fraud teaching a course like this if I didn't. Especially when I've got a group of doctors who already know more than I do.'

'Are you kidding?' Susie raised her eyebrows. 'I spend half my days writing repeat prescriptions and trying to convince people that they'd feel a lot better if they stopped smoking and lost a bit of weight. I've never used a laryngeal mask airway and I have to confess, the thought of having to perform a cricothyroidotomy on a real patient is terrifying. Wrangling three overtired kids into bed is a breeze in comparison. Especially when the husband gives me a hand like he did last night.'

Mitch closed his eyes as he took another sip of his coffee. Ollie hadn't gone to sleep at his usual time yesterday so he'd been overtired by the time Mitch had got home as well, but how lucky were they both that there was a loving grandparent on hand and bath time had clearly been a joy for both of them.

I waited for you, Daddy,' Ollie had said kindly. *'I knew you'd want your goodnight kiss...'*

And that feeling, when those small arms got wound tightly around his neck—that feeling of being *home*...

Mitch wouldn't give that up, no matter how exciting a career it could allow. He'd done the opposite, in fact, hadn't he? He could have been one of those experts on the team Jenna was working with to produce those updated clinical guidelines. He'd had the fastest-paced, most challenging job ever, running that hectic emergency department, but he'd given it up for his son and he'd do the same again in a heartbeat.

'Well, you have my respect,' Jenna told Susie. 'I think you're juggling a lot more than I do.'

'It's worth it,' Judith said quietly. 'My lot have grown up and left home now but you know what? I can't wait for the grandkids to start arriving. I kind of miss that chaos and clutter.' She smiled. 'I won't have to wait too long, either. My daughter's pregnant. Due in a few weeks. It hasn't been an easy pregnancy so we're both looking forward to the birth.'

Nobody could miss that look that passed between Judith and Susie. The understanding of one mother to another. Mitch could have nodded his own agreement that parenting was worth any struggle but, for some reason, he didn't. Because he was watching Jenna's reaction, closely enough to catch a flash of something that caught his attention. Gave his heart a bit of squeeze, to be honest. It looked like she'd lost something and it made him wonder if she'd wanted kids and had found she couldn't have them for some reason. Or if she'd lost the person she'd wanted to have them *with*.

The impression was gone in a blink, however, and Jenna was smiling now.

'I wasn't kidding when I was banging on yesterday

about how much I love my job,' she said. 'It's everything to me and I'm not about to let anything get in the way of being able to give it everything I've got. It's not that I don't like kids. I love them.' Her smile widened. 'As long as they get to go home with someone else.' She was already turning away. 'We'd better get cracking. We've got a lot to get through today.'

The stimulating effects of the strong coffee had probably worn off by the time they were into the second session of the morning but Mitch still felt alert enough to be absorbing—and enjoying—everything he was listening to Jenna saying about eye injuries that were considered to be emergencies due to their life-changing potential loss of vision.

'So the usual cause of an orbital floor fracture is when a blunt object, of equal or greater diameter than the orbital aperture, strikes the eye.' Jenna grinned at her class. 'And one of the reasons I love talking about them is that we get to use really cool words when we're discussing the signs and symptoms. Okay…quick quiz. What's diplopia?'

'Double vision,' Peter answered.

'Ecchymosis?'

'Black eye.' It was Melanie who responded first this time.

'Ipsilateral epistaxis?'

'Nose bleed on one side only,' Indira said.

Jenna was nodding at each correct answer and clicking a remote control to bring up a corresponding image as confirmation. The quiz was rapid and the class members—including Mitch—were clearly enjoying the participation.

He was enjoying more than the quiz, however. The feeling that something had changed yesterday, after that brief, private conversation with Jenna, had not worn off. If anything, it was stronger now and Mitch was feeling a lot more relaxed. As if he'd somehow absorbed some of the serenity that came from the combination of passion and knowledge that gave Jenna that very appealing glow?

Maybe it was the idea that you could look back on even catastrophic events and realise that they were the catalyst for something good that wouldn't have otherwise happened. Like him coming on this course and putting himself on the front line for local emergency service call-outs. There was a frisson of excitement to be found in the idea that his world would be expanding to include some of the things he thought he'd left far behind in his career but there was something deeper as well. The idea that he was changing more than an element of his working life? That he might become a better doctor because of this? A better person, even?

'Traumatic hyphaema?'

There was a longer pause before anyone answered this time. Mitch knew the answer but he was momentarily distracted as he watched the way Jenna caught one corner of her bottom lip between her teeth as she waited. She was loving challenging these doctors and that glow had just ramped up a notch or two.

Good Lord…had he really thought that this woman would not stand out in a crowd because of how she looked? Her intelligence was shining just as brightly and Mitch already knew how compassionate Jenna was. How empathetic. She'd known exactly how horrific it must have been for him to watch that dramatic accident scene involving a fall from a horse. He'd also been left with the impression that she more than understood what it was like to lie awake half the night being tortured by thoughts of how different things could have been.

'Is it blood in the anterior chamber of the eye?' Jack sounded a little hesitant as he broke the silence in the classroom.

'Yes…excellent!' The image that came onto the screen of a close-up shot of blood obscuring even the iris of an eye was enough to make a couple of people groan but Jenna was obviously happy as she clicked through more images and talked more about the implications of the sign.

But Mitch was still watching her rather than the screen.

If he had been looking for another woman in his life—which he wasn't—then Jenna would have been perfect.

Apart from that one little detail he'd learned over coffee this morning that meant she was actually the absolute opposite of perfect, of course. If he was ever going to share his life with a partner again, he'd have to find someone who not only loved him but would love his child as her own. The fear of risking Ollie's happiness in any way was so abhorrent it had been more than enough to let Mitch close the door firmly on even thinking about looking for someone.

Not that he'd needed an extra incentive to not get too close to anyone again. He'd loved Tegan. So much. And he'd known for a very long time that that part of his heart had died along with his wife. It was a no-brainer that he could never love another woman in a way that was fearlessly based on the confidence that they had the rest of a normal lifespan to be together. Even if that gaping hole in his heart had somehow, miraculously healed itself, he wouldn't *want* to offer that much of himself to someone else. He didn't even want to try dating anyone to try and find out how much of a relationship might be possible.

He couldn't afford to get broken again. Not when he had his precious son to raise.

But that didn't mean he didn't miss the sexual side of a relationship, did it? It wasn't normal for someone in his stage of life to be living like a monk, although it had seemed relatively easy up until now. Maybe that was why he was finding this unexpected attraction to Jenna rather disturbing. And maybe he could find a way to add the perfectly normal pleasure of sex back into his life at some point.

No…he had to dismiss that notion as he refocused on what was happening around him. A casual arrangement for a friendship with benefits would never work when he had a small child and worked in a small town. It was much safer for everybody for him to just focus on his life as a parent and his work as a GP. A life that was about to get more challenging and no doubt satisfying by him becoming qualified as a FRAME practitioner.

'Okay, last one…' Jenna's tone suggested it might also be the hardest. 'Enophthalmos?' Her grin was cheeky. 'And, yes—that does have two 'h's in it.'

Her gaze roamed over her silent students before finally resting on Mitch. The remnants of that grin were still evident in the curve of her lips and he couldn't help smiling back.

'It's a posterior displacement of a normal-sized globe

in relation to the bony orbital margin,' he said. 'Or, more simply, a sinking of the eyeball into the orbital cavity.'

'Just what I was about to say.'

Judith's wry comment made everybody laugh, including Jenna, but the look she was giving Mitch was not one of amusement. He'd impressed her, hadn't he? And he rather liked that.

Okay…he liked it a lot.

He liked *her* a lot.

And…and maybe the fact that she was the total opposite of a woman he'd choose to have as part of his life wasn't a bad thing. She'd feel exactly the same way about him, surely? With the way she felt about kids, a single father would be a nightmare scenario. But what if Jenna's incredibly busy career meant that she was as alone in her bed as he'd been for years?

What if—and the look he was getting at this precise moment suggested it could be a reality—she was as attracted to him as he was to her? Mitch knew the answer to that. It was a very simple two-word answer. Or was it a question?

Why *not*?

CHAPTER THREE

DESPITE THE TENSION that always went with an assessment scenario, being closely watched and graded by both Jenna and a consultant trauma surgeon she had invited to help sign off the latest recruits to the FRAME network, one of her students was noticeably more relaxed than he had been at the beginning.

Andrew Mitchell was flying past every tick box on the assessment sheets. He had competently assessed the imaginary scenario for safety issues, cited the ways he would manage or mitigate risks, discounted the need to instigate a major incident plan and was moving through his patient assessment. A mannequin lay on the floor beneath a picture of a badly mangled motorbike and Mitch was up to assessing respiratory effort.

'Do I have any signs of respiratory distress?'

'Yes. Your patient has a respiration rate of greater than thirty. He's complaining of chest pain but is unable to speak in sentences. Heart rate is one hundred and thirty. Pulse oximetry is less than ninety percent and you've just lost a palpable radial pulse.'

'Do I see a jugular vein distension?'

'No.'

'Tracheal deviation?'

'Possible shift to the right.'

Mitch put the disc of the stethoscope onto one side of the chest. 'Breath sounds inaudible on the left.

'I'm diagnosing a tension pneumothorax,' he said moments later.

'Treatment?'

'A needle thoracostomy.'

'Talk me through the steps.'

Mitch easily listed the steps for a procedure that Jenna doubted he would have had reason to use during his time as a general practitioner. It sounded as if he'd done one only yesterday, however, and his manner was calm and confident.

'The recommended insertion site is the second intercostal space in the mid-clavicular line but, actually, insertion of the needle virtually anywhere in the correct haemothorax will decompress a tension pneumothorax and if my patient's getting hypotensive enough for the radial pulse to have disappeared then that puts his systolic blood pressure at less than eighty and makes this a genuine emergency.'

The trauma surgeon exchanged a glance with Jenna and the slight quirk of his eyebrow told her how impressed he was. It was a bit absurd to feel this proud of Mitch but—right from the opening minutes of this course—there had been something about this man that had captured her. She'd recognised that he was the first person since Stefan that had triggered the kind of attraction she'd never expected—or wanted?—to feel again but what had been even more of a worry was how intimate that whispered conversation had seemed yesterday while he'd been having a go with the video laryngoscope.

'The needle needs to slide in over the upper edge of

the rib to avoid damage to the neurovascular bundle on the lower edge of each rib,' Mitch continued.

He was moving his hands as if he was actually performing the procedure as he was explaining the steps. It was just as well she was assessing him, Jenna thought, because it gave her a valid reason to be unable—or unwilling—to look away.

That sensation of intimacy had stayed with her last night and had only become stronger as she'd lain awake far longer than usual.

Jenna was, quite genuinely, not in the market for any kind of relationship. She'd meant what she'd said to people this morning that she wasn't about to let anything—or anyone—interfere with her commitment to the career she loved. What she hadn't bargained for, though, were the echoes of something that could only be shared by a couple who were completely in tune with each other. A particular look. A touch. The feeling of simply being held...

There was a part of her that still wanted that. So much that not having it in her life was a grief all of its own but she'd never considered trying to find it in isolation. Finding someone who wanted to hold her and touch her but nothing more than that. Maybe she was old-fashioned and hadn't approved of things like having a one-night stand or, good grief, what was that term she'd heard someone use recently—a sex buddy?

No...that notion was still enough to make her shudder but a one-off experience? With someone as attractive as Mitch? That might ease the ache of what had been missing in her life for a considerable period of time. Or it might, at least, allow her to gauge how great the effect of the total absence of physical connection with another person might be actually having on her.

Mitch would be perfect. If he was single, of course. If he was attracted to *her*.

There'd been moments in the last couple of days when she'd imagined that he was attracted to her. Like when she'd invited him to the front of the class to demonstrate the modified jaw thrust and he'd given her that almost smile when she'd praised him. And what about earlier today, when he'd been the one to answer the trickiest medical term she'd been able to come up with in relation to eye injuries?

Oh, yeah…she'd definitely seen something in his eyes that suggested this attraction was not one-sided.

So what was she going to do about it, if anything?

What would she do if she discovered he was up for something a little more personal than being in a classroom together?

What if…?

Mitch was still speaking. Still sounding—and looking—remarkably relaxed. That curious intensity that she'd been aware of when she'd first met him had dissipated noticeably. As if he'd found whatever that important thing was that he'd been searching for. Was it crazy to feel a kind of connection here that suggested that Jenna *had* been the person who'd helped him find it?

'The signs and symptoms of a cardiac tamponade can certainly mimic a tension pneumothorax,' Mitch was saying. 'You can have the same hypotension, jugular vein distension and respiratory distress but the unilateral absence of breath sounds isn't present and…'

Oh, man… It was just as well that Jenna already knew Mitch was going to pass this assessment with no problems at all because she was barely listening as he talked to her colleague about differentiating between two critical situations that needed very different treatment.

All she could think about as she listened to his voice and tried to keep her gaze on his face instead of watching those expressive hands, wondering what it might be like to be touched by them, was the answer to that 'what if' question she didn't quite dare to articulate.

The answer was pretty simple, however.

Why *not*?

She drank beer.

A boutique lager that came in a pretty, small bottle but it was still beer and not a glass of chardonnay or sauvignon blanc or maybe even an obscure cocktail that you might expect a sophisticated, intelligent young woman to choose when she was at the pub for a quick drink after work.

Mitch wasn't a bit surprised, mind you. It was just different, like everything else about Jenna Armstrong.

'I'll have what she's having,' he told the barman and, even if the beer wasn't going to be to his taste, it had been worth saying that just to catch the surprised delight in Jenna's eyes as he used a famous movie line that she clearly recognised. He also got the impression that, while she might not have expected him to watch rom coms any more than he'd expected her to drink beer, she rather liked this new piece of information about him.

Susie hadn't come to this planned gathering to celebrate the end of the intensive course and their collective success in making the grade to become FRAME practitioners. She'd apologised as she explained that her husband had a long shift that day and the nanny had her own commitments. She said that she hoped to catch up with everybody next year, when they would be due to come back for a refresher course but she looked disappointed at having to rush off.

She'd been shaking her head as she'd left with her certificate and new first aid kit. *'How did life suddenly get quite so complicated?'* she'd asked.

Mitch took a second sip of the boutique lager, which wasn't bad at all, and the baskets of deep-fried bar snacks that were arriving on the long wooden table, like tiny samosas and spring rolls, potato skins and battered scampi, looked delicious. Thank goodness he'd already warned his father that this social conclusion to the course was planned and that he might be a lot later home this evening. Ollie hadn't been bothered at all. Apparently a bubble bath was on the agenda as a treat and Grandpa was going to get *his* goodnight kiss as a bonus.

Mitch could relax and do something he hadn't done in a very long time, which was to simply enjoy the company of like-minded colleagues. Including Jenna. He wasn't a student any longer and she wasn't his instructor, which was making a surprising difference to how things felt between them.

Or perhaps that had something to do with the fact that Jenna had changed out of her uniform before coming to the pub. She was in denim jeans, white sneakers on her feet and a well-worn-looking leather jacket over a T-shirt. Her black curls had been ruffled by gusts of wind as they'd all walked to the nearest pub and it looked as though she'd used a bit of make-up despite being so quick to get changed after the course had formally concluded. Whatever the reason, Mitch was again wondering how on earth he had thought she wouldn't stand out in a crowd.

She was stunning.

And it was just as well he was sitting right beside her at this end of the long table because, otherwise, everybody would have noticed him staring at Jenna.

Or maybe not. All his fellow course attendees seemed to be involved in animated conversations. Peter and Jack at the other end of the table were talking about something that needed diagrams or possibly a flow chart to be drawn on a paper napkin. Melanie and Indira were listening to a story Ravi was telling them and, at this end of the table, Judith was frowning as she read a text message on her phone.

'Excuse me,' she said. 'It's my daughter. She had an antenatal check-up today so I'd better go and make a call somewhere a bit quieter and find out what's going on.' She squeezed out past Jenna, who moved sideways to make it easier which brought her close enough to Mitch for their thighs to touch.

It was impossible not to notice that Jenna didn't instantly move back but that was possibly because she hadn't noticed with other things that were happening, like Judith excusing herself and someone passing a basket to their end of the table.

'You guys had better get something to eat before it's all gone.'

Jenna beamed. 'Yay. I love potato skins. Especially when they're all crispy with Parmesan cheese on the top like this.' She bit into one of the snacks and Mitch had to deliberately turn away so he didn't keep watching her eat. That could well come across as being creepy, couldn't it?

'Looks like there are lots of good places to eat around here,' he said. 'Did you say you live not far away?'

'Just round the corner.' Jenna nodded. 'And you're right. I've got restaurants for just about every cuisine in the world within walking distance for take-outs. Afghani is my latest favourite.'

'Not something we've got in Allensbury,' Mitch said. 'Or not that I'm aware of, anyway.'

'You're not into take-outs?'

Mitch was taking another sip of his lager. This was a perfect opportunity to tell Jenna something about himself. That eating food that wasn't home cooked was quite a rare treat in the Mitchell household, because he was trying to keep his four-year-old son's diet as healthy as possible. He could also say that his dad was pretty conservative when it came to ethnic food but that would inevitably lead to talking about why three generations of Mitchell men were living in the same house and that would include his tragic personal history, which just wasn't appropriate in this time and space.

Being here, with this group—with Jenna—was not a part of his normal life. It was a treat. Like a take-out meal. Why spoil the enjoyment by talking about something that wasn't relevant, like why he was a single father? Especially when that information could very well change the vibe between himself and Jenna. It would undoubtedly make her move to put more distance between them and, he had to admit, if he could, he wanted to enjoy that frisson of physical touch—and the evidence of attraction that went with it—for a bit longer.

Judith came back but only to collect her bag and

coat. 'Have to go,' she said. 'Everything's okay but my daughter sounds a bit stressed out. Thanks again, Jenna. The course was brilliant.'

Peter stood up as well. 'Better hit the road,' he sighed. 'Or I might be tempted to have another drink and it would be a long walk or a very expensive taxi ride home.' He shook Jack's hand. 'Nice to meet you. Let's stay in touch.'

'I'll walk out with you.' Jack smiled at Jenna. 'Thank you so much. I reckon we were pretty lucky to get you as our instructor.'

'I'll be in touch, too,' Jenna promised. 'I check in with all our FRAME practitioners on a regular basis.'

'Good to know,' Mitch murmured.

Maybe Jenna had heard his comment given the way her gaze flicked sideways. And maybe that was the reason that Mitch was aware of the sudden electricity in the air between them. That simmering attraction had ignited in some fashion, enough to make even the air sizzle.

Melanie was the last to leave, apart from Mitch. She also thanked Jenna profusely for her coaching.

'I wouldn't have got through that assessment scenario without you, either,' she added. 'I've always hated any kind of exam.'

'You did well. I don't think many people like performing in front of an audience but, you know, you'll find that's part of being a first responder in an emergency situation. Sometimes there's a crowd of onlookers and distressed family members but you *do* get used to it.'

Melanie made a face. 'If only I didn't live so far away. I'd love to take you up on that offer of getting more experience by going out on the road for an ambulance shift.'

'Talk to your local station. You'll find they will be very supportive of any FRAME doctors and they'll make space for you to join a crew. If you run into any problems, call me and I'll talk to the station manager. You're part of our team now.'

Mitch turned to Jenna before Melanie had reached the door of the pub. 'I didn't hear about that offer.'

'It was just chatting over lunch,' Jenna responded. 'But it applies to you as well. It's a great way to keep your skills up and get used to being ready for anything. I love the shifts I do.'

'I'm not sure where my closest ambulance station would be. We don't often have to call them in to transport patients from our medical centre. I think the last one came from Guildford. Or possibly from around here, given that Croydon is our other closest hospital. I could make enquiries about picking up the odd shift in an ED, I guess. That's where I used to work before switching to general practice.'

'Yes, you said you used to work in emergency.' Jenna nodded. 'It's a good idea. Or you could come here to do a few shifts. Sometimes it's very different working out in the field—as you know.' Jenna was sticking crumbs from the bottom of the potato skin basket to her finger as she spoke so she wasn't looking directly at Mitch but then she glanced up and caught his gaze. 'You could come out with me,' she added. 'In the rapid response vehicle. You get all the excitement of being sent to every potentially critical job and plenty of opportunity to use all your skills in situations that can be more challenging than an emergency department. Plus, you skip the downtime of having to transport patients to hospital or wait your turn for a Code Blue call if you're out on an ambulance.'

'Seriously?' Mitch was holding her gaze and he could actually feel his heart rate pick up at the prospect. 'You're allowed to take someone with you as an APP?'

'I'm the boss of my vehicle. I get to make the rules.' Jenna's grin was just a brief flash as she looked away, noticed the crumbs still stuck to her finger and put them in her mouth. 'Mmm.' She picked up the basket and shook it to see if she could find any more.

Meanwhile, Mitch was letting that idea roll around in his head and it was getting more exciting by the moment. It was like stepping back in time, even, to a point in his career when he had been exactly where he'd dreamed of being—the head of an emergency department that could erupt into the kind of chaos that came when back-to-back life-or-death emergencies had to be dealt with. A passion that he'd thought he'd never be able to recapture. A way of life that, at one point—before he'd met Tegan—had been his entire *raison d'être*.

'Could you do that?' Jenna asked. 'Or do you have commitments at home that might make it tricky?'

Was she asking him if he was single? *Available?*

Oh…wow…

He might have been justified in dismissing an opportunity to tell her about his private life earlier this evening but the answer to this specific query about his home commitments could change everything and Mitch didn't want that to happen. Amidst his gathering of those tendrils of a forgotten excitement his career was capable of providing, Jenna caught his gaze again and Mitch was instantly aware of another almost forgotten, but equally seductive sensation. This was far more powerful than an unexpected physical attraction to someone. This had all the sharpness and depth of an urgent level of desire.

He wanted this.

He wanted to recapture a snatch of the career he'd once loved so much.

And more than that, he wanted to ease an ache in his life that he had been ignoring for years.

Jenna didn't want a husband or a relationship that would interfere with her freedom to pursue a career she loved more than anything. She certainly wasn't interested in children. And…she was asking him if he wanted to spend more time with her. Professionally and…possibly personally?

There was only one way to find out but Mitch had to clear his throat before he could speak and, even then, his voice was a little hoarse.

'I'm single,' he told her. 'I could make it work. It wouldn't be a problem.'

He might not be telling her the whole truth but it wasn't a lie. Ollie was perfectly happy to be cared for by his grandpa and he would be totally protected from whatever came from Mitch spending more time with Jenna because there was no connection. Nobody in Allensbury, including his father, would need to know anything about what happened here, unless he chose to tell them. They would all support his interest in his new clinical responsibilities as a FRAME doctor and Mitch had at least two days a week when he wasn't rostered on at the medical centre so it would be easy to make himself available. He wanted to make himself available.

Mitch found a slow smile curving his lips after he'd

spoken. The ball was back in Jenna Armstrong's court now. He was certainly available for a casual, professional kind of relationship. He could also be available for…what could he call that? Fringe benefits?

There was definitely a dreamlike quality to what was happening here. What had been happening for the last forty-eight hours, in fact—as if it had been scripted for a movie or something. Jenna felt like she was playing a part. That what was happening between herself and Mitch was meant to be…

He'd been a last-minute addition to that FRAME course and he'd captured her interest from the very beginning. That she was actually physically attracted to him had come as enough of a shock that if Jenna had simply met Mitch in passing, she would most likely have just kept moving. The fact that it would have been unacceptable if not unethical to explore an attraction while they were in a classroom situation with her as the instructor made it both impossible to escape and easy to deal with.

And because they had been forced to be together for those two days, they'd had opportunities to connect and that attraction had become more familiar. Less scary. Welcome, even?

That hadn't been the reason that Jenna had invited Mitch to do some shifts with her in the rapid response vehicle, however. She genuinely liked him and was equally impressed with the clinical skills and intelligence he clearly had. He'd been an emergency department doctor in the past so it was highly likely she could learn as much from him as he might from being out on the road with her.

Jenna had to admit that the attraction might explain why she'd suggested he walked home with her, mind you, under the pretext of making a copy of the printout of her coming roster so that he could take it home and choose a date for his first shift with her. Not that she was about to try and seduce him or anything. She just wanted to be in his company a little longer. To be honest, though, there was something rather intimate about leading him up the narrow staircase that led to her attic flat a few blocks away from the pub they'd left.

''Scuse the mess,' she said, as she opened her front door. 'I've been packing and sorting the paperwork for a longer course I'm heading off to tomorrow up in Manchester. When we work with nurses or paramedics to bring them up to speed with FRAME skill set requirements, we do a five-day initiation course.'

It felt like she was prattling, which she probably was. Because Jenna was suddenly nervous. She hadn't felt like this in so long, it was like time-travelling back to being an awkward teenager. She hadn't even invited a man back into this small flat and it seemed to have shrunk considerably in the last few seconds. It felt stuffy, too, as if there wasn't enough air. Maybe she should open a window?

'There's a beer in the fridge if you fancy it. I'll just find that file and warm up the printer.'

'No, thanks. Not when I'll be driving soon.'

Did he want to escape as soon as possible? Had she been reading signals incorrectly? Like when he hadn't moved his leg when she'd shifted on that seat in the pub and her thigh had come into contact with his? The thought prompted a curious glance in Mitch's direction. That touch might have felt weirdly hot on her skin, despite the layers of clothing between them, but maybe he hadn't even noticed it?

But he was smiling at her. 'A coffee would be great, though,' he said. 'Shall I put the jug on?'

Such an ordinary sort of thing to say. And it had the effect of taking all the awkwardness out of him being here. Even when Jenna joined him in the tiny kitchen to find the instant coffee and some mugs and they were so close together that Mitch's arm brushed her back as he reached to open the fridge to get the milk, it still felt okay.

More than okay…

Jenna wasn't sure if she leaned into the touch of that arm or whether it had been Mitch's choice to abandon opening the fridge and let his arm curl more closely around her body but it didn't seem to matter because, as she looked up, she found Mitch looking down at her and the expression in his eyes took her breath away.

How could she have thought for a moment that he hadn't been aware of that touch of their thighs earlier this evening? The strength of the desire she could see in his eyes was enough to create a shaft of sensation deep in her belly that felt like fireworks going off. She had completely forgotten—probably deliberately—what even an echo of that kind of desire could feel like. The reminder was enough to make her lips feel suddenly dry and she couldn't stop herself moistening them with the tip of her tongue.

Mitch watched her do that but he said nothing. The only sound in this cramped space was the bubble of water coming to the boil in the electric jug and then it shut itself off automatically with a dull click but they were still staring at each other, as if they were both caught. Wondering how or where they could find shelter from the force of what was happening here, perhaps?

It was Jenna who finally moved. Who came up on tiptoe but she wouldn't have been able to reach Mitch's lips to kiss him if he hadn't bent his head.

It wasn't a real kiss. Jenna just felt an overwhelming need to know what it would be like to touch a man's lips with her own for the first time in for ever. She even kept her eyes open as that touch happened. A touch that was so soft it was kind of like hearing the faint notes of a favourite song wafting from an open window nearby but so nice that she moved her head a little to one side and then the other, a stroking movement intended to capture a bit more of that feeling.

Pulling back, Jenna saw that Mitch had *his* eyes open as well and once again they were staring at each other. And it felt as if they were communicating by sharing nothing but ripples of emotion.

Astonishment.

Delight.

A longing for more…a lot more.

But, even with the strength of those emotions, the next touch of their lips was still gentle, although nowhere near as soft as the first time. The real difference was that they both closed their eyes. And that it morphed into a very real kiss in a matter of moments. When Mitch's hands shaped Jenna's body, however, softly cupping her breast as his thumb stroked over her hidden nipple, she sensed the same kind of wonder that she'd felt about kissing him—as if this was something new in his life again as well.

Something changed at that point. Maybe because Jenna could feel a connection that was very different to this physical desire. Was she projecting her own mixed feelings that she needed this so much but it felt almost as if she was dismissing a very important part of her past? It didn't feel wrong, though. Instead, it bestowed something positive on this. Something caring. Or at least something that, for Jenna, made it more acceptable than a casual encounter that had no significance.

Exchanging emotions wasn't enough as their gazes met this time.

'I…um…I'm a bit out of practice with this kind of thing.' Jenna's voice was husky. 'Actually, *very* out of practice.'

'You and me both.' The muscles in Mitch's throat moved as he swallowed. 'It's been…good grief…years.'

So she'd been right. This was as new again for him as it was for her. The reasons why didn't matter. Jenna remembered that odd feeling that he'd seen her as the person who could give him something he'd been searching for.

Now maybe she knew what that something was. And it was something that was also missing from her own life.

'It's because I haven't been looking for a relationship,' she said quietly. 'It's still not something I want.'

'Neither do I.'

'It makes it difficult, doesn't it? To…you know… find, um…company.'

'Mmm…'

He was watching her carefully. Waiting for what she was about to say.

But there was something else she thought she could see in his eyes. Hope…?

'Skills get rusty,' she murmured, 'if they don't get used every once in a while.'

'I've heard that.' Mitch closed his eyes as he whispered the words, his breath coming out in a slow sigh.

It was Jenna's turn to swallow carefully. 'Even if they are a bit rusty—' she needed to catch another breath '—it's possible to fix that. If…you know…you want to.'

Mitch's eyes were open again. His gaze was fixed on Jenna's with all the intensity they had been a few minutes ago before that first, butterfly wing kiss.

'Oh… I want to,' he said softly. 'But what about you?'

Again, Jenna stood on tiptoe and, this time, she reached up to put her hands on Mitch's cheeks to encourage him to bend his head so that she could kiss him.

She only had time for a single word before his mouth covered hers. Before she felt him lift her into his arms and knew he was about to carry her to her bed.

'Same…'

CHAPTER FOUR

EQUIPMENT IN THE back of the rapid response vehicle bounced and clattered as the vehicle crossed the central island in the road, aiming for a gap amongst oncoming traffic. Cars and trucks were doing their best to pull aside and make room for the emergency vehicle with its flashing lights and siren going. A warning blast on the airhorn was enough to make a pedestrian change his mind fast about the wisdom of ducking in front of them to weave through the rush-hour congestion.

Mitch was in the front passenger seat. Jenna was driving. She bounced them back over the raised concrete edges of the island as they cleared the intersection, flashing him a quick grin as she noticed him reach for the handle above the door to steady himself so he didn't lurch sideways.

'All good?'

'Couldn't be better.' He looked at the satellite navigation screen built into the dashboard. 'We're getting close.'

Jenna was accelerating as she overtook vehicles pulling to the side ahead of them. The heads of a line of people at a bus stop turned in unison to watch them go past and Mitch could imagine that there was a collective bubble above their heads asking, 'What's happened? How bad is it?'

Maybe Jenna had seen that as well in her peripheral vision. 'Any more details coming through?'

'Paramedics on scene say they're dealing with a collapsed lung. Respiration rate currently sixty and oxygen saturation levels are under eighty.'

A single nod from Jenna showed that she had taken the information on board but her focus was on getting them to the scene as back-up as quickly as possible had just ramped up. She had to brake hard enough to be sure that cars were all stopping to let them go through a red traffic light safely and then she put her foot down again. Mitch was still hanging onto the handle, to stop him tipping too far towards her, as they rounded a sharp corner.

It was a hit and run they were heading to. The sixth and possibly final job on the first shift that Mitch had come to spend with Jenna. An older pedestrian that had been clipped by a van and it sounded like he wasn't doing too well at all. A collapsed lung could be caused by a pneumothorax, with air collecting outside the lung and inside the chest wall, probably due to damage from a broken rib. It could be a haemopneumothorax with a mix of blood and air or a tension pneumothorax, like the scenario that had been used for his FRAME practitioner assessment a couple of weeks ago.

Whatever the cause, this time Mitch would get to do the treatment for real because getting precisely this kind of experience was why he had taken up Jenna's offer to join her on some of her APP single responder shifts. And, this time, someone's life could very well depend on it.

Mitch took a deep breath as they rounded another

curve and could see flashing lights and a solid wall of traffic ahead of them. A police officer waved them towards the side of the road and Jenna moved forward slowly now, with one set of wheels on the footpath as bystanders got out of the way. Mitch was totally focused. Ready for anything. Exhilarated, in fact. He hadn't felt this *alive*, he realised, for a very, very long time.

In a way, it reminded him of when he'd been a kid, about Ollie's age or a bit older, and it was Christmas Eve and excitement was building to an almost unbearable level because he knew something big was about to happen but he had no idea what it might be. What he did know was that taking up Jenna's offer to join her on the road was the best decision he could have made because it had brought an entirely new dimension into his life.

As had that single night with the woman who was driving this vehicle like an absolute pro. Not that he was about to let a single, mind-blowing detail of that extraordinary taste of a previous life derail his concentration right now but he was still feeling relieved that their first meeting today since that evening hadn't been awkward. Okay, he knew they were both thinking about what had happened in Jenna's flat—in her bed—but it had been pushed aside as something irrelevant to their professional time together today. It was only important because it had given them a connection that added a level of friendship, or maybe trust, to their imminent working relationship.

No. It was important for something even more significant than what was happening now. It was linked to the past because it had also been a catalyst for a major change in his life. Deep down, he knew that that night together was a part of this new dimension. A reawakening of the man he'd once been. Before life had derailed *him*.

'You get to run this job,' Jenna told him, as she pulled the vehicle to a halt near an ambulance that had its back doors open to reveal uniformed paramedics crouched over a figure on the stretcher. 'Pretend it's a FRAME call-out. I'll only step in if you ask me to. Or if I think it's in the patient's best interests.' She caught his gaze, pausing for a heartbeat before opening her door. 'All good?'

It was the same question she'd asked before, when the speed of their vehicle had had them lurching around. And that hadn't been the first time, either. A tiny blip at the back of his brain reminded Mitch that she'd asked it that night, as well—after the most incredible sex he'd ever experienced. It was almost like a private code between them already and what was becoming a practised response was right on the tip of his tongue.

'Couldn't be better.'

One of the paramedics on scene at the hit and run knew Jenna but he could see that she was staying behind her extra crew member and that the stranger was wearing a high-vis jacket with 'DOCTOR' emblazoned on the back so that made him the highest medical authority here.

Not that Mitch needed a label to enable him to take control. He had an aura of confidence and skill that made it automatic and Jenna found herself admiring the calm way he was gathering as much information as he could in the shortest possible time from what he could see and hear around him and the questions he was asking the paramedics who had been treating the patient for his chest trauma including broken ribs and possible internal injuries.

Sixty-four-year-old Gerald was still conscious, despite falling blood pressure and having difficulty breathing.

'I'm Mitch,' He crouched at the head of the stretcher after the rapid-fire information-sharing. 'I've got Jenna with me as well and we're going to help look after you and get you safely into hospital just as quickly as we can.'

'Okay…thanks…' Gerald's voice was muffled by his panting breaths beneath the oxygen mask.

Mitch glanced up. 'Blood pressure now?'

'Systolic still dropping. Eighty-four.'

'Oxygen saturation?'

'Seventy-eight.'

'Has he got a pelvic wrap on?'

'Yes.'

'We need another line in. Preferably central. Jenna? Could you pass me the portable ultrasound, please? And set up for the line?'

'Sure.'

It was getting crowded in the back of this ambulance as its crew shifted back to make room for the more advanced procedures their back-up medics could provide. Gerald already had a peripheral IV line in his arm but a central line was an intravenous catheter placed in a large vein near the heart and it had the advantage of letting them infuse a large volume of fluid rapidly, which their patient might well need if his blood pressure fell any further and he crashed.

Jenna could see Mitch using the probe from the ultrasound as she set out the cannula and attachments, adhesive coverings and alcohol wipes she needed to insert the subclavian line. She could sense his concentration and how fast his brain was working, not only to interpret the grainy images of what he was seeing on the screen but to weigh up every treatment option and the order they might need to be done to keep this critically ill person alive.

'Okay,' he said moments later. 'Here's the plan.' He was speaking to the medical team around him but including Gerald as well. 'You've got a collapsed lung and it's getting harder for you to breathe, so we're going to give you some more pain medication and try putting a needle into your chest. If that doesn't help enough, we're going to give you some stronger medication that will make you very sleepy. You won't know what's happening but we'll be taking over helping you to breathe for a while—until we can get you into hospital.'

Gerald nodded. He seemed to be trying to say something but his words were no more than incoherent gasps and his anxious head movements gradually slowed as the medication took effect.

Jenna had the central line in place by the time Mitch had the chest decompression needle inserted but the numbers on the monitor weren't going in the right direction.

'O2 sats down to seventy-four.' Jenna knew they were going to have to do something a lot more invasive and they probably only had one shot to obtain control of the airway and to improve how much oxygen was circulating. She'd have to step in if Mitch didn't move fast but he was speaking even before she'd finished her sentence. He'd also seen the numbers on the monitor.

'Let's have the RSI kit,' he said. 'We're going to do a crash intubation and see if we can get those sats up. I need one person to pre-oxygenate. Jenna, could you draw up the ketamine and suxamethonium, please? And I need a rolled-up towel to go under his shoulders.'

It was the first time Jenna had seen Mitch work on a real person rather than a mannequin but it was no surprise that his intubation technique was smooth and confident. It was also successful but even with the high level of oxygen being provided, the figure on the monitor remained dangerously low.

Mitch caught Jenna's gaze. They were going to lose this patient if they didn't try something else. She waited a beat to see if the procedure she was thinking of was also at the top of Mitch's list. A surgical intervention only authorised to be performed out of hospital by doctors or paramedics with advanced training.

'Finger thoracostomy?' he suggested quietly.

'It's what I'd do.' Jenna nodded.

Gerald was unconscious. Unaware of the slice of the scalpel or the pressure of Mitch's gloved finger pushing through the muscle of his chest wall. The white towel underneath that side of the chest caught the rush of blood that obviously had air pressure behind it but the bleeding subsided relatively quickly. As quickly as the percentage of oxygen in the blood being displayed on the monitor began to increase. Back into the eighties. Into the nineties when Jenna could see Mitch releasing a relieved breath of his own but then he turned instantly to the next issue.

'Blood pressure's still too low,' he said. 'Let's get more fluids up and I think it's time to move. He could well be bleeding somewhere else. Jenna?'

'Totally agree.' She nodded. 'We'll stay with him in the ambulance. Can one of you guys follow us in with our vehicle, please?'

'I could do that.' A policewoman was standing at the open back door. 'I need to come in with you, anyway. I've got a little girl here who says that your patient is her grandfather. We're trying to contact other members of her family but it will be easier to meet them at the hospital.'

Jenna blinked. Was that what Gerald had been trying to tell them when he was so anxious before they knocked him out to take over his breathing? The policewoman moved and now Jenna could see a girl who was about five or six years old. Her long dark braids were framing a very pale, frightened little face and the child was crying silently, fat tears rolling down her cheeks.

'Oh…sweetheart…' Jenna stopped packing up some of their gear in preparation for transport and stepped towards the doors. She jumped out and crouched down so that she was on the same level as the girl. 'I know it's scary,' she said, 'but Dr Mitch is looking after your grandad and we're going to take him to the hospital where there are even more doctors to take good care of him.' She reached out to brush the tears from that small face. 'What's your name?'

'K-Kirsty.'

'Can you be brave, Kirsty? And come to the hospital with…?' She glanced up at the policewoman.

'Lydia,' she supplied.

Kirsty nodded slowly.

'Good girl…'

Jenna only intended to smile at Kirsty but somehow she ended up with two small arms around her neck and legs that wound themselves around her waist as she stood up. For just a heartbeat, and then another, she pressed her cheek against that soft hair, closing her eyes as she felt and responded to that plea for comfort. When she opened her eyes again, she could see over Kirsty's shoulder into the back of the ambulance where things were moving fast to tidy up the clutter of used packaging and equipment enough to make sure they could monitor their patient and keep anything they might need for the journey close at hand.

Mitch was already seated at the head of the stretcher, holding and squeezing the bag mask to keep Gerald breathing. He had the monitor screen close by but, right now, he was watching Jenna and Kirsty and there was a concerned frown on his face. Because she was holding them up? Fair enough.

'Come on,' she said, gently disengaging the limbs of the frightened child. 'I'm going to put you in my special car because Lydia's going to drive you to the hospital. I've got to go and help take care of your grandad.'

If Mitch had shown his ability to take command of a tense medical situation when they'd arrived on scene, he was even more in his element as they rushed the stretcher into the Trauma Resus room at the hospital they transported Gerald to. The specialist ED consultant leading the trauma team took a second look as someone led the transfer of their patient from stretcher to bed.

'On my count. On three. One…two…*three*…'

There was controlled chaos behind them as everybody played their part in rearranging the attachments for an oxygen supply, replacing ambulance monitoring gear with their own, hooking up a mechanical ventilator and taking a new set of vital signs. Someone was also cutting away the remnants of Gerald's clothing to expose his entire body for a detailed examination. It would be a few moments before everybody was ready for a detailed handover.

'Mitch?' The consultant took a third glance. 'What on earth are you doing out on the road? Last I heard you were HOD at St Barnabas.'

Jenna's head turned sharply. Mitch had told her that he'd worked in an emergency department before moving into general practice but he'd been Head of Department? In one of London's most prestigious trauma centres?

No wonder he had that kind of confidence she'd seen on scene today.

But why on earth had he gone from one end of the spectrum to the other as far as fast-paced medical careers could be lined up?

Mitch was simply shaking his head, dismissing the query. His attention was on the consultant in charge of the airway and breathing who was examining the hole in the side of Gerald's chest.

'Can you feel the lung? Has it re-inflated?'

'Yes. And we'll get a tube in to make sure it stays that way. Good job sorting that in the field. What was the initial blood loss?'

'Only a couple of hundred mils. Not enough to account for that level of hypotension.'

Jenna stepped back as the lead ambulance paramedic detailed their findings on arrival at the scene and Mitch took over to cover the more advanced interventions they'd supplied. There was ultrasound gear being manoeuvred into position beside the bed, a radiographer was getting ready to take any X-rays ordered and so many other people around that she could only catch a glimpse of Gerald.

Near the half-open door to this highly specialised and equipped space, she could see into the emergency department and the central desk. Lydia, the policewoman, was standing there and she was holding Kirsty's hand. A nurse was leading a distressed-looking woman towards the pair. Kirsty's mother? Gerald's daughter? Jenna felt a lump in her throat that was actually painful as she saw the expression on the woman's face.

She knew that kind of fear.

The kind of despair that could come later as a family was shattered.

She watched the woman scoop Kirsty into her arms and remembered the feeling of having those small limbs wound around her and that made the lump even bigger. Sharper. Enough to make it hard to breathe so Jenna automatically turned away. She watched what was happening in Resus for another minute but then moved out of the way completely. She could wait in the car until Mitch came out and make herself useful by seeing what needed to be restocked with their gear and starting on their own paperwork, which would be added to the ambulance report forms.

Finding a smile for Kirsty as she walked past, Jenna sincerely hoped that the news this family would be receiving later on would be good. Or at least hopeful. It was satisfying to know that everything possible that could have been done medically to make that a possibility had been done at the scene.

And done brilliantly. Jenna would have no hesitation at all in letting Mitch lead any job she was dispatched to when he was with her. She would trust him with her own life with any medical emergency.

She had already trusted him with her body in another way, after all.

Phew… It was just as well she was already walking through the automatic doors to leave the emergency department as that thought entered her mind because it immediately triggered memories of that night that actually felt like Mitch was touching her again. She could feel the intensity of the strokes of his hands. The touch of his fingers. The glide of his tongue. She was even aware of a spear of sensation deep inside to remind her of how *that* had felt as well and a ripple that was a faint echo of just how powerful her climax had been.

Oh, *my*… Jenna was grateful for the cool air outside, knowing that her cheeks had to have reddened. She knew they'd both been thinking about it when Mitch had arrived on station and they'd made eye contact for the first time since he'd left her flat that evening but that had been okay. There had been an instant, tacit agreement that it was not something they were going to think about, let alone discuss, while they were together in a professional arena. It had felt almost like friends thinking about a shared night out of going to the movies or out for dinner or something. It had only been intended to be a one-off, after all—to see how rusty they might both have become in the area of sexual skills?

Andrew Mitchell hadn't been at all rusty. She almost wished she hadn't reassured him about that at the time because, that way, they have come to an agreement to arrange another skill refresher session.

Any disturbing feeling of being disloyal to Stefan's memory had worn off since then so Jenna didn't even try and contradict the assessment that the sex with Mitch had been the best sex she'd ever experienced in her life. But how big a part of that was due to having gone without intimate touch for so long? A starving person would probably find any kind of food delicious, wouldn't they?

There was a level of curiosity in Jenna's mind now. Would a second time with Mitch be as good as the first? Because she was still thinking about that as Mitch climbed back into the passenger seat of the car, Jenna instantly found something else to talk about. Something professional.

'How good was that? You got to tick off three major skill sets that you haven't used for a while. Needle decompression, intubation *and* a finger thoracostomy as a bonus.' She was speaking a little too fast but Mitch was smiling.

'I think he's going to be okay. They're taking him up to Theatre. Ultrasound showed some abdominal bleeding that looks like it could be coming from a ruptured spleen. He's got blood products running now, which has stabilised his blood pressure.' His smile widened. 'It was a great job, wasn't it?'

Jenna nodded. 'And I have to say, I was impressed with how not rusty you were with your skills.'

Uh-oh…that was rather too similar to what she'd said to him that night. Jenna grabbed the handpiece to her radio from its clip on the dashboard. 'Rapid Response One available,' she told Control. 'We'll return to station to restock but we're still okay to respond in the meantime.'

Mitch clicked his seatbelt into place but he wasn't saying anything so Jenna filled the silence quickly.

'Not that I'm surprised you did so well,' she said. 'There I was thinking you'd done a registrar rotation or something in an ED but you were head of department? At St Barnabas?' Jenna couldn't help the admiration in her tone. 'Bit of a career change to become a GP, wasn't it?'

Mitch shrugged. 'Crossroads in your life appear for all sorts of reasons' was all he said.

Jenna turned out of the hospital entranceway to join the heavy traffic of a late London weekday afternoon. She had to weave across lanes so it didn't feel like an awkward silence between them. She wasn't just thinking about what lane she needed to be in, however, because it was impossible not to pick up on the message that his dramatic change in career was not something that Mitch wanted to talk about.

Fair enough.

Would she want to talk about the how and why of how she'd ended up in this particular branch of her career as a paramedic?

Absolutely not. And, if he'd been nosey about her personal history when they'd first spent time together, she would have put distance between them as fast as possible and that night would never have happened. And she was very, very glad that it had happened. This connection she'd discovered with this man was very new.

It was exciting.

She'd taken a huge leap reintroducing sex back into her life again and that time with Mitch had confirmed that being close to someone like that was definitely a missing piece. Whether she could find anyone else that might be interested in an occasional, purely physical interaction was an entirely different matter, mind you. But…maybe she didn't need to…?

'Good to know that you thought my skills weren't too rusty.' Mitch was smiling at her again. 'But there's always room for improvement, isn't there? Practice makes perfect.'

Oh…man…

That *smile*…

That flash of complete understanding in her eyes. Jenna had been completely in sync with the skills he was actually talking about when he'd suggested that practice made perfect. Okay…when he'd pretty much asked if she was up for a repeat of their 'no strings', 'no pressure' sexual encounter from the other week.

Not that she'd responded straight away. No…another emergency call had been a great excuse to shelve saying anything and it wasn't until the shift had ended more than an hour later that she'd caught Mitch's gaze and suggested a debrief over a beer or coffee—at her flat— and the way she'd held his gaze had told him that she had understood his earlier, subtle invitation. And that she was more than happy to accept it.

She understood a lot of things without needing any kind of explanation, Mitch thought as he followed her up those narrow stairs again and waited for her to unlock the door to her flat. Like the way she'd known how hard it had been for him to watch that dramatisation of a nasty horse-riding accident. And that he didn't want to talk about the reasons he'd left his position at St Barnabas to become a small town GP.

He liked that she was respecting his privacy but it actually had a contradictory effect because Mitch found himself wanting to tell her the truth about why he'd given up the career he loved.

About Ollie…

Except that would change things and they were perfect just as they were. Mitch pushed the door shut behind him as Jenna dropped her keys onto a table and hung her uniform jacket over the back of a chair. She pulled pens from her shirt pocket and a tourniquet and notepad from a pocket in her trousers and then stooped to unzip the sides of her heavy boots.

It looked as though she was getting undressed already and Mitch could feel his heart rate pick up and the curl of desire in his belly grow instantly a hell of a lot more noticeable.

'Maybe I can help with that…' He walked closer to Jenna and reached for the button at the top of her shirt. 'I'm not feeling that confident in my button undoing skills. I think…maybe I need a bit of practice?'

He was watching her face as his fingers brushed her skin while fumbling with the small button. He saw the way she caught her bottom lip between her teeth but that didn't quite stop the delighted smile trying to break out. He felt the way she came up on tiptoe as that button popped free and dipping his head to respond to that invitation to kiss her was enough to drive any other thoughts from his head.

Almost…

Maybe he was trying to find justification for keeping his personal life so private because the thought that occurred to him in that split second before his lips covered hers was that people who respected the privacy of others often preferred to keep their own lives private and maybe that was a part of the trust that had made a connection with Jenna so easy.

Perhaps they knew enough about each other as it was so he didn't need to feel that he was being dishonest in some way.

They'd both turned their backs on the possibility of significant relationships and there always a reason why people did that. A big reason, usually.

They'd chosen each other—or fate had done it for them—to step out of a sexual desert they'd been in for a long time and they'd discovered something amazing.

Mitch was kissing Jenna again now. And she was kissing him back. He could taste that deliciousness that had been haunting him ever since last time. He could feel her fingers on his belt—and the buckle—and the touch created an anticipation that was just as delicious. Until her fingers brushed lower as she undid the buckle and anticipation got blindsided by an irresistible need to get a whole lot closer.

It was way too tempting to stop thinking and give in to simply *feeling*…

He would tell her the truth at some point, of course he would.

But not now. Because it was totally irrelevant.

CHAPTER FIVE

THERE WERE A huge number of towns and cities that Jenna had been to during the years of establishing the FRAME network and she'd always loved the travelling—the disruption of a normal routine and the distraction of exploring new places.

Until now.

She wasn't loving being away from London this time, despite being in York, one of her favourite cities, and this being a five-day initiation course that provided enough time to really get to know an interesting group of mostly nurses who had come from small villages and remote communities to upskill in careers they were all passionate about. Not only that, she was also doing one of her favourite things in that she was training a trainer.

Rob was a skilled paramedic in his fifties, who'd been an APP like herself but had moved into teaching due to a bad back injury and, to his surprise, found he was loving his new direction. He was engaging, often funny and his students were responding in a way that told Jenna their new instructor was going to be one of their best. He'd been sitting in on her taking most of the sessions for the first couple of days but was gradually taking over. By Day Five and the assessments, he would be running this intake alone.

Right now, Rob was wrapping up a session that had never been a favourite for Jenna.

Paediatrics.

In the early days these sessions had, in fact, provided one of the biggest hurdles she'd had to overcome but also one of the biggest incentives to train people to the very best of their abilities in the hope that it could prevent another person having to go through what she'd endured.

The anatomical and physiological stuff was easy enough, covering the major differences from adults that influenced assessment and treatment, like the larger head and shorter necks, larger tongues and higher larynx, and normal ranges for vital signs like respiration and heart rates. The harder stuff was what Rob was teaching now and Jenna automatically found herself taking a mental step backwards. Distancing herself from the session's content enough to make it impersonal.

Trying to ignore that awareness like a soft drumbeat in the back of her head. Or was it in her heart?

'So, there you are.' Rob had a scene on the screen of a small, crumpled figure lying on a patch of grass. The background was blurred but you could see it was a child's playground. 'You're first on the scene and you've got an unresponsive kid. Before we get into how we're going to assess and treat this little guy, let's run over all the possible causes of paediatric collapse.'

It was just a single word, that drumbeat. A name that Jenna could hear again and again and again.

Eli... Eli... Eli...

Even now, as year after year had ticked past, it was still there. Nothing like as painful, of course, but she knew it was never going to disappear. She didn't want it to. Memories were precious. It wasn't something she was ever going to experience again but it was a part of her history. Her story. She had once been a wife. And a mother.

Rob was doing a great job eliciting the correct answers before revealing the next line of text on the screen. Under the heading of hypoxia, there were now bullet points of airway obstruction—with secondary headings of foreign body, croup, epiglottis and asthma—anaphylaxis, near drowning and cardiac causes that also needed a breakdown into areas like congenital heart disease, arrhythmias and heart failure.

'We're missing a couple, guys. Have a think.'

An older nurse spoke quietly. 'I went to a family in our village once. Their toddler had got himself all caught up in the strings for the venetian blind. He'd suffocated.'

Rob's nod was solemn. 'That's one of them, all right. Sadly not that uncommon, either.'

'Asphyxia' came up on the screen.

'There's another condition that is not uncommon in children. It can start at any age and someone with Down syndrome, metabolic disorders or autism may have this as well. Causes can include infection, brain injury, a tumour—'

'Epilepsy,' someone called. 'They're unresponsive due to a seizure.' The answer was accompanied by a headshake. 'I should have thought of that straight off. My nephew used to get them all the time. Seems to have grown out of them, though.

'And other kids have seizure activity that's very well controlled with medication. So when would you be more likely to get called in, do you think?'

'When the medication's not working. When the seizure doesn't stop.'

Rob gave the student a 'thumbs up' sign and then the last line of text appeared. Status epilepticus. And that was the point that Jenna let her focus drift completely, even turning her head enough to look out of the window. She could see a section of the ancient city walls that York was so famous for. She'd go and walk there again when classes were finished for the day. The sights were all familiar but she loved them. She might stop and have a coffee in the little shop in Barker's Tower and she'd never miss the highlight of Clifford's Tower, the largest remaining section of York castle.

But even the prospect of revisiting a place she enjoyed so much wasn't enough to squash the nagging feeling that she wanted to be somewhere else and Jenna knew exactly where it was she wanted to be. In Croydon. More specifically, in her own flat. Or out on the road. Because, even more specifically, she wanted to be with Mitch.

She was missing him.

She'd only known him a matter of weeks. They'd only been working together in the rapid response unit a handful of times and they'd been to bed together on even fewer occasions but his company had become an important part of her life.

Jenna really liked him.

Okay…she really, *really* liked him. She admired his professional skill and his impressive intelligence but there was a lot more to his company that she was ap-

preciating more every time they were together. He had
a compassion and gentleness with his patients that was
completely genuine and he was, quite probably, the nic-
est man she'd ever met. Apart from Stefan, of course.
But he wasn't so nice he was too good to be true. She'd
seen him deal with unpleasant people in no uncertain
terms and he still had that air of mystery about him that
was intriguing. Why *had* he left such a prestigious position at St Barnabas?

She would have enjoyed Mitch's company—the satis-
faction of working together and the stimulation of having a professional conversation—without the bonus of
the sex but, if she was really honest, that was a huge part
of this pull she was feeling to be back home. She knew
that she'd been missing that physical closeness with another human being but she'd had no idea how much
more than something purely physical it could be. Those
times with Mitch could make the world stop turning for
a while. Could make it impossible to have the head space
to include anything from the past. Or the future. For as
long as it lasted, that connection—that exquisite tension
and pleasure—was all that existed. In nearly a decade,
Jenna had never found anything else that came close to
giving her even a temporary belief that life could be as
perfect for her as for the luckiest people alive.

Rob was moving on, directing the class into exer-
cises for assessing and treating paediatric emergencies and he was managing so well that Jenna knew she
could excuse herself from the room for a few minutes.
Enough time to check her rosters for the coming week
or two and see what days she might be back on the road
in South London. And to send a text message to see if
Mitch was available to share that time with her?

Yes… Even knowing when she was going to see him again would prevent that knot of tension from growing any more disruptive. What was it, exactly? A worry that this new dimension in her life might vanish as unexpectedly as it had arrived in her life? Maybe Jenna just needed to be more confident that this arrangement she had with Mitch was providing something they both wanted. That they both needed, even.

Just to be on the safe side, though, she would send that text. Holding her hand up to indicate a five-minute interval, she tilted her head to acknowledge Rob's smile and nod and slipped out of the classroom.

When his text came in response to hers, almost instantly, to say that he'd look forward to coming out on the road with her next Friday, Jenna found herself holding her phone against her heart, leaning back against the corridor wall and closing her eyes as she let her breath out in a sigh.

She felt like a teenager who'd just been asked on a date by the boy she'd had a crush on for ever.

It felt a lot like she might be falling in love with Andrew Mitchell which was most definitely not supposed to be happening.

But what if it was?

A new thought occurred to Jenna and it seemed like her entire body wanted to consider it. What if Mitch felt the same way she did about not wanting children in his life? They wouldn't need to consider anything as formal as marriage or anything but it was quite possible to imagine their connection lasting…well…for ever…?

One look at the sky as Mitch headed towards London early on a Friday made him think that if he was sensible, he'd be staying at home on his day off. It was clearly going to be stormy and the forecast had warnings of possible thunder- or even hail-storms. He could have caught up on some shopping and housework and then had a fire going so that the house was lovely and warm for when Ollie got home from school but no... he was on his way to spend a day with Jenna and there would probably be a spate of the kind of road accidents that always came with bad weather. He remembered the chaos that could accumulate back in his days in the emergency department but he'd been working inside where it was nice and dry.

Today he'd be working outside and could be getting miserably cold and wet where it would be so much harder to do something like inserting an IV or splinting a fracture and...and he hadn't felt this happy in a very long time.

He'd found himself thinking about Jenna rather a lot between the times they spent together. Sometimes he'd remember how much he enjoyed a particular conversation with her or how impressive it was to watch her work. Other times, he could remember just an expression on her face, the way a brief glance had made him feel so good or...oh, *help*...the feel and taste of her skin in those secret places. Mitch had to blow out a slow breath as what was becoming a very familiar shaft of sensation came from nowhere and obliterated any other coherent thought.

Fortunately it only lasted for as long as it took to blink but the echoes were still astonishingly strong. He must have felt the same way with Tegan but it was so long ago he couldn't really remember. This—with Jenna—felt completely new. Amazing enough to remind him of what it had been like to discover sex as a teenager. Important enough to create a hint of something that felt like nervousness because he didn't want it to stop anytime soon.

Anytime at all…?

The first spots of rain spattered his windscreen as Mitch merged with Greater London commuters. The red traffic lights ahead took so long to change from red to green that he could allow his thoughts to wander again. There was no real reason for this 'no strings' relationship with Jenna to end, was there? Not if Jenna was getting as much out of it as he was. Maybe…one day…he might even be able to introduce her to Ollie.

Mitch knew she might not want children to interfere with her career and that was fair enough, but he also knew that she was good with them—he'd seen the way she'd been with that little girl, Kirsty, the granddaughter of the man who'd been so badly injured in that hit and run. He'd been caught, not only by how easily he'd seen her win the trust of that frightened child but the way she'd looked with Kirsty in her arms. That moment when Jenna had given her a cuddle and the expression on her face when she'd looked up and caught his gaze.

It had only been for a heartbeat but, for that instant, Jenna had looked more vulnerable than he'd ever seen her. As if she'd been spotted doing something she didn't want anyone else to see. It hadn't been the first time that Mitch had wondered if there was a reason other than her career that had shaped Jenna's decision not to have children but now, sitting here at a traffic light, was the first time it occurred to him that she might feel differently about having a child that wasn't her own in her life.

That it was just possible she might welcome it?

Ollie would adore Jenna. She was funny and smart and clever and she could connect with children effortlessly.

Good grief…was he actually thinking the unthinkable? That there might be a future for him and Jenna?

Mitch brushed the thought aside as the line of cars ahead of him started to move and it was raining hard enough for his automatic wipers to speed up. One step at a time, he told himself. This thing could fizzle out as quickly as it had begun. But if it didn't…well…who knew?

It wasn't the first time that Jenna and Mitch had been despatched as first responders to a cardiac arrest and they both knew they could work seamlessly for the intense period of trying to resuscitate someone who was hovering much closer to death than life. To do it in the middle of a building site, with the man's employees trying to hold tarpaulins over the medics, certainly made it more of a challenge as they performed CPR, got the electrodes in place and then defibrillated their patient but it also made it more satisfying to have brought him back to a perfusing rhythm by the time the first available ambulance back-up arrived to transport the man to hospital.

Cranking up the heat in the rapid response vehicle to full strength helped dry Mitch and Jenna's wet clothing and warm them up on the way to their next call which was a multi-vehicle crash. The traffic was backed up for miles around the scene by the time they got near the area and even Jenna's inventive driving tricks couldn't have got them through without the assistance of police units forcing a way through for a fire truck.

They got wet again all too quickly as they moved between the vehicles involved to triage at least a dozen people but, while some people involved in the accident would need transport to hospital for moderate injuries, nobody was seriously hurt which meant that the rapid response vehicle could leave the scene and be available for the next call.

Jenna's dark curls were plastered against her forehead as she climbed back into the driver's seat and she could feel drips rolling down her neck.

'The weather's vile,' she declared, reaching to unclip the microphone on the dashboard to radio through their availability. 'Had enough yet?'

'Nope.' He was grinning back at her. 'I'm loving it. Bit of rain has never melted anybody that I've heard of.'

He held her gaze when he'd stopped speaking and, for some reason, Jenna's finger resisted pushing the button on the microphone to open communication. Mitch clearly *was* loving this but there was another very clear message in his eyes and it wasn't just the challenging work conditions that were making him so happy.

It was because he was with *her*.

That briefest of moments was enough to let Jenna know she felt the same way. More importantly, that this was what she'd wanted all along and that, despite convincing herself that it was only something physical missing from her life, she was actually ready for a lot more than that.

As scary as it was, she was ready to embrace life again. Because holding Mitch's gaze for another heartbeat was long enough for questions to be both asked and answered.

Are you thinking what I'm thinking?

Yes.

Can we trust this?

Yes...

They both broke that eye contact then, as if they needed privacy to absorb that something huge was changing here. Jenna sucked in a breath and pushed the button on the side of the microphone.

'Rapid Response One to Control. We're available.'

'Roger that' came the response. 'You can head back to station.'

'Yay...' Jenna started the engine. 'Let's stop at that nice coffee shop on the way and get some cake as well. I reckon we deserve it, don't you?'

'Absolutely.'

But Mitch was pulling his phone from his pocket, something he never normally did when they were working together. Jenna didn't need to catch the frown on his face a second later as he read a text message—she could feel the sudden tension in his body.

'Something up?'

'It's, ah...from my father. He wants me to ring him when I've got a spare moment.' Mitch sounded hesitant. 'He wouldn't ask unless it was something urgent.'

'Call him.' Jenna nodded. 'We're only on our way back to base.'

But she could still sense his hesitation and, oddly, this felt like a much bigger decision than to respond to his father's text message.

Maybe Mitch's father was unwell. Or was he calling about another member of the family, like his mother or siblings? Being reminded that she knew nothing about Mitch's life should be a warning bell but, oddly, it wasn't worrying Jenna at all. She knew *him* now and instinct told her that that was enough. That she could trust him.

She killed the engine and then turned her head. 'I don't want my partner being distracted by a family concern on the next job,' she said. 'We've got time. Call him. I'll do our paperwork.'

It was still raining heavily outside their vehicle and there were people shouting and heavy trucks revving as breakdown services arrived to start clearing the traffic jam but, inside their car, Jenna could still hear the voice of the older man on the other end of Mitch's phone call clearly enough to make out most of what he was saying.

'Sorry to call you like this,' he'd started.

'What's happened, Dad?' Mitch asked quickly. 'What's going on?'

'Nothing to worry about. I just took Ollie in to see Euan, that's all. He was jumping in puddles on the way to school and tripped over. He got a cut on his eyebrow that bled enough to need some attention.'

'Did it need stitching?'

'No, no...nothing like that. Euan just used a couple of those wound closure strips but the bleeding had already stopped by then. I wouldn't even be telling you but Ollie just wanted to tell you about it when you weren't busy. I think he got a bit of a fright, that's all. He needs his dad to tell him how brave he was.'

Jenna wasn't deliberately eavesdropping. She couldn't even hear the other end of the conversation that clearly but she caught the word 'Dad' and there was no mistaking the bell-like tones of the young child that started speaking then.

'Daddy? I fell over and hurt my head.'

'I know, buddy.' There was a note in Mitch's voice

that Jenna had never heard before. 'But Grandy told me how brave you were. I'm really, really proud of you.' He was speaking quietly but the sound was as comforting as a hug. The sound of pure love.

Jenna knew that tone so, so well. The sound of a parent speaking to their child and it cut into a place in her heart with such unexpected sharpness she actually caught her breath and had to blink back a sting behind her eyes that could have become tears. She was perfectly in control by the time Mitch finished his call only a short time later.

She was also hurt.

Disappointed.

And angry. It felt like she had been deceived. Lured into a new hope that her life could include a fairy-tale new direction that provided companionship and love and…and a passion she'd never expected to find again and now it was being taken away from her. Or rather, she had to get rid of it.

As fast as possible.

Her tone, when she spoke, couldn't have been more the opposite to that warmth with which Mitch had been talking to his son.

'So…' Jenna didn't look up from the clipboard on her lap where she had been filling in some paperwork. 'You've got a son?'

'Yeah…' She could hear Mitch take in a slow breath. 'His name's Ollie. He's four.'

As if this new information wasn't devastating enough, Jenna was aware of another alarm sounding.

'And Ollie's mother?' She glanced sideways, only to find that Mitch was staring straight ahead through the rain-streaked windscreen. 'Do you think it might be time to admit that you're married as well?'

'God, *no*...' His gaze swerved to meet hers. 'Ollie's mother died a couple of days after he was born. Good grief...' Mitch pushed his fingers through his hair. 'Do you really think I'd would have gone to bed with you if I was *married*? That I would cheat on someone?'

Jenna shrugged, looking away. She didn't want to see that shock in his eyes. To see that he might have reason to feel hurt himself. 'You didn't tell me you had a kid.'

'No.'

The agreement was a single word that fell into a silence. One that Jenna wasn't about to break because she knew she might say something she would later regret. Or maybe she didn't want Mitch to know how hurt she was. Or that she had even been dreaming of their 'arrangement' growing into something a whole heap more meaningful. At least, this way, she could get out of this with some dignity still intact.

She should start the car and get them back to the station as quickly as possible. That way she could get out of this vehicle and wouldn't have to be this physically close to him because that was becoming harder as the minutes ticked on. She was never going to get really close to this man again, was she? She was never going to be kissed by him again. Or feel that incredible touch...

She was reaching for the key when Mitch broke the silence and her fingers turned into a fist and dropped back to her side.

'I didn't tell you because I knew how you felt about kids. I thought it would put you off having anything to do with me.'

'You got something right, at least.' Jenna's tone was clipped. Icy. 'If I'd known, I'd never have…'

Her words trailed off because it was all too easy to sense that her response was surprising Mitch. Disappointing him? Was he also starting to feel angry, perhaps?

'What—invited me to come out on a shift with you? To get professional experience? You only did that because you fancied some *sex*?'

'*No*…of course not.' Jenna was appalled.

'So what possible difference could it have made that I was a father?'

The suggestion that she'd offered him the opportunity to work with her in exchange for sex was beyond offensive. And, okay, she wasn't the only one angry, here, but that accusation hurt.

Of course it wouldn't have made any difference that someone she had a professional relationship with was a father. But getting close enough to have sex with anyone had been a very big deal. Something she'd believed had been significant for both of them. Was it really only a matter of minutes ago that she'd been so certain she wasn't the only one who'd thought it could grow into something more? He'd known how she felt about including children in her life so, yeah…he *should* have been more honest. *She* wasn't the one who'd lied by omission.

This was her own fault, however, because she'd allowed herself to start dreaming of a potential future. She'd set herself up for getting hurt and, for heaven's sake, that had been the one thing she'd vowed never to do ever again.

'I made a mistake,' she said aloud. 'A big mistake…'

'You and me both.'

The anger crackled in the air between them. The sooner they could get back to station, the better. Presumably, Mitch would choose to cut this shift short at that point and go home. It was quite likely that Jenna would never see him again.

Good, she thought. She could do without this kind of angst in her life.

As if it was an extension of the atmosphere within the vehicle, the radio crackled into life.

'Control to Rapid Response One. Are you receiving?'

'Receiving.' Jenna had the microphone in her hand instantly. 'Go ahead, Control.'

'Please proceed to four-three-three Andersons Road, towards Fairleigh. Details coming through now. Code Blue, thanks. Collapsed person—not breathing.'

Jenna started the engine. The windscreen wipers sprang back to life and cleared the windscreen as both she and Mitch reached to fasten their seatbelts. The priority call they were being dispatched to was in the opposite direction to the station so it would appear that they had at least one more job they were going to have to work on together. It didn't matter how upsetting their interaction had just been, they were both going to have to forget it completely and think about the patient they were heading towards.

Hearing the wail of the siren made it easy because it was an automatic switch in Jenna's brain that allowed her to dismiss anything personal that could affect her ability as a paramedic.

Maybe Mitch had learned the same lesson during his time as an emergency department consultant. Not that it mattered. He might not have found their conversation anywhere near as disturbing as she had but if anything

emotional did affect his work he could go back to the
vehicle and stay there for the duration of the call-out,
couldn't he?

This was Jenna's vehicle.

Jenna's rules.

CHAPTER SIX

SOMETHING FELT OFF about this job.

It wasn't simply due to the exchange that had clearly ended whatever personal stuff had been going on between him and Jenna. This was something that was sounding an instinctive, professional alarm at the back of Mitch's mind. Something that was making the hairs on the back of his neck prickle as they stood up.

It was an ordinary enough looking house up a long, tree-lined drive. There hadn't been anyone waiting anxiously outside for help to arrive, to direct them to where they were needed, but that wasn't surprising either because the call had warned them that someone wasn't breathing. The person who'd called for the emergency services might be inside the house, as the only person available to perform CPR.

Neither Mitch nor Jenna were giving a single moment's thought to any personal tension between them as they loaded themselves with the gear they'd need to deal with a respiratory or cardiac arrest. The defibrillator, the pack with the IV gear, airway kit and all the drugs they might need, an oxygen cylinder and a suction unit. Both the driveway and the area outside the house had a patchy layer of pebbles and the rain was turning bare ground into mud which Mitch was trying to avoid getting onto his boots. Not that it really mattered—any relatives of someone who needed resuscitation were unlikely to complain about mud being tracked into a house by the people who were arriving to help.

'Ambulance,' Jenna called out as she opened the front door following a sharp rap.

There was no response to the call and they stepped inside to find an eerie silence in the house. That was when Mitch knew something wasn't right. Jenna obviously felt it as well because she paused before going any further into the dark hallway.

'I'll go first,' she murmured, her voice low enough not to be overheard. 'I'm not sure I like this.'

'Same.' Mitch nodded. He reached for a light switch. 'Being this dark in here's not helping.'

'Keep doors open and an escape route in mind at all times,' Jenna continued whispering. 'And hold that pack in front of you. If you need to, throw it at someone to give you a bit more time to get out.'

But there was no one presenting any kind of threat in the first room they looked into. Or in any of the other rooms that opened off this hallway until they came to a living area at the end. There didn't appear to be anyone in here, either. No one standing, anyway. There was a figure on the floor. A large man was face down and unmoving amongst overturned chairs. A broken plate and spilled food lay beside him on the floor and another half-eaten meal on the table looked as if it had been interrupted some time ago.

Jenna didn't rush in to check on the collapsed person, however. She was looking around. Doors from this room opened into what looked like a kitchen and a back door to the house was open. Rain had puddled onto a tiled floor and, as Mitch followed her gaze, the wind caught the door which made it bang shut and then bounce open again.

'Stay by the door,' Jenna told Mitch. 'Keep an eye out for anyone coming in through the front.'

She walked slowly towards the prone male figure. With gloved fingers she felt the side of his neck and for what seemed like a long, long moment, she was completely still. She lifted her gaze to meet Mitch's and gave her head a small shake. Then she reached for her radio with her other hand. It was then that Mitch noticed the blood on the hand she'd used to feel for a pulse and he could see the shadow of the dark stain on the carpet beside the man's head.

'Rapid Response One to Control. Are you receiving?'

'Receiving loud and clear. Go ahead.'

'We have a situation at four-three-three Andersons Road. Code zero male.'

Mitch knew that the code zero was used as a status for a deceased person. He assumed that Jenna was quite sure that he had been deceased for enough time to make an attempt to resuscitate him futile. She used another code he wasn't familiar with and he wondered if that was to indicate that the circumstances looked more than a little suspicious. Just as he wondered if a person responsible for this death might have been the one who'd made the call to the emergency services, something to one side of the room caught his attention. Someone was outside, looking through the window, but they were already rapidly moving out of sight as Mitch looked up.

'Someone's outside,' he warned Jenna.

'We're not alone on scene,' Jenna informed the person in the control centre. 'We require police back-up. Stat.'

'Roger that.' The radio fell silent for a few moments, as though the call taker was busy activating other calls. Jenna was on her feet as it crackled back to life.

'Return to your vehicle if it's safe to do so. Don't touch anything and don't leave the scene. Back-up will be with you as soon as possible.'

'Roger that.'

Mitch waited for instruction from Jenna before he moved.

'Try and keep to the same track we used coming in here,' she told him quietly. 'If this *is* a homicide, forensics will be all over this and we don't want to have interfered with any more evidence than we might have already.' She way she shook her head showed Mitch she was less than happy. 'I've heard about cases like this. We could be stuck here for hours.'

The wheels of the car hadn't sunk into the layer of mud at the top of the driveway but they might as well have been buried up to their rims.

They were stuck.

The property in Andersons Road had ghost-like figures everywhere. Forensic investigators wearing disposable white overalls with hoods, masks, gloves and shoe covers were coming and going from the house and working outside in the rain, trying to collect evidence before it got destroyed by weather conditions or movements of people or vehicles.

Mitch and Jenna couldn't drive away. They were waiting for their fingerprints to be taken so they could be excluded from prints that would be taken inside the house and currently they had only socks on their feet because their boots had been borrowed to record the kind of tracks they may have made going into or coming out of the house, where it had been confirmed that a murder had taken place some hours ago.

Listening to the chatter of emergency services radio transmissions only made it more frustrating that a rapid response vehicle had been taken off the road and its crew stood down for the rest of this shift. There was no indication of when they might be allowed to leave and it already felt like far too long, thanks to the fact that Jenna and Mitch were barely talking to each other.

Any distraction had been effectively diluted and the silence inside this vehicle was loaded with all the angst of the conversation they'd been having when the call to this incident had happened.

Mitch was still feeling that edge of anger. With himself as much as with Jenna. How had he allowed himself to think it was okay to simply ignore the existence of his own son just because he'd found a woman he was so attracted to? He'd already known that Jenna's attitude towards children meant that she would never be someone he would want to have involved in his day-to-day personal life but what had happened between them had felt significant in its own way. And she'd dismissed it as being a 'big mistake'? That stung.

But it wasn't entirely Jenna's fault, was it?

He'd known he was being less than completely honest and he hadn't liked that, either. A sideways glance showed him that Jenna was watching the forensic team at work but he knew she wasn't happy. She'd rather be anywhere else than stuck in the small space of this vehicle with him. Not talking to each other wasn't helping, either. It was, in fact, rather immature behaviour, come to think of it.

'I'm sorry,' he found himself saying aloud—and meaning it. 'I don't like things being like this between us.'

Jenna's head turned swiftly. She looked almost relieved. 'Neither do I,' she said quietly. 'It's horrible.'

'I should have been more honest with you.'

Jenna didn't say anything but Mitch had seen the flash of hurt in the instant before she dropped her gaze. It clearly needed a bit more than just an apology to fix an atmosphere he knew neither of them wanted to be sitting in for goodness only knew how much longer.

'I didn't expect you to offer me the chance to work with you like this,' he continued. 'And I certainly didn't expect to be attracted to you like I was and…and to find that you felt the same way was… I don't know…a kind of miracle. I didn't stop to think about anything else.'

He hadn't been thinking of anything except how much he wanted to be physically close to Jenna. A closeness that was never likely to happen again, now.

'I didn't think that my home life was relevant to anything happening between me and you,' he added. 'It wasn't as if we were dating. Or thinking about a serious relationship.'

'No.'

Jenna seemed to be staring at her hands as she responded in almost a whisper but then she glanced up and met his gaze. Just for a moment. Just long enough to remind Mitch of the way she'd held his gaze for much longer than that only a very short time ago and that he'd been quite certain that he wasn't the only one to be thinking that this—whatever it was they'd discovered together—could possibly become something more than putting a toe back into the waters of a long abandoned sex life. And then she spoke again.

'I'm sorry, too,' she said. 'I know I overreacted.'

'I doubt that,' Mitch said. 'I'm pretty sure that whatever it is that's made you feel so strongly about things is completely justified.'

Silence fell again but, this time, it was different. Mitch could sense that Jenna wanted to say something but didn't know where to start. Or whether she should say anything at all, perhaps? The only way he could help was to give her the time she needed and, sure enough, a minute or so later, she began offering words that were hesitant enough to sound as if they were coming from a very private and well-guarded place.

'I…had a son, too,' she told him, slowly. 'His name was Eli. He was four years old when he died.'

Oh… *God*… The same age as Oliver? Mitch couldn't bear to even try and imagine how devastating it would be to lose his child. How impossible it would be to carry on any semblance of a normal life.

'Oh… Jenna,' he said, softly. 'I'm *so*, so sorry,'

Reaching for her hand had been purely instinctive. That she let him take hold of it and curled her fingers around his was a response that made the crack in his heart widen. He could feel the enormity of what she had faced. Could feel the astonishing amount of courage she had needed.

The silence this time was totally different. It felt as if they were connecting on a new level. It reminded Mitch of the feeling of making up after a heated argument. Jenna still hadn't taken her hand away.

'You know what it's like,' she said. 'To lose someone you love. You said that Ollie's mother died just after he was born?'

'Mmm.' Mitch was very aware of the subtle pressure of Jenna's hand. An invitation to share? Would that open the door to hearing more of *her* story? Mitch wanted to know more—as much as she was willing to tell him.

'Tegan developed signs of pre-eclampsia,' he told her. 'She had an emergency Caesarean at thirty-one weeks but…there were complications.' He took a slow, inward breath. It wasn't often he needed to recall details that were still horrific because it was so unexpected, these days, to lose a young, healthy woman due to child-birth. 'Her blood pressure was still way too high. Her liver had a spontaneous rupture. She went into renal failure.' Mitch swallowed hard. 'She never saw Ollie. Never held him.'

'So *that's* why you gave up your position as HOD at St Barnabas?' Jenna's tone was one of complete un-derstanding.

'My life imploded.' Mitch nodded. 'The only thing that mattered was Ollie and I had time while he was in the NICU to rearrange my life around him. My dad was the rock that let me hold things together. I eventu-ally moved back into the house I'd grown up in—with my son. I'd planned to take a year off work but then the position at the medical centre came up and I thought, why not? Being a GP would make me part of the com-munity and the hours can be very child friendly for a single parent.'

He could feel the way Jenna's hand had relaxed in his as she listened to him. And she still hadn't taken it away? He gave it a tiny squeeze. 'You'd know about how important that is, I'm guessing? Or was Eli's dad around to help?'

Jenna shook her head. 'That was where it started. Stefan was a paramedic like me—we met when we were rostered on the same watch—and, after Eli was born, we juggled shifts so that one of us could be at home with him as much as possible. Eli was about six months old when Stef had taken him for a walk to the park and he got hit by a car that went out of control and onto the footpath. Hit and run. They never caught the driver.' Mitch heard the tiny hiccup in her voice.

'Stef died before an ambulance even got there but a witness said he'd done his best to protect Eli by trying to push him out of the way in his pram. That he kept asking about him until he lost consciousness completely.'

Mitch simply nodded. He would do anything to protect Ollie. Any father would.

'It undoubtedly saved his life but he still had some serious injuries, including a skull fracture. He was in hospital for more than a month and…and he developed epilepsy later that was hard to control with medication. It was a seizure that he died from. Nobody at school saw it start and he was in the playground. They think he just hit his head too hard, too many times, on the asphalt.'

Mitch didn't have to say anything to let Jenna know that he was thinking of his own son and imagining her unbearable loss. All he needed to do was to hold her hand. And to hold her gaze, eventually, when she was ready to meet his.

'How long ago did you lose Eli?'

'Nearly five years now. Which was about when I

came up with the idea of the FRAME network and threw myself into getting the project off the ground. My career was all I had left, you know?'

'I know,' Mitch said quietly. 'And you've achieved something amazing but...'

Jenna's eyes widened. *'But?'*

'But I think you're lonely. Like me...'

Jenna's lips parted as if she was about to say something but then they were both startled by a tap on the window behind her. Her head swerved and she rolled the window down enough to hear what the white-shrouded person was saying.

'We've finished with your boots. And we reckon we've got anything useful we can find out here in the way of tyre marks and shoe prints. Whatever's left is getting ruined by this rain. Sorry to have held you guys up for so long.'

'No worries,' Jenna told him.

Mitch nodded his head. He was glad they'd been trapped on scene. If they hadn't, they would have gone back to the station and he would have gone home and he and Jenna would most likely have never seen each other again. Ever. Instead, they had just discovered a kind of connection they would probably never be able to find with anyone else on the planet.

An astonishing connection.

'We still need to get your fingerprints but the team's flat out inside the house. Would it be okay if you went into the nearest police station and did it there?'

'Of course. We've got one virtually next door to our headquarters in Croydon. Would that be okay?'

'Absolutely. I'll get in touch with them and let them know you're coming.'

* * *

Jenna had been about to deny that she was lonely when that extraordinary conversation with Mitch had been interrupted but she'd had time to think about it on the drive back to her home patch.

She was still thinking about it as she watched Mitch take his turn to have his fingerprints recorded. Focusing on his hands reminded her of how it had felt to have him holding her hand while they were sharing such intimate details of their personal histories. And how it had felt to have him touch her—and hold her—in a way that she hadn't been touched, or held, in such a very long time.

As if he sensed the direction of her thoughts, Mitch looked up and caught her gaze at that point and Jenna felt the corners of her mouth lift. No more than a hint of a smile, really, but it was enough to make the corners of Mitch's eyes crinkle and create a softening in his expression that was almost like the kind of touch Jenna had been thinking about.

He waited until they were outside the police station and walking back to the ambulance station where Jenna had parked the car before saying anything.

'Just so you know,' he told her, 'you didn't overreact. I think I blindsided you in a way that must have been an absolute kick in the guts and I just want to say "I'm sorry" again.'

It was still raining. Mitch was holding an umbrella over both of them as they walked side by side.

'I kind of did overreact,' Jenna said. 'I can actually deal with kids perfectly well when they're my patients or my friends' children. I think…' Mitch was an amazing person and he deserved to know the truth, didn't he? 'I think I read too much into what was happening with our…um…friendship and that's why it hit me so hard. I could never get close to a child again. I think my ability to love anyone so unconditionally died when Eli died.'

Mitch nodded slowly. 'I get that. I've felt like that about sharing my life with another woman since I lost Tegan.'

The long glance they shared acknowledged the sad connection they'd found in each other.

'But I think you're right,' Jenna added quietly. 'I hadn't really thought about it but I *have* been lonely.' She smiled at him and made an attempt to lighten the atmosphere. 'Maybe I should get a dog, after all.'

'I've got a dog, too.' Mitch returned the smile. 'I just wanna be totally upfront about that one.'

Jenna's smile widened but Mitch's actually faded. 'I really like you, Jenna,' he said.

'I really like you, too, Mitch.'

'And, I have to say, the sex has been amazing. *You're* amazing.'

'Same…' Jenna had to drop her gaze to escape the intensity in Mitch's gaze. She remembered how she had felt when it seemed like she was never going to see Mitch again. How deeply that hurt and disappointment had reached.

'We know where we stand, don't we? And we can probably understand *why* we feel like that better than anyone else would.'

Jenna nodded her agreement.

'And…we're both lonely.'

Jenna nodded again. She couldn't disagree with that.

'Maybe…' he suggested softly, 'we can still be friends? With zero expectations of anything else? Even better friends than we were because…you know…no more secrets.'

They were almost at the station where Mitch's car was parked. They were also close to Jenna's flat.

'It's early,' she said. 'But they'll have someone else covering the rapid response and they won't put us back on duty for less than a couple of hours.' She looked up to catch Mitch's gaze. 'Do you need to rush home?'

He shook his head. 'They won't be expecting me until the usual time. Ollie's perfectly happy with his grandpa. He just wanted me to know how brave he'd been.'

'So, would you like to come back to my place? For…a coffee or something?'

Mitch hadn't looked away and, if she'd thought his gaze had been intense before, it was nothing compared to what she could see in his eyes right now.

'I would like that very much,' he said.

Mitch was tilting the umbrella so that it became a screen from anyone else in the street. He was also bending his head and Jenna knew he was about to kiss her. And she wanted him to. More than anything.

'I choose the something,' he murmured, as his lips brushed hers before settling. 'If that's all good with you.'

That did it. That private code after the intensity of how they'd forged a new level to their connection made the thought of not having Mitch in her life—or in her bed—something she didn't want to even contemplate.

Jenna felt his lips against hers, his mouth swallowing her response.

'Couldn't be better…'

CHAPTER SEVEN

MITCH HAD FALLEN ASLEEP.

This wasn't part of the new routine of the last few weeks and Jenna knew she should wake him up and she would. Soon. But he'd had such an early start to get to Croydon for the beginning of his weekly shift with her in the rapid response vehicle at seven a.m. It had been a full-on day, as well, with back-to-back call-outs until six p.m. and, even now, at nearly eight-thirty p.m., there would probably be significant traffic on the roads between Croydon and Allensbury so the drive would be safer if he just had a bit of a catnap. Ten or fifteen minutes at the most so he wouldn't be too late home.

Not that Ollie would still be awake, of course, but Mitch had had a chat to him on the phone to say good-night and he was perfectly happy at home with his grandpa. And Jenna had been perfectly happy to hear the conversation on speakerphone because she'd made the mental shift since that awful day when they had almost thrown away their friendship. Ollie was a child like any other in her life. The offspring of one of her friends. Or a patient. She could keep her guardrails firmly in place.

It was all good.

Jenna felt her mouth curve into a contented smile as she snuggled a little closer to Mitch, turning her face just enough to touch that soft skin on the underside of his arm with her lips. Mitch stirred in his sleep, making a soft sound and curling his arm around Jenna to draw her even closer. She closed her eyes and let her breath out slowly in a soft sigh.

Actually, it couldn't be better, could it?

Thanks to that intense day when she'd discovered Mitch was a father and had finally opened up about the reason it had upset her so much, there was a new connection that felt way more than 'good'. He understood. He been through a huge loss himself. Jenna didn't have to hide anything any longer and neither did Mitch so there was a new honesty there as well. An honesty that extended to them being totally upfront about what they wanted from their friendship.

Jenna was never going to be asked to include Ollie in her life in any meaningful way. The last thing Mitch wanted was a wife—or a new mother for his son—for exactly the same reasons that having another child was the last thing Jenna wanted. What Mitch *did* want was a connection with someone that could fill the space where loneliness took up residence. Jenna was more than happy to be that someone because now she didn't have to keep *doing* things or *going* places so that she wouldn't notice she was right in the middle of that lonely space herself.

And, yes, she did have other friends she could be with, as company to go out to dinner or a show or simply to hang with, but it wasn't the same because there were levels to loneliness and one of them could only be filled by a physical closeness that none of Jenna's friends could ever provide and she'd never wanted to go looking for it elsewhere.

She hadn't been looking for it when Mitch had walked into her life.

She hadn't known how much she needed it, either. That closeness. His touch. And the sex...well, she wouldn't have believed it could get any better but there was a tenderness to it now that could only have come from that understanding—that unique connection of shared loss that they had with each other.

Mitch stirred again and Jenna could feel the moment he woke up, as his muscles tensed and he drew in a sharp breath.

'Oh, no...what time is it?'

'Only eight-thirty. Don't worry, you've only been asleep for about ten minutes.'

She could feel the tension in his body ebbing. 'Phew... I had a horrible thought that I wouldn't get home before Ollie got up.' Mitch rolled onto his side and smiled at Jenna. 'We have important plans for after breakfast and before I go into work to cover the Saturday morning clinic. I'd better get up and dressed.'

'Okay...' Jenna was smiling back at him. 'I *was* going to wake you up soon but I thought you could do with the rest before you have to make that long trip home. And...'

'And...?'

Her smile felt almost shy, which was a bit crazy considering what they'd been doing only a very short time ago. 'And it was rather nice just lying here with you for a few minutes.'

'Mmm...' Mitch bent his head and placed a gentle kiss on Jenna's lips. 'I'd better not tell you how much I look forward to my Fridays these days.'

He kissed her again and, this time, she could feel those first flickers of desire building again—a sensation she was coming to recognise instantly and welcome more than wholeheartedly. Maybe Mitch was feeling it too, because he broke off the kiss with a soft groan.

'I really have to go.' He rolled away from Jenna to sit on the side of the bed. He reached for the shirt that had been thrown carelessly over the wooden post, pushed his arms through the sleeves and began to button it up.

Jenna pulled the sheet up to cover her bare breasts as she propped herself against her pillows to watch Mitch get dressed.

'What are the important plans with Ollie?' There… she'd included his son in their conversation without even thinking about it. As if it was the most natural thing in the world. It was getting easier all the time.

'It's Pets' Day at school soon and Ollie wants to take our old dog, Jet. What he's most excited about is that there's a dress-up competition for pets. Ollie's been dressing him up in weird things like hats and jumpers ever since he was a toddler and Jet is an extremely tolerant dog.' Mitch had pulled on his underwear and picked up the formal dark trousers he wore to work with her. 'It should be great fun.'

'I'm guessing Jet is a black dog?'

Mitch threw her a grin. 'Yep. A rather overweight, sixteen-year-old black Lab.'

'And what's he going to be dressed up as?'

His socks were going on now. 'A doctor.'

Jenna laughed. 'Whose idea was that? Yours or Ollie's?'

'It got decided at a family conference. But it's me that has to figure out how to make a white coat for him. We're taking the measurements in the morning and my wonderful receptionist, Josie, is going to help cut it out and sew it. We found an ancient coat in our supply room. Nobody wears them these days, do they? Josie reckons we could get clever and cut it to keep the collar and buttons.' Mitch looked up from lacing his boots to smile at Jenna. 'I've got a broken stethoscope, too. I reckon Jet will be quite happy to have that hanging round his neck.'

'He's bound to win,' Jenna said. She was still chuckling. 'I'd love to see it.'

'So why don't you come along?' Mitch's tone was casual as he stood up but he was holding her gaze carefully. 'It's on Wednesday. Didn't I hear you tell someone on station that it's your day off next week?'

Oh…it was one thing to find it perfectly natural to be talking to Mitch about his son but the prospect of meeting the little boy was something else altogether.

And Mitch clearly knew what a big ask it was. He didn't say anything but he sat back on the edge of the bed and pulled Jenna, wrapped in the sheet, into his arms. He still didn't say anything. He simply held her and pressed his lips against the top of her head.

It felt like an apology.

It felt like he understood exactly how hard that might be for her.

It also felt like he really, really cared about how she was feeling.

Mitch's arms tightened around her. 'Don't say anything,' he whispered into her hair. 'Just think about it.'

Jenna hadn't needed to be told to 'think about it'.

It was hard to think about anything else, in fact. Especially when she had several hours' drive ahead of her to get to Sheffield, where she was booked to take a FRAME refresher course for rural GPs. She'd had meetings during the day for final editing on the new set of clinical guidelines for their practitioners so it was mid-afternoon by the time she set off and it was only then that Jenna realised she'd missed lunch. Maybe that was why it was harder to focus on her driving and contributing to the reason her thoughts kept circling back to the invitation to attend Pets' Day that Mitch had issued that evening last week.

Food might help. Coffee certainly would, so Jenna pulled in to the next service area off the motorway— one of those vast places that had everything from petrol stations to motels with enough restaurants, fast food outlets and even bars or supermarkets to cater for any possible refreshment travellers might desire. With coffee already on her tray, Jenna was heading for a place where you could choose your own sandwich fillings when she passed something far more tempting.

Potato skins. Hot, crispy, cheesy potato skins were exactly what she needed right now and Jenna ordered a plateful and then carried her tray to search for an empty table to sit and enjoy her meal. It wasn't until after she sat down and took her first bite that she realised she might have made a bit of a mistake. For one thing, as soon as she tasted the potato skin, she was taken back to that night in the pub with Mitch and his classmates at the end of their course. The night that had ended with them making love.

The night that had changed her life.

The follow-on from that was, of course, remembering the last occasion they'd spent together in bed and how *that* had ended, with Mitch holding her so tenderly after inviting her to come on what could only be considered a family kind of occasion.

Actually, there was a third thing that Jenna noticed as she swallowed that first mouthful. The only available table she'd been able to find was on the edge of a children's play area. Just outside, through wide, open doors there were seesaws and swings, a wooden fort with a slide from the highest point and climbing towers joined by swing bridges with rope walls. Inside, there were parents all around her, feeding young children or enjoying a coffee and break themselves as they watched their offspring let off steam in the playground.

It was Family Central. For a moment, Jenna considered loading her food and drink back onto the tray and going in search of another place to sit. Back in her vehicle, even? No, she told herself firmly. That was ridiculous. There was no reason to move. She'd been dealing with seeing families and children for years without falling apart so why would anything have suddenly become too difficult now?

Her gaze drifted to settle on a young mother who was breastfeeding a baby as she ate a hamburger and fries with one hand. Her partner was also eating his meal one-handed as he pushed a stroller back and forth with his other hand. The toddler in the stroller was sucking her thumb, her eyes almost shut, on the verge of falling asleep.

The clarity of the time-slip in Jenna's head—and her heart—was startling. She could almost feel that soft, warm weight of Eli in her own arms as she breastfed him, sometimes dipping her head to kiss that wispy hair and just soak in the smell of him. That delicious scent of milkiness and warmth and baby shampoo. She could even feel the echo of the exhaustion of those days along with that extraordinary difference that going from a couple to become a family had created.

She could feel a poignant smile tilting her lips as she remembered how happy she and Stefan had been. How there were those moments when the love was so huge it was overwhelming. How, even then, when she'd had no idea of what was just around the corner in her life, she'd felt afraid of the idea of losing it all.

Jenna shifted her gaze to stare, unseeing, through the doors to the playground. She was remembering Stefan now and the way he would rock Eli to sleep in his push-chair while listening to music through his ear buds, or reading a book with one hand. A clever, quick, passionate young man, Stefan had loved to dance. And argue about almost anything. So different to Mitch, who was mature and thoughtful and had a kindness and empathy that could only come from experiencing the hard parts of life.

Mitch made her feel safe but Stefan…well, the light had gone out in her life when Stefan had died and what made it so much worse, if that was possible, was that she had to grieve for him as she sat, day after day, in the paediatric intensive care unit beside Eli's bed as he slowly began to recover from his own injuries.

The potato skins were getting cold on the plate but Jenna had forgotten about her food. Her eyes were focusing on what was going on outside now. She could see parents holding young children on a seesaw where the seats were on the backs of large, wooden ducks. The toddlers were laughing with delight as they bounced up and down. Her journey with Eli had had moments like that as part of the rollercoaster. He could be a laughing, singing child one minute and then, in the blink of an eye, he would be unresponsive and on the ground or floor, convulsing. There had been a new fear to live with then, on top of what should have been the worst thing that could have happened when her fledging family had been ripped apart by losing Stefan.

Eli had only been four years old. Jenna found herself doing something she hadn't done for years—letting her gaze search until she found a child that would be about that age. He'd be nearly nine years old now if he'd lived. That was the next automatic search mode and…yes…those boys who were scrambling across the swing bridges would be somewhere between eight and ten years old but she only watched them for a few seconds. It didn't feel meaningful. Eli would be only four years old for ever in her head. And her heart.

Ollie was four years old.

If Jenna went to his school for Pets' Day she would not only meet Ollie, she would be with a whole class of other children the same age. Could she really cope with that?

No.

Yes. Of course she could. In the same way she coped with the young patients she treated or played with the children of her friends. Or watched a random bunch of kids playing the way she was doing now.

Did she *want* to cope with that?

No.

Yes.

No, because it might be too hard if it came with this new clarity that felt like a filter, which prevented too much light or something being allowed through, had somehow been lifted. A clarity that felt like a direct connection to the past and all the pain that had come from losing the future she'd believed she had. With her very own family.

She wasn't hungry any longer but Jenna sipped her coffee, looking back towards the young family she'd first noticed. Both the baby and the toddler were fast asleep now and the young parents were smiling at each other. For now, at least, they were coping with travelling with young children. They were winning.

Jenna wanted that. The coping. The winning.

So, the answer was definitely 'yes'. Because she really wanted to be able to cope and not to have to fear those memories. That would be a kind of freedom all by itself, wouldn't it?

And, maybe, she wanted to go to Pets' Day because it was Mitch who had asked her. He knew exactly what he was asking her to face and, as someone who knew all about facing ghosts from the past, he believed that she could cope. A part of her wanted to show him that he was right. Or perhaps she wanted him to be proud of her?

Taking another long look at the playground was deliberate. So was searching out a child of the right age so that she could pretend it was Ollie. She waited for the kind of jolt she'd experienced when she'd first found out that Mitch had a young son but it didn't happen. The pain of Eli's loss didn't come at her like a runaway train either, so something had changed. The shift towards it being easy to talk about Ollie and accept him as part of Mitch's life had taken weeks but this shift seemed to be happening with enough speed to be disconcerting. There was no mistaking it, however. The feeling that she could cope with something like Pets' Day—if she had Mitch beside her. And that being able to cope could be the key to making life better.

Not that she'd ever choose to become a mother again. Or a stepmother, for that matter, but to be able to see life with this sort of clarity, with no need for protective filters to dull what she was seeing couldn't be anything other than a good thing. Imagine if she could actually enjoy being around children instead of simply 'coping' with it? She'd been afraid of getting close enough to another man for a physical relationship, after all, and look at how she felt about Mitch now? She certainly couldn't dismiss the comfort and pleasure and…and the sheer joy he'd brought back into her life.

Jenna already knew she didn't need to hide anything from Mitch—the way she still hid her personal history from anybody new that she met or worked with and… and it felt like her life had been fragmented ever since it had fallen apart eight years ago. As if it had been so broken, it could never be put back together. But that's what this new feeling was. As if Mitch—and Ollie— and maybe even Jet and Pets' Day might somehow be a glue that could bring those pieces of her life back together. If she could be brave enough to trust where this feeling might eventually lead her, who knew how much better her life might become?

Pushing away the plate of cold food, Jenna reached for her phone to send a text message.

I've never been to a Pets' Day. And I've certainly never seen a dog dressed up as a doctor.

Jenna took a deep breath before tapping in her next words.

I'd love to come if that invitation's still open.

* * *

Andrew Mitchell was bursting with pride.

It wasn't only because his son was standing in front of Allensbury Primary School's Reception class of twenty pupils giving a talk about his pet, although he was doing a very good job of it.

'Jet's a black dog and he's very, very old. He's sixteen, which my dad says is like over a hundred years old for a person and…and that's even older than my *grandpa.*'

Ollie's grandpa, Michael Mitchell, was the first to laugh out loud. He shook his head and shared a resigned glance with some of the other adults packed into the back of the classroom. The closest person grinning back at him was Jenna, who'd arrived just in time for the 'interesting things about my pet' presentations—the preparation of which had been the children's reading, writing and art projects for the week. Her gaze shifted to meet Mitch's and the sparkle of amusement was still lighting up those golden brown eyes and making them even warmer than usual. She seemed to be enjoying this, which was rather a big relief because he'd known that, in introducing her to his son, he might be pushing her in a direction she really didn't want to go. Not only that, she was in a classroom full of four-year-old children and that had to be making her heart ache on a level he couldn't begin to know.

Ollie was wrapping up his talk. 'Dogs need food and Jet's favourite thing is toast and peanut butter. And cuddles. And that's why I love my pet…'

Mitch's gaze slid sideways without his head moving so Jenna didn't realise he was looking at her again. He saw the way she caught her bottom lip between her teeth and he could almost feel the increased tension in her body, as if she was bracing herself, and he knew exactly what it was that she was afraid of.

The memories.

The echo of that devastating moment of loss.

But she was smiling again now and joining in the applause as Ollie tugged on Jet's lead and took him to sit on the mat with him.

And that was when Mitch realised the pride that was filling his heart included Jenna as well. He knew how courageous she was—you only had to look at what she'd done with her life in the face of a double tragedy to know that—but she could have avoided this and she hadn't. This was her first ever Pets' Day at a school. Possibly the most full-on exposure to so many children who were the same age as Eli had been when she'd lost him but she was facing it. With dignity and humour and…and that determination to really live every moment of her life that was just one of the admirable things about this woman who'd fallen into his life.

He could feel that pride, laced with his understanding of how hard this might be for Jenna, tightening something in his gut and wrapping itself around his heart. It was a poignant feeling—wanting to take that pain away from someone because he cared about them. Kind of like the way he felt when Ollie got hurt, or sick. Or when he noticed his dad looking tired enough to make it hit home that his father was getting older and wouldn't be around for ever.

People he loved…

This was more than that brief thought he'd had, when he'd seen Jenna with Kirsty at that accident scene, that perhaps there might be a future for himself that included her. Good grief…the way he'd just put his feelings about Jenna up there with Ollie and his dad made it seem as if he was falling in love with her. The thought was so out of left field—unwelcome, even—it could be dismissed in a nanosecond and Mitch could focus on what was actually real, as a small girl with a big smile, her hair in gorgeous cornrows with the braids decorated with beads, got up and carried a shoebox to the front of the class. She took off the lid and lifted out her pet.

'This is my turtle. His name is Winston.'

'That's Mia,' Mitch whispered to Jenna. 'She's Ollie's very best friend.'

They had to sit through several more pet show and tell performances but they were all so cute, nobody minded the squeeze of it being standing room only for the adult audience. Things became a little more dramatic when a cat was making it very clear that it didn't want to be in its carry box by hissing, yowling and trying to scratch its young owner through a gap in the door and a parent had to step in to rescue it. A rabbit got loose in the classroom and a small dog was sick on the carpet. Everybody was more than ready to go outside for some fresh air when they were told the last two class members had their pets tied up on the playing field.

'Oh…' Jenna's jaw dropped as they rounded the corner of the school building. 'Ponies?'

'Allensbury's the centre of a rural community. There are quite a few small farms and lifestyle blocks around here. One of the GPs I work with, Euan, has a smallholding where he keeps a Highland cow. A prize-winning bull, in fact.'

'Really?' Jenna blinked. 'Is it somewhere around here, with one of his kids?'

Mitch shook his head. 'Euan's not remotely interested in having children in his life. Probably why he's still single.'

It occurred to Mitch that Euan might think Jenna was the perfect woman and maybe he should introduce them to each other. The thought that followed, however, was a silent but incredulous huff of dismissal. *As if…*

Jenna was distracted again. 'And there's a donkey over there…' She crossed her hands on her chest in an enchantingly childish gesture of delight. 'I *love* donkeys.'

'I love donkeys too.' Ollie, with Jet plodding patiently beside him, caught up with them, his grandfather right behind him.

'This is Jenna.' Mitch introduced her to his son and father.

Michael's smile was warm and welcoming. Ollie's eyebrows had almost disappeared under the spikes of his hair. 'Are you Daddy's girlfriend?'

Jenna hesitated for a second, shooting a quick glance at Mitch, as if unsure what he might have told Ollie, or more to the point, his father? He hoped his smile was reassuring. There was no pressure here. No expectations—just as they'd agreed.

'A girlfriend is a bit different to a friend, Ollie. Jenna's my friend. And I go and work with her sometimes.'

'But she's a girl.' Ollie looked puzzled. 'And she's your friend. Mia's *my* girlfriend.'

'You're right.' Jenna was smiling now. 'I'm Daddy's friend. Just like Mia is your friend.'

Ollie nodded. He knew he'd been right. 'He told me you were coming. Because you want to see Jet in the fancy dress competition.'

'I do indeed. I can't wait to see Dr Dog.'

Ollie turned to his father. 'Can we put his clothes on now, Daddy?'

'Not yet, buddy. We're going to have lunch first. There's a big sausage sizzle, remember? Don't forget you promised not to let Jet eat too much. We don't want him being sick like Aiden's puppy.' Mitch was looking around. 'Where's Mia?'

'She had to put Winston back in the car. And her mummy said she had to have her puffer before she came near the ponies. In case she's…'llergic.'

'Ah…' Mitch nodded. 'Of course. Mia's asthmatic,' he told Jenna. 'They haven't sorted out what all her triggers are but she did have a serious attack and needed admission to hospital after she had a pony ride last year.'

There were pony rides happening at Pets' Day as part of the activities that were on offer during the relaxed picnic and barbecue lunch. A lot of parents must have taken time off work, Mitch realised, because many children had both parents there, along with siblings who were still too young for school. There was an overwhelmingly family feel to the day and while this was the Mitchell family's first Pets' Day, it still felt very different thanks to having Jenna with them. And he wasn't the only one noticing the difference, it seemed. Mitch was aware of the curious glances coming their way from people who knew him in the community.

He knew they were referred to as 'the Mitchell men'. Three males from three different generations that had forged an unusual family unit after tragedy and people cared about them. He couldn't blame people for being curious, either—this was the first time he'd ever been seen with a female companion in public. He could only hope that Jenna wasn't aware of the interest she was generating, which she might interpret as a level of pressure she would rather avoid.

She certainly seemed to still be enjoying herself. Mia's mother, Hanna, had joined them to sit on the grass on the playing field and she was talking to Jenna about her daughter's asthma.

'The ambulance people were wonderful when they came that first time when she was only ten months old. I was so worried about her.'

'I know. It's such a scary thing when you know your baby's having trouble breathing.'

'They thought it was an infection then. Bronchiolitis?'

'It's the first diagnosis I would have considered myself in a baby.'

'Then they said it was reactive airways disease, but the last attack was so bad she ended up in intensive care and they did a lot of tests and said it's definitely asthma so now we have all the inhalers and spacers and an action plan and even a nebuliser at home.'

'She doesn't look like she's having trouble with all the different animals around her today.' Mitch joined the conversation. 'She and Ollie are having great fun.' He was smiling as he lifted his phone to try and capture the moment in a photograph.

The children were giggling as they rolled around, pulling up handfuls of grass to throw at each other. They both had grubby hands, grass in their hair and smears of tomato sauce on their faces. Jet was taking advantage of the lack of supervision and was crawling over the grass on his stomach to snatch up the half-eaten sausages rolled in bread.

The adults exchanged glances and smiles. No one was about to growl at them for getting messy or forgetting promises not to let the dog eat too much food. This was one of those moments in life. One of the small things that made life as good as it could be. Throwing grass. Laughter. Being with friends and family.

On impulse, Mitch shifted his focus and caught a photo of Jenna watching the children with a smile as big as Mia's on her face. In this moment she didn't look as if she was tormented by past memories at all. She looked like she was loving this. No one who was watching her right now would ever imagine the pain and grief in her past. Maybe she'd even forgotten it herself in the joy of this moment? No one would think she was afraid of loving anyone like that again, either.

And…maybe…if she got used to it bit by bit, she might forget that herself?

Because that feeling—the one that gave him that knot deep inside and squeezed his heart like a vice—had come back and he couldn't simply dismiss it by distracting himself this time. Especially not when he lowered his phone camera to find Jenna turning towards him, with that gorgeous smile still tilting her lips.

His gaze snagged on those lips and another sensation joined the mix he was aware of as he remembered the softness and taste of Jenna's mouth and what it was like to hold this woman in his arms.

That was all he wanted to do now. To hold her.

To say *I think I'm falling in love with you, Jenna…*

Just as well he couldn't do either of those things here because Jenna would run a mile. He'd be breaking their agreement—the one where they'd both been honest in saying that they didn't want a future with each other that had even the hint of a partnership like marriage. Jenna never wanted to be a mother to someone else's child and Mitch would never risk Ollie's happiness by including anybody in his family that didn't love his son as much as he did.

All he could do was to return Jenna's smile. To be relieved that a bell rang in that moment, signalling the end of the lunch break and that it was time to prepare for the Pets' fancy dress competition and to be thankful that it hadn't been a huge drama for Jenna to join a family occasion.

Because that was what it felt like.

Family...

CHAPTER EIGHT

'HE'S BRADYCARDIC.' JENNA had had her fingers on the man's wrist even as she greeted the patient they'd been called to see. Her glance up at Mitch was brief. 'Let's get some leads on for an ECG.' She turned back to the man, who was slumped on a bench seat in the waiting area of this barber's shop. 'How are you feeling, Bruce? Apart from the chest pain?'

'A bit dizzy. And…like I might be going to be sick.'

The barber stepped back swiftly. 'I'll find a bowl,' he said.

'Thanks.' Jenna looked up at the onlookers, a couple of whom were still wearing capes that suggested their haircuts and shaves had been interrupted. 'Could one of you please go outside so you can flag down the ambulance that's coming as well?'

'Blood pressure eighty over fifty,' Mitch told her as the reading came up on the life pack. He was rapidly sticking electrodes on Bruce's chest, pulling his unbuttoned shirt aside to attach the final leads that circled the left side of his chest to end under the armpit line.

The blood pressure was far too low. Jenna reached for the IV kit. 'I'm going to put a small line in your arm,' she told her patient. 'Just in case we need to give you some fluids and medication. Is that okay with you?'

'Sure…if you think I need it… Am I having a heart attack or something?'

'That's what we want to find out.'

'Hang in there, Bruce,' an onlooker said. 'You'll be all right.'

'Heaven help the rest of us if he isn't.' The barber was back, holding a stainless-steel bowl. 'He's the healthiest bloke here by a mile. He even ran the London Marathon last year.'

'I did.' Bruce leaned his head back on the seat cushion. 'Feels like a million years ago right now.'

'Do you have any medical conditions we should know about?' Jenna asked. 'Like your blood pressure or anything to do with your heart?'

'Don't like doctors,' Bruce said. 'Haven't been for a year or two.'

'Are you allergic to any medication that you know of?'

'No. Don't like pills, either. Haven't even taken an aspirin that I can remember in recent times.'

Mitch was printing out a piece of paper from the life pack and Jenna bent her head to see what might be revealed by the twelve lead ECG documenting the electrical activity of Bruce's heart.

She expected to see the wide spacing between beats due to the slow rate. She wasn't surprised to see that Mitch's finger was touching the squares that were abnormal in rapid succession, his voice no more than a murmur.

'Look at that PR interval,' he said.

'Mmm. First degree heart block.'

'And here…and here…' He touched the capital W and M shapes showing in the chest leads. 'Left bundle branch block. I wonder if it's new or old?'

Jenna was wondering too. As a new development it could indicate that Bruce was, indeed, suffering a heart attack and it could be a serious one. 'I'll get that IV line in. Could you draw up some atropine?'

'Sure. I'll set up an adrenaline infusion, too, shall I?'

'Please.' Jenna's fleeting glance was the only appreciation she had time to show. How good was it to be working with someone who knew more than she did about how to deal with a situation that could potentially turn to custard at any moment? Someone that she trusted probably more than any crew member she'd ever worked with in the past.

How good was it that it was Friday? Her day—and at least part of her evening—with Mitch? Not that this was the time to allow even a momentary thought about what she knew that would include but her body knew and, somehow, it gave her even more energy and focus for the task at hand. Having Mitch with her out on the road always had this effect—as if it only took his presence to turn up the volume on anything in her life. Work, sharing a meal, conversation…making love…

Today, like most days with Mitch as her crew partner, was flying past and cardiac call-outs seemed to be the theme for this shift. They'd already been to a chest pain with an apparently non-cardiac cause and an episode of angina that wasn't responsive to the elderly woman's normal medication so she had been taken to hospital for further tests. A drug overdose on the back seat of a bus had kept them busy for long enough to create a large traffic jam on a busy road and put them in the right area of the city to be the rapid response for the urgent call from this barber's shop.

'Sharp scratch,' she warned Bruce. She slid the cannula into his vein, blocked the end of it while she screwed a Luer plug into place and then put the clear, sticky covering over the line to protect it, turning to look over her shoulder at the screen of the life pack. Mitch was filling a syringe from an ampoule but he was also watching the screen.

'PR interval's stretching,' he said quietly. 'We're losing the P wave in the T wave.' He taped the ampoule to the syringe barrel and handed it to Jenna. 'Atropine, zero point six milligrams.'

But Bruce's abnormal rhythm wasn't responsive to the first drug. Or to the adrenaline they tried next as an infusion. His rate, in fact, was dropping.

'Rate's in the twenties.' Mitch was supporting Bruce as his level of consciousness dropped to the point where they needed to move him onto the floor. 'Shall we pace him?'

Jenna nodded. Even if the ambulance arrived in the next few seconds, it would be unsafe to transport Bruce to the hospital when his heart rate was now too slow to be life sustaining. External pacing, by delivering electric shocks to stimulate the heart, could be effective but painful. About to ask Mitch to draw up a powerful analgesic, Jenna's heart sank as an alarm on the life pack suddenly sounded.

'He's in VF.' Mitch pushed the button that would charge the defibrillator and the increasing pitch of the new sound was added to the alarm still bleeping.

Bruce's heart was in the process of stopping completely. This had suddenly become a cardiac arrest and the change in the tension of this call-out was all the more dramatic as the ambulance crew arrived, two paramedics and an observer who looked young enough to be a medical student. Due to the medical hierarchy, Mitch automatically had the position of leading this resuscitation but it didn't feel like that to Jenna. They had become so tightly welded as a team over the many weeks they had been doing these shifts together that they could virtually read each other's minds and have equipment ready or drugs drawn up so that the protocol became a seamless performance.

'Stand clear…'

'Clear.' Jenna wriggled back on her knees. She needed to, anyway, to reach the airway kit that was going to be needed to intubate.

'Shocking…'

She could hear the gasp from Bruce's barber shop friends behind her. Some crews would try and clear an area of spectators when something was happening that might not end well but Jenna's opinion was that if they weren't children, they weren't in the way, and they wanted to be there, witnessing that everything possible was being done for someone could make the experience less traumatic.

And it was one of those all too rare occasions when it looked as if the audience was going to witness a successful resuscitation because, with just the first shock of the defibrillator, there seemed to be a rhythm appearing on the screen as the interference from the shock faded. Mitch held up his hand to stop the paramedic about to start chest compressions.

'Wait. Let it settle…'

Yes. They could all see the spikes of a normal, sinus

rhythm. Still too slow but enough to keep blood circulating and keep Bruce alive. They definitely needed to get him to hospital as soon as possible, however, and he was going to need very careful monitoring and medication dosages.

Minutes later, they had Bruce on a stretcher and Jenna was happy he was stable enough to move.

'Dr Mitchell and I will come in with you,' she told the ambulance crew. 'Can one of you bring my vehicle, please?'

'I can do that as soon as we're loaded.' One of the paramedics stepped forward to take the keys. He turned to the observer. 'You can come with me. You don't want a crowd in the back of the truck if things need to happen fast.'

Jenna nodded in answer to the unspoken query from the other paramedic. 'Yes, we can load. Mitch, can you stay with him? I need to make a call and find the closest hospital with available, emergency PCI facilities.'

'Is he going to be okay?' The barber wasn't the only person looking pale here now.

'We're going to take the best possible care of him,' Jenna assured them all. 'And we'll be taking him to a hospital that can treat him for whatever's going on.'

The hospital with the ability to deal urgently with a life-threatening blockage of coronary arteries was a little out of Jenna's usual patch for her rapid response vehicle but the longer drive towards Central London gave them enough time to stabilise Bruce's condition and he was regaining consciousness as they handed over to the cardiology team waiting for them. A short time later, as the team prepared to rush him into the catheter laboratory to diagnose and treat any blockages in his coronary arteries, he was awake enough to recognise Jenna and Mitch.

'Thank you,' he said to them, his voice shaky. 'I think I owe you guys one…'

Walking to find where the vehicle had been parked to one side of the ambulance bay, Jenna smiled at Mitch.

'That doesn't happen often, does it?'

'Someone waking up after a cardiac arrest and saying "Thanks"?' Mitch grinned. 'No, it doesn't happen often. That was a great job.'

'Be even better if it's the one we can finish the shift on but I don't like our chances. It's going to take a while to get back to station from here, which means plenty of opportunities to be needed somewhere.'

'I'll have to come back this way later, too, so I hope we don't run late. Dad and Ollie are at the zoo.'

'Oh… I'd completely forgotten you told me about that school trip coming up.' Jenna climbed into the driver's seat. 'Good grief…we've been so busy today I hadn't even asked how the family is. It's been ages since Pets' Day.'

'I don't expect you to remember everything in my family diary,' Mitch said. 'They came in on the train but I've arranged to pick them up. We'll have dinner in town and then I'll take them home.'

So they wouldn't have the couple of hours of private time together that had so quickly become the highlight of Jenna's weeks. That the disappointment was so sharp should be a warning, Jenna thought. Was she getting too dependent on Mitch's friendship? That hadn't been a part of the plan. She would never intentionally become dependent on anything or anyone again. Because that meant trouble if it disappeared and she'd had enough of coping with that kind of adjustment in her life already. So she squashed the disappointment.

She had no claims on Mitch's time. If he was available to be with her, that was great. If he wasn't, that was no big deal and, after all, he was spending his whole day with her. Come to think of it, that had to be a big deal for Mitch, being with her rather than his son.

'You're missing a school trip with Ollie?' Her tone revealed her astonishment. 'To come out on the road with me?'

'Well…apart from how much I love my Fridays with you, there was a limit of how many parent helpers could go. Dad won Rock, Paper, Scissors, so he got the day at the zoo. Actually, I would have let him have the treat, anyway. He deserves it—he does so much for me and Ollie.' Mitch reached for his seatbelt. 'He always has. My life would have fallen apart completely after Tegan died if he hadn't been there for me.'

'He's a lovely man, your dad. I really liked him.'

'He really liked you, too,' Mitch said. 'So did Ollie. They're both still talking about how excited you got when Jet won the fancy dress competition and Ollie's been asking when he's going to see you again.'

'Has he?' Jenna's heart gave an odd little squeeze at the idea of Ollie remembering her, let alone asking to see her again. Being with Ollie, along with so many other children, on Pets' Day had had its moments of challenge but, overall, it had felt like a positive step in a new direction. Knowing that she had become someone that Ollie was talking about when she wasn't there was disconcerting, however, and Jenna wasn't sure if that squeezing sensation was pleasant or not. It felt like it could go either way if it got any stronger so it might be a good idea to change the subject.

'Was your mother around as well?' she queried.

'No. She died when I was fourteen so it was just me and Dad after that.' Mitch let his breath out in a sigh. 'They say history doesn't repeat itself but it kind of felt like that when I went back home with my motherless baby and it was me and Dad running the show.'

'You were lucky to have the support. My family—and Stefan's—were thin on the ground and living too far away.'

'I'll bet you coped brilliantly,' Mitch told her.

'I had good friends.' Jenna nodded. She caught his gaze. 'Friends are gold, aren't they?' Maybe she wanted to reassure him that it wasn't a big deal that they couldn't be together this evening. That this was a friendship that wasn't held together only by a sexual connection. 'Especially the ones who step up in the bad times,' she added, remembering her close friends that had been there for her when Stefan—and then Eli—had died. 'The ones who are there for you, no matter what.'

Mitch was holding her gaze. 'I'll be there for you, Jenna,' he said softly. 'Anytime. Don't ever forget that, will you?'

Oh, man…that squeezy feeling around her heart had suddenly made it impossible to take a new breath. This was it, wasn't it? The thing that had been missing from her life. It hadn't been simply about the lack of physical touch and closeness, it was this—having someone who cared enough to make a commitment to be there. To share even a part of her life for the foreseeable future and then some. Jenna remembered that moment in the motorway service area when she'd been watching that

young couple and their children and she'd compared
Mitch to Stefan.

She'd thought the light had gone out of her world
when she'd lost Stefan and that Mitch was quieter and
more mature and…maybe less exciting? But he had
brought a different kind of light into her life, hadn't he?
Maybe not fireworks, but a steady, comforting light that
gave warmth as well. She had to close her eyes for a
heartbeat with that realisation and find that new breath
because it felt, absurdly, as if she wanted to cry. And
Mitch had obviously noticed.

'Tired?'

'I wouldn't say "no" to a coffee, that's for sure.' Jenna
made sure her tone was upbeat. 'Have we even had a
break since our lunch got cut to less than ten minutes?'

'Don't think so.'

Jenna picked up the radio handset and called in their
availability. She also told her friend, Adam, in the control centre that she was suffering from caffeine with-
drawal. He laughed.

'No promises, Jenna, but go and get your coffee fix.
I'll keep you on standby as long as possible.'

There was a coffee shop well positioned to take advantage of hospital staff patronage so it was only minutes until they were sitting back in their vehicle with
paper cups of delicious coffee and some homemade
blueberry muffins. Even if this break only lasted a
few minutes, she was going to make the most of it.
The warmth of Mitch confirming how important their
friendship was had added yet another layer to the connection they'd forged since they'd first met each other
and that was helping to make up for any disappointment
about this evening.

'So you're going to go and pick up your dad and Ollie straight after our shift?' Jenna managed to sound perfectly cheerful as she spoke around a mouthful of muffin. 'Is that early enough? If we get back to station soon, I'm happy to take any last call solo. What time does the zoo visit end?'

'The others are all heading back to the train station at four p.m.' Mitch looked at his watch. 'So that's only half an hour away, but Dad said he and Ollie would go and get an ice cream somewhere and wait for me. Or they might go and feed the squirrels in Regent's Park. It's no problem. We haven't booked anywhere special for dinner, we're just going to find a place we like the look of.'

And then Mitch would be driving his family home. Away from London. Away from her. Okay…maybe that disappointment hadn't been entirely made up for. It was normally easy not to even think about being in bed with Mitch while they were on duty, or even having a bit of a break from being on active duty like they were at the moment, but right now, it was filling Jenna's mind and the pull towards touching Mitch became suddenly overwhelming so it was just as well she had her hands full of coffee and muffin. They shouldn't even touch, let alone kiss each other when they were in the rapid response vehicle but there was nothing to stop them sharing a glance.

A long glance that could say such a lot. Mitch could let her know that he was going to miss their time together later just as much as she was. Then he cleared his throat.

'What would you say if I suggested we went away

sometime? Just for a weekend break. Somewhere… nice…'

Somewhere nice? Was that a euphemism for somewhere 'romantic'? Jenna took a slow sip of her coffee as she thought about that. Would she want it to be? Judging from the way her heart rate suddenly picked up, the answer to that question seemed to be affirmative.

'You mean, like Paris?'

Mitch made a face. 'Maybe not Paris. I proposed to Tegan there, on top of the Eiffel tower. How 'bout… Barcelona?'

Jenna shook her head. 'Stefan and I went there on our Spanish honeymoon.'

The wry smile they shared was acknowledging more than crossing potential weekend destinations off a shortlist. It was also about understanding how important the memories were of the people they'd loved enough to marry. That they would always be a part of their lives and…maybe that, because this was a friendship with no expectations on either side, it wasn't a threat to those memories. They didn't have to feel disloyal. Maybe, Jenna needed to dismiss that idea about time away being romantic so she didn't undermine that trust.

She dropped the rest of her muffin into her empty coffee cup. She started the engine but didn't immediately pick up the radio microphone to call in their availability. She didn't pull out into the traffic, either. She felt like she was holding her breath to hear what Mitch was going to say next.

'I think we need to find somewhere just for us. Somewhere neither of us has ever been.' Mitch finished his coffee. 'Can't be too far away, though. I'm quite confident that Ollie and Dad would be delighted to have their first weekend alone together but that wouldn't give us enough time to get to the Antarctic. Or the middle of Africa.'

'I've always wanted to go to one of the Greek islands,' Jenna said. 'Like Mykonos. The pictures always make it look like paradise. White buildings and blue, blue sea and sky, fishing boats and pelicans and a taverna right on the beach.'

Oh… Dear Lord, how romantic would *that* be? And why wasn't that thought being shut down as quickly and completely as she knew it should be?

'Let's do it,' Mitch said softly. 'Just for a day or two. Just us…'

And there they were again, looking at each other and saying things silently and…the pull was irresistible. Jenna had to lean closer and it seemed like the magnetism was working on both sides because Mitch leaned towards her at exactly the same time. It wasn't a real kiss—that would have been utterly unprofessional— but the brief butterfly brush of their lips was just as powerful.

It reminded Jenna of their very first kiss in her kitchen that evening, after Mitch's FRAME course had finished. For ever ago. If she'd known that she would be sitting here a few months later with butterflies of excitement in her belly at the thought of a romantic weekend away with Mitch, she would have run as far and as fast as possible away from him that night. How on earth had the idea of their friendship growing into something more not only become acceptable but something she actually wanted?

She remembered this kind of feeling. Those butterfly

tendrils of sensation that were excitement and yearning and desire all tumbling together.

It was the feeling of falling in love, that's what it was.

And even that realisation wasn't enough to scare her as much as she might have expected. Because part of her wanted to fall in love. To feel that astonishing kind of magic again. She had to turn away swiftly enough that Mitch didn't see even a hint of that flash of thoughts. It wasn't as if she was sure about it herself, anyway. And it certainly wasn't part of their agreement. If Mitch knew, it might spell the end of their friendship and Jenna didn't want that to happen. She *really* didn't want that to happen. And yet, in that nanosecond before she'd broken the gaze they were sharing after that almost kiss, she could almost swear that she could see a reflection of her own thoughts in Mitch's eyes.

And that thought was too much to take in just yet. Reaching for the radio microphone, Jenna turned up the volume of background radio transmissions as well, as if it could distract them both from whatever disconcerting potential change in their friendship that might be happening.

Not that Mitch was showing any signs of being disconcerted. Or scared off.

'It sounds like a plan,' he said. 'I reckon we both deserve a bit of a break and how nice would it be to sit on a beach and soak up some sun? Let's talk about it again next Friday. In the meantime, why don't you come with us tonight? For dinner?'

'I can't crash your special family dinner.'

The beeping from the radio was a city ambulance responding to a call.

'Roger that. ETA five minutes for London Zoo.'

The mention of the zoo did more than catch the attention of both Mitch and Jenna. She reached to turn up the volume even more. Mitch froze.

Beep... Beep... 'Any further patient details?'

'Coming through on your pagers. Sixty-eight-year-old man with severe chest pain and shortness of breath. He's just inside the front gates.'

Mitch had gone pale. 'Dad's sixty-eight,' he said.

Jenna pushed the 'talk' button on the side of her microphone. By chance, she was connected to Adam again.

'Rapid Response One available. I'd like to respond to that cardiac call to London Zoo as back-up. My crew partner's father is there at the moment. Same age.'

'Understood,' Adam said briskly. 'Logging you in.'

The call came through on their radio only seconds later. 'Control to Rapid Response One. Code Blue, please, to London Zoo. Chest pain.'

'Rapid Response One to Control. Roger that. On our way.' Jenna hit the switch to start the beacons flashing on the roof. She also activated the siren. She kept her gaze firmly on the heavy traffic around them as she pushed her way through. She didn't want to look at Mitch because she knew she'd see the fear in his eyes.

It was not just a day for a run of cardiac calls.

It was, apparently, a day for feelings that Jenna hadn't experienced in a very long time. A rollercoaster of emotions, in fact.

The warmth of feeling that close connection to someone.

Disappointment that they wouldn't get that special time together.

The flicker of the kind of intensity that only came from falling in love.

And…now the fear. Of the kind of loss that only came from losing a loved one.

Jenna didn't want Mitch to have to go through that again. Surely life could never be that unfair?

She pushed her foot down on the accelerator as they hit a clearer stretch of road. She knew only too well that there were no guarantees of life ever being fair. She also knew that there was only one reason why she was feeling this so intensely.

It was because she cared so much about how this might affect Mitch.

Because she cared so much about *him*.

This was love. Maybe not the bells and whistles that went with the 'falling in love' process and all the romantic gestures but this was real.

As real as it got…

CHAPTER NINE

'IT'S NOTHING. I don't know why everyone's making such a fuss.'

'Chest pain is never something to ignore, Mr Mitchell.'

The senior ambulance paramedic was sticking ECG electrodes in place on Mitch's father's chest as he and Jenna stood to one side, having arrived a minute or two later than the ambulance crew. He still looked pale, Jenna thought, and Ollie, who was in his father's arms, looked even more worried. His dark eyes looked enormous in that small, pale face and he had a flop of soft hair hanging over his forehead that made her want to reach out and smooth it back before it got too close to his eyes. She didn't, however. She, like Mitch, was waiting anxiously to see what might be revealed on the twelve lead ECG that was about to be recorded.

'Call me Mike. Please.'

'Sure. Do you have any other problems with your health that we should know about, Mike?'

'*Other* problems? You mean a bit of indigestion isn't enough?' Michael Mitchell's wry smile faded as he realised his attempt at humour had fallen flat. He shook his head. 'My GP, here, can tell you anything you want to know.'

'He's treated for high cholesterol and hypertension,' Mitch said. 'Blood pressure's well controlled, though…' He glanced at the reading on the life pack beside where the lines of the ECG were showing. 'It's a bit higher than usual at the moment.'

Jenna could hear the layer of anxiety beneath the calm words. Never mind brushing Ollie's hair out of his eyes. She found herself shifting a little closer to Mitch and had to fight the urge to touch his hand with her own. To let her fingers curl around his in the hope of offering support. To let him know he wasn't alone.

'Are you surprised?' His father asked, irritably. 'I didn't want anybody calling an ambulance. I'm wasting everybody's time. If I hadn't told the teachers to get going, the whole school would have missed their train back to Allensbury.'

'You're not wasting anybody's time,' the paramedic assured him. 'We'd much rather get called and find there's nothing wrong than not be called when there is.'

But Michael didn't seem to be listening. He made a sound that could have been a stifled groan and rubbed at the centre of his chest.

'How bad is that pain, sir?' the paramedic asked. 'On a scale of zero to ten with zero being no pain and ten the worst you can imagine?'

Michael shrugged. 'About a four.'

'Translate that as being at least six,' Mitch said. 'He's not one to complain about anything. I'd make it an eight, actually, judging by how green around the gills he's looking. Is the pain just in the centre of your chest, Dad?'

'Where's he green?' Ollie asked. His question was a frightened whisper but Jenna could hear it as clearly as if he was in her own arms, rather than Mitch's. 'I can't see…'

'It's just an expression, sweetheart,' Jenna whispered, seeing that Mitch's attention was firmly on his father. 'He's not *really* green.'

'It does kind of go through to my back,' Michael admitted.

'What's the matter with Grandpa?' Ollie sounded on the verge of tears now.

Mitch shifted Ollie in his arms so that they could see each other's faces. 'Grandpa's not feeling well,' he said gently. 'He's got a sore bit. Like that sore tummy you had a while ago, remember?'

Ollie nodded. 'I was sick. And then I felt better. You said I had a bug. A round bug.'

Jenna found herself smiling. 'A "round" bug? How did Daddy know what shape it was?'

Mitch caught her gaze and she could see a gleam of amusement amidst the anxiety. 'I suspect I said that Ollie had a bug that was going around.'

Ollie nodded again. 'Maybe Grandpa has a round bug, too.'

'It's just a bit of indigestion, lovey,' Michael told him. 'I expect I ate too many of those bacon sarnies for lunch.'

Both Jenna and Mitch stepped closer to the paramedics as the ECG trace was printed.

'Can't see too much to worry about there,' the paramedic said.

'No.' Mitch caught Jenna's gaze as if her opinion mattered as well. She liked that. It was like when they worked together as a team and he always made her feel like an equal partner.

'How's the pain?' she asked Michael.

'Getting better by the minute,' he told her. But when he moved, his face made it very obvious that he was playing it down.

'We'll give you something for that pain.' The paramedic reached for his kit. 'And then we'll take you into hospital so they can find out what's going on.'

Michael looked horrified. 'No. I'm fine. I can go home with my son.'

'Just cooperate, Dad.' Mitch's tone was patient. 'We need to know what's going on. They'll run a few tests and rule out anything we need to worry about.'

He still had Ollie clinging to his neck and maybe Michael could see how frightened his grandson was.

'I'll go—but only if you and Ollie go and have that dinner we were planning. I'm not going to spoil a special day out by having you hanging around a hospital for hours. You can come and pick me up later.'

'Don't be daft. Of course we're coming with you.'

'That's not fair on Ollie. He's worried enough as it is, without seeing everything that goes on in an emergency department.'

Jenna could sense a standoff happening. She could also sense that, underneath his bravado, Michael was probably as worried about his own health as his family was. She could see how tense Mitch was and…as for Ollie, well…her heart just went out to the scared little boy.

'I could look after Ollie,' she offered. 'My shift's about to finish and the vehicle's not needed back on station any time soon.'

The swift glance from Mitch told Jenna that he didn't want her doing anything she might not be comfortable with. That he knew how big a deal this was.

'You don't have to do that,' he said quietly. 'We'll be fine.'

'I know I don't.'

And even yesterday, maybe she wouldn't have made that offer, even though she had chosen to meet Ollie and attend Pets' Day because it was a big step to changing her life for the better. This was something else. Another huge shift and it was happening because of how she was feeling about Mitch. This was about finding out whether she could cope with being with Ollie as a parent figure, because, if she couldn't, there was no point in dreaming about falling in love with Andrew Mitchell or of them having any kind of future together. And the part of her that was longing for that seemed to be growing.

Jenna found a smile. 'I wouldn't have offered if I didn't want to. We'll stay within easy reach of the hospital. You'll be able to text whenever you want me to bring Ollie back.'

His glance was asking silently if she really thought she could cope. By way of responding, she turned to Michael. 'Will you go and have those tests done, Mike, if I'm looking after Ollie? So that everyone can stop worrying about you?'

'If it's really okay with you, Jenna.'

Jenna still didn't meet Mitch's gaze. 'That's settled then,' she said brightly. Ollie? Do you want to come with me in my car or ride in the ambulance with Daddy and Grandpa to the hospital?'

'I want to go in the ambulance.' Ollie's eyes were wide. 'Can I do the siren?'

'We'll see about that.' The paramedics shared a glance. And a smile. 'Maybe just a blip when we get outside the gates. We don't want to scare the animals, do we?'

'So…what would you like to do first?'

Ollie was still staring through the automatic glass doors that led from the ambulance loading bay into the emergency department of the same hospital Mitch and Jenna had brought their last patient to, even though the stretcher carrying his grandfather had now disappeared from view. His father had also disappeared from view and Jenna knew that this little boy had to be feeling lost. When his small hand crept into hers she froze just for a heartbeat because it was the first time since Eli that she had held the hand of a child that wasn't a patient.

She took a quick, inward breath. She'd told Mitch she could cope. And she could. This was a step she wanted to take, she reminded herself. Like Pets' Day, this was a step towards a better future. A life that she could live to the fullest. With both Mitch and his son, if he ever felt the same way.

She gave Ollie's hand a gentle squeeze. 'Are you hungry?'

A small face tilted up towards her. A small head nodded.

'What do you like to eat? More than anything else?'

'Hamburgers.' Had Ollie noticed the group of shops across the road that included many of the most popular fast food outlets? 'And chips. The ones that come with a toy.'

Jenna grinned. She knew exactly which child-friendly chain he was talking about. 'Are you allowed to eat hamburgers and chips?' Maybe she needed to text Mitch and check.

'Only sometimes,' Ollie admitted.

Jenna didn't want to disturb Mitch unless it was for something important. She knew that blood samples would be being taken as part of the examination his father needed. And another ECG. Maybe a scan or X-rays as well. There was still the concern that it could be a cardiac pain and it had just been too early in the process for the ECG changes to have shown up at the zoo.

'I think this is definitely a "sometimes",' she told Ollie. 'There's a playground in there, too, isn't there? Look... I can see the big pipe that comes out the side of the building from here. Is that a slide?'

'You climb in it.' Ollie's grip on her hand tightened as they started walking away from the hospital. 'I can show you, if you like.'

It felt like he was offering Jenna his trust in that handhold. As if, just for the moment, she was the person that mattered the most in his world. That was a reminder of just how big this step she was taking was, but it was actually easier to take a new breath this time.

'I'd like that very much,' she said.

They both ate hamburgers and French fries. Ollie was thrilled with the toy car that came with his meal and drove it round the table between the hamburger boxes and along a road he made out of leftover fries. When he realised he was making engine noises he glanced up at Jenna, as if he was worried he was being too noisy, but when she smiled his face lit up and he went back to driving the little blue car.

Jenna was perfectly happy to sit and watch. She

needed the time to take this in. To let herself be in the moment and know that this was Ollie, not Eli. That this was about the future and not the past. That it was okay to have a part of her heart that ached but it was also okay to have a part that could find joy in a small boy's happiness.

Ollie wanted Jenna to watch him try out everything the playground had to offer after that. He waved at her from the windows in the climbing pipes, bounced on seats set on huge springs, played in the pit full of brightly coloured balls and finally came back to where Jenna was sitting.

'Will you read me a story?' he begged. 'In the quiet corner?'

'Of course.'

It was the perfect way to fill in the rest of the time that she needed to care for Ollie. Having let Mitch know where they were and that Ollie was happy, he had texted back to say that his father had been cleared of any cardiac issues and that the diagnosis for his chest pain was likely to be a severe dose of gastric reflux. They were waiting at the pharmacy to pick up some medication and then Mitch would order a taxi for the three of them to get back to his car and they would come and collect Ollie when it arrived.

Ollie curled up in the soft cushion of one of the over-sized bean bags near the bookshelves and leaned his head against Jenna's shoulder as she read. He still had the little blue car clutched in his hand and he was clearly worn out from all the playing because she could feel his head getting heavier and his body softening against her arm. And…she could smell a faint whiff of, what was it? Oh…yes…*baby shampoo*…

Her voice faltered as she tried to keep reading and then trailed into silence but it didn't matter because Ollie was too sleepy to notice. And Jenna had a whole new idea to grapple with—the knowledge that it would be just as easy to fall in love with this child as with his father. That maybe she was a lot closer to that point than she realised. The thought was too big to allow herself to go there and Jenna could almost feel mental doors slamming shut in an effort to protect her from the fear that was hovering. Waiting to step in and force her to flee.

So she simply sat there without moving a muscle. Letting Ollie sleep. Holding herself together until she could find a new level of calmness. This wouldn't last long. Mitch would be here any minute to collect his son and then she could get herself home to her safe space and maybe then she could step back far enough to think about this new shift in her thinking.

Seeing Mitch coming through the restaurant area made her even more confident that she was coping with this. Seeing the smile on his face as he saw Ollie asleep beside her was enough to make her feel very proud of how she was coping. Shifting to give Mitch room to scoop Ollie up was enough to wake the little boy but he wasn't upset by the interruption. He sat up and blinked and then smiled happily, first at Jenna and then at his father.

'I'm the same as Mia now, aren't I?' he said.

'Are you?' Mitch raised his eyebrows as he shared a glance with Jenna.

Ollie nodded. 'She always has her mummy to watch her playing. Now I've got one, too.'

Again, Mitch glanced at Jenna but she dodged the

eye contact. Her mouth had just gone very dry. This had gone way too far. Way too fast. She couldn't keep those doors shut any longer and she could feel panic closing in on her. She couldn't do this, after all. The enormity of those emotions and that fear that came with them was too much.

The last straw was Ollie starting to climb out of the squashy bean chair and losing his balance. Or maybe he was just wanting a cuddle. Whatever the reason, the thought of having those small arms winding themselves around her neck was instantly unbearable. Without even thinking about it, Jenna pushed him away, scrambling to her feet as she blindly reacted to the instinct to run. Ollie tried to hold on, fell back into the chair and then rolled off to land with a bump on the floor, whereupon he burst into tears.

Jenna froze, appalled at what had just happened. She could feel that Mitch was just as horrified, although he calmly stepped forward to lift Ollie into his arms.

'Come on, buddy. You're okay…'

'I'm sorry…' Jenna bit her lip. 'I didn't mean… I…'

What was she trying to say? That she hadn't done it on purpose? Surely Mitch couldn't possibly think that was the case anyway?

But there was an edge of anger in the steady gaze Mitch was giving her over the head of a still sobbing Ollie.

'I get it,' he said slowly. 'But I'm not about to let my son get hurt by it. You said you could cope…'

There was something else that was being said silently, as well.

How could you?

'I'm sorry…' she said again.

'Yeah… I know. Me, too.' Mitch was turning away. 'It's time I got Ollie and Dad home. 'Bye, Jenna.'

The farewell had a chilly edge that generated a new fear in Jenna. 'You'll be back next week?' It was a plea as much as a question. 'For our shift?'

Mitch turned his head. 'I don't think that's a very good idea,' he said slowly. 'For any of us. Do you?'

Jenna didn't say anything. She didn't move as she watched Mitch carry his son out of the restaurant. Away from her. She ducked her head as she fought back tears and it was then that she noticed the little blue car lying on the floor. Without thinking, she stooped and picked it up. She could feel the sharp edges of the toy cutting into her hand as she walked out herself but she welcomed the physical discomfort.

It was so much easier to handle than the emotional pain she knew was waiting for her.

CHAPTER TEN

IT SHOULD HAVE worn off by now.

This horrible, empty feeling.

Missing Mitch so much it was an actual physical pain that was, predictably, there at times like being alone in her bed in those wakeful hours in the dead of the night but could also sideswipe her at unexpected times, like now—when Jenna was sitting up late to check the content of tomorrow's planned teaching sessions.

She needed to simplify the session on ophthalmic emergencies. That quiz of medical terminology might be fun for a group of highly trained doctors but it was very likely to be obscure for the paramedics and nurses that were here to so the five day introductory FRAME course. Throwing in one or two, for interest's sake, like diplopia and ecchymosis, was fine but even amongst experienced doctors, Mitch had been a standout in knowing that enophthalmos was the displacement of an eyeball.

It was suddenly so much harder to focus on the Day Three programme she was checking as Jenna fought off yet another wave of that pain. For heaven's sake... how long was it going to take? It had been weeks now.

'Stick to the basics,' she muttered aloud, as she deleted a slide of the presentation and added a different one. 'Recognition and initial management of the most common eye injuries. There we go…corneal abrasions, foreign bodies, chemical injuries, blunt trauma…'

She had to focus on making this course the best it could possibly be because it was special. Jenna was in Northern Ireland for the first time, as the FRAME initiative was expanded yet again and the interest from medics wanting to do the course and the wider public was huge. A film crew had sat in on a session or two on the first day and had interviewed the course participants. Clips of Jenna teaching and her class revealing what an exciting addition to their practices this qualification would be had been shown as part of her appearance on breakfast television early this morning to explain the reason the FRAME initiative had been developed in the first place and the measurable difference it had made to the outcomes in medical emergencies in rural areas.

Not that Jenna had explained that the main reason FRAME had been developed had been her desperate need for a new direction in her career that could give her a purpose in life during those dreadful, empty months after she'd lost her precious son. Or that throwing herself, heart and soul, into the formation and delivery of the initiative had become her entire life. That it was now in every part of the United Kingdom was something to be very proud of and being here, in Belfast, taking the very first course should have been the absolute highlight of her career so far.

And it was. Of course it was. Jenna was immensely proud of what she'd achieved since she'd started this journey but…but it didn't come close to filling that empty space in her life.

That wave of missing Mitch hadn't completely worn off and the thought of lying awake yet again tonight after such an early start and a long day since was so unappealing that Jenna did something she never normally did when she was travelling for work. She went to the mini bar in her room and took out one of the half-sized bottles of wine. Just a glass, she promised herself, because it might help her to sleep, if nothing else.

For the minute or two it took to open the bottle and pour herself the glass of wine, she had to do without the distraction that working on her session content or catching up on emails could have provided and Jenna was too tired to resist the direction her mind was determined to take her.

Back to that course when Mitch had fallen into her life. Back to that moment when she been captured by this man. Not by something as shallow as his physical appearance but by that aura of being able to take command of any space or situation he was in. By the impression that he was searching for something of significance and that perhaps she was the person who could help him find what he was looking for.

Most of all, by him being the first man she had been attracted to since Stefan.

Jenna unscrewed the lid of the bottle and opened a cupboard to find a glass. The way she was feeling now was her own fault, she reminded herself. She was the one who'd talked herself into following through on that attraction. Had she really been naïve enough to believe that it was simply an experiment that would not necessarily have any negative impact on her life? She'd recognised that there was a gap in her life, no matter how satisfying her career was, and the experiment was to find out whether the addition of a physical connection with another human could fill at least part of the void she'd learned to live with and have the opposite of a negative impact.

And it had. It had filled it to the point of overflowing. To the point where Jenna had not only not wanted it to end but she'd wanted more. A lifetime of more, preferably. And now she had to try and learn to live with the flipside of that kind of connection—the loss and loneliness of finding herself right back in that empty space.

Jenna poured the wine into the tumbler she'd taken from the cupboard. She hadn't heard from Mitch since that awful day when he'd walked out of her life with his crying son in his arms. She'd hurt Ollie and she could understand that he would not permit that to happen again. She would have been just as protective of Eli so she could also understand that another apology from her would make no difference.

If he'd chosen to see her again as something that had no connection to his personal life—or even just come out for a shift with her again—she would have believed that things could have been fixed but he hadn't made contact. He didn't want anything to do with her any longer so there was nothing she could do about that empty space other than to learn to live with it. To try and find her way to leave it behind far enough to fence it off. She needed to try and find those protective filters that she used to view life through, which had somehow been lost during her time with Mitch.

Having been through coping with loss before didn't

make it any easier, though. The void felt bigger, if anything and, in moments like this, Jenna felt as if she was actually falling into it and would become instantly and heartbreakingly lost.

It was so empty.

So lonely.

The experiment had backfired. Jenna had found exactly what was missing from her life and it wasn't anything as simple as sex.

It was love.

It was that feeling of family.

Oh…help… Tears were imminent now. Jenna picked up the glass and took a large mouthful of the wine. She felt her face crumpling as it hit her taste buds, however, and seconds later, she was leaning over the basin in the bathroom, to spit the wine out. Even then, she needed a mouthful of water to try and get the incredibly sour taste from her mouth. Despite being a wine she'd had and enjoyed in the past, this particular bottle was horrendous.

Corked?

No. It had a screw top.

Maybe she was coming down with something?

A 'round' bug, perhaps?

Jenna felt a tear escape and roll down the side of her nose at that memory of Ollie and then something shifted into place at the back of her mind. A memory of the only other time she'd ever found a mouthful of wine so revolting she'd had to spit it out before it made her sick. She could almost hear Stefan laughing at her and what he'd said afterwards.

I bet you're pregnant… Let's do a test…

No…

No, no, no. It couldn't possibly be why the wine

tasted so bad. She and Mitch had taken precautions. It wasn't even as if she was late with her period but, just to double-check, Jenna went to her diary and began counting the days. When she went past twenty-eight days, she felt a cold trickle of fear down her spine.

She was never late.

Ever.

But she was this time. Her period should have started at least two days ago and she didn't even have a hint of the cramps that always came as a warning. Stunned, Jenna sat unmoving. She couldn't even begin to imagine what this could mean in her life. If she could have chosen one thing that she never wanted to happen ever again, it was this.

Being pregnant.

Knowing that one day, in the not too distant future, she would be holding another baby in her arms.

She couldn't do it.

But she couldn't *not* do it, either.

It was almost funny, in retrospect, to have thought that a glass of wine might help her sleep but Jenna's huff of laughter wasn't amused. It felt rather more like despair.

His patient was only in her early sixties but it was clear that she was suffering a potentially catastrophic neurological event—a stroke or an aneurysm perhaps. Shona Barry was well known at the Allensbury Surgery due to her frequent visits to manage the kind of problems that came with a lifelong struggle with obesity, like high blood pressure, diabetes, respiratory and cardiac issues. The main problem right now, however, was that

Shona's weight was going to present a huge challenge for Mitch to intubate her to secure her airway.

A helicopter had been dispatched from a London hospital that had a dedicated emergency unit for stroke patients but it was still ten minutes away. Mitch had been paged as the local FRAME doctor and had arrived at the same time as their local ambulance service to face dealing with precisely the kind of case that had prompted him to go to that course in the first place.

Having to deal with a difficult airway.

He had positioned Shona's head and one of the two paramedics was pre-oxygenating her, the other was drawing up the drugs needed. Mitch had a cricothyroidotomy kit unrolled as an insurance policy because he knew that this was likely to be a difficult intubation and if he wasn't successful within the maximum three attempts, he would move swiftly on to creating a surgical airway. He also had his video laryngoscope and the stylet to help shape the endotracheal tube as it was manoeuvred past the vocal cords.

As focused as he was on his task, Mitch was also aware of something that wasn't even here.

Jenna.

Part of his brain was back in that classroom, using this equipment with a mannequin. He could sense the same anxiety of failure but could also feel the confidence that Jenna had exuded. That belief that he was going to succeed. He could actually hear an echo of the calm advice she had given him, regarding the shape of this stylet, when he'd found it difficult to advance the breathing tube through the vocal cords and into the trachea.

Try popping the stylet off with your thumb, back it out a bit and then try advancing the tube...

And, just like it had with that mannequin, the action made it possible to slip the tube into place, check its position and secure it and then move on to everything else that was urgently needed to stabilise Shona's condition before transport to hospital. One of the flight medics took in the challenging size of their patient and the successful intubation and nodded at Mitch.

'Good job,' he murmured. 'I'm sure that wasn't an easy one.'

News that Shona had undergone emergency thrombectomy to remove the clot in a cerebral artery and that she was expected to make a good recovery made that call-out all the more satisfying. The only downside of that interruption to his normal clinic, other than running late for the rest of the day, was that Mitch hadn't been able to shake off that awareness of Jenna. She was just there, in the back of his mind, along with that now familiar ache of missing her.

Getting home was usually enough to be able to shake it off because he had the reason why he'd had to walk away from her right in front of him. Ollie. Mitch would always do whatever he needed to do in order to protect his precious son. Even if it meant giving up a woman he'd fallen in love with. An amazing woman that he was missing with every breath he took, even weeks after that unfortunate incident in the playground of that fast food restaurant.

He'd expected the ache to have faded by now because it had been weeks but today had let him know that it might take a lot longer than expected. Still, he would cope. It was definitely better than that first week, when he'd been so upset by Ollie being so blatantly rejected, worried about his father's health and fighting the urge to contact Jenna when he knew he shouldn't. He had to put Ollie first. He'd vowed to do that when he'd been sitting beside his dying wife.

'I'm going to take such good care of our son,' he'd whispered. 'I'll keep him safe. As healthy and happy as it's possible to be and...and I'll love him with all my heart. I'll never let anything get in the way of that...'

Ollie was healthy, thank goodness. And happy. Mitch could hear his giggles as he played with Jet in the garden when he arrived home that evening.

'Heard about Shona,' Michael Mitchell said, when Mitch arrived home. He was tossing a salad and there were salmon steaks on the kitchen bench waiting to be grilled. 'Makes you think, doesn't it? You never know what's just around the corner. Could have been me, if that chest pain had been a real heart attack.'

'You're going the right way about improving the chances it won't happen for real.' His father had lost a bit of weight since that scare with the chest pain, modified his diet and was taking some medication. 'That's a nice healthy looking dinner you're making.' Mitch went to the fridge. 'Fancy a beer?'

'Good idea. I imagine it's been a long day for you.'

'Mmm…' Mitch pulled out two bottles of lager. 'It has.' And it wasn't over yet. The feel of those icy bottles in his hands had just triggered a memory of that night in the pub with Jenna. That pleasant surprise of finding that her choice of beverage was just that bit different. The amusement that had danced in her eyes when he'd said that he'd have what she was having. It inevitably morphed into a memory of what had come later that evening when they'd made love that first time and the fresh awareness of what was missing from his life was more than an ache—it was an actual pain.

He stared through the window as he swallowed a mouthful of beer. 'Ollie looks happy.'

'Hmm.' Michael was looking at Mitch rather than his grandson. 'Wish I could say the same about you.'

'I'm fine, Dad.'

'You don't look it. You haven't looked happy for weeks, son. Ever since that visit I had to hospital. You not worried about *my* health, are you?'

Mitch shook his head. 'You're looking better than you have in a long time.'

'So why are you hanging around home so much, then? You loved your days being out in that rapid response vehicle.'

Mitch shrugged. 'I only did that to get back up to speed with the kind of skills I might need in emergencies here.'

'Oh…' His father turned away to get on with his dinner preparations. 'That'll be why you invited Jenna to Pets' Day, then, I guess? Why you've looked happier in the last couple of months than you've been ever since Tegan died.'

Mitch was silent.

'I'm not stupid,' Michael added quietly.

'I know that.' Mitch took another mouthful of his beer. He knew his friendship with Jenna had made enough of a difference in his life that it was no surprise others had noticed.

'You might be, though.'

'What?'

'If you let Jenna disappear from your life like this.'

'Ollie comes first,' Mitch said. 'And Jenna rejected him. End of.'

Ollie had come through the kitchen door as Mitch was speaking. 'What's '"jected"?' he asked.

'Rejected.' Mitch ruffled his son's soft hair. 'It means that you don't want to accept something that someone's trying to give you. Like a cuddle, maybe. That's what I was talking to Grandpa about—that Jenna didn't want your cuddle.'

Ollie's shrug was so like one of his own gestures that it made Mitch smile.

'Sometimes I 'ject cuddles,' he said. 'If I'm cross. Or sad. You have to be ready for cuddles.' He was heading for the pantry. 'Jenna was sad. Can I have a biscuit, Grandpa?'

'Nope. We're going to have dinner very soon. You can have a bit of carrot, though. Here…' Michael held out a strip of the carrots he was cutting but his gaze was on Mitch.

'Out of the mouths of babes,' he murmured. 'He's not stupid, either.'

But Mitch was frowning. Had he missed something important? That looking after Ollie had made Jenna sad, perhaps? How much worse had he made it, if that was the case, by accusing her of deliberately hurting his son? By not accepting her apology? Not even trying to make contact with her?

Ollie was feeding the carrot stick to Jet. 'Let's go outside again,' he said to the dog. 'And find sticks to throw.'

'Hang on,' Mitch called. 'If it was okay that Jenna didn't want your cuddle, why were you crying so much?'

Ollie didn't bother turning around. 'I lost my car,'

he called over his shoulder. 'The blue one that Jenna gave me. And I was sad because it was my favouritest.'

Mitch turned to find himself under his father's steady gaze. 'Maybe Jenna knows where it is,' he said. 'You never know, it might be worth asking.'

Oh…the thought of talking to Jenna. Hearing her voice again gave Mitch an odd feeling in his chest. A tightness that made it noticeably hard to pull in his next breath. He didn't want the concern he could see in his father's eyes though because the thought that his father still felt the same way about him as he did about Ollie was enough to give him a prickle of tears at the back of his eyes. So he turned away, lifting his shoulders in a half-hearted shrug.

'Maybe…'

Jenna had learned how incredibly long a day could seem many years ago. Back when she had been trying to take life one day at a time. Again and again, she'd told herself she only had to get through this one day in order to survive but it felt like it went on for ever.

This had been longer than any of those days.

She wasn't about to try and unpick the emotional threads that were contributing to the crushing weight she was carrying because that would have meant thinking about a future she wouldn't have chosen again in a million years. Another child. Years and years and years of that fear that something terrible could happen and she would have to face the kind of devastation you surely couldn't survive more than once.

It was much better to have something else to focus on and Jenna put everything she had into making the sessions for her class today as memorable as possible as she covered spinal and head injuries, blunt trauma and management of burns. To keep herself busy throughout the evening, Jenna decided to revamp her entire folder of triage scenarios, spending many hours making new cards that listed the injuries and condition of a good variety of patients that could be attached to the mannequins she would arrange tomorrow to look as though they'd been in a bus crash, an explosion or under a collapsed building in an earthquake. Her course attendees would arrive on scene and have to prioritise the patients in order from those who needed immediate, life-saving resuscitation through to those who were so badly injured they were unlikely to survive despite major intervention.

It was a case of rinse or repeat to get through the second to last day of the course where she covered the session on triage along with fracture management, soft tissue injuries and safety around helicopters. It was ironic that the last session of the day was about critical incident stress management when she noticed she had some of the physical symptoms of that kind of stress herself. Slight dizziness and a headache that could be caused by her blood pressure being higher than normal. Chest pain… No. It was more like abdominal pain.

Cramps.

'Excuse me for just a minute,' she said. 'Talk amongst yourselves and come up with the types of situations you think you would struggle to cope with. I'll be right back.'

Except she wasn't. Jenna had to spend more than five minutes just sitting on that toilet seat, her head in her hands, breathing through the relief that she wasn't going to have to face the situation she'd known she could never deal with.

She wasn't pregnant.

And she'd never been so relieved in her entire life.

So why was it that, when she got back to her hotel room that evening, she could still feel like she hadn't shrugged off that weight of despair? Why did she feel a kind of grief, even, that she wasn't pregnant? This was crazy. So confusing that Jenna had to give up even thinking about it because it was too exhausting. She lay on the couch and closed her eyes, so drained that surely she would fall asleep and be able to escape in a matter of minutes.

She almost did. But it was in that space just before you fell asleep—that half-dream, half-reality space—that Jenna thought about Ollie. She could feel the weight of him falling asleep against her arm. She could smell that whiff of baby shampoo. And she could hear Mitch…that tone in his voice—not when he'd been so angry with her but way before that, the day that she'd found out he was a father and he'd been speaking to Ollie on the phone and she'd heard that note that had pierced her heart so sharply—the tone of a parent speaking to their precious child.

The sound of love.

Jenna opened her eyes as she felt the tears streaming down her face. She knew what the problem was, here. Despite a crippling fear that had made her avoid any kind of significant relationship in the last eight years and had made her believe that having another child was the last thing she would ever want, it had been nothing more than an extreme form of self-protection.

And it was a lie.

A baby would have been the best thing that could have happened for her.

A baby with a father like Andrew Mitchell would have been an absolute blessing.

Being a parent alongside Mitch—as partners, as *lovers*, perhaps even as husband and wife—would have made anything possible. Could have given her the courage to face all those fears.

Was it possible to feel something this big if it was only one-sided?

Was Jenna brave enough to try and find out?

This time, as her eyes drifted shut, Jenna knew she would be able to sleep peacefully. She had learned something about herself that, if nothing else, gave her hope in a future she hadn't known she'd wanted so much.

Was she brave enough to find out whether that was a possibility with Mitch? Whether what she'd thought she might have seen in his eyes that day, after they'd shared that butterfly's wing kiss, had been as real as the plans they had been making for a romantic getaway to a Greek Island.

Yes…but she needed to think about it. About how to do it. And that was when inspiration struck. When she got back to London, she needed to have a hunt in the glovebox of her vehicle. It was where she'd put that little blue car when she'd stumbled out of that restaurant having given Mitch enough time to carry Ollie well away from her.

Maybe it was still there.

Maybe Ollie might like it back?

CHAPTER ELEVEN

THE LITTLE BLUE car was sitting on the dashboard of the rapid response vehicle. Maybe that was why Ollie was the first thing to cross Jenna's mind when a Code Blue priority call came through on her radio to go to an incident with a critically ill child at the medical centre in Allensbury.

She was already past the outskirts of Greater London, on that side of the city, with her last call to a cyclist who had been knocked off her bike by a van in a village about halfway between Allensbury and Croydon. That patient was now being transported to a trauma centre by the helicopter that wouldn't be available to be dispatched to Allensbury for at least fifteen minutes.

Jenna was twenty minutes' drive away under legal speed limits but she knew she could do it in less than ten. She activated the siren and beacons with one hand as she pushed her responding button with the other. Then she pushed her accelerator to the floor. There was a hard knot in her belly that was rapidly getting bigger. Harder. It felt like fear. Was this fate trying to remind her of why she's been prepared to believe, for years and years, that she never wanted to be a mother again? Or a stepmother—especially to a child as adorable as Ollie?

A flash of blue caught in the periphery of Jenna's vision as she hurtled along in the fast lane of the motorway. Maybe it was just as well she hadn't quite found the courage to do something with that toy car in the few days since she'd been back from Ireland. This horrible fear couldn't be dismissed. Fear for Ollie. Fear for Mitch. And…yeah, fear for herself, even though she'd thought she'd kept herself safe from ever feeling fear like this again. If she'd needed any confirmation of just how deeply she cared for both Mitch and Ollie, this was it. This meant everything.

'Not Ollie,' she found herself whispering aloud. '*Please*…let it not be Ollie…'

But Ollie *was* the first person Jenna saw as she rushed through the front doors of Allenbury's medical centre a short time later. He was in the waiting room, on his grandfather's lap, and Michael Mitchell had his arms wrapped around the frightened looking child. He saw the alarm on Jenna's face but shook his head.

'Ollie's fine,' he told her quietly. 'Just scared. It's Mia that's sick.'

She didn't have to pause to try and give Ollie a reassuring smile and give his grandpa a nod of thanks for the information. Jenna kept moving, her arms full of the medical gear and drugs she was hoping she wouldn't need to use. The receptionist, with 'Josie' on her name tag, was pointing to a door.

'In here,' she urged Jenna. 'Dr Mitchell's with her. Her mum's here, now, too.'

It was Hanna who was sitting on the bed in Mitch's

consulting room, in fact, but it was very clear that the patient was the small girl she was holding in her arms. Mia had a nebuliser mask on her face and Jenna could see what hard work it was for her to breathe. She was hunched forward, breathing at a rapid rate with her nostrils flaring, and she was using accessory muscles in her neck and chest. More worryingly, she looked very different to the happy little girl Jenna had seen rolling around and throwing grass at Pets' Day. This Mia was so lethargic, she was barely conscious. She didn't even look up when Jenna arrived.

Mitch did look up as she entered his consulting room and that first shared glance set the pattern for a current of non-verbal communication that did nothing to undermine what needed to happen here for Mia but did everything to let Jenna know she was in the right place at the right time for more than professional reasons.

I'm so glad you're here, Mitch's gaze told her.

I'm so glad I'm here, too.

Mitch's tone was calm as he spoke aloud. 'Mia was playing at home with Ollie after school. This could be an exercise-induced asthma attack although Hanna said she's had a bit of a runny nose for a day or two so it might be something viral. She didn't respond to repeated doses of her inhaler so Dad brought her in fast. Currently, she's tachycardic, tachypnoeic and breath sounds are decreasing despite the nebuliser. I'm about to get IV access.'

He already had a tourniquet around a tiny arm. Jenna knew it wasn't going to be easy to find a small vein in such dark skin but also knew that Mitch's confidence in being about to achieve a result was not misplaced.

His glance was adding something else, however. *I'm really worried. Mia's not doing well. We both know how quickly a severe asthma attack can become life-threatening.*

Jenna nodded. 'We could try some intramuscular adrenaline if there's any delay with getting access.' She held his gaze for a heartbeat. *We're a good team, Mitch. We've got this.*

Mia didn't make a sound as the small needle pierced her skin. She was looking up at her mother, holding her gaze fiercely. And Hanna was cuddling her, making the kind of soothing sounds mothers always made when comforting their child.

'You're doing a great job, Hanna,' Mitch told her. 'It's helping a lot.'

Hanna simply nodded and Jenna could understand how she might not be able to find any words. How terrified she probably was. As she finished adding a bronchodilator to the nebuliser mask's chamber to keep up the continuous mist of medication to be inhaled, she touched Hanna's arm, catching her glance to let her know she agreed with Mitch—and that she understood exactly how hard this was.

Mitch was securing the IV line. 'I'll give an IV salbutamol bolus. And could you draw up some hydrocortisone for me, please?'

Jenna nodded. She'd noticed that Mia's lips were starting to look blue when she'd lifted the mask to fill the medication chamber. Mitch had a fleeting glance for her as she reached for the drug ampoule.

I know how hard this is for you, too. I'm sorry, Jenna...

It's okay... I'm fine.

'She's so drowsy.' Hanna's couldn't hide how afraid she was. 'Is she losing consciousness? How can we get her to hospital in time?'

'The helicopter will be on its way now,' Jenna assured her. 'And it's great they can land just across the road on the common. In the meantime, Mitch and I have got more that we can do to help.'

'Please help her...' It was no more than a desperate whisper. *'Please...'*

Minutes flashed past because there was so much to do. Listening to Mia's chest as her lung sounds got alarmingly quiet. Getting electrodes on to monitor her heart rate and rhythm. Monitoring her blood pressure and oxygen saturation. Administering more drugs. Thinking about what they didn't want to discuss out loud yet—that if Mia's condition continued to deteriorate they might have to go to what was a last resort of intubating and manually ventilating her and that carried a very real risk of complications. Death, even.

This time, it was Jenna that needed the silent reassurance when she glanced towards Mitch and she got it instantly.

We've got this, Jenna... You and me...

If Jenna hadn't been there with him, it would have been too hard to hold on to that confidence as the tension escalated, let alone to have enough to share. Thank goodness Mitch had recognised the severity of the situation as soon as Michael had run into the medical centre with Mia in his arms and he'd called for help. Thank goodness, by some extraordinary stroke of luck, Jenna had been dispatched and had been able to arrive in a remarkably short period of time. And thank goodness managing this life-threatening asthma attack didn't have to include intubating Mia.

In the last minutes before the air rescue crew arrived at the medical centre, their young patient's condition started to improve. By the time the intensive care flight medics were in the room and taking over to transport both Mia and her mother to a specialist paediatric hospital, the little girl was a lot more awake and, while her breathing was still too fast and laboured, she wrapped her arms around Hanna's neck as she was lifted and even found a smile.

Hanna also managed to find one.

'Love you, baby girl,' she said. 'We're going for a ride in a helicopter. That'll be something to tell Daddy about later, won't it?'

It was controlled chaos moving the stretcher with two occupants, IV set-up and bag of fluids and all the monitoring gear and attachments swiftly and smoothly out of the medical centre, across the road and into the helicopter. Jenna's vehicle was also parked on the Allensbury Common side of the road. Mitch was helping her carry some of her equipment back to her vehicle and a couple of officers from the local police were making sure bystanders were keeping a safe distance from the helicopter.

His father and Ollie were amongst those bystanders, standing on the footpath, hand in hand, not far from Jenna's car, and Mitch saw the moment that Jenna was caught by the fear on Ollie's face. She dropped the backpack she was carrying on the footpath and crouched, holding out her arms. And Ollie let go of his grandfather's hand and ran to Jenna, hurling himself into those waiting arms and then clinging to her like a little monkey as his voice hitched and wobbled.

'Is Mia going to come back?'

'It's okay, Ollie. I know how scary it is but she's feeling better already and the people in the helicopter are taking really, really good care of her.'

Mitch was looking at those two dark heads so close together and their total focus on each other in this moment of seeking and offering comfort and his own heart felt like it was about to burst. It was hard to tell where the boundary was between where his love for Ollie finished and his love for Jenna began. Maybe there was no boundary. They were distinct parts but inseparable from the picture being created here.

A family picture.

Ollie didn't notice him stepping closer, putting down the gear he'd been carrying. 'But when can she come and play with me again?' he was asking.

'The doctors will want to look after her for a wee while,' Jenna told him. 'They might want to try some new puffers and medicine to see if they can stop something like this happening again.'

The rotors of the helicopter were picking up speed and the noise level was increasing but Mitch was close enough to still hear what Jenna was saying.

'How 'bout if I go and see Mia as soon as I can and I'll text Daddy to let him know how she is and then he can tell you?'

Mitch stepped even closer. 'I might go to the hospital myself very soon and see Mia and her mummy.'

He caught Jenna's gaze and was doing his best to convey a private message.

We need to talk. Please...asap.

'That's a great idea,' Jenna said. But her gaze was also responding.

Yes...there's so much we need to talk about.

'Can I come too?' Ollie raised his voice. The question was for his father but it was his grandfather on his other side who answered.

'We'll stay here, Ollie. I think your daddy and Jenna can look after everything all by themselves.' Michael was smiling quietly as he looked from Mitch to Jenna—as if he'd heard that silent exchange they'd just shared.

Perhaps Ollie heard an undercurrent to what was actually being said, as well. He still had his arms wrapped around Jenna's neck but he unfurled one to reach out to his father. He still looked pale and worried and Mitch could see in his eyes a plea for touch. Closeness. The comfort of knowing you had someone who loved you enough to make the world a better place.

And then his gaze shifted a fraction to catch Jenna's and he could swear that he saw an identical plea in *her* eyes and Mitch could actually feel some jagged pieces in his soul shift a little. Enough that things were settling into place. A new place, perhaps, but that was okay. Better than okay.

He crouched down so that Ollie could wrap that free arm around his neck. He still had Jenna caught by his other arm so the most natural thing in the world was for Mitch to put his arm around Jenna as well. A group hug. They could feel the vibration of the helicopter's rotors gaining enough speed to lift off and the sound was covering any voices but it seemed like Mitch could hear what Jenna was saying as she suggested that Ollie should wave because Mia might be able to see him watching. As Ollie raised both arms to wave, she smiled at Mitch. He couldn't hear her now but he could lip read her words so easily.

'All good?'

Now it felt like there was hope that everything was going to work out in the best way possible. For Mia and her family. For his family, too. Ollie and his dad, himself and Jenna. He smiled back.

'Couldn't be better.'

They met in the observation ward next to the emergency department of the paediatric hospital.

Mia was sitting up in bed, eating ice cream. Her parents were sitting on opposite sides of the bed but holding hands across it. Hanna was brushing a tear from her cheek as she told Jenna about the enormous relief that Mia hadn't needed to be taken to the intensive care unit—that she had improved enough to be only staying to be monitored overnight and then she would be able to go home, as Mitch came in to stand beside Jenna. He'd heard enough to know all was well.

'That's great news.' He smiled. 'I'll have a chat to the doctors tomorrow. I'm thinking we might need a new action plan for Mia.'

Hanna nodded. 'They want to get all the results of the tests they've done this afternoon and they said they'll go over the plan with all of us. I'm so glad you came in, Mitch. I don't know how to thank you for what you did this afternoon. And you, Jenna.' She had to brush away another tear. 'You have no idea what it means…'

Mitch's gaze locked with Jenna's. 'Oh, I think we do,' he said quietly. It looked like it was an effort to break the eye contact. 'That looks like yummy ice cream, Mia.'

'Mmm…' Mia had ice cream over both cheeks and her chin.

'Ollie's going to be so happy to hear that you're feeling better. Hey…why don't we call him so he can say "hi" himself?'

The benefits of technology meant that it was only seconds before the two children could see each other on a phone screen and it was so lovely to see that wide grin on both their faces that Jenna had to swallow a rather big lump in her throat.

'Will you get me an ice cream on the way home, Daddy?' Ollie asked. 'A big one, like Mia's?'

'I think you'll be asleep by the time I get home,' Mitch told him. 'I'm going to take Jenna out to dinner first.'

Ollie's clear voice made all the adults smile. 'Because she's your girlfriend?'

'I think so…' Mitch said.

He was smiling at Ollie on the phone but his gaze was on Jenna and the question in his eyes was unmistakeable. She caught her bottom lip between her teeth as she nodded. Just once, but it was enough.

'Yeah,' he added. 'Because Jenna's my girlfriend.'

Perhaps it was because they had such big things to talk about that neither Jenna nor Mitch wanted to be enclosed in a restaurant. It was a pleasantly warm evening, so they began walking in the direction of Hyde Park to look for a takeout meal and, when they saw the familiar signage of the fast food outlet, it felt like a circle was being completed. Their relationship had ended at another branch of this same restaurant so maybe it was the perfect segue into forging something new.

Something better?

'I don't suppose you ever eat junk food like this normally, do you?'

'Only sometimes.' Jenna felt her heart squeeze as she remembered Ollie telling her that. 'And I think this might well be a "sometime".'

'Do you want to eat here or go into the park?'

'I'd love the park.'

'Same. What would you like to eat?'

'Surprise me.'

Mitch was back with a large paper bag in no time and a minute or two later they'd found a bench just inside the park grounds, with a lovely view of grass and huge trees and…squirrels.

'They'll take that hamburger out of your hands if you don't eat it fast enough,' Mitch warned.

His eyes were dancing with amusement and something else. Something huge that told her he didn't want to be anywhere else in the world right now. Or with anybody else. Which was exactly how she was feeling herself and her heart was so full that, curiously, she wasn't very hungry any longer. She broke off a piece of the bun for her hamburger and held it out. Sure enough, a bold squirrel ran forward to pluck it from her hand, which made them both laugh. Then they looked at each other and the laughter faded instantly but neither of them looked away.

'I love you, Jenna,' Mitch said softly.

'I love you, too,' she whispered.

Mitch didn't seem to be hungry any longer, either. He put the hamburger he was holding down on the bench beside him and didn't even notice the squirrels that appeared from nowhere and stole it because he was so focused on Jenna.

'Really? Oh, my God… I hoped so but…but I didn't dare let myself believe…'

'Same…'

It was Jenna that discarded the food in her hands completely this time but she wasn't aware of anything other than the way Mitch was looking at her. The way his hand came up to cup her chin and cheek. The way he touched her lips with his own with that gentle whisper of a kiss that was becoming her favourite thing in the world—a promise of what was to come next. And, yes, the 'real' kiss that followed took her straight into another world. One that only she and Mitch inhabited. Where time stopped. Where anything that wasn't good could be put aside for the moment, with the knowledge that when they went back into the 'real' world, it would be easier to cope with, because they would be coping together.

Maybe it was a vague awareness that they weren't alone by any means in this park that pulled them back to reality. Or maybe it was the squirrel that ran along the back of the bench in search of more food. Not that they pulled apart entirely. Jenna's head rested in the hollow beneath Mitch's collar bone. He tilted his head so that it rested on hers.

'I was going to call you,' he said softly. 'I was just waiting for the right moment. I'm not at all happy that Mia got so sick, of course, but I can't tell you how happy I was to see you again.'

'I was so scared when that call came through,' Jenna told him. 'My first thought was that something had happened to Ollie.'

'He was that scared as well. He adores Mia.'

They sat in silence for a breath or two and Jenna soaked in the solid feel of Mitch's chest beneath her cheek. The steady thump of his heartbeat.

'I thought I was keeping myself safe, you know. Not letting anybody too close in my life. It was easy to avoid a relationship with a guy because I genuinely wasn't interested. Until I met you...'

'I get that.' Jenna could feel Mitch's head move against her own as he nodded. 'I felt the same way after Tegan. If I saw a woman even looking at me twice, I'd think, Can't you see that that's never going to happen? *Ever?* Having Ollie to focus on made it even less likely. It felt like a life-saver.'

'And I had Eli for a long time...' Jenna let her breath out in a sigh. 'Enough time to get through the worst of my grief over Stefan. It was a lot harder after I loss Eli, though. I might have been able to see an attractive man and not be remotely interested or affected but...seeing children and babies everywhere—that was something completely different. It was unbearable...'

Mitch's arms tightened around Jenna. 'Oh, I get that, too. I knew how big an ask it was for you to come to Pets' Day but I was *so* happy that you did. Because I thought it could be the first step towards something bigger. Something that I realised I wanted very, very much.' His voice cracked. 'A future with you.' He was pressing his lips to Jenna's hair. 'A family...'

She twisted her head enough to look up at him. So that she could see the truth of what he was saying aloud. And so that he could see the truth in her eyes.

'I wanted that too,' she whispered. 'And I really believed it could happen.' One day—soon—she'd confess how she'd felt when she'd thought she was pregnant, and how she'd felt when she'd found out she wasn't. But that could wait until an even more intimate moment. 'Then Ollie fell asleep when I was reading him that story and…' She had to clear her throat. 'And I could smell baby shampoo and then, when he said he had a mummy to watch him like Mia did…'

'Oh, darling.' Mitch's tone was raw. 'It can just be a tiny thing that triggers grief and, for that moment in time, it feels like the worst just happened yesterday, doesn't it?'

'I got scared,' Jenna admitted. 'It was just that moment, but I didn't think it would be possible to survive it happening again. And then you were angry with me and I totally understood why…' Her breath hitched. 'I'd hurt Ollie. I'd made him cry.'

'No…' Mitch was smiling at her. So tenderly that Jenna could feel her eyes filling up. 'You know what he told me?'

'No…what?'

'That he knew why you didn't want a cuddle. That it was because you were too sad.'

Jenna blinked. 'He's four years old. How could he possibly know something like that?'

Mitch's smile widened. 'He's smart, I guess.'

'Like his dad.' Jenna smiled back at Mitch. 'But why was he crying so much?'

'Apparently, he'd lost something he loved. A little blue car?'

'Oh…' Jenna sat up. 'I know exactly where that is. Maybe I should give it to you to take home for him?'

'No…' Mitch stood up and held out his hand to

Jenna. 'I think you should give it to him yourself. You should come home.'

And Jenna took his hand and let him pull her to her feet. Pull her right back into his arms, before they started walking anywhere. For another one of those kisses that stopped coherent thought for as long as it lasted. There was time for a very clear thought in the heartbeat before their lips touched, however.

Jenna knew with absolute clarity that she would follow this man she loved so much anywhere he wanted to take her. But the best place she could possibly go with him was home. A home that she would share with Mitch. And Ollie. And his dad and Jet and maybe even another baby one day.

Their home.

The place she wanted to be in for the rest of her life.

Mitch held her gaze as he lifted his lips from hers and Jenna could see a promise that felt like one of those butterfly kisses. A promise of so much more to come.

'All good?'

Jenna swallowed what felt like it could be the last of a fear she'd lived with for too long.

'Couldn't be better...'

* * * * *

FLING WITH THE CHILDREN'S HEART DOCTOR

BECKY WICKS

MILLS & BOON

Dedicated to Liz Wicks, my mum,
who didn't have the chance to visit Amsterdam
in 2020 because of the pandemic.

CHAPTER ONE

THE REVAMPED SEVENTEENTH-CENTURY hospital building spanned the length of an entire street, with an old black-brick church at one end and a small tree-lined park at the other. Bicycles took up every spare inch of space outside, chained up almost on top of each other between the sycamore trees. Dr Freya Grey passed a red-haired woman in a staff lanyard and polka-dot jacket, who was jabbering into a phone on the steps outside, and pushed through the double doors to Reception.

Huge seven- or eight-foot-high red and purple tulips covered the walls. Each had a long green stem that seemed to sprout from floor to ceiling. Impressive paint job, she thought to herself, making for the lifts.

The Happy Hearts Clinic, where Freya Grey was going to be spending the next six months as the new paediatric cardiologist, was on the top floor of the Anne Frank Children's Hospital. Shifting her feet on the black-and-white-tiled floor and watching the people milling about, she wondered why on earth she was so nervous. She'd moved from job to job in the US and elsewhere without a backward glance for years and had never felt as much as a flutter in her belly, and the vibe here was a thousand times more serene than any hospital she'd ever seen before.

Looking back, she hadn't known anyone at the start of her fellowship at the children's hospital she'd worked at in Boston. *Or* when she'd signed up to the mission projects in Cambodia and South Africa. There was nothing more exhilarating than diving head first into a new adventure. Solo ventures weren't what made her nervous. *This* move felt different. Despite the six-month contract, which meant she was technically free to move on again at the end of the year, she had history in Amsterdam, both good and bad.

And from this point on, she had two jobs keeping her here in her childhood stomping ground—this one at the hospital, and the other one renovating the old canal house she'd inherited from her gran, Anouk. She'd never had the pleasure…or torture, it was too soon to tell…of renovating a house before.

The shiny elevator door slid open. A young child hooked up to an IV in a wheelchair was pushed out carefully by a woman around her age and Freya stepped back with a smile to let them pass.

'Excuse me! Hold the elevator, please!'

The woman in the polka-dot jacket had finished her phone call and was rushing towards her across the chequered floor tiles. She looked rather flustered as she rammed herself through the doors and let out a huge sigh as they shut behind her. 'Thanks!'

'You're welcome.' Freya could read the woman's lanyard now. 'Nurse Joy? Oh, you're at Happy Hearts, too? I'm the new cardiologist, Freya.'

'Oh, hi! Good to meet you. We really *need* you. You're from America?' She must have heard the accent, just as Freya could tell Joy was from somewhere in Ireland.

'I've just come from Colorado. I was at the Children's Hospital in Aurora for a year, but I moved about quite a bit in the US before that. Maybe I picked up an accent from talking to patients and their families all day, but I spent my childhood between here and the UK, actually.'

Joy still looked flustered. She ran a hand through auburn spirals and shuffled out of her jacket, revealing her pale pink sundress. 'Getting hot now, right? It's warmer than it normally is here in June and it's still only seven a.m.'

'Climate change,' they muttered in unison, and they both smiled. Freya liked Joy already. It was always good to meet someone you liked on your first day in a new place.

More tulips greeted her from the walls on the top floor. Three small patients no older than seven were sitting cross-legged in a circle in a designated play space, engrossed in a puzzle. One little girl with a tube in her nose looked up and waved at them, and Freya watched Joy's face soften as she raised her hand in greeting, unwittingly creating a polka dot flag above her head from the jacket.

'She's the sweetest thing, but unfortunately she spends more time in here than at home, poor Violet,' she whispered to Freya.

'What's she in here for?'

'She was born with an Ebstein anomaly and an ASD. It's a lot but you wouldn't know it, she has the whole place wrapped around her finger. You should see Lucas with her. She loves him. He's so great with all the kids.'

Freya watched Violet from afar, feeling her heart go

out to her. She had diagnosed an atrial septal defect in a young boy in South Africa on her last medical mission and she was still in touch with him and his lovely family. She also didn't miss the almost dreamy singsong way Joy had mentioned Dr Lucas Van de Berg. The heart surgeon Freya was going to be assisting as diagnostician.

Lucas was something of a hero. He'd been at the helm of a team that had brought a new transcatheter aortic valve replacement technique to the operating table. It meant they could fix a severely narrowed aortic valve without the need to open up a patient's chest. It was giving new hope to children who'd normally have a much smaller chance of survival. She'd heard him talking about it on a podcast on the plane over from Denver, which secretly had been an excuse to hear his voice again. She'd found the sound of his Dutch lilt quite intoxicating during their phone interview a week or so before she learned she'd been hired by Happy Hearts.

'I have fifteen minutes till I'm meant to meet Dr Van de Berg. It didn't take as long to get here as I thought it would on foot.'

'You're staying nearby? A hotel?'

'I have a house here.'

Joy looked taken aback. 'I thought you just came from America?'

'I actually just inherited my gran's house,' she explained, but the words from her own mouth brought more uncomfortable memories flooding back. 'Anyway, do you know where I can wait for Lucas?'

'You could wait here, or you could just come with me to the staffroom. He'll go there eventually for his coffee. Where's the house you inherited?' Joy asked interestedly, leading her through a set of double doors.

'In the Jordaan, it's across three floors. I forgot how many stairs you had to climb to get to the top. I guess it was more fun as a kid, you know, like climbing a ladder. It's not as much fun when you have to lug three suitcases up there all by yourself.'

There it was again, a flutter of discomfort, just remembering the time she'd spent in that house growing up. As the child of a Dutch teenage mother and a wealthy British tax lawyer twenty years her senior, Freya's childhood had been complicated. Her parents had tried to make it work, living in the UK together, but she'd been taken back to Amsterdam by her mother at two years old, presumably after they'd both had enough. After that, she'd pretty much been raised by her mother's mother, Anouk, until her dad had stepped in and enrolled her at an elite boarding school back in Surrey, when she was just five years old.

It wasn't till her mother had met Stijn and fallen pregnant again with Freya's half-sister Liv a decade later that Elise Grey had finally learned how to be a responsible parent. Liv had got a proper mother…in fact, she'd got all Freya had ever wanted. By then, though, Freya had already decided her own fate was to keep on moving, wherever her heart might desire, instead of waiting around for someone else to make her happy.

Liv was trying to call me last night, she remembered guiltily, realising she had zoned half out of Joy's introduction to the hospital social schemes and in-house school, and the cinema, all of which she'd read about online already. Liv had gone to live in the UK four years ago, to be with her boyfriend.

'You get three cinema passes a month, so you can catch the best movies free,' Joy explained, leading her off into one of the rooms, which appeared to be some sort of office-slash-staffroom. A worktop above a fridge offered a clutter of mismatched mugs, cutlery and a coffee pot. The wooden polished floor looked original, as did the stained-glass motifs above the huge rectangular windows.

She watched her new guide hang her jacket and handbag on a coatstand by a velvet couch. 'The cinema passes can be given to friends, too. You can even take your husband for free.'

'Oh, I don't have a husband,' Freya said, noting a jar overflowing with sweets on the desk, more cheerful flowers in vases, and the framed certificates on the walls. One of them was a recent gold-framed tribute to the work of Lucas Van de Berg—Netherlands Paediatric Surgeon of the Year.

'Boyfriend?' Joy probed behind her. Freya laughed under her breath, wondering absently yet again what Lucas Van de Berg was like in person. She already knew he was articulate and well respected, rich and successful, and had a list of accolades a mile long. She'd been excited to work alongside him, just listening to him talk at the conference from his place on the interview panel, and on the podcast.

Joy was still waiting to hear if she had a boyfriend.

'No, I don't have one of those either. I move around too much for that,' Freya said.

'Well, we're lucky to have you here for the next six months.' Joy beamed, and Freya forced a smile in return. She was excited about this position, and the free cinema passes, but no amount of perks would keep her from packing her bags once the house was sold, she knew that much for certain. Already she felt out of her comfort zone, being back once more in a place where no one had ever really wanted her.

Joy leaned over a chair behind the desk and scanned the computer screen in front of her, whilst hurriedly pulling on a white coat over her sundress at the same time. 'Oh, Lord, today is looking busier than I thought.'

'Don't let me hold you up,' Freya started, although a very tall man with dark chestnut hair in a side parting had just stepped into the room and stolen all her other words away. She knew it was Lucas, before he even said a word, but the deep husky baritone of his voice confirmed it.

He took in the room with a single sweep, his blue eyes settling on nothing before finding hers, and holding them.

'Hi,' he said. He stopped a foot from the doorway and pulled the phone he was holding away from his ear. She felt like a fish who'd just been hooked.

'Lucas, there you are. Look who I found. This is Dr Freya Grey, our new cardiologist.' Joy gestured to Freya proudly, like she was a treasure she'd just unearthed especially for him, but Lucas was already appraising her with his mouth curved in a slightly mysterious half-smile that did something funny to her stomach.

'Dr Grey,' he said coolly.

He had kind, almond-shaped eyes, framed by soft, chestnut brows that matched his hair, which was slightly longer at the front than the back. A typical Dutch look, yet there was something extra striking about him. His face was clean shaven, and serious, and she noticed a pair of glasses peeking from the top pocket of his shirt.

She took his outstretched hand and shook it. *No ring*, she noted. Interesting. The heart surgeon was single. Or at least not married. Not that she cared either way, she reminded herself. She was here to work, not for the men.

Out of the corner of her eye she saw Joy reach a hand into the jar of sweets on the desk and fill one pocket of her white coat, but Freya couldn't look away from Lucas. He was dressed in navy trousers and a crisp pale blue shirt. The laces in his expensive-looking loafers defied his sensible demeanour and clothing. They were the kind of comical bright green that might make a sick kid smile.

He ended his call and put the phone into his trouser pocket, before sliding casually into the seat behind the computer. Joy offered Freya a coffee.

'I'm fine, thanks,' she replied. Lucas's mouth stretched into a lazy smile, revealing very good teeth. Freya had a thing about men's teeth, probably from all the years she'd spent in America. Once last year she'd gone on a date with a guy she'd met online—the only date in a long time—and the second he'd smiled in real life she'd regretted it. His teeth had been a total disaster zone.

'OK…well, I should get to my rounds now.' Joy placed a hand lightly on Freya's arm on the way past with her own coffee. 'You're in good hands with Lucas.'

I have no doubt about that, Freya thought as she found herself alone with Lucas. Suddenly she didn't know what to do with her hands, and she cursed herself for refusing the coffee. He gestured to the seat in front of him, then trailed a finger round the rim of his cup as she sat opposite him, urging her own hands not to betray her by fiddling with her hair. She quickly clasped them in her lap.

'Finally we meet,' he said. 'I take it you're settling in OK, getting over the jet-lag?'

'Oh, yes,' she said, swallowing hard. She hadn't anticipated him being quite so handsome. 'I'm pretty used to jet-lag by now, that's not what keeps me awake at night.'

She watched his eyebrows rise in interest as he rested on his elbows and leaned forward slightly. 'Sleepless in Amsterdam already? I forgot, you mentioned you had plans to renovate a house here. I imagine that must be a lot of work.'

Freya recalled they'd spoken briefly about her other 'job' here during their phone call. She fought the fresh twinge of anxiety from showing on her face. Grandma Anouk's house was so full of clutter. A clause in her will had stated it shouldn't be touched by anyone except Freya and her elderly friend who lived in the house next door, so it had been left exactly as it was since her death almost a year ago.

Now, with her own stuff on top, she could barely move in it around all the boxes. Doing up the house and selling it was going to be a far bigger project than she'd anticipated. Just the thought of it had kept her awake most of last night, and she prayed she didn't look tired on her first day at work.

'It won't affect my work here, Dr Van de Berg,' she assured him, noting his long, lean fingers reach for a pencil on the desk and pop it back into a jar of pens. She could imagine him in the operating room, stitching up patients she herself would have diagnosed and cared for, from start to finish. They were on the same team now. The thought brought new excitement, amping her up without the need for caffeine.

'Call me Lucas,' he said, his blue eyes still luring her in like deep oceans. 'And I'm sure you can make time for all the things you have to do while you're here. If you have any concerns about anything, we have a very supportive team in place—myself included. All you have to do is ask. Understood?'

'Understood and appreciated, Lucas, *dank je*.' She found she felt unaccountably hot despite the air-conditioning. She'd been entirely unprepared for this man's undeniable sex appeal.

'How's your Dutch?' His question came out of the blue. 'Conversational, as I remember from the interview?'

'Mijn Nederlands is oké, maar het kan beter,' she replied. *My Dutch is OK, but it could be better.*

'Well, you grew up here so I'm sure it will all start coming back to you. We already have you signed up for the refresher lessons we spoke about before.'

'That's great,' she said. 'If only for any new slang I might have missed, being away so long. I'd like to be as confident speaking with Dutch patients as possible.'

'You'll be fine. Did I hear you mention you speak Italian too?'

'I do,' she confessed, and she registered a rare flicker of pride in her linguistic abilities as he nodded in what seemed like admiration, and sat back in his seat. 'We were all encouraged to be over-achievers at boarding school.'

'Ah, boarding school in England, that's right.'

'Yes, my father sent me when I was very young,' she said, recalling how he'd freed her from poor Anouk's care at the same time. She'd loved term time at St Cuthbert's, because at school she had almost been able to forget that in the outside world she was nothing but an inconvenience. It had only been in the holidays, when she had been swiftly shunted back to Amsterdam, that it had truly hit home.

Her father had been too busy for her, her mother hadn't cared *where* she was, and Anouk, although she'd done her best to keep an eye on her, had been working full time, too. Not that she would say any of that to Lucas; she was far too busy getting lost in his eyes.

'And your parents, are they in the UK, or here in the Netherlands?' he asked.

'They separated when I was a toddler. My mother lives here with her second husband Stijn...in a town called Weesp,' she said.

Lucas let out a short laugh. 'How funny, my parents live pretty close to there.'

'I haven't seen my mother in a long time,' she told him, picturing his parents, who were obviously still together. Were they as tall as him, as good looking, as charismatic? 'My father died almost seven years ago. He was bitten by a spider in his sleep on a trip to Thailand. He developed a fatal kidney infection as a result.'

Lucas's face fell suddenly and gone was his air of professional authority. 'I'm so sorry, Dr Grey...'

'Freya, please.'

'I didn't mean to drag up the past like that. And to lose your father that way, I can't even...'

'I know,' she said shortly, feeling the electric storm between them pass in a flash and settle into something verging on awkwardness. She might not have been so forthcoming with such details if he hadn't been so damn handsome, staring at her like that with his vivid blue eyes. He was unnerving her, to say the least.

She sat up straighter in her seat, determined not to let things get any more personal. She was here to work after all, not to be thrown by a surgeon who for all intents and purposes looked more like a movie star than a medical professional. 'Time heals everything, in my experience. Almost everything anyway. There's no point in dwelling on the past. Should we get back to my introductory session, Lucas?'

CHAPTER TWO

A WEEK LATER, Lucas was observing Freya from across the room. She was crouched on the floor of the play space, laughing with little Violet and her mother over something in a book.

'If only my hair would look that glossy at this hour,' Pieter said, appearing at his side in the hallway. Lucas could always tell it was Pieter. It was as if he made his shoes squeak on purpose when he walked, just to be noticed.

'She's definitely the hottest cardiologist we've ever had here,' Pieter's boyfriend Ruud whispered, coming up between them. The two of them always arrived together. 'Joy says she's single. We should set her up with someone. What about Lucas here? Is his dating profile up to date again yet?'

Pieter rolled his eyes. 'Ruud, he's still mourning his Indian bride-not-to-be, you know that. Don't be so insensitive.'

Rudd let out a *pffft* noise. 'He has to move on from her eventually. It's not like she's ever coming back…'

'Guys, I'm standing right here.' Lucas shot them a look. They were speaking in Dutch, but he didn't want *any* of his patients to hear them. Or Freya, who clearly didn't need refresher lessons as much as he'd thought she might—he'd heard her talking quite fluently to their young patients all week. As much as he respected Pieter and Ruud's work, the dietician and social worker duo liked to offer their observations a little too often, especially regarding his personal life, and especially at work.

Then again, if they were taking too much interest in his love life, that was his fault. He'd become pretty good friends with them more recently, and he'd never made a habit of becoming friends—or lovers—with colleagues. Not until Roshinda had shown up at the clinic to shadow him. The medical illustrator had been sent from India nearly two years ago to document his work for a journal. Things had been so good with her, at the start at least, that he'd been much happier in general. He'd got closer to his other colleagues at the clinic while she'd been around, Pieter and Ruud included.

The guys had been a huge support after she'd left six months later, but they still didn't know the whole truth about why she'd gone. Roshinda had always had an arranged marriage to go back to. It had been set up long before her arrival in the Netherlands, and a fiancé she'd met just once had been waiting for her at home.

Lucas had tried hard not to, but he'd fallen for her anyway, and she him. He supposed he'd spent their whole relationship hoping she'd change her mind about going ahead with the marriage, although she never had. A year and a half after she'd left, he was starting to come out the other side, but moments like this brought it all back.

'Touchy,' Ruud quipped, no doubt seeing the look on his face. 'You know we have your best interests at heart, Doctor. Get it? Heart doctor? Oh, she's coming over. Tell her I like her shoes.'

The pair took their leave as Freya stood up and made her way towards him. 'Good morning, Lucas.' She stood at least a foot shorter than he was. 'How are you today?'

'Good,' he said simply, frowning after Ruud and Pieter. 'We'll check in on Rolf first.'

'You look tired. Was it a big night?' Freya said, just as he was thinking how shiny her long, brown hair really was. Her observation took him by surprise, and he was a little irritated with himself at the way what she thought bothered him.

He'd been spending a lot of time admiring her over the past week, not least wishing he hadn't put his foot in it before, asking about her father. How was he to know the man had died like that? He prayed to God it would be a long time before he'd have to know what that was like; losing his father. He'd sworn to be more careful with what he said to new recruits from now on, but Freya had got him flustered the second he'd walked into the staffroom and seen her face with its large pansy-like eyes in a shade of brown he'd never seen before, and her petite figure that would probably look great in anything.

She wasn't what he'd been expecting. In fact, he'd had no time to wonder much about her beyond the fact that she'd seemed perfect for the position, but the moment she'd met his eyes, he'd seen something in her that he really hadn't wanted to. Something interesting and magnetic.

'I suppose it was a big night,' he replied slowly, realising how tired he felt. The homeless shelter was usually busiest on Tuesday nights when he took the helm in the kitchen. He'd found a new sense of purpose at the chopping board, and putting creative recipes together from the leftover boxes of food the supermarkets dropped off; a different kind of science from his skills in surgery.

Freya was looking at him inquisitively but he didn't elaborate. No one at work knew he was still volunteering at the shelter, it was a takeaway from his time with Roshinda that he'd kept to himself. Talking about the shelter meant talking about her, and he'd been trying not to.

They swung into Neonatal. Eleven-month-old baby Rolf was on ECMO for a congenital diaphragmatic hernia. The state-of-the-art technology known as extracorporeal membrane oxygenation supported the heart and lungs by replacing the heart's pumping function and the lungs' oxygen exchange. Rolf was doing well with it so far, but his face was still pale and he still wasn't moving his fingers when they peered down at his tiny frame.

'We had a child with a congenital diaphragmatic hernia at one of the hospitals I worked at once,' Freya told him sadly. She started adjusting the blanket around the baby's arms and he watched her long fingers fold the fabric softly around his tiny shoulders. 'We couldn't save him.'

'We're saving this one,' he said firmly.

'Little Rolf is going to be fine,' Joy confirmed, coming over to them. 'He's a feisty one, he is. Was the other little baby back when you were in South Africa, Freya?'

Lucas flicked through the notes, listening to them talking with interest. He knew all about Freya's penchant for travel—she'd spoken of these missions in her interview process and they'd hired her partly for her international experience—it wasn't just the Dutch they served at this hospital. He'd never been farther than the south of France, himself, though not for lack of interest. He'd just never found much time for travelling.

'It was, yes,' Freya said, and he heard the slight despondency in her voice. 'I did a three-month paediatric cardiac surgical mission with an NGO. That was pretty eye-opening. I was told we were lucky there was an operating room nurse and a consultant anaesthetist at the centre. Juanita, our consultant intensivist, said she'd been on missions in Asia where the surgeon had to do it all.' She looked like the flashbacks of memory still upset her.

'Sadly there were a lot of kids who suffered because of the lack of facilities. You can only do so much for people with limited tools and equipment, you know? I'm always so grateful when I'm working somewhere we can offer children the best chance of getting better.'

'Like here,' he interjected. 'That's our aim here.'

'I know, that's why I applied,' she responded, and the look in her eyes suddenly told him she was a woman who could keep a team…and a man…in check. Freya was quite a force to be reckoned with, he thought with an inward smile.

'What about you?' she asked. 'I've seen your certificates, Dr Van de Berg. Being the top children's heart surgeon in the Netherlands must have kept you busy. Have you had the opportunity to work on a medical mission anywhere yet?'

'No,' he admitted, watching the sunlight catch her hair again through the stained-glass balloons above the windows. It was interesting, the way she'd said 'yet', as though going off to do things like that was for everyone. 'I haven't done too much travelling, for work *or* pleasure,' he told her enquiring eyes. 'I guess I always tell myself it's something I'll do later.'

Freya looked puzzled by his response, as though the notion was absurd. 'How do you know how much "later" you have left?'

Lucas cleared his throat. She'd said it with a certain kind of intensity in her narrowed brown stare that he wasn't used to and it both unnerved him and turned him on in equal measure. 'Where in South Africa were you?' he said, to distract them both.

'Right in the heart of the Zulu area,' she said, and her voice softened more as she ran a thumb softly across Rolf's cheek. 'Communities there were made up of all sorts of people, from refugees, to tribes, to people in rural areas who had no access to healthcare at all. Some of them lived in so much poverty you couldn't help letting it all out sometimes, even though you knew you needed to be their strength.'

Joy pressed a hand to her heart and let out an anguished sound. 'You're making me want to go there.'

'You should, at some point,' she urged, casting him a glance that told him she meant him, too. 'They need every qualified medic that they can get. We all had to do our breaking down behind the scenes, we couldn't let them know how hard we found it. Seeing their pain, and realising the consequences of our world's indifference over matters of life and death, that's life-changing. Those people, Joy, they have hardly *any* help. Some of the kids came in as heads of their households after their parents had died, some of their family members were too sick to get to us themselves. I really should go back on the next mission trip…'

The things Freya must have seen throughout her career so far had intrigued him from the start, since their phone interview, in fact, when she'd told him one of her best achievements to date was spending six weeks on another medical mission in Cambodia, mostly keeping the wild monkeys at bay. She'd said the monkeys had been trying to steal supplies from their camp.

He remembered he'd wanted to ask her more about all the places she had seen and been, but the panel had had three other people waiting to be interviewed for the same role on the same afternoon, so he'd had to cut their call short. He wasn't sure he'd have been able to do that had the interview been in person. Freya was beautiful and beguiling on top of her impressive list of qualifications. He'd been struck by her presence the second he'd seen her.

Joy was looking at Freya like she'd just switched on a light-bulb inside her. Lucas hoped she wasn't getting any ideas. As much as Freya's work was impressive, inspirational even, he didn't need his team to start disappearing off to South Africa, or anywhere else for that matter. Maybe it wasn't the same as heading to Africa but he…all of them…had enough people to help here. More than enough.

His life was different now, and had been ever since his father had been diagnosed with Alzheimer's eighteen months ago. Now Fred Van de Berg couldn't concentrate on a conversation for more than five minutes, which was driving his already crazy mother, Mira, even crazier. She was putting on a brave face but it was getting harder by the day.

There was Martijn, too, at the homeless shelter. Martijn was only fifty-five, a once proud family man who'd served his time in the military before losing an arm in an aircraft manufacturing accident at a factory up near Rotterdam. Then he'd lost his wife, both kids and his home thanks to the depression he'd suffered after the accident.

It was a self-appointed position, to be doing what he did for *Inloophuis*, meaning Walk-in House, one, sometimes two nights a week. Sometimes he wished he didn't care so much about Martijn, especially when he showed up at the shelter and found the guy passed out drunk outside next to his dog, Shadow. But when Martijn was sober, he enjoyed talking to him and Lucas had seen a steady transformation in Martijn's attitude towards life and recovery that countered his father's slow but steady decline. One made him sad, the other lifted his spirits, so he'd come to rely on Martijn as much as Martijn relied on him.

His father Fred had the rest of their family around, who loved him dearly and protected him. Martijn had nothing. No one. Like many of the people Freya had met on her travels, probably.

'You look like you're miles away,' Freya observed.

He shrugged and turned away from her piercing eyes, cursing himself. He hadn't told anyone at the hospital about his father's illness, not even Pieter and Ruud. If he did, they'd be urging him to spend less time working so hard at the hospital and more time with his father, and there was just so much to do here. His team didn't know he worked at the shelter either, but he was too involved now to stop and he juggled it all well—most of the time.

'I'll see you later,' he told Freya, resisting the urge to get lost in her eyes again. There was something about her…

Sometimes it felt like everyone needed a piece of him. He couldn't leave the Netherlands even if he wanted to.

CHAPTER THREE

'I DON'T KNOW why you won't just let me come and help you with the house. You can't do all that on your own, Freya, it's a huge task!'

Freya lowered herself to the grass and lay on her back and stared up at the solo wispy white cloud that seemed to be hovering over her head in Vondelpark. Her half-sister Liv had finally caught up with her. Or rather Freya had guiltily decided to answer one of her calls.

'I told you Liv, I'm fine. Thank you for offering. I'll be working all day at the hospital. It's long hours, you know that, so you'd be by yourself most of the time, and it would be very boring…'

'Freya, Anouk was my grandma too. I know she left the house to you, but I want to see the place we spent all that time in. I want to help you go through her stuff. Besides, me and Jed just broke up.'

Wincing Freya squeezed her eyes shut. 'Oh, Liv. I'm sorry to hear that.'

She really was. Liv and Jed, both twenty-three, had been an item for four years. He was the reason Liv had left the Netherlands and moved back to the UK. 'I thought you guys were rock solid?'

'He did to me what Johnny and Beatrice did to you,'

Liv said through clenched teeth. Her thick Dutch accent permeated her English still, but she always made a habit of speaking in English to Freya. 'Can you believe it? I don't know how women can be so cruel to other women. Maybe I'll just come home. It might be fun, now you're there too.'

Liv worked as an accountant, so technically she could work anywhere, like Freya.

Freya bit her tongue and focused on a dog with long, bouncing ears, who was scampering after a red ball in the grass, followed by a giggling toddler. Her heart was thudding now, the way it always did when she was rudely reminded of how her best friend from St Cuthbert's had made a move on Freya's American boyfriend, who'd been all too happy to reciprocate, nine months into med school.

'I mean, at least you were only dating Johnny for a few months before he got together with your friend...'

'Nine months, Liv,' she reminded her stiffly. 'That was a pretty long time.'

'OK, well, I just wasted four *years* on Jed. I'll never get that time back. What if they get married, like Johnny and Beatrice did?'

A few ducks waddled past on the grass, quacking loudly as bicycles whizzed past on the gravel tracks beyond. Liv went on about her boyfriend's betrayal and Freya found herself witnessing her own experience all over again in her mind's eye: Johnny with his hands in Beatrice's hair as he kissed her passionately, still dressed in most of his soccer kit; her best friend's long legs wrapped around his middle. Their wedding photos, three years later, had been all over Facebook. Their mutual friends had all been invited. She'd deleted her account after that.

'You should visit first rather than come back here permanently, Liv. It's a big move and your break-up is still fresh. Give me a few more weeks to get my head around everything here and we'll talk about it again,' she said.

'OK. Have you spoken to Mum since you arrived there?'

Here we go again, Freya thought. 'No, not yet.'

'She's back from Reykjavik now.'

'Reykjavik?'

'Stijn took her there for a holiday, I told you that.'

'Did you? I don't know, it seems like she's always going somewhere…'

'Not unlike someone else we know.'

Freya pulled a face. 'Liv, I've been so busy…'

'She knows you deserve Anouk's house, Freya. There's never been any dispute over that, in case you were wondering.'

Freya kept her eyes on the dog with the ball, and heard her half-sister sigh down the phone at her silence. She knew Liv was disappointed that she barely ever spoke to their mother but Liv was oblivious to the fact that Elise had barely noticed or cared about Freya till after Liv had come along. Ugh, it was too nice a day for these bad memories, but unfortunately for her Amsterdam was full of them.

'I have to go,' she said quickly. Lucas Van de Berg had just appeared in the park, looking impossibly handsome. He held up an acknowledging hand from where he was jogging along the track beside the bike path, and changed direction to head her way. 'I really am sorry about Jed. If it's any consolation, you will meet someone else who's worthy of you. You'll get over it. I did.' she added.

'Get over what?' Lucas had reached her on the grass. He carried on jogging on the spot in front of her as she shoved her phone back into her bag, taking in his workout clothes—a tight black gym shirt with neon yellow bands around the arms, and track pants with black sneakers.

His damp, dark chestnut hair hung over his blue eyes before he raked a hand across his forehead. She blinked up at him into the sun, realising she'd never seen him in casual clothes, let alone workout gear. She couldn't help admiring his impressive physique even more now. He was as hot as a model in his scrubs but in gym clothes… he was making the back of her neck break out into a nervous sweat.

'You jog on your lunch breaks?' she heard herself say, trying not to notice his long, lean calves, the way his muscles gave extra definition to his tanned skin in the sunlight.

He raised an eyebrow. 'Sometimes. You sound surprised.'

'I am,' she admitted. 'Most surgeons I know say they don't have the time to exercise.'

'Well, we're all busy enough,' he said, still jogging. 'Everyone's busy, but if you don't make the time to look after yourself, you're not in the best place to give health advice to others, are you.' He said it like a statement, not a question. She smiled to herself. This was the Dutch way. Blunt. She actually admired it.

Lucas dropped to the grass on his haunches and started stretching out one leg. 'So, who has to get over what?'

'You're nosy, aren't you?' She could see the delineation of his six-pack through his shirt. Lucas was definitely not your average surgeon and she hoped humour would distract him from the fact that she was clearly staring at his abs. She wished she wasn't so drawn to him. If he carried on being so sexy on top of everything else, things could get very complicated for her.

'I like to think interested, rather than nosy,' he said, and Freya struggled not to stare at his biceps flexing rigidly as he tossed the ball, which rolled over and sent the dog speeding after it.

'That was my half-sister, Liv. She just found out her boyfriend of four years did something pretty unforgivable.'

Lucas scowled at the grass a second. 'Did he go off and marry someone else?'

'What?' Freya emitted a snort through her nose. 'No, of course not.'

Lucas was frowning at his kneecap now, stretching out the other leg.

'He cheated on her with a friend they both know,' she told him, raising her eyes to the sky at an orange plane zooming low over the park from Schiphol airport.

'You said she'd get over it, like *you* did?' When she turned to him, Lucas was looking right at her, which made her feel even hotter. She stopped her hand from wiping a bead of sweat from her forehead and contemplated being just as blunt; telling him she didn't want to talk about it. Why drag up the past in a new place? But he seemed genuinely interested, and honestly? When was the last time a guy this hot had offered her his complete undivided attention?

'I had a best friend called Beatrice, my only friend, really, back then,' she relented.

'When?'

'At boarding school. I kept myself to myself as a kid, till we met. We did everything together. Anouk—she hated being called Gran—was our inspiration. She was a medical researcher and *her* mother was a paediatrician in World War II. She cared for children with rheumatic fever mostly, that being the biggest cardiac problem they had to deal with back then.'

'I know,' he said. She felt her mouth twitch again with a smile. Of course he would know that.

'Well, Anouk was the one who made us both want to get into medicine, when Bea used to visit me in Amsterdam. We got it into our heads that we wanted to study in the US together. I don't know, maybe we watched too many medical dramas on TV. Come to think of it, I just wanted to move as far away as possible from…' She trailed off. No need to mention her mother. 'We both got places at medical college in Wisconsin.'

'Wisconsin?'

She smiled absently, remembering how excited they'd been, packing their bags, practising bad American accents. 'We applied to a bunch of places. I got into them all, but that was the only college that offered us *both* a place. It felt like a dream came true, getting to move there together.'

Lucas was staring at her mouth, she noticed, while she spoke, and she wondered if he found her attractive. The thought that he might made her nervous, but so did the thought that he might not. Then he sat down fully, cross-legged on the grass. 'So, what happened at college with Beatrice?'

She swallowed a lump in her throat, more at his proximity than having to relive her story. 'We moved into the halls of residence. A shared apartment. Our roommate Johnny was… Well, Johnny was a lot of things. Mostly he was Texan.'

'You fell for his accent? Or was it the gun he kept in his locker?'

'Very funny.' She smirked. 'Actually, he was the kind of guy who'd bring pots of homemade ceviche to a party when everyone else brought potato chips. He knew about art and books and…' She realised Lucas's eyebrows were knotting together, like she was reminding him of something that wasn't particularly pleasant. 'Anyway, I ended up dating him. I thought it was getting serious after nine months together, but it turned out he'd fallen for someone else, right in front of my nose.'

Lucas pulled at the grass between them with his fingers. 'I sense a betrayal coming on.'

She smiled wanly, still trying to ignore how his presence out here in the sunshine was actually unnerving her more than the memories she was recalling.

'I came home early from class one afternoon. The *worst* part was that I pretended to be a delivery guy, to surprise them. I'd got us all pizza, sneaked up to the window outside and banged on it. That's when I saw them, all tangled up in Bea's dress on the couch. The best friend and the boyfriend. Is there anything more clichéd?'

Lucas raised his eyebrows, dragged a hand through his hair again. 'It's a cliché precisely because it happens all the time.'

'Don't tell me *your* best friend stole your girlfriend and finally took up his rich parents' offer of a penthouse suite in a private apartment block off campus?' she teased.

'Not exactly. So, did Beatrice move into the penthouse, too?'

'Yes, three weeks later.' Freya had no idea why she was opening up to him with all this information. She wasn't used to sharing so much so soon with people she didn't really know, and she rarely invited the same from others, she realised, letting her eyes linger on the form of his muscles in his shirt for another moment. He already knew she was staring at his body, she was sure of that. But he wasn't exactly trying to cover it up.

'What happened to you, then?' she asked now, noticing how he was pulling harder at the grass between them. 'Do I sense a betrayal coming on?'

His mouth kind of twisted for a second. 'I thought I'd met the woman I would marry. I guess I was wrong. I don't want to bore you with the details, Freya. She's back in India now.'

'Back in India, huh?'

She watched a look of mild discomfort at her question cross his face, which made her wonder exactly how much this woman from India had hurt him, right before he pulled a buzzing phone from his pocket. So, the doctor had a girlfriend from India...or used to. Someone who'd caused him difficulties and pain.

Freya caught herself. It wouldn't do to start speculating about Lucas Van de Berg, even though she'd told him enough about herself already. Maybe it was being out here in the sunshine, seeing him dressed like a normal, regular guy that had made her feel more like opening up. If he didn't want to answer any of *her* questions, she couldn't force him to.

'They're sending a three-year-old girl called Maeve to the hospital, she's on her way in the ambulance,' Lucas said now, interrupting her thoughts. He held his hand out to help her up. Registering the thud of her heart at the gesture, as much as the emergency that must have befallen an innocent toddler, she waved his hand away and stood up herself, gathering her belongings and her thoughts.

'Go, go,' she told him. 'I'll catch you up on my bike.'

CHAPTER FOUR

'MAEVE IS STABLE, but acute decompensated heart failure, or cardiogenic shock due to severe aortic stenosis, is a pretty bad diagnosis in anyone, let alone a child, as you know, Frey—Dr Grey,' Lucas said, correcting himself.

He glanced up when the door shut, meeting her soft brown eyes over their masks. The harsh lights were shining solely on little Maeve. As discussed in her interview, she was observing his work, poised with her notebook and a pen wedged sexily behind her left ear. He wondered if she knew how hot she looked.

He cleared his throat, adjusting his glasses on his nose.

'Operative risk in patients like this is exceedingly high, even here, where we have far more opportunities to help patients than anywhere else you've been on your travels, I'm sure.'

'No doubt about that,' she said, stepping closer. 'We had nothing like this in Cambodia. I'm pretty sure there won't be anyone with your skills in Vietnam either.'

'Vietnam?' He was only half listening. Lucas had performed thousands of transcatheter aortic valve insertions, and while every procedure performed on a child carried an immense amount of weight on his heart, he'd grown pretty good at keeping his emotions at bay. Under Freya's watchful eye the pressure was piling up anyway, so he was having to fight for extra focus.

'Just somewhere I'm thinking of taking my next contract,' she said absently. 'It's a long way off, anyway. What do we have here?'

Lucas frowned to himself; six months *wasn't* that long a time in the grand scheme of things, and he hadn't been aware she was even looking at alternative destinations already. Her announcement both irritated him and filled him with a sudden sense of apprehension, but he needed to pull himself together and concentrate.

He kept his tutorial going, pretending he was only marginally aware of her presence, her shadow, the sound of her shoes on the floor tiles, and the revelation that she wouldn't extend her six-month contract if there was something better she could be doing in Vietnam.

'So…this has proved to be a safe procedure in comparison to surgical aortic valve replacement… We know that the chances of bleeding are less with the kind of transcatheter aortic valve insertion I bring to the table, using this.' He held up the stent, one of a set they'd had made especially in Sweden. 'Renal failure and the need for dialysis is also far, far less than with your regular catheter-based procedures…'

'Such as emergency balloon aortic valvuloplasty,' Freya mused, chewing her lip as she got up close to observe it under the same light. Freya's brown hair was back up in a professional-looking bun, but he couldn't stop replaying the sight of her in the park, out of her white coat, the glossy tumble of her hair across her shoulder blades.

He could almost feel time stop as their breathing synced. He had a flashback suddenly of he and Roshinda in a similar situation, working so closely...sometimes too close for comfort, especially back when he had been trying, and failing, to stay away from someone he knew could never be his.

Freya was single, no marriages arranged that he knew of. Yet somehow she was even more unreachable than Roshinda had been, always flying away somewhere new. He knew he should stay away from her at all costs. But, damn it, her ambitions made her even more desirable.

'Dr Van de Berg operated on Maeve with great success.' Freya scanned the face of the dark-skinned, sleep-deprived mother, Mrs Vasque, and the equally worried father from her place opposite them on the plush couch.

'She was in the very best hands possible, I witnessed it myself. She's still unconscious so she's not in any pain, and we're monitoring her twenty-four seven until the anaesthetic wears off. That's when we'll run more tests. Nurse Joy, who you met outside, will be on constant watch, on rotation with Dr Bram— Oh, here is Dr Van de Berg now.'

She looked up in surprise as Lucas entered the room and felt a jolt of adrenaline like a lightning bolt, just seeing him. 'Just checking in,' he said, catching her eye and nodding as he strode towards them and held out his hand. 'I know you asked to see me, Mrs Vasque?'

He'd changed out of his scrubs and was dressed in the same dark navy trousers and a different pale blue shirt. He took a seat next to her on the couch, and Freya felt his leg brush the fabric of her coat momentarily against her thigh before she crossed her the legs the other way, conscious of the sparks. He was still wearing his glasses. Good God, he looked sexy as hell in them.

'Yes, I did. Thank you so much for everything you did, Dr Van de Berg, you have no idea what this clinic means to us.' Freya watched in pride and surprise as Mrs Vasque reached for his hand and squeezed Lucas's fingers hard. 'Our Maeve might not be alive if it wasn't for you.'

Lucas seemed to brush off her praise. 'I was honoured to be able to do what I do best for your daughter.'

'Can we see her?'

'Of course you can see her. Maeve is a little sleeping beauty,' Freya said, smiling. Their little girl had a shock of black hair, thick and dark, like Liv's when she'd been born.

'With a little bit more time we'll know more about what we can expect to deal with going forward,' Lucas interjected. 'But she's a strong little lady. And our team here will be right here for all of you, whatever the outcome, whatever comes next.'

Freya listened as he answered their questions, happy to accept his opinion and expertise under the circumstances. She could tell Lucas was as careful with hearts as she was...but now she couldn't stop seeing him with washboard abs and the sun on his face in the park. Maybe she was starting to like him a little too much already and that was probably why she'd just casually brought up going to Vietnam, she thought to herself. She'd been creating distance between them, even though his closeness was intoxicating. She was still wondering about his ex in India. Who was she? Why had she left a man like Lucas?

Her phone started flashing on silent. The words *Mother. Don't answer,* sent a jarring bolt of adrenaline through her, just as embarrassment flushed her cheeks. She'd been meaning to change that.

Reaching to end the call on the table in front of them, she was quick to turn the phone face down and refocus on the Vasques, but she didn't miss the look Lucas shot her while he was talking. She almost mouthed, 'Sorry', but she kept her head high and her back straight.

Lucas was still watching her. It made her feel nervous. She cared what he thought, whether she wanted to or not.

Of course she would have to talk to her mother eventually. But the fear of all the words that had been left unspoken for so long filled her with dread. How sad was it that she could be like this for other people—open, direct, honest and unwavering—but when it came to her own mother and addressing their fractured relationship, she could never seem to find the right words to say?

Freya was just about to leave for the elevator when she realised she'd left her book in the staffroom. At the end of another busy shift she was making a mental note of all the things she now had to do back at the house. The boxes certainly weren't unpacking themselves, and she still had to pack the 'vintage treasures' she'd promised to sell to some bargain hunter on an online marketplace.

But when she stepped through the door, she was surprised to find Joy, Pieter and Ruud huddled around the desk with the computer on it, all looking at something in a box.

'What are you lot doing?'

Pieter put a hand to his heart and drew a short, sharp breath. 'It's you,' he stated in relief.

'Still me.' She swiped her book from the table and dropped it into her bag. 'Who were you afraid I was?'

Joy handed her a medical journal from the box on the desk. 'We don't know if Lucas has seen it yet,' Ruud said cryptically, perching one butt cheek on the arm of the sofa and adjusting his tie and his shirt collar. Both he and Pieter were wearing matching purple ties with characters from *Sesame Street* on them.

'Maybe she had some separate copies sent straight to him at the houseboat,' Pieter wondered out loud.

'Houseboat?' Freya asked, intrigued.

'The gorgeous, state-of-the-art, totally humongous houseboat Lucas lives on,' Joy explained, as if she should already know. 'It's more like a luxury apartment with three-hundred-and-sixty-degree views of the water from floor-to-ceiling windows. Did you know he even has a grand piano in it? And he had Banksy design his bathroom wallpaper.'

'Lucas knows Banksy?' she heard herself saying in awe.

'That was just a joke,' Ruud said, tutting loudly. 'Lucas wasn't being serious when he said that about the wallpaper, Joy.'

'How would *you* know?' Joy shot back, but Ruud didn't respond. He was frowning to himself, pulling at an imaginary beard on his chin. 'Why would she make two different deliveries all the way from India? No, this must be the only box of journals she sent. I bet Lucas hasn't seen it yet.'

'Well, it doesn't matter, he's still booked to give a

speech about it at the presentation on Friday. It's in his calendar, I checked,' Joy said.

'What is it?' Freya remembered the email in her inbox about the event on Friday night. It was a black-tie dinner for cardiology professionals. Part of a three-day medical conference at a hotel in Dam Square, Amsterdam's historic central point. They'd been promised great food, as well as speeches by various medical contributors, blah blah.

She'd been to several such events before and usually sat there wishing she'd declined the invitation. They were often excruciatingly dull. She'd been contemplating not going, given that she had so much to do at the house. Now she realised that was probably the wrong attitude.

Still, she failed to see why the *Rhythm Medical Journal* in her hands was causing such excitement amongst her colleagues. She turned it around in her hands and read the blurb. It was all in English.

The Netherlands is putting the heart into cardiology. Exploring new experimental aspects of paediatrics with genetics, devices, drugs and surgery by Dr Lucas Van de Burg. Illustrations by award-winning Rajasthan-based medical illustrator Roshinda Acharya.

Freya flicked through the pages, taking in the immaculate, detailed drawings, which seemed to document the surgical techniques involved in Dr Lucas's breakthrough heart replacements. Something clicked from their conversation in Vondelpark.

India… Hadn't Lucas said his ex-girlfriend had gone back to India? The one he'd thought he would marry?

'She did a great job,' Ruud said from the couch. He was flicking through the pages, admiring each image up close. 'No matter what she did to Lucas's heart in reality.'

Freya looked up. 'Roshinda?' she probed without thinking, though she already felt a little ruffled by the revelation, much to her annoyance.

'We don't talk about her.' Pieter's fingers caught around Elmo's face on his tie. He sounded almost sad, and her heart upped its thudding, remembering the look on Lucas's face in the park just at the mention of his ex being back in India. Maybe he wasn't over her yet. Seeing these journals certainly wouldn't speed up the healing process for him either—not that she should be tracking the extent of Lucas's recovery after a failed relationship at all, she reminded herself.

Still…they must have worked pretty closely together to do all this. She looked through the journal again. It must have taken months to do all these illustrations. How long had they worked together before getting physically close? she wondered, noticing the way her stomach seemed to tie itself into jealous knots most unexpectedly.

Had he been with Roshinda out of hours in Amsterdam's most beautiful places? Had they once sat in the park together with the sun on their faces during their lunch breaks? She turned to the photo on the inside cover, feeling another pang of envy. Roshinda was beautiful, with hair just as long as Freya's was, piercing dark brown intelligent eyes, and eyebrows to die for.

Ruud made a disapproving growling sound over her

shoulder. Then he shut the journal with a snap. 'Ro-shinda was—'

'An asset to our team.'

Lucas was standing in the doorway. Blood rushed to Freya's cheeks as he strode towards their little huddle and stopped at the desk. It felt like time stopped as he hovered there a moment, jaw ticking. Pieter put a hand on his arm in apparent consolation, but Lucas ignored him.

'I need to look at this before Friday,' he said gruffly, and his eyes met hers. She tried to convey her apologies with just one look. It wasn't like her to involve herself in gossip or even a staffroom huddle. She hoped he didn't think badly of her. She felt like saying she wouldn't even be here if she hadn't forgotten her book. But Lucas picked up the entire box of journals in his arms and without a word left the room with it. She swore the room grew colder as he shut the door behind him.

CHAPTER FIVE

LUCAS WATCHED THE breeze send ripples through the reflections on the swimming pool's surface from his place on the swish poolside tiles. The waiter stopped at his side and offered him a glass of wine. He refused.

It was hard to find a swimming pool in central Amsterdam, but the one on the rooftop of the Royal Palace Hotel was special for many reasons. It was a mirror for the setting sun, the spires of the Nieuwe Kerk, and the mint-green globes and gargoyles on the facade of the seventeenth-century palace. It was certainly impressing the two hundred medical experts who'd flown in for the three-day conference.

He checked his watch. He should probably stay another thirty minutes or so. So many people were still vying for his attention with questions about his work after his speech so it wouldn't do to run off yet, even though he'd promised Martijn he'd stop by the shelter with a book they'd been discussing. He didn't want to let the older man down.

'Lucas?'

Freya was heading towards him from where she'd been talking to Joy over by the bar. He'd caught her eye and found himself appreciating her lovely figure in the tight blue satin dress at several points through-out the evening, and now he registered a slight twinge of discomfort at the way his body still insisted on re-acting to her.

In spite of telling himself over and over since her ar-rival that he didn't find her overwhelmingly dazzling, both to look at and listen to, he'd been lying to him-self. Beauty and brains were a fatal combination for his heart, damn it.

Still, he nodded curtly as she stopped in front of him. 'Freya.'

'Lucas.' She almost smirked, like she knew as well as he did that they'd both been waiting for an opportu-nity to talk out here.

'Listen, Lucas, I wanted to apologise for the other day in the staffroom. I'd hate to seem like I was encour-aging or participating in any gossip.'

He said nothing, though it was his turn to smirk now, letting his eyes travel along the slit in the skirt of her satin gown from her ankle right up to her slender hip. Why did women always insist they hated gossip when they revelled in it—all of them? It hadn't annoyed him, seeing her participating in that little staffroom huddle, but he'd noticed Freya first, like he always did, and at that moment the last thing he'd wanted her to think was that he wasn't over Roshinda, which concerned him. Why get attached to someone else who had no inten-tion of sticking around?

Her hair was shinier than ever tonight. It annoyed him no end that he'd even noticed that. His efforts to keep her at a professional distance and think of her only as a colleague were probably futile. He let his eyes linger on her lips next as she took a sip of wine from the glass she was holding.

'I mean, it's none of my business if you dated the medical illustrator you were working with on the journal.' She gestured to the issues of *Rhythm* that were propped on a silver podium by the pool, next to a giant poster of him in scrubs, advertising the Happy Hearts Clinic.

'You're right, it's no one's business,' he agreed.

Saying Roshinda's name tonight in his speech in front of all these people without letting on with his face how close they'd been once hadn't exactly been the highlight of the night. It had taken so long for the journal to be published. They'd had to finalise the plans, the illustrations, the bilingual blurbs and corresponding DVDs, the legalities around publishing in multiple countries...and it had felt like everyone and everything involved had dragged out their broken relationship along with it. Still, now it was over and the journal was finally out, perhaps he could put it behind him once and for all.

He motioned for Freya to walk with him away from the crowd. Her high-heeled shoes tapped behind him on the tiles around the pool before she joined him in leaning against the balcony railings. The sun was a fading glow that was quickly disappearing behind a building.

'I told you my ex was back in India,' he said, watching the traffic snaking through the narrow street below. 'You would have figured out we'd worked together on that journal even if Joy and Pieter weren't the biggest over-sharers in Amsterdam.'

'Probably. I am pretty smart,' she agreed, and he felt the smile break out fully on his face for a second, just as he took a dizzying hit of her perfume.

'I did like your speech, though, Lucas. You managed not to let on that you dated her. From the crowd's reactions I'm assuming most people didn't know you were together while she was documenting your work with all those drawings. Was it a secret?'

'I like it that *that* is what you were thinking about while most people were lost in the details of my surgical procedures,' he said lightly, tightening his hands on the ornate railings. She had basically just offered proof that she'd been wondering things about him and his past relationships, which caused a sudden desire to snake an arm around her shoulders and escape with her down the stairs, maybe invite her to find out more about him, so to speak.

That would be entirely inappropriate, he told himself ruefully.

'So, was dating your colleague a secret to everyone *except* the team?'

He blew air through his lips, shaking his head. 'You don't like gossip, eh? Could have fooled me.'

'I'd rather hear it from you.'

'Damn, you're persistent.'

'When I want something, yes, I am.'

She offered him a secretive smile and he groaned inwardly at her not-so-subtle flirtation, watching the shape of her lips, noticing how the alluring fragrance she wore sent his mind first to the clouds and then to the bedroom. 'To tell you the truth, the fact that I dated a colleague is irrelevant,' he said, reining his mind back to the moment. 'What bothers me is that I dated her at all, when I always knew she'd have to go back to India. Deep down, I guess I always knew she'd leave. '

He looked at her pointedly. Freya wasn't biting.

'Why did she *have* to go back?'

He fixed his eyes on a cyclist in a neon-green vest below them, weaving through a line of cars backed up in traffic. He was dying to get out of his suit jacket. Instead he loosened his tie while Freya's velvet eyes lasered his profile.

'We were from two different worlds. Her family manages a chain of restaurants in Jaipur. They got rich and started an outreach centre, feeding the poor. She got into medicine because of that, and then she travelled all over the world…like you. But ultimately I think she loved her home too much to stay away for too long.'

'It's nice that she knows where home *is*. Some of us don't.'

He shrugged. 'I think home can be anywhere you decide you want it to be.'

'Well, no offence, but sometimes it's not that easy,' Freya demurred. 'Anyway, you can't have been that different if you thought she was the one you would marry.'

'You remember that.'

'I do.'

They stood in silence a moment, watching the cyclists and cars. He could tell she was mildly disappointed that he wasn't opening up to her to the same extent that she had done in the park with him, but that wasn't his style. He was starting to feel like Freya was inching her way into his thoughts faster than Roshinda had, without her even realising it, and he felt his heart might be heading for the danger zone. Maybe he should start trying harder to protect himself, he thought.

'So your family…' he started, in an attempt to change the subject. 'You said before how you haven't seen your mother in a long time, even though she lives close to here?'

She bit her lip, looked away. 'That's right, in Weesp,' she said. It sounded like *Veysp* in Dutch, and he liked the sound of her voice when she switched from English to Dutch. He had a thing for accents. Roshinda's Indian lilt had been bewitching at first, like she'd carried the exotic thrill of somewhere new into every room and filled it with promise. Freya's accent was different yet again. She sounded American, but there were often bits of British in there too. She didn't drag every word out like some Americans he'd met, but she was neither one thing nor the other. A puzzle.

'I bet you can't wait to have them both at the house after all this time, your mum and your half-sister.'

Freya sipped her wine again, looking across at a formidable-looking gargoyle. He almost mentioned her phone, what he'd seen on the screen back when they'd been with the Vasques.

Mother. Don't answer.

It was obviously a difficult topic for her to talk about, but he was intrigued to know more of her story.

'Honestly, Lucas, sometimes I think I'm avoiding my family on purpose. To tell you the truth, my mum wasn't exactly there for me as a kid, shuttling me between boarding school and Anouk while she did whatever she wanted. Anouk was my unofficial parent, really, even though she spent a lot of time at work. She was only thirty-eight when Mum had me. Cancer took her last year.'

'I'm sorry to hear that.' He was. It sounded like Freya

had had it tough growing up, in comparison to him at least. He'd had what most people might consider an idyllic childhood, encouraged by his parents, surrounded by love, and no great losses…yet.

'I do miss her, she was kind of what made Amsterdam my second home. I'm still planning to sell the house, like I told you at my interview, but it needs a lot of work. Maybe more than I anticipated. You should see the windmills on the kitchen tiles.'

He raised his eyebrows. 'That's a classic Dutch look, you know.'

'I know.' She pulled a face, put her half-full glass back on the waiter's tray as he passed. 'But between you and me, Lucas, I have no clue where to start.'

'I know some people who can help, if you want,' he offered. 'I sold a house before I bought my houseboat.'

She chewed her lip and he could tell she was considering whether that would be a good idea or not, committing to spending more time together after hours, and for a second he thought she was going to shut him down.

'That would be great. I'm a little out of the loop,' she said after a pause, and he felt her acceptance like a little victory, even though he knew it might well land him in trouble.

He was trying to pretend he hadn't noticed Joy watching them from the bar with Pieter and Ruud. He folded his arms across the railings. Freya mirrored him at his side, at least a foot below him. Her lily scent lingered in the warm air. If he escaped now, they would all see him running away. He cleared his throat, his fingers still itching to touch her.

'So what about *your* family?' she said.

'My own family is spread all around,' he offered.

'Are you close?'

'I'm very close to my parents, but I don't see as much of my brother Simon as I did when we were growing up. Life gets in the way, I guess. He's the CEO of an ad agency in Rotterdam. We have a lot of love and respect for each other, but we're pretty different.'

He paused. This wasn't the time or place to get into the other reasons he and Simon hadn't seen eye to eye lately. In fact, the thought rather ruined his mood. Simon had suggested putting their father in a home, even though neither of their parents wanted it. There were too many ears listening here to bring it up, not that he needed to involve a colleague in his private life anyway. He'd already decided that.

Looking at Freya now, though, he wanted to tell her suddenly. He was starting to see her as more than a colleague, more of a confidante. A very sexy, dangerous one...

She pushed her long brown hair over her right shoulder, causing a curl to bounce back around her face. 'Still, you're lucky to be so close to your parents,' she said.

'There's still time for you to reconcile with your mother now that you're here.'

'Maybe.' She looked uncomfortable now, and he regretted pushing it. Then she said, 'I don't know why Anouk left that house to me and not her, Lucas. I mean, Anouk knew I'm not exactly the kind of woman who lives in a multi-storey heritage home in Amsterdam. I haven't even *been* here for years.'

'You're here now. Maybe, after all your travels, she thought you might want to put some roots down.'

Freya flinched. 'Well, she picked the wrong person to try and pin down, if that's what she had in mind.'

Lucas had never thought of it that way before. 'So you think that staying in one place is like being pinned down, do you?'

'Oh, there's nothing wrong with putting down roots, Lucas…not at all. I just prefer having wings.'

'Is that why you're already planning on leaving for Vietnam?'

Freya looked away. He felt it then, the pang, just as he could practically see the giant red flag waving above her head. This was a warning to his brain to stop before he even started: to put his heart on high alert and protect it with everything he had. But his body seemed to have other plans. He reached out a hand to tuck the stray curl behind her ear. 'Are you planning to fly away already, Freya?'

Freya opened her mouth to say something; maybe to defend some predetermined decision, but she seemed to think better of it. Her cheeks flushed slightly, like the faintest physical contact had touched her on a deeper level—just as it had him.

In the corner of his eye he saw Joy looking at them curiously. Hell. Had she seen him, just now, putting a hand on Freya's hair?

Leaning down, he lowered his voice and spoke in her ear. 'How far can you walk in those heels?'

'Not very far. Why?'

'I thought so. Do you want to get out of here?'

CHAPTER SIX

FREYA CLUTCHED HER bag to her shoulder. She suddenly felt overdressed in the satin gown as the evening breeze played with her hair on the street outside the hotel. But Lucas was already saluting the security guard outside, making a beeline for the busy square.

'We'll cut through Dam Square.'

'You haven't said where we're going,' she reminded him. The cobblestone streets were threatening to make her topple already, but something was making her follow him anyway. Their conversation on the roof had been both intimate and awkward, and she couldn't tell which aspect had intrigued her the most. She supposed feeling anything at all for a guy was part of the reason—she just wasn't used to it. She wasn't used to letting people in at all.

There was also the fact that he looked so damn good in his suit. Tall, lean, composed, he took each step in a way that commanded the people around him to stop and pay attention. Even a woman on a bicycle turned around to look at him over her shoulder and nearly ran into a lamppost.

In under a minute they found themselves together in the middle of Dam Square. With Lucas at her side she stopped abruptly at the towering white memorial in the centre—built, if she remembered rightly from her chats with Anouk, in memory of the Dutch soldiers and members of the resistance who'd died in World War Two. Cyclists seemed to float past her as she followed the structure skywards with her eyes.

'I used to come here with Anouk to feed the birds,' she shared. She could feel the warmth of his hand so close to hers by her side, an energy buzzing between them that fizzed in the growing darkness. 'She used to tell me how she bought flowers from the hippies here in the sixties. This was where they all hung out.'

'Must have been fun in those days.' He smiled.

She nodded, letting her eyes wander past a group of Australian guys singing over beer cans to the waxwork museum just beyond the memorial. Madame Tussauds.

In a flash she saw her mother laughing like crazy with Liv over the printouts of photos they'd taken together of themselves inside with waxwork versions of celebrities.

'I never went in there,' she told Lucas, wrapping her arms around herself to stop herself from reaching for his hand. She hadn't wanted to touch someone so much in ages. Just feeling his fingers brush her hair like that, back on the roof—it had taken all her strength not to respond in some way. Maybe she would have if they hadn't been surrounded by people.

She focused on the museum with its gaudy facade. 'Did you?'

'You never went into Madame Tussauds? It's like… the biggest tourist attraction here. Bigger than the Anne Frank House!'

'Liv went in there with Mum,' she said, 'and Stijn. I didn't go with them.'

'Why not?'

'I was such a stubborn kid whenever they asked me to do stuff like that with them.' She let out a sigh, shaking her head at herself. 'I guess I took offence that my mum only seemed to want to have fun as a family after Liv came along. I made things difficult because I felt…'

'Hurt? Rejected? That's understandable.'

'Maybe I denied myself a few experiences, looking back.'

'You were just a child.' Lucas suddenly put a hand on her shoulder and gave it a small squeeze that felt like an invitation for her to lean in, to absorb the comfort she'd been seeking. Instead, she froze.

She shifted her focus to a lone pigeon swirling round the top of the memorial. When she finally met his eyes, his words from before played over in her head. *Are you planning to fly away already, Freya?*

She hadn't known what to say to him. Was she really giving off the vibe that she didn't want to be here at all? Standing here now with Lucas, she did, but she could also see the mistakes she'd made in this city rearing up like angry horses, making her want to flee.

She'd refused to go into Madame Tussauds because her *mother* hadn't pushed her to go. In an effort to seem independent and indifferent she'd made up some story about having homework to do. Liv had been upset, let down by yet another refusal. It was Liv who had suffered. She could have been a better sister. And daughter.

But what if it was too late to fix things with her mother? Elise hadn't exactly been beating down the door to see her either. A few phone calls, basic small talk…that's all they'd allowed each other ever since Freya had left for America. Maybe her mother was angry underneath, too, at how spoilt and sullen her daughter had seemed back then.

'Freya?' Lucas was looking at her in concern now, but she swiped at her eyes, realising suddenly they were wet.

'I'm fine. I shouldn't have had the wine,' she told him, embarrassed.

He frowned at her. 'You barely touched it.'

She turned away from him, started walking. The flock of pigeons took fright at a passing blue and white tram and fluttered off to the rooftops and she prayed her mascara hadn't streaked her face in that sudden emotional replay. It wouldn't do to let him see her cry, for so many reasons.

He caught her elbow. 'Hey, I was going to suggest you come with me somewhere but if you'd rather I took you home instead…'

He trailed off, searching her eyes. She wanted nothing more than to continue being with him tonight, but she was feeling emotional now, and she wasn't entirely sure it was a good idea. Her thoughts were so muddled. Luckily he seemed to sense it.

'Let's just start with a ride.' He placed a hand gently on the small of her back, just to guide her in her high heels. Her mouth went a little drier.

'A ride?'

'You'll see.'

They were approaching another canal. This one was narrow and flooded with pink and yellow neon lights—the Red Light District was pumping as usual. Her feet were starting to redden around the straps of her heels, but thankfully Lucas soon stopped by a ladder leading down to a tiny wooden jetty.

'Take those off and follow me down,' he told her, motioning for her to take off her shoes whilst pulling a set of what looked like twenty keys out from his jacket pocket. He made easy work of climbing down the ladder rung by rung till he reached the jetty. Once on the wooden slats he held up a hand to help her.

'I'm OK,' she said quickly, pulling off her shoes and hoisting up her dress to knee height.

'As you wish,' he said. It sounded like he gave an amused sigh as she started climbing down by herself.

When she'd made it down the ladder with her dignity thankfully still intact, he was already climbing aboard a small motor-powered boat. This time she accepted his hand to help her, but only because she might have fallen into the canal without it.

'Your house is on the Prinsengracht, right? Where, exactly?' he asked, taking a set behind the wheel.

She told him, eyeing another group of people watching them from the bridge, eating chips from paper cones. Two ducks scrambled closer in the water in a flap of feathers, hoping for scraps, as he started the engine and they chugged away from the jetty.

'Is this yours?' she asked, running a hand along the smooth side of the boat. It was small but definitely expensive. The finish was all polished wood and varnish and the floor was an engraved map of modern Amsterdam.

'It's Ruben's. He's an old school friend, he's up north of here with his family in Groningen right now because his wife Anne Marie is pregnant with their second child, and I think this was their last chance to go before the baby gets here. But I have keys to most of my friends' boats.'

'Is that right?'

'It's good to have a ride whenever you need one.' He said it like it was the most natural thing in the world to climb onto someone else's boat and steer it away.

'Do they all have keys to *your* boats, too?' She said *boats*, not boat, as a joke; as if he'd have more than one.

'Of course,' he said simply. 'We share.'

She hid her smile behind her hair, crossed her legs a little awkwardly in the dress from her place at the bow, looking out at the line of elongated storybook houses huddled shoulder to shoulder along the canal, like a giant's doll's house collection. 'So…you *live* on a houseboat?'

'That would be correct. It used to be on the Prinsengracht actually, but I moved it.'

'Why did you move it?'

'I had a few kids knock on the door and ask for a tour. I guess you can see some interesting stuff through the windows. It was safer and more private to move it somewhere else. It's less exposed now anyway, moored under some trees."

'That sounds like a good thing.' She was itching to ask what people could see through the windows. Did he really have wallpaper designed by Banksy in his bathroom? She bit her cheeks to stop herself asking. Of course he didn't. Then again, he *was* stupidly wealthy…

'My mother said a bit of bird poop probably helped my tomatoes to grow, but I have my doubts about her theories.'

'Her theories?'

Lucas rolled his eyes with a smile. 'Mum likes to believe everything she reads or hears. I think she's just got a busy mind. She gets bored easily with the real world… or just…maybe she needs an escape from things sometimes. She's convinced elves are real.'

Freya let out a snort. 'Elves?'

He made a noncommittal sound as he took off his tie and she let her eyes run over his smooth jawline down to his Adam's apple and back up over his lips. 'She met this woman at her life-drawing class who told her all about elves. They grant wishes, did you know that?'

'I did know that.' She swallowed as he draped his tie over the steering wheel, revealing a small tuft of hair that peeked from his shirt. Damn, why did he have to be so freaking sexy?

'Anyway, Mum went home and built some kind of elf house for them in the back garden out of flower pots. She got pretty annoyed at the cat when he knocked it over, even though the same woman told her there are no elves here in the Netherlands.'

'How does she know there are no elves here?' Freya asked, with a straight face.

Lucas frowned, playing along. 'That's a good point. Maybe they're just hiding.'

'Or maybe they're just really small.'

'Who knows. Anyway…the houseboat… It's better where it is now, on the Amstel just off the canal ring.'

Freya was still laughing to herself, picturing his mother shouting at a cat over an elf house. She sounded fun, she thought with a stab of envy. 'What does your father think about elves?' she asked him.

Lucas went quiet for a moment. 'I don't know if he always knows what's real and what isn't.'

'What do you mean?' she asked, confused.

He shrugged. Falling silent, he steered the boat expertly under the next bridge, leaving the Red Light District behind, and his words niggled at her conscience. She sensed there was something else under the surface that he wanted to say about his father, but he clearly wasn't about to tell her.

The night was darker and quieter instantly. Crossing her arms around herself, she peeked at his profile in the passing streetlights. 'So, you grow vegetables on your roof? That sounds ambitious,' she said to fill the silence.

'It was Roshinda's idea. She preferred to cook with fresh ingredients.'

Freya flinched. Hearing him mention Roshinda again made her feel jealous, much to her own annoyance. 'Do you miss Roshinda?' she ventured anyway, wondering if they'd lived together on the houseboat. 'She sounds like she made quite an impact on the team.'

'I did miss her for a long time. Both professionally and personally. You know what it's like after a relationship ends, certain things bring it all back.' He met her eyes. 'But time heals, right? You said that yourself, not long ago. It's been eighteen months since she left and most days now I don't even think about her.'

She nodded slowly. She'd admired him quietly during his speech for many reasons, even as she'd spotted Joy openly swooning. It was clear her new friend had a crush on the heart surgeon, though Joy had once admitted to Freya that she knew she wasn't Lucas's type.

Freya had figured that if she couldn't keep Johnny coming back for more, she didn't stand a chance with a man like Lucas either. Being as rich and successful and handsome as he was, he could have any woman he wanted. But a smile danced in his eyes, seemingly just for her, and her stomach filled with butterflies all over again. Maybe she'd been wrong.

A rumble of thunder. A sudden howl of wind. Lucas stopped the engine, throwing them into total silence. Night seemed to envelop them as he reached for a blanket under the seat and wrapped it around her shoulders. Just the action made her groan inwardly and this time, when he stood close behind her with his hands on her shoulders, she let her head fall back against him. Clutching the blanket around the thin dress, it felt like just enough of a barrier between flesh on flesh.

This is safe enough, just staying like this. As long as nothing else happens.

'It's getting late.' Slowly, he turned her in his arms to face him.

Her breath caught in her throat as he cupped her face in her hands, and his eyes held an expression that made her heart sing, and freak out at the same time. 'I wouldn't normally be here like this with a colleague, Freya, but I have to admit I like being around you.'

Blunt as ever. Totally gorgeous. She ran her eyes over his lips, so close she could almost taste them. 'I…don't know what to say, Lucas.'

She didn't want to say anything, she so badly wanted to kiss those infuriatingly sexy lips but she couldn't do it. Something was holding her back. 'Maybe we shouldn't be doing this either.'

'Yeah?' His expression was half amused, half something else she couldn't quite read. Disappointment, maybe? Liv's voice was back inside her head again: *'You always push people away. Even the good ones.'*

She closed her eyes, pressing her palms to his chest. Lucas pulled her close under his chin, and she allowed herself a deep lungful of his cologne and the warmth of his comforting embrace…just for a moment.

Then he stepped away respectfully, back to the wheel with a long exhalation. 'You're probably right,' he agreed. Instantly she wanted to retract her refusal.

It was tempting, very, very tempting. But no. It definitely wasn't a good idea to blur any lines between work and pleasure when she wasn't even going to be sticking around for that long. He certainly didn't need another failed romance with a colleague behind him. This was for the best for both of them…wasn't it? Keeping things less complicated?

Minutes later, he was helping her off the boat at a jetty at the end of her street. 'You should get inside your house before it rains. Don't forget these.'

Their fingers brushed for another second over the velvet straps of her shoes, and her heart rocketed to her throat. What had just happened? 'Weren't you going to take me somewhere?' she asked him, feeling a wall springing up between them that, admittedly, she had built herself. This was very confusing. His very smell had been flooding her senses with delicious promises only seconds ago, and now, standing just a metre away from him, she felt cold and alone.

'Maybe another night. I'll see you tomorrow, Freya,' he said briskly, tossing the rope back into the boat and taking the wheel again.

'OK, thanks for the ride, Lucas…' Her voice trailed off in the breeze. He was already steering away.

CHAPTER SEVEN

Lucas heard the yelling from halfway down the corridor. It was coming from the consultation room. Freya was inside, clearly dealing with an emotional parent. He was about to walk on by and not interrupt her session when the noise erupted again.

'Dr Grey?' he said, knocking on the door in concern. He opened it, despite not being invited to. 'Everything OK in here? I heard some commotion.'

Freya stood up from where she'd been sitting opposite two women, presumably a mother and daughter, the younger of whom made a show of ending a phone call and slamming the phone back into her bag with a huff.

'We're OK,' Freya told him, crossing to the door and causing his heartbeat to speed up in the process. The room smelled of the lily-scented candles that Freya liked to use, and it took him back to that moment a week ago on Ruben's boat, when the heady scent of her perfume and the glistening wonder in her eyes had almost tempted him into kissing her. He had a feeling she was avoiding him now, but that was probably for the best. She clearly had a stronger sense of self-preservation than he did.

'Angela was just having a… conversation…with her

husband. Unfortunately he couldn't make it for their son Antonio's surgery.'

Her eyes told him these were difficult patients, but nothing she couldn't handle. He was about to excuse himself again when the young mother, Angela Regio, stood up from the couch. 'Dr Van de Berg?'

He hovered in the doorway, not wanting to step into Freya's territory. He hadn't seen her outside the hospital all week, or been alone with her without the team around. If Freya wanted to distance herself from him, and that almost-kiss on the boat, he would accept it, even if he didn't really want to.

'Now that you're here, perhaps you can describe the procedure to my mother here?' Angela said, fixing him with wide, deep brown eyes rimmed with red. 'I know you told me and Stanyo, Doctor, but he's obviously too busy with his new girlfriend to be at his own son's heart surgery appointment. What is aort…stemu…what…?'

'Aortic stenosis,' he corrected her, as Freya crossed her arms and averted her weary gaze to the polished floor. He'd overheard her saying to Joy she'd been unpacking boxes till late, and that that was all she ever seemed to do when she wasn't at work. He'd been planning on following up with his offer of helping in some way, but she hadn't approached him about it either.

They seemed to have reached a tense stalemate, and he was getting increasingly more annoyed with himself for still not being able to get their almost-kiss out of his head.

'Please, do explain, Doctor.' Angela's mother was in her mid-fifties. Her ruby-red lipstick had stained a paper coffee cup, which she'd placed on the table.

'I'm sure Dr Van de Berg has to prep for surgery,'

Freya cut in, walking back over to them. 'We do have some illustrations here that might help make things clearer.'

'Nurse Joy is taking care of things for now,' he said, and he thought he saw a flicker of annoyance cross her face. Still avoiding his eyes, she picked up a copy of the journal featuring Roshinda's work and leafed to a page with a full-colour illustration of what he was describing.

The journals had bothered him up to a certain point but now it was Freya's determined refusal to acknowledge their chemistry that was getting under his skin. He crossed to the couch in interest, wondering how she'd use them.

'When a child has aortic stenosis, the area where blood exits the heart's lower left chamber…right here… is too narrow, and the left heart has to work much harder to pump blood around the body…'

He peered over Freya's shoulder. She straightened up at his proximity, and somehow he could tell he was making her nervous. Like he had done on that boat.

Pure panic. That was the only way to describe what he'd seen in her eyes, right before they'd come so close to kissing he could almost taste her. He'd gone over it in his head afterwards on the way to the shelter. In spite of her candour, she had walls up a mile high. She seemed to have issues even accepting his friendly gestures… like when he'd offered to help her down the ladder. He was only being a gentleman, but she had made it pretty clear she didn't need one of those in her life, thank you very much, and backing away from that kiss had just proved she had no intention of taking their simmering attraction any further.

'Dr Van de Berg will place what we call a stent-based

tissue aortic heart valve into here…using a catheter that he'll insert right here…but the difference is, it will go in through a tiny incision in Antonio's leg. Then it's threaded up to the heart through the arteries…'

'So very clever,' Angela's mother pronounced, looking at him in awe. 'These really do work, Doctor?'

He nodded curtly, pushing his glasses up his nose. He'd stood over Roshinda's computer while she'd been drawing these exact illustrations. He could still see her giant computer screen casting a white glow on his black marble dining-room table and their wine glasses, while her pen moved expertly over the mousepad, rendering, reshaping, colouring. She'd turned his profession, which he'd always considered scientific, into art.

Lucas had to admit that while Roshinda had a way of making something incredibly complex, like the human heart and other body parts, look nothing short of beautiful, and simple, Freya had a way of bringing it even more to life with her words.

Her phone buzzed in her pocket.

She pulled it out and swiped yet another of her mother's calls away, looking at him in annoyance, or embarrassment, or both, he couldn't tell which. Did she ever talk to the woman, or just ignore her all the time? He could tell she was stressed over it—why didn't she just answer the phone and put herself out of her misery? More to the point, why did Freya's broken relationship with her mother bother him so much?

He assumed it was because spending time with his own father was so precious these days and he couldn't imagine ever shutting a parent out on purpose. He frowned. He was getting far too invested in Freya's life when she'd clearly indicated he should butt out.

'I should get back to work. I see everything is under control here,' he said coolly, before he could take her aside and speak his real thoughts out loud.

'Sorry you had to hear me shouting at Stanyo, Dr Van de Berg,' Angela said, looking sheepish.

'No need to apologise,' he assured her. 'Ladies, I will see you and Antonio very soon.'

Freya simply bobbed her head in his direction as if he were a stranger—another attempt to douse the sparks he damn well knew they could both still feel. They were more like painful prickles now.

Leaving for the neonatal ward, he wondered if she'd ever let a man back into her heart since that guy Johnny had ditched her for her best friend, back at college. Maybe it was a good thing she'd put a stop to their kiss before it had even started, he considered. A woman like Freya would be all too easy to get involved with, but not only was she altogether emotionally unavailable, she had her eyes on her next destination already, too... just like Roshinda had.

With his father's mental health going downhill, he really didn't have the time to chase after another woman with wings, even if he wanted to. He should just put Freya out of his head for good.

Little Antonio was wide-eyed and smiling, sitting up in bed in his private room, oblivious to the fact that he'd soon be under in what Joy called, in her Irish sing-song voice, the HAC-HOR. Their 'highly advanced cardiac hybrid operating room'.

'He's being such a brave boy, aren't you?' Joy crooned, tying Antonio's blue gown behind him. Freya noticed Joy had Minnie Mouse laces in her trainers today, which matched her red polka-dot headband.

'You're in great hands, little man,' Freya followed up with a smile, just as Lucas entered the room. She bit the inside of her cheeks as he strode up close, and the scent of his cologne made her feel giddy, just as it had earlier when he'd intervened in her consultation room. She'd picked up Roshinda's journal just to test him, maybe. To see if he'd flinch, or leave the room, but she'd only felt his thoughtful eyes on her.

It made her feel guilty for even testing him. She wondered if he had been thinking about that night on the boat as much as she had.

She'd been trying to stay away from him because now, more than ever since their almost-kiss, she was confused around him. It was like his very presence sent her straight off her carefully navigated course and wreaked havoc with her plans to be a strong, independent, man-free zone whilst she was temporarily living in the place she hadn't much wanted to come back to. She hadn't succumbed to the temptation to kiss him, but she might as well have done. It was all she'd been thinking about.

'Are you ready, Superman?' Lucas said, wriggling the child's little toes gently in his Superman socks. Antonio giggled and said something in Italian.

It was clear Lucas didn't understand, so without thinking Freya translated. 'He said he's happy to be getting a new heart from you.'

Lucas was looking at her surprise and admiration. 'Boarding school, I forgot,' he said, and she nodded brusquely, trying to ignore the way her heart still all but imploded every time he met her eyes. It was why she'd been trying so hard not to look his way.

'I think the heart you have already will be just fine,' Lucas replied, letting Freya translate again, and his fingers brushed against hers on the bedside railings as he went to ruffle the kid's hair. It set off a Catherine wheel in her chest that took her straight back to her dream last night, when they'd done far more than kiss until she'd woken in a sweat with her heart pounding.

'Should we find out where your heart is, Superman?' she managed to say in Italian. 'Is it here?' She placed a finger softly on the boy's forehead. Antonio giggled and shook his head.

'Is it here?' Lucas said next, moving his finger to Antonio's belly button, and the boy laughed again.

'Here?' Joy asked, picking up his foot. Antonio was almost beside himself, giggling. The laughter was infectious and this time she did look up at Lucas. In a heartbeat she realised why these new feelings unnerved her so badly. She already liked him more than she had ever liked Johnny, and look what had happened there.

She winced internally as her phone buzzed yet again.

'Go talk to your mother,' Lucas said in a lowered voice, glancing at the screen over her shoulder. 'It might be urgent.'

'I'll call her later,' she told him, careful not to sound as annoyed with herself as she felt. She said 'See you soon, Superman,' to Antonio in Italian, and then wished Lucas a good operation in English, feeling the heat race to her cheeks at the frown on Lucas's face, just for her.

He wasn't annoyed at the phone ringing, she could tell. He was annoyed that she never answered it, which of course she didn't, not at work anyway. It wasn't like she ignored *all* her mother's calls…although, if she was honest with herself, she didn't exactly look forward to them either, considering the stilted, almost painful small talk they always seemed to involve.

Still, why did Lucas care so much what she did, or *didn't* do, with her mother?

CHAPTER EIGHT

THE EVENINGS WERE long now, as summer was in full bloom. It didn't get dark till eleven p.m., which was great because cycling all the way from Jordaan to Amsterdam North two weeks after Antonio's successful operation with two bags of trinkets for her bargain-hunter took longer than she'd anticipated. She must have got herself lost about four times in the narrow, winding streets on the way to the ferry behind Centraal Station.

Maybe her internal homing device wasn't quite as accurate as she'd thought. Then again, a lot of things were new to her here now. Sometimes it didn't even seem like the same city she'd grown up in. Guilt made her stomach churn every time she thought about how she still hadn't confirmed with Liv that she could visit.

Poor Liv didn't realise how badly Freya had been affected by the way their mother had ignored her, prior to getting pregnant for the second time. With her break-up and everything else going on, it wasn't fair to involve her now. It wasn't Liv's problem anyway—it was hers and Elise's.

She pushed her bike onto the ferry, along with what felt like two hundred other people, and watched the other shore grow closer as the music from a band on a rooftop swirled across the water to her ears.

Most of what had been built north of Amsterdam Centraal, beyond the river Ij, was new to her. Before, when she'd visited Centraal Station with Anouk or Beatrice, there had been hardly anything to look at across the river. Now there were tower blocks and apartment buildings, parks and a film museum. Pieter and Ruud had even invited her and Lucas to a virtual reality experience over here, somewhere in a huge hall.

'Let's all go put sexy goggles on and shoot zombies together. Then we'll eat dinner in that nice Mexican restaurant—the one with the fancy tacos that cost fifteen euros each. Unless you want to cook for us all, Lucas?'

Ruud had turned to her then. 'He used to have legendary dinner parties on his houseboat, you know. Have you cooked for Freya yet, Lucas?'

Lucas had said something about their schedules not matching up, and being busy, which she knew by now was everyone's reason for not doing something they just didn't want to make time for, and the guys had thrown each other knowing glances. About what, she could only imagine. They were probably trying to set them up in their most unsubtle, unnerving way, but Lucas was having none of it.

The ferry chugged noisily beneath her. Clutching the handlebars of her bike, she thought of Lucas. They still hadn't spent any more time together outside the hospital. Maybe she *had* pushed him away, like she seemed to do with anyone who threatened to get too close, she thought, watching a seagull cut through the sky.

It's better this way anyway. You're here to work, and sell a house, and then leave.

Where would she go next? Back to the States? It didn't seem like an option right now. There had been a time when all she'd wanted was a Green Card, but now most of her friends there were green with envy over her European passport. As a European with her qualifications, she could now work anywhere. There *was* still the job she'd seen, starting in the new year, in Ho Chi Minh, Vietnam. She was too busy to think about it properly just yet, but what was life if she didn't have *some* vague travel plan on the horizon?

A life without Lucas's handsome face in it, she thought, without meaning to. It made her cheeks flush and a vague twinge of nausea swirl through her stomach that she chose to blame on the boat crossing.

Something was off when she pulled up at the location she'd been given by the guy she'd arranged to meet—Tom. There was no one in sight.

Still on the saddle, she dug in her bag for her phone to double-check the address. Her heart did a funny leapfrog in her chest when she saw a missed call from Lucas, but she swiped away the notification. This wasn't the time. Had she gone off track again and ended up at the wrong place?

Her map said, no, she was exactly where she was meant to be. Tom had said it was a brasserie, which it was, but she hadn't expected to find it closed.

Parking her bike, she flipped the stand down and wandered towards the restaurant entrance. The doors were bolted, bound with heavy chains. Weeds sprouted messily through cracks in the paving slabs out front. Cardboard boxes and bins full of bottles greeted her as she walked around the back.

'Hello? Is anyone here?'

A bird took flight, and something in the bushes scuttled off, but otherwise she could have heard a pin drop. 'Hello?'

Where was Tom?

'Talk about a waste of time,' she muttered to herself, peering over an overgrown hedge to look through the window. Nothing. The place had been stripped bare. 'What the...?'

She jumped at a sudden sound out front. Footsteps on the asphalt. 'Hello? Is that Tom?'

Hurrying back the way she'd come, she scaled another pile of boxes, only to see the back of a guy with shoulder-length dark hair in a red striped sweater and army combat pants. 'Hey! Tom, is that you?'

The guy didn't look particularly surprised to see her. He looked more annoyed than anything. The second he noticed her, he jumped onto her bike and flipped the stand up.

'What are you doing?' Freya sprinted towards him in her sneakers and sundress as realisation hit home. She had left the bags of stuff for Tom in the basket. 'Tom? Did you bring me here to steal my bike?'

'I did,' he said simply. 'Sorry.'

She stopped short in shock. '*Sorry? Are you serious?*'

Quick as a flash, he sped off, leaving her chasing after him across the empty courtyard in vain. 'I don't believe this! I'm calling the police!'

'Thanks for the bike, lady!' he called back.

'You're a terrible human, Tom, if that's even your name!'

Chocolate-bar wrappers and newspaper coupons swirled up in the breeze as she stopped on the barren street, panting and fuming. His red sweater shrank to a dot in the distance, then disappeared.

Her phone was ringing. Lucas again.

'Sorry to call again,' he said when she answered, still out of breath. 'Pieter says you're the only one who knows where the lily-scented candle supply is. I don't know what he wants them for right now, but he doesn't have your number.'

'The candles?' she echoed, feeling confused. Where was the ferry? Suddenly every direction looked the same and she couldn't remember now which way she'd come. A siren wailed in the distance.

'Where are you?' Lucas sounded concerned now.

'I… I don't know…'

'There's an app for that,' he said.

'I can't use it when I'm on the phone, can I?' she huffed back. She dragged a hand through her hair, turning around again. She was fuming and embarrassed. 'Sorry,' she said quickly. 'The aromatherapy candle supply ran out, that's why he can't find them. I haven't had time to get any more…'

'What's happened?'

She swallowed back a growl. 'Some guy just stole my bike,' she told him, starting to walk towards the gap in the buildings up ahead. The river must be somewhere around here. 'I thought I was selling someone some stuff from Anouk's place but when I got here…'

Lucas let out a long groan. 'Damn, Freya, you fell for the oldest trick in the book. You didn't make any bank transfers, did you?'

She prickled at his words. Sometimes he was just *too* blunt. 'Don't hold back, Lucas. And, no, I didn't, thank goodness.'

'Did they lure you somewhere remote? Somewhere in the north?'

'How did you know?'

'It's the quietest place, less security, not as many police. You can't be too far from a bus.'

'The ferry is around here somewhere.' It was Freya's turn to groan now. She felt like such an idiot.

'I'm just finishing up at the hospital, then I'm heading that way on the boat,' he said. 'I can come and get you.'

Instantly her defences were back up. She didn't need help from anyone. She'd got herself into this mess, she would get herself out of it, eventually. 'There's no need, thank you, I'm totally fine.'

She almost heard him roll his eyes. 'I know you are, you always are. I'll meet you at the ferry.'

CHAPTER NINE

THE GUY FREYA had arranged to meet had since deleted all traces of their conversation from the marketplace app they'd been chatting in. Lucas watched her eyes move over the box of clothes on the floor of Ruben's boat. They were heading from the river back towards the canal belt.

'Sorry to tell you this, Freya, but this kind of thing happens all the time. It's easier to get another bike than stress yourself out filling in forms and filing reports, and all that. I can take you to the police station, but as they already said when you phoned them, I can pretty much guarantee you won't be getting that bike or your stuff back. It would be a waste of your time.'

Freya grimaced at a passing cruise boat and he admonished himself for delivering the news so matter-of-factly when she'd just had a terrible evening. It was probably a defence mechanism on his part; he wasn't too proud of himself for sailing to her rescue like Prince Charming when they'd barely spoken, other than to discuss work, in weeks.

Then again, women who didn't appear to need him were his weakness. And leaving her lost and alone out here had not been an option. She was an attractive and vulnerable woman, and it was getting dark. No way was he leaving Freya alone anywhere.

She let out a sigh, and he realised she was looking him up and down in his shirt and jeans, with something he could've sworn was pent-up frustration in her eyes. 'So you're still using your friend's boat, I see?'

He patted the wheel with both hands. 'Ruben likes to keep it moving, it stops the engine rusting up.' He paused, feeling the slow acid burn of not knowing and unease start up again. 'It's not like him to miss a summer night like this, cruising the canals, but they went to Anne Marie's parents' place again. I think she's pretty nervous about something the obstetrician said to her, and she wanted to be with her mother.'

'I remember you said she's pregnant, yes?'

'That's right.' He was trying not to worry before it was necessary, but it was hard. 'She had a blood test this morning and Ruben told me their obstetrician prescribed a level two ultrasound in order to get a better view of the baby's heart.'

'I hope nothing's wrong,' Freya said, putting a voice to his innermost fears. It made him feel colder despite the warm breeze. Just that morning they'd said goodbye to little Antonio Regio after his final check-up—yet another success story. As far as *this* baby was concerned, however, his friends were counting on his involvement, in every way possible—they hadn't even had a diagnosis yet, but he'd been the first doctor, the only heart doctor, Ruben had thought of right from the start.

'We'll know soon enough, they'll be at the hospital again on Monday.'

'At least you'll be close by then.'

Lucas couldn't entertain getting any bad news about

their baby. Ruben meant too much to him; he was like a second brother to him. The look on Freya's face told him she was thinking about it too. His problems were her problems where their patients were concerned. His heart softened again. He had missed her these past few weeks.

'If you want, you can come with me to the shelter,' he said. The words were out before he could even think to change his mind.

'What shelter?'

'It's called *Inloophuis*, which means Walk-in House. The homeless can stay there for up to three months, usually while they're waiting to get settled in an apartment or some other permanent place further out of the city. I have to take those clothes.' He pointed at the boxes on the bottom of the boat. 'There are some pretty interesting characters over there. Everyone has a story.'

'Where do you get all the clothes?' Freya asked curiously. 'Are they yours?'

'People leave them for me to collect, and I take them myself.'

Two women above the bridge he was heading for waved down at Freya, but she didn't see them. She was looking at him thoughtfully. 'I can probably make some donations too, I have plenty more stuff at Anouk's house. If only I'd known about your shelter before the last lot just got stolen...'

'Your house,' he reminded her. 'It's yours now.'

'Not for long,' she said, pulling her sunglasses down over her eyes. She sat back in her seat, like she was trying to create more distance between them all of a sudden. He forced himself not to push it as he didn't want her crawling straight back into her shell now that she'd just opened it a crack again.

Lucas steered the boat under a narrow bridge, watching a flock of birds scatter in their wake. 'Roshinda took me to the shelter first,' he said. 'As soon as she moved here from India she was looking to get involved with something beyond the hospital, something for people in need like her family does at home. Even though Roshinda left, they still need me...so I keep going.'

'You're a busy man.'

'I do what I can.' He wasn't entirely certain he was doing the right thing involving her in the shelter, for many reasons, but it was too late now.

'My sister's calling,' Freya announced suddenly.

He almost said, *What's new?* but didn't want to rock the boat even more.

'I texted her to tell her what happened with that thief, and she's been calling me a lot more since her break-up so...sorry.'

'Don't apologise.'

He listened to her talk as he steered the boat towards the Bilderdijkstraat, where the homeless shelter was. There were a lot of long pauses. It seemed like Liv was doing most of the talking.

'Well, I still have to check my schedule, you know things are pretty crazy, and now I have to get a new bike... I'm not sure it's the right time for you to come just yet... No, I'm not saying you should *never* come, I'm saying I'm still not ready for guests. The house is such a mess and... Yes... Liv... I know you want to help me.' She lowered her voice. 'I'm not making excuses.'

She paused, and it seemed like she was embarrassed he was having to hear this personal conversation. He was simply thinking Freya looked hot as hell in her dress. The cut of it showed off her slim waist, with just a hint of cleavage. But he didn't want a repeat of the last time she had backed off from blurring the lines of their relationship, so he would make sure to keep things professional. His heart would only thank him for it, anyway.

'No, I haven't arranged to meet Mum yet,' she said now. All her usual serenity was gone. He heard her let out another sigh. 'I know... Liv... I know she wants to see me, I was thinking we could all meet up together when you're here.' She closed her eyes, as though Liv was giving her a hard time on the other end of the line.

'Listen, Lucas is taking us to the homeless shelter now, so I have to go...'

She paused again like she'd been cut off, and glanced at him suddenly, narrowing her eyes. 'Well, that's a very good question,' she said cryptically. He realised she was half smiling mysteriously in his direction. 'I'm discovering new answers to that question every day, actually.'

The Inloophuis building was an old converted car mechanic's shop. It was big enough for fifty beds across several dorms, a canteen and kitchen, a shower block and a big community area. Encouraging posters adorned the walls around a scattering of colourful cushions on the floor. There must have been twenty or so people of various ages milling around.

'There are fourteen staff, everyone keeps to a schedule,' Lucas explained now, stopping by the jobs board in the communal area. She eyed the posters shouting about health and free clinics and career opportunities, some in English, some in Dutch. In another world she would be at the police station now, spending hours waiting around or filing reports.

Freya's evening had done a three-sixty. Lucas had rescued her, much to her initial embarrassment, but he was impossibly sexy behind the wheel of a boat and she'd been grateful for the unprecedented interruption in the end. She had missed their growing rapport, even though she'd been the one to step back from it. She hadn't been able to stop looking at him in his white shirt, half open at the neck, and now he'd invited her into another element of his personal life.

A Dutch voice behind her. Freya turned to see a woman in her mid-twenties coming up beside her in black jeans and trainers and a blazer three sizes too large for her slim frame. She had cropped brown hair, and a set of uneven, browning teeth. Freya read 'Kate' on her name badge.

'You know, I had blood poisoning because I self-harmed,' Kate shared, looking between herself and Lucas with shifting blue eyes. 'It was serious. This place was my last resort. Wouldn't be here without it. The people here…the number of people *this* man has helped by coming here…me included.' She looked at Lucas like he was a god or something. 'I'd be in prison if it wasn't for this guy. How do you know Lucas?'

'We're colleagues.' Freya said, introducing herself as Lucas excused himself to unpack the box he'd brought in with him from the boat.

She watched him hand a navy-blue T-shirt to a man with a name badge reading 'Martijn'. The guy must have been in his mid-fifties and the stump showed he'd lost his right lower arm in an accident, rather than through illness or a birth defect; he still had half a military tattoo on show, down to his elbow. Was there anything Lucas didn't do for people? She was in total awe of his participation in this shelter already.

Kate was scanning her up and down with her eyes like a barcode, a semi-smile on her thin lips. 'You're a doctor too?'

'I'm a paediatric cardiologist,' she said, tearing her eyes from Lucas's tall frame the second he glanced her way.

'I work in a shed, potting plants,' Kate replied unapologetically. 'I guess we both dig around in things, huh? You in people, me in the earth.'

'I…suppose that's true.' Freya had never thought of it like that before.

'Lucas was a big part of getting me my new job, and my place. I come back to help cook, and eat the food, it's the best on Tuesdays—that's when Lucas works in the kitchen.'

Freya was busy taking all this in. Lucas was a star here, no doubt about it. How had no one at the hospital mentioned this?

'I've been in a lot of homeless shelters, in a lot of places, and most of the money goes to the people at the top, not to the homeless,' Kate told her, dropping to a couch and flipping open the top of a soft-drink can. When Lucas took over here he made sure that changed.'

Freya felt her jaw drop. 'He took over here?'

Kate swigged from the can, swallowing loudly. 'He calls himself the creative director,' she said, swiping her mouth with the back of one hand and pulling her legs up under her. 'He got the walls painted, new beds for the dorms, blankets…and put the new team together on top of all he does for those sick kids. Lucas made sure we have the facilities to provide almost twelve thousand beds a year, across all three shelters. He arranged for the Happy Hearts Clinic to offer free check-ups to anyone who wants one.'

She tapped the can on her knee, leaned forward as if to share a secret. 'In the last eight months more than twenty guests from here have gone into full-time employment. Not a cent comes from the authorities. That's more than creative direction, that's life-changing.'

'I agree.' Freya was amazed. There was a lot she didn't know about Lucas, clearly. She looked over at where he was still talking to the one-armed guy, Martijn. A black and tan German Shepherd dog was wagging his tail and sniffing Lucas's pockets. She watched as he pulled a treat out of his jeans and fed it to him.

'He says he found us by accident through his ex-girlfriend, but Fayola says the universe sent him our way by whatever means it had, because we needed him so badly. 'That's Fayola,' Kate said, motioning to a large black woman lying belly down on a pink floor cushion, reading a book. 'She owned a vintage clothing store that got burned down. She used to live in it, but after the fire she lost everything, no insurance, no family. She had nowhere to go, so now she's here. So, are you Lucas's new girlfriend, or what?'

'What? No.' Freya's head was spinning. All the people here had such tragic stories, and they clearly all liked Lucas a lot. What was not to like, though? she thought, realising it was near on impossible to stop herself from being so attracted to him, which felt more like a teenage infatuation with every passing day. It had been years since she'd thought about a man so incessantly, and admired his body as much as his brain.

'Who's Lucas?' Liv had asked on the phone earlier. She'd told Liv she was discovering new answers to that question every day, because every time she decided not to let her heart get involved he stepped up with a different side of himself to admire. Lucas Van de Berg was a dedicated doctor and friend, he adored his mother, and now she'd discovered Lucas was funding and reviving this homeless shelter.

He'd flooded it with help and hope and what sounded like a fair amount of his personal money. All this time she'd been talking about her missions, she realised suddenly, and the need to help everyone else out there in the world, when Lucas was doing all this, right here in his home city, where just as many people, if not more, were benefiting in a multitude of ways.

'You're mending hearts off the operating table too, you know that,' she said to him when he wandered back over to her side. Self-conscious suddenly, she felt like he could see her feelings magnified in her eyes, but she didn't look away. 'You're making such a difference. People like you give me hope for a better world.'

Lucas's smile radiated pride and affection for her at the same time, and she felt an undeniable burst of butterflies explode in her belly. 'I could say the same about you,' he said. She was done for.

She had never considered staying in one place, there had always seemed to be too much to do out there in the world, but had she ever really tried? she wondered. No, she had never focused and committed because she'd been too busy running away from everything and everyone she'd been hurt by, instead of finding what was great about the present moment. Lucas made being in one place seem as though it was not only possible but just as rewarding, just as fulfilling. What might she have been missing this whole time? she wondered uneasily.

'You want a tarot reading, pretty lady?' Fayola was beckoning her over, sitting upright, bosom heaving in her loud magenta dress. Her hair sprang frizzy and full from her round head in greying dreadlocks, and she wore a chunky necklace made of moonstones and rose quartz.

'You really should, she's very good,' Kate said, though Lucas just shook his head in silent amusement.

Before she could refuse, Freya was being urged onto a floor cushion and made to shuffle a set of yellow cards.

CHAPTER TEN

LUCAS DIDN'T BELIEVE in things like the tarot. How anyone thought a spread of cards could tell the future, or even help you tap into your intuition, like Fayola said they did, was unfathomable to him. Not that Fayola was some end-of-the-pier charlatan, but he was a man of science after all.

Even so, he'd watched Freya on Friday night at the shelter, and had seen the colour drain from her face as she'd studied the spread, all the swords and hearts and kings. Shadow had demanded his attention, Kate had started talking recipes for Tuesday's dinner, and the next thing he knew, Freya was standing up, telling him she had to go.

He'd offered to take her home, but she told him he'd been heroic enough for one night. *'Thank you so much anyway,'* she'd said, and had refused to let him accompany her.

'What happened the other night?' he asked her now, closing the door to the conference room. It was just the two of them mid-morning on Monday, and she looked like she'd barely slept all weekend.

She went to the drawer for the candles, before obviously recalling there weren't any. 'I got my bike stolen, remember,' she said ruefully, as if he could forget that.

'I meant with Fayola. You couldn't wait to get out of there.'

Freya shut the drawer, kept her back to him and stared at the vase of tulips on the table, reaching out a hand to stroke one absently. 'She just said some things I wasn't exactly expecting to hear. Sorry, I didn't mean to run off like that.'

He frowned. He'd wondered if she'd become worried he had pulled her too far into his world again, and had rushed off to avoid getting in any deeper. 'What did she say?'

'Just some things…family stuff. I'd rather not discuss it now.'

'Family stuff. Did she know about your mother? How you don't talk about anything that really matters?'

Freya was silent.

He resisted the urge to walk over to where she stood highlighted by the patch of sunlight streaming in through the window. He wanted her to confide in him, to know she could trust him. He had been thinking all weekend about how nice it was to finally share his other life at *Inloophuis* with Freya. He'd ended up going home and telling his father all about her; her work on the mission projects, the difference she was making to the patients at the hospital; the way he hadn't felt this burning urge to be with anyone since Roshinda.

'You need to hold on to this one,' his dad had observed through the fog of disarray that constituted his thought patterns these days.

He studied the back of her head now as she arranged her tulips in the vase. He doubted Fred would remember them talking about her, his memories waning and warping the way they were. Wishing he could have agreed with him, Lucas had instead assured his father that he wasn't about to get involved with anyone else from work, let alone someone who wasn't intending to stick around for more than a few months. But his father's words had resonated with him. Maybe he *would* have tried to hold on to Freya if she didn't keep putting up walls faster than he could knock them down.

'Freya, this is crazy. We need to talk,' he said now, and this time she turned to face him in surprise, right as the foetal cardiologist, Femke, rapped on the door. 'Sorry to interrupt you, Lucas, but I thought you and Freya might want to know the results of your friend Anne Marie's ultrasound.'

'HLHS,' Freya said with a sigh, studying the scans. 'Hypoplastic left heart syndrome with an intact atrial septum.' She was all too aware of Lucas's presence at her side. She could smell the fresh scent of his post-workout shower. He didn't even know it but he threatened to undo her resolve not to kiss him every time he looked at her over the scans. He'd been overwhelming her even before this but when he'd suddenly said they needed to talk, her heart had practically leapt from her chest.

They were facing a new dilemma now, though.

She'd learned in the US that heart defects occurred in eight out of every thousand newborn babies and HLHS was among the rarest types. Ruben and Anne Marie's baby was missing a natural hole in his heart. It was a devastating diagnosis and she wasn't looking forward to giving it to one of Lucas's good friends.

'We can operate,' Lucas said with confidence, perching on the corner of the desk and adjusting his glasses.

She nodded, resisting the urge to remind him that if they waited till the baby was born, the chances of saving his life weren't very high. He'd need to be transferred to the neonatal intensive care unit right after birth, then undergo the emergency procedure to create the hole in his little heart.

Very few babies survived this, most dying during the procedure, some right after a resulting heart transplant. This could be trauma after trauma for the parents, Lucas knew that. He was a scientist at heart, like her. He just wasn't saying so right now.

This wasn't the time to continue anything personal between them, she told herself, making for the door.

'Freya, wait.' He followed her out into the hallway. 'Talk to me,' he urged, stepping close to let a wheelchair go past.

'I'm concerned for your friend's baby,' she said, running her hands through her hair. 'You know it's a tricky procedure, operating while he's still in the womb.'

'I can do it, you know that. So trust me. We'll give them what hope we realistically can for a successful outcome. 'I meant talk to me about what happened on Friday. Are you still worried that some random spread of cards said something discouraging about you and your mother?'

She scowled at the floor. His persistence on the matter was unwelcome here, though it made her heart ache knowing he still had the capacity to be concerned for her, on top of what they'd just discovered about Ruben and Anne Marie's baby. 'Forget about it, please,' she said, and to her dismay her phone buzzed again.

Lucas put his hands in the air. 'I guess that's your mother, or your sister, and you're just going to ignore them again.'

'Leave it Lucas…' she replied, walking away, but he stopped her again, standing in front of her.

'Only *you* have the power to fix your relationships, and you should do it while you still can, Freya. You're smart enough to know that, no matter what some random spread of cards told you.'

'I said leave it.' She hated the way her heart had started hammering against her ribs; his suddenly impassioned stance making her feel helpless, like he was stripping her down without ever putting a hand on her, pinning her.

She scanned his eyes, seeing the tarot cards all over again in her mind's eye. She had pulled The Lovers—two naked people baring all—crossed with the ominous Ten of Swords—the ultimate 'stab in the back' card. She could see Fayola's knowing smile.

'There's someone you've been baring your soul to, someone you want to trust, but somehow you still can't fully trust them, can you?'

Lucas crossed his arms, leaning against the wall over the bottom of a clown's foot. Pieter walked past with another patient, a teen in a tracksuit, and she plastered a smile to her face for his benefit. She was practically pressed up against the wall on one side. Again, her heart did a backward flip. Why was it, after all these years, she still saw every guy as Johnny, just waiting to stomp on her heart the second she as much as thought about giving it away?

She knew why…

She didn't *want* to believe in anything Fayola might

have claimed to see in a few random cards but the next thing she'd said had shaken Freya, despite herself.

'Swords mean internal conflict, and more breakdowns in communication,' Fayola had said. 'I sense this is concerns your mother...either that or something is causing you to cease communication with a close female family member. This battle, whatever it is, is with your own feelings. You're getting trapped inside your own head and it's affecting everything around you. Everyone who crosses your path.'

'I'm sorry,' she said now. He was so close she could see the flecks of green in his vivid blue irises. 'I need to focus on how to tell Anne Marie—'

'You live your life for the good of every mother who comes in here with a sick child. Why don't you ever just talk to *your* mother?'

'It's none of your business. Why do you even care so much?' she shot back, annoyed. 'You seem to pick and choose what to tell me about your life, Lucas, but when it comes to mine you're all over it!'

'All I'm saying is you don't know how long your parents will be around for and you don't want to have any regrets.'

'What?'

He suddenly flipped the handle on the storeroom door, pulled her inside by the elbow and closed it hard behind them. Darkness enveloped them in the small, enclosed space. She found her hands pressed to his chest in his coat as a patter of footsteps passed by outside.

His lips were an inch from hers, intoxicating, passionate. 'Your phone keeps ringing. Your mother obviously wants to see you, your sister too. So why don't you just put everyone out of their misery? Put yourself out of this misery? I don't like seeing you like this, it's the reason you don't want to stay here in Amsterdam, isn't it? Why you're still thinking about going to Vietnam after this contract ends, instead of renewing it.'

She swallowed. She had sworn no man would ever get to her like this again, but her fingers betrayed her and started clasping the fabric of his coat around the lapels and pulling him towards her. Lucas let out a frustrated groan before his forehead lowered to meet hers. He urged her closer still, drawing her hips flush against his.

'You're something else, you know that?' he told her, right up against her lips. The sound of his raspy voice was like liquid adrenaline being mainlined into her bloodstream right before he kissed her.

Freya almost forgot where she was as pure animal instinct took over. He was strong, and in one swift movement he claimed her small frame in his big, muscled arms and urged her up against the wall. She was conscious of his hands hoisting her coat up around her middle, and her own dashing through his hair, along his face, down his back, cupping his delicious backside…

She ran her hands around his front and pressed her palms to the firmness of his torso, God…she couldn't get enough of the way his muscles flexed against her touch. The smell of his aftershave enveloped her just as much as his arms did in the enclosed space and left her feeling dizzy. She sucked in a breath, letting her hands play in his hair as she found his lips again. He tasted better than she'd ever imagined.

Lucas met her mouth with fierce desire, drawing her harder against him, one hand tangling in her hair as their kiss grew deeper... And then...a flailing limb... an almighty crash.

They sprang apart.

In seconds, the door creaked open. 'I can't find those spare candles,' Freya mumbled breathlessly, trying to cover up what they'd been doing and fumbling through a box of what felt like baby bottles as her swollen lips threatened to give her away. Pieter was standing there open-mouthed in the doorway. He adjusted his dinosaur-patterned tie, looking her up and down in amusement, while Lucas struggled with the fallen item.

'The vacuum cleaner...appears to be broken,' he announced hoarsely in the semi-darkness.

'I wonder how that happened.' Pieter smirked.

CHAPTER ELEVEN

'PENNY FOR YOUR THOUGHTS,' Joy chirped behind her in the staffroom. 'You were zoning out for a moment.'

'Was I?'

'Thinking about your house still? How's all that going? You know, the offer is still there for me to come over and help you. I have some special cookies that would make it more fun.' She threw her a wink over her shoulder, pouring hot water from the dispenser into a mug that held a teabag.

Freya felt worse, suddenly, than she'd been feeling all week since her accidental, hot, unforgettable, embarrassing kiss with Lucas. She was certain their excuse about looking for candles had been accepted as the final word on the incident—at least, Pieter hadn't done anything more than throw her a knowing look or two in passing. But she'd kept her head down since and had politely declined at least four more invitations from Joy to do things after hours.

She hadn't had much experience with female friendships since Beatrice but then again, she thought, looking at Joy now in her happy polka-dot headband, maybe it was time to make a conscious effort to stop pushing people away.

'You know what?' she said now, as Joy dug her hands in the candy jar and refilled her pockets with lollipops. 'That would actually be great. I need to clear out and paint one of the spare rooms at least, to make some space so my sister can visit.'

'Oh?' Joy arched a plucked eyebrow. 'Is she coming to stay from the UK?'

Freya shrugged distractedly. 'I haven't arranged a date yet, but yes.'

'That'll be lovely,' Joy enthused, popping a sugary sweet into her mouth. 'Will you take some time off to spend with her?'

Freya made a noncommittal sound. 'I'll see how busy things are.'

She'd taken on board what Lucas had said. Hearing the woman in the homeless shelter tell her that she was trapped inside her own head, and that her lonely past was affecting everything in her present, had shocked her. Hearing pretty much the same thing from Lucas had forced her into action.

She still hadn't discussed with him the issue at heart exactly—that she'd grown up feeling more or less abandoned by her mother, even if teenage hormones had played a small part—but she'd invited Liv to visit with a mind to also asking their mother and Stijn to visit the house and clear the air at the same time. They'd be a family unit for the first time in years.

The thought both excited her and made her feel nauseous, which was probably what was preventing her from setting a date with Liv for her visit. What if she finally confronted her mother about her lack of maternal instinct and Elise was offended, or refused to admit she'd done anything wrong, or severed ties with Freya altogether? She'd be worse off than she was now…abandoned all over again.

But, regardless of the outcome, everything was pointing to the fact that she at least had to try to take control of her own narrative. She would have thanked Lucas for the intervention—so to speak—but she hadn't seen him.

It had been a week since their little spat in the hallway, followed by the best kiss she'd ever had, and he'd since taken personal leave of his own. She had no idea why—maybe he regretted it? Time off hadn't been scheduled into his calendar before, but the surgeries that needed his exceptional skills had been postponed; the others being covered by the locum surgeon.

She was aching to know what was going on with him, but just the fact that she was bothered to this extent worried her. It wasn't something she was used to, and she hadn't come here to feel like this for a guy— even one as gorgeous as Lucas— so she hadn't tried to call him, which was just as well, seeing that he hadn't contacted her either.

'I can't wait to see the house,' Joy said, sipping her tea. 'Doing up one of those heritage houses would be like my dream renovation project. If you need any help, I'd be happy to share my idea boards with you…'

Freya said thank you, and listened politely to her suggestions for furniture stores and vintage markets around the Netherlands, but her head was still lost in Lucas. She'd gone over the possible reasons for him not contacting her a hundred times, whilst telling herself she didn't care.

Maybe the humiliation of Pieter walking in on them had been too much for him, though in fairness Pieter hadn't seemed all that shocked. He'd been trying to set them up together ever since she'd set foot through the hospital doors.

Maybe Lucas was regretting getting personal with another colleague after being involved with that medical illustrator from India who'd gone home... She never had found out the details of exactly what had happened there. Lucas had been pretty evasive, as usual.

Anyway, it was highly unprofessional of both of them to have exchanged heated words in the hallway, and then given into their raging desires, even though she and Lucas had been dancing in circles around each other for weeks. It had always felt inevitable that something would snap eventually.

That night, she arrived home late and exhausted, on two tired feet. Her elderly neighbour, Jolene, called out to her through the shutters of her chocolate box house next door. Jolene was sprightly and lithe as any Dutch woman in her seventies who'd spent her whole life cycling in the open air. She reminded Freya of Anouk—the two had been good friends.

'Freya! *Je hebt een levering*...a delivery for you. I keep it inside, in *de gang*.'

'For me?' Freya racked her frazzled brain, but she was sure she hadn't ordered anything.

'*Wacht hier*...wait there, I'll bring it out.'

Seconds later, Jolene's front door burst open, and she emerged from the hallway wheeling a bright red, brand-new bicycle. She propped it on the pavement on its stand next to Freya and they both walked around it in the streetlights, admiring the reflectors in the pedals, the gears and dynamo lights, and the silver bell. Jolene dinged it with her finger. 'Nice,' she enthused.

There was even a black wire basket on the front, and a ribbon tied around the leather saddle. Freya was stunned. 'Are you sure it's for me?'

'That's what the note says.' Jolene pointed to the sealed envelope with her name in block capitals on the front. Two separate chunky chain locks sat coiled next to it like snakes in the basket. 'Someone must like you a lot.'

The butterflies zoomed straight back into her belly as Jolene squeezed her arm affectionately and left her alone.

Freya crossed to the bridge over the canal and leaned across the wrought-iron railings, feeling the tickle of the purple petunias against one leg as they waved from their decorative box. Sliding the notecard from the envelope, she found she was holding her breath as she read it. Lucas had sent it—but why would he vanish after kissing her and then send her such a lovely gift? If he was trying to distance himself from her, this was a strange way of going about it.

'Dr Van de Berg! Over here!' Little Violet was sitting up in her bed, clutching a pink frizzy-haired doll to her chest while Joy adjusted her tube. 'I heard that podcast you did the other day, Dr Van de Berg. My mum listened to it twice in the car.'

Lucas caught Freya's eye. She was chatting with a teenage patient and his parents at the next bed, and her long hair was once again piled up on the top of her head in a bun.

He watched a flicker of surprise cross her face, no doubt over his appearance after being gone for over a week, but Violet was tugging on his sleeve, urging him closer so she could whisper in his ear. 'She said you have a nice voice, I like it, too.'

'Well, thank you very much, Violet. You have a very nice voice too.'

Joy told the girl jokingly not to inflate his ego and Violet grinned with gappy teeth. The child was the nine-year-old queen of the ward. Their last cardiologist had diagnosed her Ebstein anomaly and ASD, but rare abnormalities with her heart's tricuspid valve meant in spite of two surgical procedures she was on constant watch for congestive heart failure. Her parents had taken to rushing her in every time she as much as coughed, but she lived like nothing was wrong with her at all. An inspiration, if ever he'd met one. She'd been on the transplant list for a while now and he was hopeful she would get her new heart soon. He looked forward to another successful transplant, and seeing her live a full, healthy life away from this place once and for all.

'Good to have you back, Doctor.' Joy adjusted her hair behind her ears, while Violet reached for another doll and started brushing its blue hair, indifferent to the blood coursing visibly through her tubes.

'I hope you got some rest while you were away?' she added, as if he'd been sunning himself on a beach in the Caribbean instead of launching a family-sized search party for his missing father. 'I heard your podcast, too.'

'Which podcast was that?' Freya was at his side now.

'"The Heart of It" podcast,' Joy carried on, plucking a stray piece of lint from Lucas's coat and making him smile as they moved from Violet's bedside. He saw Freya watching them, a frown appearing on her face momentarily then vanishing just as quickly.

As she walked at his side he was struck by a flashback of her lips on his, her hands in his hair…how he'd wanted to taste more, so much more of her. While he'd been away, she'd been there with him at night, in his head and his dreams at least, although he'd been operating at maximum capacity by day with no time to act on his romantic desires.

His family was in shreds, deciding the fate of his father. Fred Van de Berg, a man of formidable intellect and pride, was now in the stage of his debilitating disease that meant he'd spent three days AWOL. No one had been able to find him until two nights ago. His brother was now adamant they put him in a home. His mother was beside herself with worry, and Lucas still had to appear at work as if everything was normal.

'He was on a panel, talking about what differentiates a successful surgeon from a not-so-successful one. He said…if you don't mind me saying, Lucas… that you have to go into the zone where you're calm and collected, even if a child is dying before your eyes. It almost made me cry; the things you must have had to put yourself through.'

Joy carried on as though she'd memorised the entire podcast. He had to remind himself to stay in that zone now, the one where he was calm and collected, but Freya's eyes were searching his with new curiosity and questions. Now he was back in her presence, he realised he should have called her after what had happened in the storeroom. He just hadn't known what to say to her, especially while he'd been distracted by his father.

He'd arrived at the conclusion that it was better not to say anything to anyone about what was going on at home until it was absolutely necessary. He didn't want everyone constantly asking him how he was every five minutes, or thinking he had something on his mind when he was conducting life or death surgical procedures, especially as Anne Marie and Ruben were going to be in and out over the following weeks, discussing their baby's diagnosis. It was as shocking to him as them; he knew they'd been trying for a second child for months.

He didn't need anyone doubting his professional focus for any reason at all, especially not Freya, though *she* was on his mind, whether he wanted her there or not.

Joy was still talking about the podcast. "'A surgeon has to be proficient physically, as much as mentally…' I liked the way you said that, Lucas. I bet a lot of people don't think about that when they start out on the road towards becoming a paediatric surgeon. If you don't apply that knife, or put that stitch in exactly the right place, you could lose a child.' She lowered her voice even more. 'Any one of these children…'

He stopped by the door, checking his watch. 'What I said was, it doesn't matter what your IQ is, or how many books you've read. You have to keep your wits about you, or you could totally fall apart, do something unprofessional in front of your team…'

'I can't imagine you doing that,' Freya said, her voice almost forcing his eyes to hers. 'You would never do anything unprofessional in front of your team, would you, Doctor?'

She arched an ironic eyebrow at him. Freya was referring to the way he'd pulled her into that storeroom and kissed her…

Maybe he shouldn't have done it, but she'd been driving him nuts, and he hadn't been able to help himself.

He almost hadn't sent her the bicycle either, but that was something she needed; a necessity to get to work on time.

The impulse purchase was a result of seeing her so lost that time, stranded on her own. He hated to think of her in that situation. Even someone as independent as Freya needed help sometimes and if he could afford to do that, he would.

That's what he'd told himself anyway.

'Well, sometimes we all do things we regret,' he stated. It was true, he regretted what he'd said to her about her mother. It had been driven by his own fears about losing his father—something that was becoming ever more real. He didn't regret the kiss, however—good idea or not, it had been one of the hottest encounters of his adult life.

'I guess we do…do things we regret,' Freya said thoughtfully, and Joy scrunched her nose up, looking between them, like she was trying and failing to connect the dots.

'Are we still talking about the podcast?' she asked.

CHAPTER TWELVE

Due to the surgery schedule, Freya didn't see Lucas again all day, not even to thank him for the bicycle in person. She'd sent a message on the night he'd had it delivered, but he hadn't replied till the next day and even then all he'd written was *Graag gedaan*—You're welcome.

She knew he'd been busy recently, though, even more than usual. He'd just performed an operation on teenage football star Valerie Maijer-Schrot. She had already been through a series of consultations and now Lucas had performed a minimally invasive procedure using new, revolutionary methods on her sunken chest.

The operation would ultimately leave little to no scarring, but thanks to Valerie's incessant tweeting and praise for her 'handsome Dr Van de Berg' it had invited a media frenzy outside the hospital and given most of the staff a headache.

Freya had had to fight her way through a crowd after work, having accepted Joy's invitation to grab some dinner at one of her favourite restaurants across town.

'This is amazing,' Freya enthused, when they were sitting at a table covered in a red and white checked tablecloth. They each had a plate of *stamppot*—steaming mashed potato, gravy and meatballs. 'Like a hug from the inside,' she noted.

Joy bobbed her head, chewing on her food with a look that reflected her name. 'It's my absolute favourite,' she said, reaching for her wine. 'Not as good as the one Lucas used to make, but pretty close. Did you put some cranberry sauce on it? That really sets it off.'

The mention of Lucas made adrenaline pulse in her veins but Freya tried not to show it. 'Lucas used to have dinner parties, I heard that.' She took a sip of her own wine, trying to appear indifferent.

'He held a lot more when Roshinda was around. What do you think he did during his personal time off, by the way? Did he tell you if he went anywhere?'

Freya shook her head, and busied her mouth with a forkful of mashed potato. She hated to gossip, but that had been before Lucas had kissed her and then gone AWOL, which had upset her more than she had admitted, even to herself. She'd been thrown by their kiss, and confused about her feelings enough, without him disappearing on her too. 'Maybe he just needed a break,' she offered after a moment, leaving out *from me*.

Joy made a *pffft* sound. 'He never takes time off. I hope he's OK. Poor Lucas, he works so hard. He's probably having a rough time knowing he might have to operate on his friend's baby. Ruben's great…'

'You know him too?'

'Yeah, we met at one of Lucas's parties. We really should get Lucas cooking again on his houseboat. If you're lucky he'll get his snake out!'

Freya almost choked on her wine. 'What?' She dragged a hand across her mouth, scrambling for her napkin.

'A python. He gets it out sometimes for people…'

Joy giggled to herself like she was amused by her own innuendo. 'What did you think I meant?'

Freya was sure her cheeks must have flushed scarlet. Joy didn't know about their kiss, and she couldn't bring it up. Lucas clearly regretted it, he'd said it himself in so many words. Earlier on the ward he'd said, 'Well, sometimes we do things we regret,' and he'd been looking straight at her.

'You know...something pretty bad must have happened with his ex to make him close his houseboat off to his friends.' Joy pushed the last forkful of mash around her plate thoughtfully. 'They seemed so happy one minute and the next she was gone. No explanation. I mean, why would she just up and leave a man like *Lucas*?'

'Maybe it was his snake?'

'Oh, my God.' Joy burst out laughing, and several people turned from their tables. Her laugh was infectious and Freya couldn't help joining in. It felt good to be in a restaurant, laughing with a friend, even if she still couldn't quite get away from the subject of Lucas Van de Berg. She was wondering yet again why Roshinda had left 'a man like Lucas', which was annoying. It was bad enough she was thinking about him so much after his absence, she didn't want to be thinking about his past relationships, too.

'So...' Joy clasped her hands together under her chin. 'Enough about men. When is your sister getting here? You mentioned she might visit.'

Freya pushed the salt shaker to the next square on the tablecloth. 'That's a good question.'

Guilt flooded in again. Why couldn't she just book Liv a damn ticket? They could see their mother together, it would all be fine. She was making a big deal out of nothing…that was how Lucas probably perceived it anyway, seeing her cancelling calls and feeding excuses to poor Liv. She didn't know why else he was so wound up over her cancelling the odd call to her mother in front of him. Then again, there *were* still things he wasn't telling her about his father; that much she was sure of.

What a mess.

Unexpectedly Joy reached a hand across the red and white checks and placed it over hers. 'I'm guessing something happened with your sister?'

'It's more our mother, actually,' she confessed, feeling a lump spring up in her throat at Joy's kindness. 'We're not close, me and Mum.'

Joy squeezed her hand. 'Well, if you ever need someone to talk to about it, or just to take your mind off it, I'm right here.'

'Thank you, Joy.' Freya realised she had tears in her eyes suddenly. She could hear Anouk's voice now, loud in her head, as if she were sitting with a plate of meatballs at the next table: *'A problem shared is a problem halved, Freya.'*

Just airing things out loud to someone, a female friend, was nice. She'd missed that since college. She was realising now that when it came to her so-called 'failed' relationships, maybe Beatrice had broken more of her heart than Johnny had.

'He's going to require three open heart surgeries, one right after birth, one at about four months, and the third one could be at about two or three years old…'

'And what about after that? Be honest with us, Lucas.' Anne Marie's eyes were pleading, and Lucas tried not to look at Freya. It wasn't easy delivering news like this to anyone, let alone friends, and he was already doing his best to keep his emotions in check, knowing his own family needed him more than ever, while he was here at the hospital dealing with everything from famous teenage football stars like Valerie, to the underlying tension between him and Freya, to this.

Freya cut in suddenly. 'After that, well, we would do everything in our power to keep him going, and strong enough for a heart transplant.'

'A heart transplant, when he's just a toddler?' Anne Marie's eyes flooded with desperate tears.

'Unless you want to schedule the prenatal surgery, which, as you already know, is very high risk, then those are our options.'

'It's all high risk,' Lucas said. 'It's not fair on you for us to sugar-coat it, guys. With the intact atrial septum on top of the defect, his chances of survival without the prenatal surgery are small...minuscule. With no left ventricle his lungs would be filling with fluid from the get-go, and with all that congestion there's a slim chance he would make it to the first surgery after he's born.'

'I've been researching this condition for hours already.' Anne Marie put a hand to her swollen belly and made a weary sound as her back hit the couch.

'She has. I can't get her away from the laptop.' Ruben arranged some cushions behind her and took her hand, and Lucas watched Freya stand and cross the room. She lit another aromatherapy candle, but he wondered if it was more for her own benefit, to soothe her own busy mind in a tricky situation.

This was a lot for her to deal with too. As well as the chemistry between them that they were trying to ignore, it was tough, having a personal connection to a patient, even through him.

Anne Marie sniffed. 'We just don't know what to do.'

'Lucas is the best surgeon for the job,' Freya interjected. 'I'm sure you know that. If you want to know what I would do, I would go for the foetal intervention.'

He met her eyes, and she nodded, as if permitting him to continue explaining. She had invited him in here for this consultation after all, it being a special situation. 'I use ultrasound to help guide a catheter through the baby's abdomen,' he told them. 'We go in, poke a needle through the septum, expand it with a balloon, and place a stent in there.'

'We'll have to run more tests to see if the baby is eligible for the procedure,' Freya said, taking a seat again beside him. 'We need to see if the atrial septum is likely to withstand the pressure first, and check that the left atrium is developed enough, otherwise the needle could pierce through the other side of the heart, which would mean more complications.'

'I'm sorry for all the waiting,' Lucas said. 'But if the baby is eligible, I'm confident I can perform the procedure successfully.'

'We just need you to be aware of every single potential outcome, no matter what you choose to do,' Freya added.

'You're doing everything you can, both of you.' Ruben was composed, but Anne Marie was looking at Freya, lips trembling. 'So…if he's not eligible for the foetal intervention, we might just get to hold him for a few seconds after he's born, and then he'll be gone?'

'We would try for the open heart surgery, with your consent, of course,' Freya explained, but Anne Marie didn't seem as if she'd heard. She was sobbing uncontrollably now with one hand on her belly and one over her eyes, and all they could do was watch helplessly as she left the room.

'I'll go after her. Sorry, we'll be right back,' Ruben muttered, racing after her.

Freya paced the length of the room, hands on her hips.

'It's a lot to take in,' he said, needlessly.

She swiped the strands of loose hair from her bun behind her ears and looked at the ceiling fan. 'It's always so hard,' she said in a choked voice. 'You know… you try and put yourself in their position, at least I do, as a woman. Carrying a child that might not make it, just the thought almost scares me off even trying to have a baby…ever.'

'Really?'

She screwed up her nose. 'I don't know why I just said that, sorry. This isn't about me, I know they're your friends.'

'You can tell me,' he said.

'Maybe it's not just my work that stops me wanting children,' she ventured after a second.

He waited for her to expand, perhaps admit that her transient lifestyle might be the real reason she wouldn't feel comfortable about bringing a baby into the world, but she said, 'Maybe I also think being a bad mother might run in the family.'

He sighed through his nose and stood up. What she'd said was utterly ridiculous. 'Freya, your mother wasn't the best mother, I get it, and I'm sorry if I sounded so… insensitive before, when I said you should just talk to her—'

'You had a point,' she cut in.

He was thrown for a moment. 'OK…well…anyway, like I said, whatever happened between you and your mother is nothing that can't be fixed. It's not too late. She's still alive, isn't she?'

He fought the urge to tilt her face up to his and kept his hands to himself. 'She's still calling you, wanting to talk, even if you're too afraid to face what she might want to say. And as for not wanting kids… I'd hate to see you ruling that option out because I think you're great with children. It's clear to everyone in this hospital that you're a natural with them.'

She scanned his eyes without moving away, like she didn't know whether to be offended or flattered. Then she walked to the window.

Lucas picked up Roshinda's journal for something to do with his hands, but it suddenly felt like a hot coal so he stood and tossed it into a drawer behind the desk.

'So, how are you doing?' he ventured, when the silence got too loud.

'I don't know how to answer that, it feels like a loaded question,' she answered, with her back to him. 'I guess we're both trying to forget what happened between us…in the storeroom.'

He rubbed his jaw, taken aback by her bringing that up. 'I assumed it was a one-off, caught up in the moment kind of thing,' he said finally.

Freya spun around. 'So, why did you buy me a bike?'

He couldn't read her now. Was she mad about the bike? She'd texted him to thank him and she hadn't sounded angry. Women were so complicated. 'I thought you needed it,' he said cautiously.

'I did, thank you, but I could have bought my own bike.'

'I know that.'

The sigh that came out of her mouth was like pent-up steam from an ancient kettle. 'You kissed me, Lucas…'

'It was a *great* kiss,' he said, allowing a smile to cross his lips just thinking about it. 'You're a very kissable woman, Freya.'

An answering smile played on her mouth for a second before she rolled her eyes and crossed her arms. 'This past week, it was pretty unexpected, you just *not* being here after we kissed like that…'

'I had some family issues,' he said simply.

'Is everything OK, Lucas?' Freya was looking at him in a way that made his jaw clench.

'It's not really something I can discuss here,' he said after a beat, seeing his dad again in his mind's eye, the way he'd been when they'd found him. Fred had no recollection of how or why he had driven himself to the cabin they used to spend summers in as kids, way down in Gelderland. He had been banned from driving anywhere now.

'I see,' said Freya. 'You can't talk about it, of course.'

He tensed. He'd told himself to keep his distance, to keep his family's issues private, but they were a team above anything else, now more than ever. He didn't just want her to trust him now, he needed her to, as a colleague, even if she'd never be anything else. He couldn't have her thinking he didn't trust *her*.

'It's my dad, Freya. I haven't told anyone here yet…'

'Your dad?' Her voice was softer, worried. 'Lucas, what's happened?'

The door swung open slowly. Ruben was back. 'We'll talk, I promise, but not here,' he managed quickly, right as Freya tore her eyes from Lucas's and hurried to assist a tear-stained Anne Marie back towards the couch.

CHAPTER THIRTEEN

THE NEXT DAY Freya lugged a box of clothes down the three flights of stairs, past the now cleared-out kitchen on the lower floor and into the street. It just about fitted into her bicycle basket, even though most of it was bulging over the sides and spilling over with Anouk's sweaters and shoes.

'I'm going to the shelter again,' she explained to Liv. The phone was still pressed precariously to her shoulder and she fumbled with her headphones.

'Again?' Liv sounded suspicious. 'Let me guess, this has something to do with your heart surgeon?'

'I just have to drop some things off. And, yes, I will talk to Lucas if he's there. It's hard to talk at work about private matters, as you can imagine.'

'Private matters? You have private matters with Lucas now, do you?' Liv was teasing her.

'We barely get any time one on one, when we're not with patients and their families,' she explained as she started making her way on two wheels along the cobbled streets in the direction of *Inloophuis*.

'One on one, hmm…'

'I think he wants to tell me something important,' she confessed.

'I'm sure he does…' Liv trailed off with a laugh, and Freya felt her nerves fray even further, taking a left along the canal. 'You seem very invested for someone who's always so…'

'So what?'

'So *anti* having a man in her life.'

Freya cringed. Was that how she really came across?

'So listen.' Liv was getting down to business. 'You told me to come up with some dates for my flight. Did you get the email I sent with my options?'

'I did. Joy's going to help me get the room ready for you. It won't be too much longer now.'

Liv tutted and blew air through her lips. 'Fine. I guess we're getting there slowly, but you're still way too busy for your own good, Freya. Is Joy a new friend of yours?'

'She works at the hospital.'

'You haven't talked about a girlfriend in a while. Does she know you'll be packing your bags soon, never to be seen again? Does *Lucas* know that?'

'Very funny. I'll speak to you later. Enjoy your night!'

'I have a date,' Liv cut in excitedly. 'He's an artist. I'll let you know how it goes. We all know artists are cheap, though, not like your heart surgeons…'

'I'm really glad you're moving on, Liv. Bye!' She hung up, narrowly missing a dog walker with her front wheel.

Liv certainly knew how to push her buttons. Freya started thinking about the job in Vietnam again. Maybe she should think about applying. The start date was early in the new year but there would be interviews and a site visit first…and then she'd have a deadline for starting another exciting new adventure.

She held up a hand to the lovely lady at the flower stall, who recognised her and waved back. That was definitely still her intention—to leave. Wasn't it?

'No tulips today, Freya?' the lady called as Freya passed, dinging her bell over the precarious box in her basket. She was packing up her stall for the night, stacking buckets by the roadside.

'I'll be back for some tomorrow!'

She'd taken tulips to the consultation room most days since she'd started at the hospital. Lucas always stopped to smell them, as if he was trying to gauge if they were real…

She caught herself.

Lucas.

They'd talked about the kiss at least. He'd said it wasn't why he hadn't been at the hospital for over a week.

It wasn't just a box of shoes and sweaters that was propelling her forward tonight, she forced herself to admit. It was the prospect of seeing him, talking to him. He had finally started to open up and she hoped that whatever the problem was with his father, it wasn't too serious. She feared it was, though, and that it could be the reason he'd been so hell bent on her mending her relationship with her mother.

At the shelter, Lucas was chopping carrots like a pro on a giant red chopping board. The kitchen at the end of the huge dining hall was buzzing with action, and the air was rich with the comforting smell of tomatoes and garlic. It made her stomach growl.

'Doesn't he look cute in an apron?' Kate said on her way past with a raw carrot to nibble on.

Lucas did indeed look cute in his denim apron. He was wearing jeans and a burgundy striped T-shirt that showed off his muscled arms. Even sexier was the fact that he seemed to be in full control of a group of nine volunteers, ordering them to chop and sieve and stir a series of bubbling pots and sizzling pans.

'Hey, Freya.' He put his knife down when he saw her. Everyone turned to watch as he slid the door open at the serving hatch and made his way out to her. 'What are you doing here?'

'I bring gifts,' she said, dropping the box on the end of one of the long steel tables. She caught the eye of the guy she'd seen here before, the guy with one arm and the military tattoo. Martijn. He winked at her, like he knew something she didn't, then winced for some reason, turning back to the sink, where he was rinsing lettuce in a colander.

Lucas had stopped in front of her, his six-foot-something frame blocking the bustle in the kitchen. He seemed to be unsure of how to greet her. In the end he lowered his head and dropped a sideways kiss against her left cheek, and the move left her throat dry and her stomach swooping again.

'You kept your promise. Thanks for this.'

'There's more where that came from,' she said, avoiding the intensity of his blue eyes. She could still feel his hands in her hair, and hers cupping his glorious backside as they'd kissed furiously. They'd totally broken the vacuum cleaner in a fit of passion and suddenly she felt an uncontrollable urge to kiss him again, properly, in private, where they couldn't be interrupted.

'So, what are you cooking?' she asked, when she realised they were still standing there staring at each other with everyone trying to pretend they weren't watching.

'Tonight is spaghetti night. We add whatever veggies get dropped off—nothing goes to waste on my watch. Do you want to help?'

Freya allowed herself to be led to a space at the worktop, next to Lucas. Before she knew it she was clad in a matching apron, spreading butter over what felt like a thousand white baguettes, ready to be made into garlic bread. The high ceilings didn't do a lot to help the temperature. Lucas swiped the back of one hand across his forehead. *Hot, to say the least.*

Lucas gave orders to the team every now and then, crossing items and duties off a giant whiteboard on the wall by the industrial refrigerators and dishwashers. He seemed to know just what he was doing, and she enjoyed the happy chatter all around her, even if it was mostly in Dutch. It took the edge off being alone with Lucas.

'So, you started telling me something about your dad,' she said quietly. 'Is everything OK? I wasn't even sure if you'd be here tonight.'

'Every Tuesday,' he said. 'I'm here without fail.' He glanced around him and put down his knife, wiping his hands on his apron. His expression was sombre now. 'But, yes, I was with him when I was on leave. Well, I was *looking* for him, actually.'

'Looking for him?'

Martijn let out a cough over by the sink. It was so loud she sprang from Lucas's side, realising now that she'd stepped even closer to him to talk. Her bare arm brushed his in her T-shirt and she shivered at the slightest contact, goosebumps spreading up her forearm. Why on earth did he have this effect on her?

'Are you OK, Martijn?' Lucas was looking at the guy in concern, over her head. Martijn had his one hand pressed to his chest.

He said something in Dutch. 'Indigestion?' Lucas replied. 'You haven't even eaten anything yet! Go sit down, man, if you feel bad.'

Martijn shrugged, winced again slightly, but carried on rinsing things with one hand under the giant hose of a tap.

'Stubborn fool,' Lucas muttered, and Freya smiled, noting the German Shepherd sitting patiently by the door to the dining room with his tongue lolling out, sniffing the air. Martijn's dog.

'So, yeah, we had to look for my dad. He was gone for three whole days. My mum's now under strict orders not to let him have the car keys any more, which is tough as they've always had so many social obligations, even more since Dad retired.'

'Why can't he leave?'

There was a long pause.

He has Alzheimer's,' he said finally.

Freya's hand found Lucas's arm. Her fingers curled halfway around his biceps. 'I'm so sorry.'

'It's getting worse. Initially, he was diagnosed with mild cognitive impairment. Then we got the updated diagnosis of Alzheimer's. Mum thought he was just becoming a little forgetful, and Dad thought he was just a bit foggy, till he filed a paycheque in one of her cookbooks. Fast forward to last week. He got into the car and drove without knowing where he was going. Then he got there and forgot to come back.'

Freya swallowed. She could tell by the look in his eyes that he was devastated. She'd been too wrapped up in her own thoughts, especially after that encounter in the storeroom. At one point she'd even entertained the thought he might have taken leave just to avoid her! How egotistical was that?

'I don't want the team to know,' he said resolutely, turning to her. 'Not until they really need to.'

'But they'd all understand. They respect you, they admire you. They'd totally appreciate the need to be with your family right now, if it's taking time off that you're worried about.'

'It's not just that,' he admitted, piling chopped carrots into a huge silver bowl. 'We both know we need to focus while we're at work, Freya, there's a lot at stake right now. My dad has the family around him, we're a tight-knit unit.' He paused a moment, swiping his forehead with the back of his hand. 'Even though Simon, my brother, still wants to put him in a home. It's the first time we've had a serious disagreement in years, but he knows I'm right. Dad needs to stay with Mum as long as possible—they'd both go crazy without each other.'

Freya picked up her knife again. It sounded like his parents were still very much in love. 'I can't imagine losing someone slowly to a disease that steals your memories,' she said. 'To think I try so hard sometimes to block so many memories out.'

'I think we all do that,' he admitted quietly.

An almighty clatter from behind them made them both spin around. 'What the…?'

Martijn was on the floor, clutching his chest, surrounded by chopped-up lettuce that had fallen from the giant bowl. Shadow was barking and leaping at the serving hatch, trying his hardest to get to him. 'Martijn!'

Lucas was on his knees in a heartbeat. Freya dropped beside him, rolling him over to his side. Martijn was trying to speak, streams of Dutch that Freya was sure were incoherent, from what she understood anyway. 'Everyone back,' she heard Lucas yell. He called an ambulance while she placed Martijn's head on a folded towel, and the shocked crew in the kitchen scattered.

CHAPTER FOURTEEN

LUCAS GRABBED A pair of kitchen scissors from the hook
on the wall, but Freya took them from his hands. 'I'll
do it.'

He switched to being Martijn's head support as her
hands worked efficiently, quickly, cutting at his T-shirt.
It was the navy-blue one he'd given the man himself.

'Stay with us Martijn,' he urged, but Martijn's eyes
fluttered shut.

Nausea started to claim his stomach, which up until
a few seconds ago had been growling with hunger for
home-made spaghetti.

'He's breathing, but it's shallow.' Freya had switched
to medic mode. This was it. The worst-case scenario
he was supposed to be prepared for, but wasn't. His
hands worked on autopilot alongside Freya's, tipping
Martijn's head back, double-checking for a breath, even
an alcohol-soaked one, as was Martijn's wont.

'His heart rate's slowing,' he heard himself say.
Somewhere in the background someone was gasping
and sobbing. Freya rammed her hair back into a ponytail. 'The paramedics are on the way.We need the defib.'

'We're running out of time.'

He forced himself back into the zone he'd been talking about not so long ago to an audience in the podcast recording studio. He entered that zone every time a parent put their child in his expert hands in the OR. *Focus. Focus.* Not so easy when it was someone you knew, though, lying at your mercy in a critical state. The calm and centred stillness was eluding him now.

'We have to start CPR,' He was surprised that his authoritative tone conveyed no hint of what he was feeling inside.

It felt like hours passed in slow motion as he pumped Martijn's chest, feeling the rest of the room slip away, even as the heat in the kitchen threatened to choke him. 'Come on, man, breathe!'

A trickle of perspiration slid down his temple. Freya's brow was glistening too, but she ignored it. She was the one in the zone now. She was helping him as much as Martijn, but they seemed to be losing the fight.

Her hand landed steady on his shoulder. 'Let me,' she said, and he shifted aside, almost skidding on some lettuce as she took over the compressions, urgent, yet measured at the same time, as if she'd done this hundreds of times.

Suddenly it hit him. He hadn't met half the people she had, or been in half the situations she had, places with barely any medical care or equipment. Now he was glad of it, in awe of her skill. His heart was a painful, heavy lump in his chest.

Come on, Martijn, you've already survived so much. You're not going down because of a stupid heart attack now, are you? he thought desperately.

Somewhere in the distance a siren began to wail. He felt like he was dreaming, watching Freya's hair tumble down around her eyes as her ponytail came loose. He took over from her on autopilot, another set of compressions, but Martijn's lifeless body was already draining of colour. Two halves of his one-time favourite T-shirt were draped like tattered curtains on the floor on either side of his torso, where Freya had scissored it off him.

Why hadn't he seen the signs?

'Cardiac episode.' Lucas stood as the paramedics raced down the aisle of the dining hall towards them with a stretcher. He knew one of them, a guy called Jan. 'He's not responding to CPR. He said he had indigestion, and that was it.'

'No,' Feyola called out from the other end of the room now in her trademark bright magenta dress. This was the first time Lucas had noticed her tonight. 'Earlier, in the communal area, he said he felt weak. I thought he was just drunk again.'

Martijn's body was clear, apart from the shock pads the paramedics were now applying to his exposed chest. 'We did several rounds of compressions,' Freya explained, and he felt her hands clutching one forearm as she tried to urge him backwards, their duty done. It was no longer up to them to try and save Martijn. But he couldn't move further away than a few inches; his eyes and feet were glued to the scene. Why hadn't he seen the signs? He'd been with Martijn for two hours already, making jokes, trying to take his mind off his own family issues. Now this.

'Lucas, they're doing all they can for him.' Freya's hand found his now, and he observed the scene from a distant place outside his body as his friend's heavy chest rose and fell with each burst of power, like it was nothing but a useless sack of potatoes.

'Come on, man,' he urged again out loud. Shadow

was still barking. Somewhere at the other end of the dining hall Fayola and Kate had gathered the guests and volunteers, and several people were whimpering.

'Go again,' the paramedic yelled. Shadow whined helplessly and his heart broke. The dog knew something was very wrong.

'There's no response.' Jan shuffled around Martijn's body on the cold, hard floor. Freya flicked several leaves of lettuce aside with her feet, in some effort to preserve the homeless man's dignity.

Someone stood to attend to a pot of pasta that was boiling over, while someone else turned off the tap that Martijn had switched on moments before he'd keeled over.

'I can't believe this,' he muttered in Dutch. Freya's fingers tightened in his. He didn't have the capacity to speak in English right now, but her hand was like a lifeline, rooting him to her side, and to normality. He knew in an instant that if she wasn't here he might just crack open and then she'd see the full extent of his emotions...

He didn't even want to think about it.

The paramedics were yelling at each other now. More shocks were administered to Martijn's chest and still Lucas gripped her hand, realising he was actually praying, pleading to a God he rarely even thought about, let alone spoke to.

'There's nothing more we can do. He's gone. I'm sorry.'

Jan's words echoed around his skull as if they were coming from miles away. He felt hot and cold at the same time, staring at Martijn's bearded face turning pale. His lips were an eerie grey, almost blue. Just moments ago the guy had been winking at Freya, chopping a lettuce. What the hell…?

'Lucas?' Freya was talking to him now, standing in front of him, hands on his shoulders. He hadn't even heard what she'd said. He was watching Jan drape a sheet across Martijn's face.

Martijn was gone.

'Lucas.'

His anger rose and fell inside him like a tidal wave, blending with an epic sense of failure. He'd failed his friend…and himself.

Pulling his hand from Freya's, he tore off his apron and tossed it on the counter, forcing his legs to extract him from the scene and somehow get him to the exit.

The ambulance left to take Martijn's body to the hospital morgue for an autopsy, and Freya found Lucas outside with Shadow. The night was cooler now than before. A full moon threw a spotlight across the water, broken by ripples. It looked too idyllic a scene to have witnessed what had just happened. 'Lucas, I'm so sorry…'

'I should have picked up on the signs,' he insisted, shoving his hair back from his face.

'What? How could you have seen the signs, you said yourself he was stubborn, and didn't say anything to anyone.'

'He told Fayola he felt weak.'

'She wouldn't have known to think anything of it. Lucas, this is no one's fault, certainly not yours.'

He was sitting on the bench facing the canal, and she slid to his side, putting a hand tentatively on his arm again. Lucas looked exhausted and shocked and she could tell how much Martijn had meant to him. It was up to her to provide him with some modicum of strength at this moment, though she was trembling herself with adrenaline and despair.

Lucas hadn't let it show until the very end when he'd removed himself from the situation, but he was clearly devastated to have lost a friend. This, on top of what he'd told her before about his father. Her heart was going out to him.

'They asked about next of kin,' she said. Her voice came out choked. Lucas just shook his head. 'He had no one. No one but us.'

His shoulders sank a little lower and she placed a hand on his back, feeling helpless. 'It's a tragedy, Lucas. I'm so sorry. Is there anything I can do?'

'We have to go back in there... People still need to be fed.'

He made to stand up, but she pulled him back down with a strength that arose from nowhere. 'Fayola's taken over. She said it was the least she could do. They'll make do with what was already cooked... Lucas, you shouldn't even be thinking about that right now. We've given our reports, we've done all we can.'

He sucked in a breath and clasped his hands together on his knees. She knew there was nothing she could say or do except try to be there for him, if he wanted her to be.

Shadow let out another soft whine, shifting his fuzzy, heavy head to her feet. She put one hand down to stroke him, wondering momentarily what would happen to him now. He reminded her of a dog Anouk used to have and she remembered she'd seen boxes of pet care items at the house in her clear-out.

'I have some dog food and a bed for this guy at the house. I can take him with me.'

'That's good, because I left Sheba out at my place,' he replied, looking down at her hand on his knee. She hadn't even realised she'd put it there, but before she could move it, he flattened his palm on hers and brought her fingers to his lips, pressing a soft kiss to the back of her hand, letting his mouth linger there. 'Thank you for everything you did in there, Freya.'

'I'm just sorry it wasn't enough to save him.' Freya paused a moment, feeling the warmth where he'd kissed her hand start to creep up her arm, along the side closest to him. 'Your bike is here too, right? Why don't you come back with me and Shadow for a while? I can... make us some tea.'

Her invitation hung in the air like a star and he seemed to contemplate it. Either that or he hadn't even heard her through the thoughts that must have been whirring around in his brain. She stood and held a hand out, half expecting him to refuse, that he had to go home. 'I just kept seeing my father lying there,' he said instead. His voice was a rasp, like he was swallowing tears and fighting an urge to throw something at the same time.

She sat down again, surprised at how her eyes pooled just hearing him.

'He was so strong once too,' Lucas said. 'Now he's just... I don't know what the future holds for him. I don't even know if he has much of a future left. I can't help him fight his disease any more than I could help Martijn back there.'

'You can't think like that,' Freya told him sternly. 'Lucas, this just has to be a lesson, right? Make every moment count, do as much with your time together as you can. That's what you did with Martijn. He was probably so grateful and happy to have found your friendship for however long he had it.'

Without thinking, she rested her head softly against his shoulder. His hand came up slowly, almost hesitantly around the back of her neck, and she thought she felt him drop another kiss, as gentle as a feather, on the side of her head. It sent a lightning bolt of desire through her entire body.

This was one of those moments she'd remember for ever. It was tragic, impactful, but shared. Neither of them would have handled tonight the same without the other and she'd never, ever felt this way before, so connected to someone but so afraid of losing that connection at the same time. He probably wasn't looking for anything serious either. At least he hadn't implied it. And she'd gone out of her way to assure him of her desire to be alone, because being alone was safer—no one could hurt her with her walls up. After everything they'd been through, they were still at an impasse.

'Who is Sheba, by the way?' she asked eventually.

'My python,' he replied.

CHAPTER FIFTEEN

THE LIVING ROOM of Anouk's house with its high beamed ceilings felt too big, even with Lucas in it. Shadow made himself busy, sniffing around the space she'd cleared for him under the spiral staircase, as she carried two mugs of tea across the faded carpets. Lucas moved a folded bit of cardboard under one leg of the coffee table to steady it.

'Thank you. Like I said, there's a lot of work to do here.'

'I like it,' he said, and his eyes burned like hot coals into her side as she felt him watching her put the mugs down. To her surprise he caught her hand again from his position on the green velvet couch and held it tight, stroking one thumb with his. She stood there, feeling the room get smaller, and smaller. Then, tentatively, she sat beside him, drawing her legs up under her. They were both still in the clothes they'd worn earlier.

'I can order us a pizza,' she offered now, aware of his hand still in hers as much as the open bedroom door, which revealed the quirky four-poster bed and its old-fashioned drapes. She'd been sleeping in the downstairs room because it was Anouk's old bedroom, and the only one not rammed with stuff.

'The kitchen isn't really…well…' She motioned behind her to the kitchen with its unplugged oven and taped-shut cupboard doors, and Lucas gave her a half-smile.

'Those windmill tiles are a feature, you know,' he said. 'I already told you some people would pay a fortune for originals like those.'

'Well, maybe I'll leave them if they add to the value. I'll see what the estate agent says.'

He nodded thoughtfully. 'Do you have an estate agent yet?'

'I made a few calls,' she told him. It was the truth, though she hadn't followed up on their calls.

'Joy's helping me paint this weekend. We're getting one of the rooms ready for Liv,' she told him instead.

'Making friends, and amends, huh?' Lucas studied her eyes. 'That's really good to hear, Freya. Best news I've had all day, considering.' The sound of her name on his lips, in this house, somehow did funny things to her heart. He rubbed his temples with his fingers and let out a deep sigh of exhaustion, and she resisted the urge to tell him to lie down or something.

'Have you spoken to your mother yet?'

'Not about the stuff that matters,' she admitted, raking a hand through her hair and recalling the last brief call she'd answered, when her mother had said something about seeing her after taking a trip to see a favourite band in Miami. That had been right before Freya had explained she was busy and had to go. 'So, about that pizza…'

'I'm not hungry any more. Are you waiting till your sister gets here to talk to your mother?'

Freya raised a hand to bite her nails, then remembered she didn't do that any more. 'Maybe I thought having Liv with me would make it easier.'

'It's none of my business, you're right,' he said quickly, releasing her hand.

She struggled with what to say, staring at his trainers on the carpet, next to hers. 'You're helping me see I really do need to fix things with my family,' she said eventually. 'Anyway, why are we talking about me? I'm so sorry about tonight. I know Martijn meant a lot to you, and your ex too, right? You met him through her?'

She clutched her mug closer. *Why did you have to mention his ex?*

She knew why…they were getting too close, they were too alone. She was vulnerable with her feelings for him exposed, seeing his disappointment over her still not speaking to her mother, maybe because losing his father slowly to Alzheimer's made that almost as much his issue as it was hers.

She still had a healthy, thriving mother for all she knew, while his father was wasting away mentally. More than any of that, he cared about *her*.

She was just reprimanding herself for building up another wall between them when Lucas said, 'I should probably tell Roshinda what happened to Martijn, yes. To be honest with you, we don't speak. We haven't spoken since she left. She's married now. She's living her life, I'm living mine. You know how that goes.'

'She's married?' Freya reached down to pet Shadow as he dropped at Lucas's feet. This was news to her. Joy had said they'd seemed happy, but that Roshinda had left suddenly. Something Lucas had told her once in Vondelpark came back to her. 'You asked me once if my ex went off and married someone else. I thought you were being funny.'

'You remember that?' He seemed half-amused.

'I do.'

'You really do have a good memory, Freya.'

'To my own detriment, I can assure you. So she moved on from you pretty fast, then.'

'Does that surprise you?'

'Maybe,' she said. He shifted on the couch to face her. 'OK, yes, it does. You're kind of amazing.'

'Freya…'

Her heart started thudding at his close proximity. His blue eyes were seeing all of her, heart and soul, exposed. He placed a hand on the back of her neck again and drew her closer, pressing his lips to her forehead and inhaling long and hard against her skin, as if breathing her in was keeping him alive, or awake, maybe both. It was late.

'I really didn't want to like you, you know. You're Freya with the wings, after all.'

'And you're Lucas with the roots.' Her hands came up over his like she didn't have a choice in the matter. She wasn't sure what she was looking for; maybe a reason not to kiss him, but it felt like an age passed as she still sat there frozen, waiting.

She wasn't sure if she pressed her lips to his exquisite mouth first, or if Lucas initiated it, but before she knew it they were kissing passionately and furiously, channelling all the pain of the evening into something else, something that might make them both forget.

As they fumbled their way to the bedroom she felt his lips on hers, as full and strong as they had been when they'd crashed together in the storeroom that first time, only now with added intensity on all counts. She could feel without a doubt that there was more he wanted—needed—from her and she would only be kidding herself if she pretended it wasn't mutual.

Tumbling to the bed, Lucas tugged at her shirt and she lifted her arms, letting him worship her with kisses to her breasts and stomach as her blood fizzed to the centre of her being. He lowered her to her back and the passionate kisses turned slow, loving, tender as his hands tangled up in her hair, and his thumbs caressed her cheeks and left tingles on her lips.

They lay there like that for what felt like for ever, exploring each other's mouths with a newfound delicious intimacy. It was the kind of connection some long-dormant part of her had been longing for, and pushing away for so many years, with so many guys who'd dared to like her. They didn't speak, not with words at least, as her desire finally got the better of her, and her hands made swift work of unbuckling his jeans.

Lucas straddled her, and she shivered at the burning desire in his stare, feeling his blue eyes grazing her body in appreciation. He exuded a special kind of hunger that was usually reserved for encounters like this. Strangely, she wasn't self-conscious at all. She was naked in so many ways already, after what they'd just experienced, after everything she'd already told him.

He brushed her cheek with a finger, so soft yet it still left sparks, and looked deeply into her eyes. Something had shifted back at the shelter, not just because of losing Martijn. This was grief, but so much more.

'I want you,' he half growled, lowering his muscled chest to half an inch above her naked breasts, to suck on her lower lip, then her nipples in a way that made her groan and reach a hand out to grip a bedpost.

'I don't want you at all,' she heard herself teasing, as if her actions weren't showing him how much that *wasn't* true. His breathing was coming heavier, more desirous, and when he reached behind him and pulled a condom from his discarded wallet, something told her their long night wasn't going to be over for a few more hours yet. He was tender with her, taking his time getting started, and she savoured the feeling of the length of him, feeling every part of her start to buzz in utter bliss, so much bliss she almost forgot the horror of the evening they'd just endured.

Maybe he was feeling the same. Maybe he was losing himself in her, trying to block what had just happened from his mind.

She didn't let those thoughts get in the way of what she was feeling; so what if he was? Wasn't she doing the same thing? He kissed her lips and their tongues danced as he moved slowly, gently, inside her, the shadows of their bodies making new shapes together on the patterned wallpaper.

The glare of a streetlamp cast a faint orange glow over their entwined limbs, almost confusing them for one entity, moving together. The euphoria she was experiencing was unlike anything she'd known in a long, long time, maybe ever, she mused to herself, feeling a smile find its way to her lips beneath his kisses.

Their bodies found a delicious rhythm as they moved, changed positions, utilised every inch of the four-poster bed. She lost track of time as they explored a new-found intimacy and his body changed before her eyes from that of something sexy to look at to something that offered shelter, protection…unadulterated bliss.

When she felt him shake and shudder with release, she let the ecstasy overwhelm her too, and she clenched her hands around the posts on either side of the bed, trembling with reaction as he finally pulled away.

'Wow,' they both said at the same time.

Lucas let out a quiet laugh that felt like a gentle wave washing over her and laid his head against her shoulder, one arm splayed over her naked breasts. Their legs had somehow got tangled in the top sheet and a warm breeze soothed her sweaty skin from the open window.

They were both breathing heavily, coming back to earth, and they indulged in the satiated silence as Shadow's paws made pattering sounds on the hardwood floor around the rugs.

'I think I want to do that again,' she heard herself say.

'It would be my pleasure, Doctor.'

CHAPTER SIXTEEN

'You saved my life, Dr Van de Berg. I just wanted to say thank you.'

Valerie Maijer-Schrot's blonde ponytail bounced through the ring of her baseball hat as she thrust the giant bouquet of flowers at Lucas. He watched Freya's face break into a smile behind the teen as he pulled out a brown, fuzzy toy bear from the depths of the polythene and petals.

'A bear...very cute... Oh, and it's wearing your football team's T-shirt.'

Valerie took it from his hands. 'My team got together to get you this. You can put it here to remind you of us. Next time we win a match, we'll have you to thank. And when I play in the Women's Championships, I'll also have you to thank.'

She sat the bear up against the vase of tulips by the window, which Freya had arranged that morning. He'd bought the tulips for the consultation room this time, when they'd walked past the stand on the way to the hospital together. It was the third time he'd stayed at her house in as many nights this week, under the pretence of helping her walk Shadow.

He knew full well he was walking the edge of a

cliff—she still hadn't said anything about extending her contract here in the new year, and he knew he could be getting in too deep with her considering her track record for flying away, but he couldn't deny himself the delicious tangle of limbs and the taste of her when they ended up in the bedroom…every single time.

Maybe they could just enjoy a fling?

He cleared his throat as Valerie took a photo of the bear with the flowers on her phone before taking back the seat next to her mother on the couch. 'So how are you feeling after your operation?'

'Great,' Valerie enthused. 'I should be able to get back to training soon, right?'

Her mother put a hand out to tug affectionately on her daughter's ponytail. 'Honey, you know Dr Van de Berg won't encourage that.'

Valerie scoffed, crossing her arms over her Cougar Football League shirt. 'I feel fine, Mum. He fixed me, didn't he?'

'Dr Van de Berg…' Mrs Maijer-Schrot looked at him beseechingly. 'Please will you just tell her? She keeps asking me when she can train.'

The mother of their patient had short blonde hair cropped close to her head, and a scarlet red sports jacket zipped to the neck that belied the warm weather. Freya perched on the edge of the couch close to Lucas—so close he could have pulled her onto his lap. He could see a hint of her bare leg and the blue of her pencil skirt, and he suddenly ached to be back in bed with her again.

'As Dr Van de Berg explained before,' Freya said, just the sound of her voice causing momentary flashbacks to them writhing naked, early that morning, making the most of the ten-minute snooze button she'd just pressed on her alarm clock, 'the minimally invasive procedure he performed on your pectus excavatum, or your sunken chest—'

'I prefer the first one, my coach said it sounds like a magic spell—*pectus excavatum*.'

'OK…well, the procedure went very well. The operation took only two small incisions and forty-five minutes of operating time, but even though you experienced much less pain, and minimal blood loss, *and* you're healing much faster than you would have done if another doctor had performed a more invasive surgery, you have to remember, Valerie, your body still went through a huge trauma with this condition. You need to give yourself time to heal. I would advise you to postpone all training for at least three months.'

Valerie looked outraged, then close to tears. Her bottom lip quivered as she struggled with Freya's proposal. 'Three months?' She turned to her mother. 'Mum, you know I can't afford to leave it that long, the team needs me on board. I can't take three months out. Coach will have to replace me. My life will be over.'

'You just said I saved your life,' Lucas interjected, arching an eyebrow.

Valerie opened her mouth to argue but closed it again.

'I would listen to Dr Grey's advice,' he said into the teen's narrowed green eyes. 'Three months, no football. After that we'll review the situation.'

Valerie swiped at her eyes, then stood dramatically. 'I need to rehydrate,' she announced, making for the door.

'Stay off that Twitter thing!' her mother called out. 'Not everyone needs to know *everything*, you know.'

When she was gone, Mrs Maijer-Schrot exhaled the

longest sigh he'd heard from anyone in weeks, including himself.

It hadn't been the easiest of times following Martijn's death. Losing someone to a heart problem was an unfortunate part of his role, one he had come to accept was bound to happen from time to time. But Martijn hadn't been a patient, he'd been a friend, and worse than that he hadn't known anything was wrong with Martijn. He doubted Martijn had known either.

Thinking about Martijn lying lifeless on the floor still rocked him into silent grief from time to time, even amidst the success stories. People knew him only as a highly skilled surgeon with an unprecedented success rate on paediatric patients like stubborn teenager Valerie, but no one here knew the concern he still felt over his inability to have helped poor Martijn three weeks ago. No one except Freya.

Seeing her face every day, working as a team at difficult moments like this, and burying himself in her most nights wasn't eradicating his grief entirely, but it was like a soothing balm to his wounds. A convenient distraction. He wouldn't allow himself to think beyond that right now, and he was certain *she* wasn't either.

'She wants to get a scholarship,' Mrs Maijer-Schrot told them, playing with the zip of her jacket. 'Did she tell you that?'

'She didn't,' Lucas said, watching Freya as she took his giant bouquet of flowers to the desk in the corner. She went about arranging them in the vase as they spoke.

'She's sports-mad, as if you didn't know. It's her life. She's been talking about getting that scholarship for years. She's worried that if she doesn't she won't be considered.'

'She has plenty of time to think about that,' he said.

'She's very ambitious,' the woman enthused. 'She isn't used to hearing she can't do something.'

'We'll have to see how she progresses. If she gets enough rest, there's no reason she won't be able to realise those ambitions.'

'Do you really think so?' Mrs Maijer-Schrot looked weary. Freya spoke now.

'I'm not going to lie,' she said, crossing back over to them. 'One of the most difficult but most frequent questions I get asked by parents like you, wherever I am in the world, is what's going to happen to their child—not just tomorrow, but in three to five years, and even beyond that. You're not alone to wonder things like this, Mrs Maijer-Schrot.'

'That's absolutely right,' Lucas added. 'Parents ask me things like will their son or daughter live to take a solo trip, or walk down the aisle or, like Valerie, go to university. And most of the time unfortunately they really do anticipate those things not happening…'

'Sometimes, they're right to think that,' Freya continued. 'Especially in developing countries, where they can't even afford to dream the kind of things we dream. In fact, I'm considering applying for a role at a hospital in Vietnam where there are a lot of kids Valerie's age who might not have fared so well with her condition, for many reasons.'

Lucas heard the word *Vietnam* as though it came from a great distance, and he let the word sink into his brain, with everything it represented. Freya kept on talking, and he watched her pink lips, gritting his teeth.

'Mrs Maijer-Schrot, my point is, we're in a privileged position here to have been able to help your daughter. And Valerie is in a privileged position to have all the care she needs going forward, making it very likely her ambitions won't suffer long term. We can't make any promises, but…' she turned to him now, but he didn't look back at her '…she doesn't seem concerned about her scars, which is a good thing…'

'On the contrary, she's proud of those,' her mother said. 'Did you not see her photos? I think she tagged you in some, Dr Van de Berg.'

'Fortunately not. I don't have much time for social media,' Lucas answered abruptly, getting to his feet. 'If you'll excuse me, I have to get to my next appointment. I'm sure Dr Grey can finish addressing any remaining concerns you may have.'

'Of course,' Freya said with a slight frown.

He picked up his phone and notes from the table and again avoided her eyes.

He'd seen the printouts about the role in Ho Chi Minh on her cluttered dining table. She hadn't tried to hide them, but she hadn't thrown them out either. This only confirmed what he'd already strongly suspected. Their new sexual relationship was just a fling. Freya saw the end of it already, just as he'd been telling himself, so why did he suddenly feel so betrayed?

Freya heard his voice in the hallway before she turned the corner. Lucas was standing with his arms folded across his chest, talking to a woman she'd never seen before. The woman was older, animated, in her mid-sixties and tall. Her purple summer scarf and red cropped trousers were so bright they looked as if petals from the giant tulips had bounced off the white walls onto her. She was gesturing enthusiastically as she spoke, but stopped when she saw her, lowering her silver-rimmed glasses down her nose to check her name badge.

'Oh, it's Freya Grey!' she rejoiced. 'Fred's been asking about you. I'm Mira Van de Berg, Lucas's mother. How wonderful to meet you.' She extended her hand and Lucas stepped back. Mira's grip was firm. Freya racked her brains. 'Fred?'

'My father,' Lucas said, but he looked as surprised as she was. He lowered his voice, walked them both over to the corner. 'Mum, how can Dad have been talking about Freya? He's never met her.'

Mira put a hand on his arm, wriggling her eyebrows. 'Your dad's not entirely senile. He has his moments, yes, but other times he's still very sharp. He said you were talking about Freya weeks ago, like you were interested in dating her...'

'Mira, please, we're at work.' Lucas seemed to be struggling to maintain his usual dignified demeanour all of a sudden, but Freya couldn't help laughing in spite of herself. She crossed her arms to mirror him, looked at him sideways. 'Is that right?'

'And I can see why,' Mira said, taking off her glasses to emphasise another appraisal. 'What a goddess you are. And a doctor too. I keep saying, Freya, that Lucas really needs to find himself a good woman, one who's actually going to stick around and—'

'OK, Mum, thank you. Aren't you going to be late for the acupuncturist?' Lucas took his mother's arm and all but marched her towards the exit, but Mira was giggling now, and so was Freya.

'Oh, don't be so sensitive, Lucas.' Mira stopped short

by the door and removed her elbow from his grip, just as Ruud pushed through with Pieter. They both looked delighted to see her.

'Mrs Van de Berg! How long has it been?' they cooed in sync, and both guys made shows of air-kissing her cheeks and making small talk about the weather and loving her outfit.

'She used to come in a lot to say hi, she has regular acupuncture appointments for her arthritis in the next building,' Lucas explained to Freya. 'But I think it's her way of spying on me.'

'You're quite correct. I have no life of my own at all.' Mira rolled her eyes at the obvious lie, then straightened the lapel of his coat. Pieter and Ruud exchanged amused looks before excusing themselves.

Mira Van de Berg was hilarious, and she was clearly a force of nature. She was at least five feet eleven, with short cropped grey hair, a husky laugh, and an infectious sense of humour. It didn't take much to picture her making homes for imaginary elves.

'I do like those boys,' Mira said with a sigh when they were gone. 'So very polite. I'd invite them to dinner too…'

'No, don't invite them to any dinners, Mum, they don't know about Dad's condition.'

Mira looked affronted. 'Why not? Having a family member with Alzheimer's is nothing to be ashamed of or to *hide*, Lucas. It's not like he's developed bubonic plague.' She put a hand over her mouth suddenly, turning to Freya. 'Are you not supposed to know either, for some reason?'

Lucas dragged a hand through his hair, then checked his watch. 'Freya knows. But she's the only one, and you know I'm not ashamed of him. I'm not the one who wants to put him in a home. There's just a lot going on here right now and I need my team to know I'm on the ball.'

'Well, Freya should come to dinner, then,' Mira said, ignoring him. To Freya's surprise the woman reached out and pressed a thumb to her upper cheek and wiped something away firmly in a motherly fashion she wasn't used to.

'You had a touch of mascara there,' Mira said kindly, patting her arm. Her eyes were the same shade of blue as Lucas's, warm, brimming over with love. The similarity stunned her into silence. 'Listen, *you* must come over tonight. We're making one of Fred's favourites. I'm trying to remind him of all the things he loves, and I know he'd love to meet you after hearing so much about you…'

At the look on Lucas's face, Mira held both hands in the air as if to surrender. 'OK, OK… I'll leave you to your work. See you both later, yes? Eight p.m.'

'I um… I can't, I'm sorry,' Freya said, finally finding her voice. 'I have to feed and walk the dog.'

'Oh, bring him! Fred loves dogs,' Mira enthused. 'Lucas, do bring that lovely wine again—oh, and the cookbook you borrowed? Thank you. OK, see you both later.'

With that she bustled off and Lucas was left looking at his green shoelaces like they were the sole survivors of the hurricane that had just blown through.

'So, you've been talking to your dad about me, have you?' Freya said, surprised at how the thought made her feel warm inside, a new kind of affection that had nothing to do with lust or carnal desire, or any of the other things he'd been making her feel since they'd decided to indulge in their heated sexual encounters. A fling felt good, and well deserved. Even if he wanted nothing more, she'd be OK with that, she told herself. Probably...

Every time she thought about leaving, she felt torn. It was strange; she'd never felt like this before.

'I'm surprised he remembers,' Lucas said gruffly. To her shock he seemed suddenly colder, distant.

'Is something wrong?'

His jaw was spasming, and she couldn't read his guarded expression. She had a terrible, unsettling feeling that he was about to retract his mother's lovely invitation, when she was quite excited to see the enigmatic Mira Van de Berg again.

An even more frightening realisation hit her next. She would care a lot if he didn't want her there, and over the past few blissful weeks in his arms she had decided not to let real feelings get in the way of their fling.

She watched his face for signs of things he wasn't saying. 'Do you not want me to come to your parents' house for dinner?' she asked.

'No,' he said. 'I mean, I want you there. I'll only face Mum's wrath if you're not.'

'Are you sure?' She tried to read his eyes. He didn't sound totally convinced.

'I'll pick you and Shadow up,' he said resolutely, though he was looking at Joy approaching them now from the other end of the hallway.

'In the boat?'

'No. We need the car to visit my parents' place. I'm pretty sure it's not what you're expecting.'

Before she could ask what he meant, he was gone, and Joy had stopped in front of her.

'Hey,' she said. 'Violet is asking for you.'

'I'll go see her. Thanks, Joy.'

Joy held her back by her sleeve. 'Did I just hear you say you were going to Lucas's *parents'* place?'

Freya held her breath. 'Yes,' she admitted after a moment. 'His mother just invited me.'

Joy nodded, biting the corner of her mouth. 'I had a feeling something was going on...the way you look at each other.'

Freya put her hands on Joy's shoulders as her heartbeat rose to her throat. 'I would have told you, but I don't even really know myself what this thing *is*. I mean, other than a fling...'

'Pieter told me already. I asked him why the vacuum cleaner was broken. I just didn't want to believe him.'

Freya frowned. *Pieter.* She should have known.

'You'd just better not hurt him,' Joy warned, taking her by surprise. She put her hands over Freya's quickly. 'Don't get me wrong, I'm glad we're friends, and you're a good woman, the kind of woman he *needs*, maybe...'

Joy released her and sighed, as if coming to terms with the fact that her crush on Lucas would always be one-sided. 'What do I know? Maybe all he wants *is* a fling this time. God knows, he went through enough with his last serious relationship.'

A wheelchair ploughed through the double doors, breaking them apart. The word 'fling' coming from Joy's mouth was tugging at her heart suddenly. It was just a word, one that had carried no real weight up till now—she'd even said it herself. It saved her from having to face what she feared this thing between her and Lucas might turn into: something much deeper, something that would seriously hurt her if she lost it. But now it sounded even more shallow, considering everything else she and Lucas had shared.

CHAPTER SEVENTEEN

'YOUR PARENTS LIVE in a windmill?' Freya's face was a picture as Lucas steered the car into the sweeping gravel driveway in Abcoude, about a fifteen-minute drive from busy Amsterdam. He hadn't told her ahead of time about the unconventional family home. He'd guessed it would be a nice surprise for someone who hadn't been in the Netherlands for as long as Freya hadn't.

'It was fully active in the eighteen-hundreds. They bought it after they got married and had it converted so, yeah, this is where we grew up.'

'It's beautiful,' Freya gushed as he let her out the passenger side. Shadow squeezed through to the front seat and leapt out after her before he'd even had the chance to open the back door.

'Everything you see is their property,' he told her, as the dog bounded straight for the fence that had been keeping the neighbouring sheep out of the front garden for over thirty years.

The summer evening sun cast a warm light on the windmill's white painted brickwork. It was all so familiar, but a sense of dread lingered low in his belly. Everything was *not* the same. His father was deterio-

rating, devoid of the freedom his car used to offer him.
His memories were fading, twisting, colliding. No matter how cheerful his mother was trying to be. Tonight
would be tough.

He put a hand on Freya's lower back to guide her
in her heels.

'Welcome, welcome, good to see you again!'Mira
greeted Freya like a long-lost daughter. He realised it
had been a pretty long time since he'd brought a woman
home.

'Mother, the cake smells incredible,' he enthused,
pushing the thought from his head as he circled an
arm around Mira's shoulders and dropped a kiss on
her cheek.

'It's vegan,' she said proudly.

He nodded at the eggshells on the counter. 'Really?'

'Oh, I didn't use the yolks, just the whites,' she explained. Freya hid a smile, and he rolled his eyes at
her, shaking his head. Freya was dressed in a mid-calf-
length dark green dress that hugged her waist with a
wraparound tie, and tan-coloured shoes with a wedge
heel. She looked hot as hell in heels. He would have to
keep his hands off her tonight, though, with his family around.

He listened to her chatting with Mira about her cas-
serole and fake vegan cake recipe, allowing the comfort of his old home to soothe his tired brain a moment.
Freya was quite a lot shorter than his mother, but he
liked her height compared to his family's. He liked how
small she felt in his arms, how she seemed to need him
at times, when she was so damn independent to the rest
of the world. He liked her altogether too much, considering she was already planning her escape.

'Did you bring my cookbook?' Mira broke into his thoughts. He noticed she'd dressed up for the occasion too; a typical Mira look, an oversized white cotton shirt and pale blue slacks, with the matching blue beads Fred had bought her on one of their cruise stops somewhere in the Caribbean.

'Of course.' Dutifully he opened the satchel he was carrying and placed the book on the counter. He held a wine bottle up too, and placed it beside the book.

'You're a superstar. Right, you two, leave me in peace to get on with dinner. Dad's in the lounge.'

'Did you ever use that cookbook?' Freya asked him when they were out in the hallway.

He shrugged, feeling conflicted by how at ease she seemed to be already in his family home, the way her heels clipped the whitewashed floor as he led her towards the lounge. Classical music was blaring; his dad's favourite. 'I haven't cooked at home in a long time,' he said. 'Only at the shelter.'

'Why?' She stopped to study the photos on the walls.

'I don't really like to cook for one,' he told her. 'Too much goes to waste.'

Her head bobbed in understanding as her eyes scanned the pictures in the frames—him at his graduation throwing his hat in the air, him and his brother Simon kicking their legs up like kung fu fighters on a trampoline, his mother and father on their wedding day outside the Oude Kerk in Amsterdam.

'But you used to cook, right? With your ex? Dinner parties,' she said after a moment. He knew from her tone that she didn't want to appear like she was fishing, even though she was.

'You heard about those, did you?'

'Apparently, they were legendary.'

He shrugged, putting a hand on the back of her neck under her hair and leaning down to kiss her. 'Are you hinting I should hold another one before I sell the house-boat?'

She turned in his arms abruptly and he realised he probably hadn't mentioned he was thinking of selling up, moving somewhere different. He'd only started thinking about it recently. It held too many memories of things that no longer served him. 'Why would you sell the houseboat?' she asked, frowning up at him. 'I love it there.'

'I could ask you the same thing about selling your heritage house and moving to Vietnam,' he told her, di-verting the subject by easing her shoulders back against the wall and pulling her closer by the hips. He knew how much she loved his houseboat—in fact, on the few occasions Shadow had been taken in by Freya's neigh-bour and she'd stayed over, they had christened every room. She didn't even mind Sheba…she said she'd seen plenty of snakes on her medical mission trips and in America's national parks.

The thin fabric of her dress was too easily lifted up above her knees. He ran his palm seductively, deliber-ately along the smooth, warm flesh of her thigh, tracing his fingers along the hem of her underwear, savouring the burning desire that flickered in her eyes.

Mira dropped something in the kitchen. Shadow let out a bark from somewhere out in the yard. 'Why don't you take me up to the miller's suite?' she teased in a whisper, and grinned under his mouth.

'Stop changing the subject,' he groaned as Freya took his face in her hands and pressed her lips to his.

He couldn't stay away from her even if he tried. He lowered his lips, leaving a trail of kisses down her cheek that made her moan softly in his arms. He knew that once he kissed the soft, sensitive flesh of her collarbone she would all but crumble. All it took was a few delicate butterfly kisses and her hands would fall down his back, then go up to his hair in an echo of desire. He was starting to get to know what aroused her, and it always left him wanting more.

'Seriously, why would you sell it? What would you do with your python? That's her home now, and you know how much she loves it.'

As she said it, Freya's hand travelled round the belt of his jeans and slipped inside the front. He pressed his mouth to hers again, feeling himself grow dangerously hard. He was way too turned on, considering where they were.

'You're not making me feel too much like talking,' he told her, almost forgetting to whisper, and she pressed a finger to his lips to silence him, giggling before drawing him in for another kiss, digging her hand further into his jeans, stroking him while dancing slow, delicious circles around his tongue with her own.

It felt illicit and forbidden in the middle of the hallway, like being a teenager again under his parents' roof, and he gave a muffled groan, urging her back to the wall. They only broke apart when their frantic kissing meant her head made a photo go crooked.

'Tell me later, when we go back there,' she said, straightening her dress while he adjusted himself in his jeans. Maybe he shouldn't have mentioned it at all, he considered. He barely thought about Roshinda any more, but having Freya at his home still felt a little strange somehow, like having her at the hospital did sometimes.

Two worlds colliding.

He wanted to start afresh, come back to a place that was just his again, where he could start building new memories. He still hadn't told Freya he'd been with a woman who he'd known full well had probably been going to leave him. Why was it still so hard to talk about it when he was over it?

Watching Freya leading him towards the living room, where his father was, the thought was like having ice tossed at his libido: despite all her warnings, and her open admission of wanting to leave Amsterdam, he was walking head first into making exactly the same mistake again.

'Fred has always been the strong, supportive one, you know, he was in charge of everything… But now that's up to me,' Mira said in confidence. 'I think losing his ability to drive has been the most difficult thing. Sometimes he's still angry about it but we can't risk letting him on the roads.'

Mira reached for the bottle of wine across the table, but Freya put her hand over her glass. 'Oh, no, thank you.' She'd probably had too much already, but she was enjoying the way Lucas's mother was confiding in her like an old friend around their rustic wooden dining table up on the deck beneath the old stationary sails.

Fred was a lovely man and she could see where Lucas got his good looks from. He was cheerful and positive, but it was worrying, the amount of stuff he was forgetting or getting wrong.

The view of the setting sun across the flat expanse

of countryside was spectacular, however. Lucas had asked if she'd mind taking a photo of them all on her phone, with the timer, and the lighting had been picture-perfect. This was the first time she'd ever dined under the sails of a windmill. 'More wine?' Mira was wielding the bottle again.

'Are you trying to get Freya drunk, Mum?' Lucas scolded affectionately from the other side of the table.

'That's how I got your father to open up to me,' Mira said. 'Remember that, Fred? Our first date, when you finally admitted you still lived at home with your parents?' She put her head in her hands and turned to Freya with blue eyes twinkling. 'We were only eighteen. I knew he was the one for me long before he did. We shared a bottle of whisky up on the deck of this old mill. We talked about buying it together, even on our first date.'

Fred was just staring at his hands now. Speckled and weathered from what looked like years spent outdoors. He shook his head, running a hand slowly and apologetically through his greying beard. 'I don't...'

He tapered off, as if searching the void and coming up with nothing. Lucas's expression was one of pain and sadness suddenly; Freya wanted to reach out and comfort him, but she appreciated that he was being strong for his family.

Mira fiddled despondently with the stem of her wine glass. Lucas put a hand reassuringly over his father's. 'It's OK, Dad,' he assured him, when it was clear Fred's memories of his and Mira's first date were gone. The gesture, as well as his tone, almost moved Freya to his side of the table again. Fred had been remembering things that had never happened and confusing things that had all evening. She could tell how frustrating it was for both Lucas and his mother, but it was clear their bond was tight. Envy flared deep in her veins over this kind of closeness. It was a closeness she hadn't realised she'd been missing when it came to her mother and Liv.

'So, tell us about this dog,' Mira said, looking towards Freya for a lighter topic. 'How long have you had Shadow?'

'A few weeks. I'm just fostering him, really,' she explained. Discomfort snaked around her suddenly.

As if reading her mind, Lucas said, 'Freya can't keep the dog, Mum. She doesn't know how long she's going to be in Amsterdam.'

'Oh?' Mira looked intrigued.

'She's thinking of taking a role at a hospital in Vietnam.' Lucas looked at her pointedly over the table and her heart began to thrum.

'I was in Vietnam once,' Fred said, perking up.

'No you weren't, darling,' Mira corrected gently. 'But we've both always wanted to go.'

Freya smiled as best she could. She had to admire Lucas's checkmate. She'd mentioned the Vietnam role a few times before, and she'd expected him to ask her more about it. In a way she had wanted him to. She wondered if, subconsciously, she'd wanted to hear him say that he didn't want her to go. But he hadn't.

'Nothing is arranged yet, I have to sort some things out here first. Like selling the house I inherited,' she said. 'And…um…my mother lives near here, too,' she added tentatively, 'in Weesp.'

'Oh, it's a lovely place, isn't it?' Mira clapped her hands together. 'I go to my life drawing class there every Friday afternoon.'

'I've never been there,' Freya admitted. Something about Mira's eyes brimming with concern for her made her continue. 'We're not that close, Mira, we haven't been for years, or ever, if I'm honest, and…maybe some of it is my fault but I'd like to try and amend that while I'm here, if I can. If it's not too late.'

Mira took her hand and squeezed it. 'Oh, honey, I'm sorry to hear you're not close. What happened?'

'She probably doesn't want to go into it here,' Lucas interjected, probably seeing her tense up. He got to his feet and put his hands gently on her shoulders from behind her chair, and the look of compassion in Mira's eyes almost broke her. 'Freya, come down to the kitchen with me?'

She almost didn't let him take her hand and guide her back down the steep windmill stairs from the deck in her heels, but she relented halfway down. 'I apologise, I'm an idiot,' he said when they were standing face to face in the kitchen on the parquet floor. 'I shouldn't have brought that up in front of them, I should have talked to you in private about your plans for Vietnam.'

'It's OK,' she said wearily, rubbing her eyes. 'I should have talked to you about it before now. I guess I just don't know what this is…'

'I know, and I got a little defensive seeing you talk with my parents. Let's just say I've been in this position before with someone I knew would eventually leave the country, and I'm not too excited about it happening again. But for what it's worth, it means a lot that you're here right now.'

'Oh, Lucas, I'm so sorry. I haven't stopped to consider what my leaving does to other people, how it makes them feel… I didn't even tell my own mother I was leaving for America when I got my place at university.'

'Come here.' Lucas pulled her against him, in the middle of the floor. He held her tight, wrapping his big arms around her, and she closed her eyes, breathing him in. Suddenly tears were streaming down her cheeks.

'I'm sorry I'm being over-emotional, this is not my usual style.'

'I know that. That's how I know how much all this is affecting you.'

She took his hands in hers, like anchors. He knew her better than she'd thought he did. He was starting to care for her, like she was starting to care for him. But Freya was still surprised at herself for bringing up her mother like that.

'There's something about being here with your parents, Lucas, and you. Your dad is losing so many precious memories and I can't even… I keep telling myself to do something about this rift with my mother. I promised myself I would after Martijn died, but I still keep making excuses. Liv will be here soon…'

He ran a finger along her bottom lip to wipe away a tear. 'It's been a long time, and you're scared to rock the boat without your sister here, but maybe you should see your mother alone and clear the air.'

'I know I should try.'

'Freya, just make the call to your mother. Better than that, I'll drive you to see her myself—would you like that? We can go whenever you like, just say the word. We could even go right now.'

'Now?'

'Why not? No time like the present, right? I'll take

you to her door, and I'll wait for you. Weesp isn't far from here.'

Freya shook her head, pressing her hands over his. It wasn't so much guilt racking her now over maintaining such a distance from her mother for so long without trying to sort things out. It was sadness and regret. 'You would really do that for me?' she managed.

'Of course I would,' he said, wrapping his arms around her again. 'We'll tell Mira and Fred right now and we'll leave Shadow with them, they love having him here, and we'll go and see your mum. You can finally be at peace.'

'I don't deserve you,' Freya said, nestling back into his shoulder.

She couldn't squash or deny the dizzying wave of something that felt a lot like love, blowing in with the bleat of a sheep through the open window, but she stepped away, almost too quickly as it threatened to spill over into tears. A fling wasn't love, she reminded herself quickly. He didn't love her, he was just being… Lucas. She'd simply got caught up in another moment.

CHAPTER EIGHTEEN

FREYA'S NERVES WERE shot to pieces the whole ride to Weesp. What if she got there and her mother didn't want to see her? It would be justified, perhaps, but mortifying. She often thought that maybe too much time had passed to patch things up with Elise anyway. They were fundamentally different people.

Their relationship, which had never really got off the ground in the first place, was irrevocably broken. But at the same time she longed to look fondly at the woman who had given birth to her. It would be nice to tell stories about funny stuff she'd done, like Lucas could do. It wasn't much fun to keep dwelling on the past when it had been so unhappy.

'Are you OK?' Lucas asked. He reached a hand across the gearstick and held her hand on her lap. For a second she thought about not taking it; she had no clue what was happening between them but it felt like their relationship was morphing quickly into something she couldn't control. Something that could do more damage to her than any other hurt she'd ever experienced.

'I'm OK,' she said, forcing herself to take deep breaths. It was still light out, but it was only nine o'clock. Maybe her mother would be making a last cup of tea before bed, or pouring a gin and tonic. Maybe she'd be doing yoga, or constructing furniture—she had no clue what her mother might be doing after all this time because she didn't really know her.

'I just hope she wants to talk to me.'

'Of course she will, she's your mother.' He indicated right and swung onto the tree-lined Appelstraat, the street where her mother lived with Stijn. 'Are you ready?'

She pulled a face to indicate she wasn't, and he pressed a kiss to the back of her hand that made her insides contract with lust again. Then she took more deep breaths.

'Nice place.' Lucas slowed the car outside the house. It was old but charming, probably built in the mid-eighteenth century. Chunky yellow bricks were offset by quirky green window shutters and a low-hanging thatched roof. The front garden was manicured and surrounded by plants and flowerbeds, a bird table, a set of black wicker garden furniture. She could make out a dreamcatcher in one of the front windows.

'I'll wait just around the corner,' Lucas said. She nodded and went to take off her seat belt. Before she could open the door he caught her arm. 'Remember, no matter what happens, at least you will have seen her, and I'll be right here.'

She wanted to kiss him, like she had at his parents' house in the hallway before her emotions had turned things on their head and forced her to re-evaluate what was real and what about their fling was just an excuse to run away from her issues.

Walking down the path, the world seemed to move in slow motion. She was finally here. The scent of jasmine floated around her nose, and somewhere frogs were singing. Her mother had built an idyllic life, it seemed, in a serene small town of green. A total contrast to the chaos she'd been swept up in as a child.

The front door was red. A statue of two cheeky-looking elves sat amongst lavender in a plant pot on the doorstep. It reminded her of Mira and she silently drew strength from Lucas's wonderful mother as she pressed a finger on the doorbell. And waited.

And waited.

And waited.

She wandered to the window. A faint light was on, making silhouettes of a piano and more plants, a comfy-looking couch, and an easel with a canvas on it. But no more lights came on. Disappointment and mild relief washed over her, right before a voice made her jump.

'Can I help you?'

Freya spun around, her heart pounding. 'Mum?' She hadn't expected her to come from around the back of the house, but the woman was approaching her now across the grass, holding what looked like a bowl and a plastic bag.

'Mum? You mean, you're Elise's daughter?' The woman stepped up close to inspect her. She was young, maybe mid-thirties, dressed in overalls over a crop top, and flip-flops. She had blue dreadlocks. Freya almost laughed.

'I am her daughter, yes, my name is Freya.'

'Well, it's nice to meet you Freya, but Elise isn't here, she's in Miami. I'm Olga, the neighbour. I'm just feeding the cats while she's away.'

'Your mum's kitchen is a lot like the kitchen I always dreamed about having, growing up,' Freya said, accepting the cup of tea Lucas handed her. 'The low beams with all the ivy and plants, the giant spice rack. That mosaic floor… I didn't tell you, because I was too busy breaking down back there.' She winced at the way the dinner had unfolded, putting the tea cup down. 'What a night.'

'What a night,' he agreed.

'I still can't believe I forgot my mum was going to Miami. She only just got back from Iceland.'

'You've had a lot on your mind,' he said, offering a smile. 'Sounds like your mother likes to travel. Like mother, like daughter, huh?'

Freya chewed on her lip, deep in contemplation. 'She didn't tell me exactly when she was going, but she told Liv.'

'Maybe that's because you never pick up the phone.'

He wondered if this fact had gone unacknowledged by her, the same as his reminder that both mother and daughter seemed to be inflicted by the travel bug. But then she sighed deeply and said, 'You're right.'

'Anyway, about this kitchen,' he said, changing the topic, 'I didn't know you cooked, too.' They were sitting on the loveseat on the deck of his houseboat, gazing over the canal. They could see three bridges from here, his favourite Dutch restaurant, and a family of geese beneath the weeping willow on the other side. It was quiet and peaceful, just out of the city.

'I don't really cook, but that doesn't mean I don't deserve a nice kitchen for someone else to cook for me in,' Freya said.

Lucas wrapped an arm around her and drew her closer. For a second she seemed to resist his touch and he waited for her to add some sort of disclaimer, like,

One day, I mean, when I decide where I want to live. But she didn't, and to his relief she leaned in and pressed a cheek to his shoulder.

He felt so bad for her, that of all the times they could have picked to go and see her mother, she hadn't been home.

Her face was pale in the moonlight and her feet were bare where she'd kicked off her shoes.

'Listen, Lucas, I was just thinking how you said you'd been through this before. With someone you *knew* was going to leave the country. You meant Roshinda, didn't you?'

His hand went to his chin, then his hair. She might subconsciously choose to block her mother's words out at times, but her memory was too good when it came to him. She seemed to remember everything, every word he'd ever said. She must have been thinking of Roshinda being in his kitchen with him while they cooked up their famed dinners for guests. He knew people at work must have mentioned them too. Joy was always hinting he should host more dinners again. 'Yes, I meant Roshinda.'

'How did you know she would leave you?'

'I knew because she was never really mine in the first place,' he admitted, looking into her eyes. If he didn't tell her now, he didn't know when he would tell her. What was the point in hiding his past mistakes anyway? She knew everything else that was bothering him, and he knew the things she kept from other people, too.

He still felt bad for bringing up her plans for Vietnam in front of his parents. Freya hadn't known how close he was to them; they talked about everything together. He'd had a stern word with himself for his moment of selfishness at the dinner table, which had sprung from a deep-rooted fear of another woman he had feelings for leaving him.

'She had an arranged marriage to go back to,' he said. 'I knew about it when we got together, it wasn't like she didn't warn me.'

Freya just blinked at him, no doubt letting it sink in. 'An arranged marriage?' She uncurled herself from the loveseat to face him. 'Are you serious?'

'In Jaipur; he was a family friend, I think. Her father thought it would be good for the business.'

'And you knew about it while you were dating? But… I thought you were in love.' Freya looked bewildered, to say the least. He moved his gaze to the geese, who were flapping and fussing over something by the willow tree.

'I don't think her love for me ever came into it. She'd made up her mind to go through with the marriage to appease her family and no one was going to change that decision. Not even me. Looking back, I just didn't want to admit it to myself. She left for India the same week Fred was diagnosed with Alzheimer's.'

'What?' Freya looked mortified on his behalf.

'I haven't heard from her since. Not one word. Well, she sent the journals, I guess, but they weren't specifically addressed to me.'

'But didn't *you* try and get in touch? Couldn't you have just talked to her family, I mean? Lucas, she wasn't bound to another guy with a ball and chain!'

He shrugged, admiring how she was taking his side in the situation, even though it had long been over and done with. He pulled her to her feet, noting how right her hands felt in his. He had no attachment to the memories he was discussing now, he knew he had met the one woman who *was* right for him, even if she didn't agree. 'She didn't want me to talk to her family.'

'But *you* wanted to?'

He met her beseeching eyes. 'I did want to, for a while. Then I cut her off, the same way she cut me off, I assume. I had to put my family's needs first, here in the Netherlands. I have a feeling her family and her husband don't want me knowing where she is anyway.'

'Don't you ever wonder?'

He studied her face. 'Not any more. There are lots of other things to wonder about instead.'

'So you never once considered getting on a plane, at least to go and talk to her?'

He swallowed a growl, feelings his buttons being pressed. 'How could I have gone to India, Freya? I'm needed here.'

She was quiet for a moment, her eyebrows knitted together. He knew what she wanted to say. He could read her silence now. She wanted to tell him that if he'd ever really loved Roshinda, he would have made more of an effort to find her, talk to her or fight for her. These were all things he already knew, but something had always stopped him from doing any of them; more than his father's illness, and more than his work here.

'It wasn't just the timing,' he said. 'I was angry at myself for a long time for getting so involved with her. I walked right into something I knew deep down wouldn't last.'

'It wasn't just you, though, Lucas. She did that too. She knew she would be marrying someone else.'

He considered that, scanning her eyes. He'd never allowed that thought to permeate before; he'd shifted all the blame onto himself and carried it around for so long.

This would have been a good time for Freya to reiterate that perhaps she wasn't going to leave the country after all, but a pained look crossed her face and he knew she wasn't going to. He knew this thing between them…whatever it was…wouldn't last either.

'No one's been here since she left, really,' he said, when she still didn't speak. 'I suppose Sheba is a part of that. Not everyone is a fan of her, but she's really cool, as you know, very gentle. Unless you're a mouse.'

Freya barely smiled at his effort to lighten the conversation, she just turned to gaze over the water and exhaled deeply. 'You didn't have to tell me all that, but I'm glad you did,' she said, her tone flat. 'About Roshinda's marriage, I mean. I understand you can't be with anyone who doesn't know exactly where they want to be, Lucas.'

His fists clenched at his sides. What could he say to that? They were at a crossroads, they both knew it. But they each cared about the other too much to say it, or even address it right now.

'Let's just make every moment count, then,' he said with as much conviction as he could muster.

'That's probably the best thing to do,' she agreed. Then she paused.

Here it comes, he thought. Just as he'd grown to predict, her walls were coming back up, blocking him out the second she caught herself getting too close. 'I do still have to focus on renovating the house, getting it ready to sell.'

'OK,' he said. He ran his thumbs across the back of her hands in his. It wasn't good to push a woman, especially one with wings who might just fly away, maybe even before she needed to. 'Want me to help you?'

Freya looked surprised, then flustered.

'I told you before, I know a lot of good people—designers, fitters, agents—'

'Um…well, there's no rush,' she cut in quickly, and he bit back a smile. It wasn't that she really wanted to sell the house, he'd guessed that much by now. She didn't want to risk getting hurt either, the same way her ex had abandoned her, the same way her mother had ignored her. He was starting to see things about Freya that maybe she couldn't even see herself.

He took a risk, sliding his arms around her waist again, and to his relief she leaned back against him. With his chin on the top of her soft head he made his embrace even tighter. Freya was just so used to running from her past she didn't know any other way to be. Maybe, if he played his cards right over the coming weeks, he could show her another way.

CHAPTER NINETEEN

FREYA GASPED AND felt the breath she hadn't even realised she'd been holding leave her body. Her arms looped around Lucas's strong shoulders as he lifted her up, and her legs encircled his middle as she sank against him into the pure unbridled pleasure of his passionate, powerful kiss.

She travelled to a different place whenever they did this, lost herself in a head-spinning carousel ride that she'd have happily stayed on for ever, somewhere slightly outside her real life. Lucas always seemed to be hungry for her, and he was kissing her now like no amount of kissing her would ever be enough.

Somewhere in the back of her head she knew she was in the darkened movie theatre in the hospital, using all her free passes at once, languishing in the kind of behaviour even her teenage self would have frowned on. But it was dark, and he was sexy as hell, and she just didn't care.

There wasn't even a movie playing. Lucas had just pulled her in here, locked the door shut after them and torn off her white coat. 'I couldn't wait,' he whispered against her breasts and she grinned, feeling the stress of another day start to melt away, even though it was barely one p.m. and she had a consultation in an hour. 'I've hardly seen you this last week since your sister got here,' he said in a gravelly, raspy tone that seemed to echo between her legs and make her ache for him. Until…

'Liv!' Freya cried, coming to her senses and scrambling off Lucas's lap.

'What?' Lucas was breathless, shirt undone, his white coat draped somewhere over another red plush chair. She hurried to do her blouse buttons up, looking around in the darkness for her coat. 'Liv is meant to be meeting me here at the hospital. I was going to take her to lunch in the cafeteria with Joy and give her the tour. Oh, God, she's probably waiting for me right now…' She shuffled down the row of seats to the aisle as fast as she could, leaving him to pull his own coat on.

'And just like that, she flies away,' she heard Lucas groan behind her.

'To be continued!' she called back.

Liv smirked at her ruffled hair as Freya took her plastic seat at the lunch table. She was already in the cafeteria with Joy, with a can of soft drink between her hands. Liv and Joy had met earlier in the week for dinner at Lucas's place. He'd cooked a special seafood dish for them all that he'd said had come from Mira's imagination, but that dinner had been the only time Freya had seen Lucas outside work since Liv had arrived. She supposed she had been using Liv's presence as a bit of an excuse for some time out from whatever they were calling this thing between them these days.

In the absence of any word from her mother, still, she'd tried to focus on the house instead. She'd called some of the designers Lucas had kindly put her in touch with, finished up the rest of the painting with Liv. Busy, busy, busy. Selling the house would be easy, so everyone said, but she wasn't too concerned if it took till after Christmas.

'Glad you could make it, Liv,' she said, smoothing down her hair.

'I could say the same thing,' Liv shot back with a grin. 'And where is Lucas?'

'Yes, Freya, where is Dr Van de Berg?' Joy had the look of a sly cat now too.

'Getting ready for surgery,' she said, without looking them in the eyes. It was half-true. If he wasn't doing it just yet, he would be just as soon as he got all his clothes on again. She could still taste his lips on hers, his musky scent was on her fingertips when she moved a hand to her mouth momentarily. Staying away from him was tough…near on impossible, actually. He was just as bad as her, keeping the fling going in spite of them both potentially heading in different directions.

Hearing Lucas talk about his ex's arranged marriage had hit home how careful she was supposed to be being with his heart, too, but there were moments, like just now, when her raging hormones still got the better of her.

'What did you do this morning?' she asked Liv, taking the cold can Joy passed to her and quenching her thirst. It had been hot in the cinema.

'I took Shadow out, walked around. Did you see what they've done to the Pijp now? It used to be so dodgy, now it's like…well, not quite as bad. Remember when we went to that store and bought those green lollipops, and you said you didn't know why you felt floaty and light after you'd eaten yours? Mum laughed so hard! She didn't even tell you off.'

Freya had forgotten that. Her mum had laughed with her that time. In fact, Liv had reminded her of several occasions when happiness had edged its way into her teenage angst all those years ago.

'It's good to be back here.' Liv beamed, resting her elbows on the table just as Freya was thinking the same thing; it was good to have Liv here. 'Oh, I also took another box of stuff to the homeless shelter for you. I got a tarot reading while I was there.'

'Oh?'

'Yeah, I'm not sure I believe in that stuff, but Fayola saw a wedding coming up. I asked if it was mine and she said no. The artist was a waste of time, so I guess I knew it wasn't my wedding, I'm too single. Happily single, mind you. Unless you have any more hot surgeons around here?'

Freya smiled to herself, 'You're definitely over your break-up,' she said, thinking back to her own tarot reading with Fayola.

She was tentatively learning to trust Lucas, but this thing with her mother wasn't going away and it still dominated everything. Her sister had been in town for a week now. It was good to see her, except when she brought up old memories involving all the lovely 'family' times Freya herself *hadn't* shared.

'There's so much of Anouk's old stuff still down in the basement. I thought we could sort through that together with Mum when…if…she's able to make it when she gets back from Miami.'

She'd done it again. It wasn't Liv's fault, this city held only good memories of their mother for Liv, but Freya hadn't heard anything from her mother except a text to say she was sorry to have missed her when they'd driven round to see her. This time the communication breakdown wasn't all on Freya.

She wondered whether her mother really was sorry for how she'd behaved when Freya hd been small. Or was she avoiding her now, like Freya had avoided her for so long?

'When does she get back from Miami?' she asked, as Joy excused herself.

'I don't know when she's back, I lost my phone, re-member,' Liv grumbled. Freya had forgotten, admittedly. Liv had left it on the tram yesterday and was still waiting for someone to get back to her, even though Lucas had reminded them both that miracles like that rarely happened.

'Oh, look who it is. I thought you were getting ready for surgery.' Liv's face broke into a grin as Lucas came up behind her and put two hands on the back of Freya's chair.

'Not yet,' he told Liv. 'I have an hour or so before that to catch my breath.'

Liv cocked an eyebrow. 'Is that right?'

Freya felt her cheeks flush.

'Friday is the big one,' Lucas said, sliding into the seat beside Freya's. He took her can and drank from it, at least three huge, thirsty swigs, and Freya caught her sister staring at his mouth around the can, feeling smug that *she* was the one who got to kiss him. She knew exactly why he was so thirsty. 'On Friday after-noon, we'll be doing what we can for Anne Marie and Ruben's baby,' he said.

'Lucas can save their baby via foetal intervention.

It's a breakthrough process he's done before, several times,' Freya explained to Liv. Liv just looked at Lucas like she'd never met anyone so dreamy and Freya rolled her eyes.

Ruben and Anne Marie had agonised over the decision, and had finally decided that surgery before birth was the preferred option, even though it was going to be a tricky procedure.

'I'm confident,' Lucas announced, swigging from the can again. But she knew his eyes by now. She knew the lines of his face and how they betrayed his words in ways only she knew and felt. After Martijn had died he'd been lost for a while. His confidence had taken a knock, and he'd even blamed himself a little for not reading the signs, if there had even been any. Lucas Van de Berg wasn't a man who let things get him down too long, but he was still going to find it tough, operating on a friend.

'I hope the baby is OK,' Liv said thoughtfully, putting a hand to Lucas's arm suddenly and squeezing it. He nodded quietly, then Freya watched him put a steady, big, warm hand over Liv's on the table.

Another memory.

Freya struggled to un-think it, but Beatrice immediately flashed to the forefront of her mind, with her ex, Johnny. They'd been in a club in a darkened corner, whispering and giggling the way they'd taken to doing without her, reminding her of how her mother used to do the same with her friends, always whispering, always planning to go places and do things without her.

Not that Liv was Beatrice, she reminded herself. Liv was just being nice. So what if her single half-sister had gushed several times since her arrival that, 'Lucas is so *hot!*'

Freya stood. She would not let her stupid demons in here. She was only thinking all this now because her mother's silence was still unsettling her, and if she was being totally honest with herself, she couldn't make Lucas any promises.

She didn't really want to think about it, but if she wasn't staying in Amsterdam, she had no claim over him. She knew that and so did he. What if he moved on from her even faster than he'd moved on from Roshinda? She felt ice-cold just thinking about him being with someone else, especially her own sister. But at least Liv would be emotionally and physically available. She'd been talking about moving back to Amsterdam permanently.

'Should I give you the tour, then?' she said to Liv, trying to smile at her.

She couldn't quite shake the persistent, upsetting thoughts from her mind as she showed her sister around, from the staffroom to Neonatal, to the playroom and the school.

Lucas didn't deserve to have someone else he cared about leave him. He hadn't exactly asked her to stick around, so maybe he didn't have particularly deep feelings for her? She could have thrown caution to the wind by now and admitted that maybe it *was* time for her to put some roots down somewhere. Sometimes, when she got lost in his eyes, she badly wanted to.

But the words wouldn't leave her mouth because she still felt so unsettled and torn, and not only because she still wasn't sure what Lucas really felt for her. If her relationship with her mother was as broken as it felt it was, if she really couldn't fix it, then she didn't want to be here amongst all the memories that stabbed like knives at her growing happiness. She just didn't think she could do it, not for anything or anyone. It would hurt too much.

CHAPTER TWENTY

'I TRUST YOU,' Anne Marie told him, taking both his hands from her place, sitting up in bed. 'But I'm terrified.'

'Try to relax as much as you can,' Lucas told her kindly. He was treating her with the same professionalism he would treat any patient before surgery, and trying to forget the number of times he'd shared dinners and drinks and nights out making trouble with this couple, before and after they'd got married and had their first baby.

He'd been slightly envious of their easy partnership over the years, but he'd never thought for a second that they'd all be here now, with their second child's life in his hands.

'Where's Dr Grey?' Ruben asked, walking into the room. He was holding a bunch of flowers wrapped in Cellophane, which he placed on the bedside table. Lucas could tell his friend was nervous too—he missed the table and the flowers fell on the floor. 'Sorry, sorry!'

'I'll get them,' Lucas said, but Joy was already on her knees, picking them up.

'It's all good.' Gathering up the scattered tulips and roses, she threw him an empathetic glance, and Lucas was thankful for her calm control, especially as he had no idea where Freya was.

Somewhere in the next room a baby was crying. It seemed to be making Anne Marie more nervous. He checked the tulip-shaped clock on the wall. Freya was late for the pre-surgery consultation, and that wasn't like her.

'I'm sure Dr Grey is on her way,' he said. 'She must have just been held up. We have our physician assistant Dr Rosenthal close by to describe the post-operative course again in more detail, if you need her. Freya not being here won't affect anything in the operating room. We're all set up for you in there.'

'I'm so grateful it's you doing this,' Ruben said, and Lucas nodded, portraying the confidence he felt over operating and not hid concern over Freya's absence. He'd seen less of her lately, thanks to Liv being around, but she'd never missed an appointment.

Five minutes ticked past.

Ten minutes.

Eventually, they couldn't wait for her any longer.

Freya breathed in the calm of the afternoon as she cycled towards the hospital, and tried her best to extend it through non-physical means to Anne Marie. She'd been putting herself in Lucas's friend's shoes all morning. What if it were her, carrying a poorly baby? What if it was her child's life and blood forming inside her, with only half a heart?

Maybe it would be a true reflection of how she'd been living, if that happened, she thought to herself. How long had she spent giving only half of herself to other people? She couldn't even commit to poor Shadow, though he seemed to be loving life between her place and Lucas's parents,' place. Fred adored him.

Her thoughts about Lucas's wonderful family were interrupted by her phone. Pulling to the kerb on the side of the canal, she fished it out, and her whole heart did a dance.

'Mum?'

She almost couldn't believe it. Elise sounded out of breath on the other end of the line. 'Freya? Oh, there you are. Sorry, I'm a bit jet-lagged. I'm at the house right now. I came straight from the airport. You said you wanted to talk?'

Freya flipped the stand down on her red shiny bike. Her knees were suddenly shaky as she swung her leg over the frame and stood on the pavement. A tourist boat drifted past beneath her under the bridge, rooting her to reality. 'Which house?'

'Anouk's...your house,' her mum said.

'Mum, I'm just on my way to—' She cut herself off. Her mother was at the house, looking for her. It was so surreal. But she'd shown up unannounced, just when Freya had somewhere *very* important to be. 'Liv should be there,' she heard herself saying. 'She can let you in. I just have to get to the hospital.'

'Liv isn't here. I'm outside, ringing the bell. And her phone is switched off.'

'She lost her phone,' Freya explained, although it was strange that Liv wasn't there. She'd been there when she'd left just ten minutes ago, and her sister had told her she would be staying in to finish her book out on the balcony.

Her mother sounded undisputedly tired. 'Look, if you don't want to see me, I'll just carry on home in a taxi. Stijn has already gone. I just thought, seeing that I was passing through Amsterdam…'

'No, Mum, it's OK. We do need to talk.' Sucking in a breath, Freya made a snap decision. Lucas would understand, and there was no clear expectation of her presence. Anne Marie's surgery wouldn't be affected, and this was important too. She'd call the hospital on the way and explain.

'OK, I'm coming back,' she said. 'Wait there.'

In a way, Lucas was grateful for Freya's absence. It meant he was too busy wondering what had happened to her to let the intricacies of the procedure get to him. It was supposed to take two hours, but they were already ten minutes over that.

He knew Ruben would be waiting outside, worried sick. But his hands did careful, efficient work as he took himself into the zone. This baby's little heart was less than perfect, but he would do everything in his power to ensure it kept on beating, now and long into the future.

The zone was his safe place and Lucas almost forgot it was Anne Marie he was operating on. The human body was a work of art, each canvas unique on the outside yet strangely the same underneath. Roshinda had taught him that. Her art in those journals had only emphasised the beauty of the human body, which he was lucky enough to witness, retouch and help to flourish on a daily basis.

The only thing he couldn't even begin to fathom was the mind. Freya was the one making him wonder about that. *Her* mind, specifically. She'd been busy with Liv, adamant she'd sell the house, but remaining quiet about her decision to stay or go. The less she offered him, the more he seemed to want her. Why was it always that way for him? Why hadn't he walked away from her already, when he'd been down this pointless road before?

He'd asked himself this hundreds of times.

There was only one answer, really. Roshinda hadn't been the right one for him. But Freya was.

Ruben's face was a picture of relief. 'The operation was a success,' Lucas said, pulling off his mask and making his way down the hallway to where he was waiting. 'Anne Marie did so well, the stent will do its work nicely. All in all, it went smoothly.'

'Oh, man, thank you, thank you. I was getting worried.' His friend threw his arms around his shoulders—something he'd never ever done sober.

'She's in Recovery, she might be out for a while but she's safe and well, and your baby is going to be fine.' Lucas took the plastic seat next to Ruben. He was tired after such intense concentration under the harsh operating lights and his brain was a little frazzled but there was no time to get sleepy. He had somewhere to be pretty soon.

'I bet baby Oscar can't wait to meet us, and his new godfather,' Ruben said, letting out a huge sigh of relief next to him.

Lucas smiled, 'You chose the name Oscar.'

'We didn't want to name him till we knew…you know.'

Lucas put a hand to his shoulder. 'Oscar's a great name. Who's the godfather?'

'You are,' Ruben said, looking at him sideways. 'If that's something you think you might want to be.'

Lucas was touched. 'Man, I would love nothing more.'

'Lucas!'Joy poked her head through the doors. 'Dr Grey called just after you went into Theatre. She said she's terribly sorry, but something important came up.'

Lucas frowned up at her, unbuttoning the top of his scrubs. He wouldn't go into it with Ruben present as he didn't want to ruin the moment. He was going to be a godfather.

With everything he had planned for later still on track, he was trying not to think that it was looking increasingly likely that Freya-with-the-Wings really wouldn't be around to meet his new godson.

Freya and her mother had been talking and walking for the best part of five or six hours. After meeting at the house, and putting a brand-new Miami Vice magnet on the refrigerator, courtesy of Elise's last-minute airport shop, they'd taken advantage of the sun and made their way down cobbled streets, past parks and cafés, along canals and into Westerpark, where they'd sat on a bench, side by side.

At first, it was small talk about Freya's work, and Elise's trip to Miami, but as the nerves began to dissipate and she'd excused herself from her shift at the hospital, Freya was surprised to find talking to her mother was easier with every passing moment.

'I appreciate you coming straight over, when you're jet-lagged,' she said again.

'I just had a feeling somehow that if I didn't I'd miss the only opportunity I had to talk to you like this in person, just the two of us,' Elise admitted. 'I know I wasn't the best mother to you, growing up.'

'You made me who I am today' was all Freya could

think of to say to that. 'And that's not all bad, so some people say.' Of course, she was thinking of Lucas.

Her mother nudged her shoulder softly. Elise didn't look all that different from the last time she'd seen her. A few more lines around the eyes and mouth, but she looked well and happy. Something in her mother's smile and frown was exactly the same as what she'd seen in the mirror every day of her own life.

'I admit I didn't know what I was doing when I had you,' her mum said now, reaching for her hand. 'I was way too young, I was unprepared for motherhood and instead of enjoying you…us…and going with the flow, I chose to see myself as inadequate and I ended up pushing you away. It's a slippery slope when that happens. I thought I was giving you a better life by allowing your father to send you to that posh boarding school, but I should have kept you with me.'

'Maybe we're not so different,' Freya mused, watching a youth launch an old-fashioned kite into the sky.

'I never realised how far I had pushed you away until you left for America with Beatrice.'

When she turned to face her, Elise looked nothing short of regretful. Freya felt a pang of compassion. 'I was hurt,' Freya admitted, 'but I pushed you away too. After what Beatrice did to me, I just couldn't cope unless I had a plan of my own that no one could swoop in and take away from me. You know she married Johnny, right?'

'I did know that,' her mother said, shaking her head. She held Freya's hand over her knee. 'But America was good for you in the end. Look at all the experience it gave you. And there are some beautiful places there…'

They talked about their travels, and life, and love,

and by the time the after-work crowd started spilling from the park's bar onto the sun-flooded patios and grass, Freya realised her jet-lagged mother was yawning, struggling to stay awake. She also realised that for the first time in a very long time she felt completely at peace.

'You know, you can come and stay at the house in Weesp any time,' Elise said, when they were standing on the train platform at Centraal. 'I have a nice bedroom all made up…you and Liv can both come. Come now?'

'I can't. Not now. I have somewhere to be,' Freya said. Her mother had kept her talking so long she hadn't even found out how the operation on Anne Marie had gone. She owed Lucas a call. Better than that, she'd go over to his place. 'But thank you, Mum, that means a lot to me. I'm glad we had this chance to talk face to face.'

'Me too. More than you know, my beautiful daughter. I'm so proud of you.'

Freya was surprised when her mother reached out and pulled her close in a hug. She swore she heard Elise's voice break slightly, too, when she said goodbye.

She took the long walk towards Lucas's place, resisting the urge to call him on the way. She had a feeling the op had been a success, otherwise he would have tried to call her, or at least send her a message. He knew she'd taken her late shift off by now, because she'd told Reception, and she was taking a moment out to enjoy this new sense of peace and serenity.

Of course, one afternoon of talking didn't make up for a childhood spent feeling so alone, but she had to admit she had done some of the pulling away herself, maybe just as much as she'd been pushed. Oh, the stories she had told herself just to preserve her heart. Now she might actually have a chance at building a new relationship with her mother.

Lucas wasn't at the houseboat. Maybe he was still somewhere with Ruben, or his father, she thought absently.

Walking all the way home, she was positively floating. For once, everything felt good, great even. Who knew just a few hours in the sun with her mother, of all people, could cement such a feeling of belonging after all this time.

She stopped in front of the house. Prinsengracht looked beautiful in the late afternoon light and she had an epiphany. What if she stayed here? What if she didn't sell…for a while at least. Give it one more year, just to see what happened between her and Lucas? What if she did even better than that, and was completely honest about her growing feelings for him? There was no excuse now not to be around him. No excuse not to tell Lucas Van de Berg how much she…

Lucas.

He was in her house. She could see him clearly through the top upstairs window in the kitchen.

What was he doing inside?

There was someone with him. Liv, of course, back from wherever she'd gone. They were laughing together at something, as clear as day. Freya stood there motionless in shock and horror as she watched Liv place a hand lightly on Lucas's shoulder and point at something across the room. Lucas was laughing too, leaning very close to Liv, and she could see his silhouette shaking at something her sister was obviously saying. Lucas and Liv. A cold sweat had broken out on her forehead;

a new sense of foreboding. She had been here before, in this exact situation. Was this Johnny and Beatrice all over again?

Freya didn't hesitate. She turned on her heel and hurried back towards the train station.

CHAPTER TWENTY-ONE

'WHERE IS SHE?' Lucas was really worried now. 'She's not answering her phone.'

'Well, I can't call her, I have no phone at all,' Liv retorted. She was crouched on her haunches, placing the finishing touches to the wall stencils in the downstairs bedroom. Lucas had called for pizza, hung balloons, and now he just felt like a fool. Freya had gone completely AWOL.

'This isn't unlike her, you know,' Liv said, and Lucas swallowed a heavy sigh. 'I mean, I love my sister as much as you, but she's done this kind of thing before.'

'I know,' he said bluntly, leaving the room. He didn't want to be having this conversation with Liv, he wanted to speak to Freya. He stepped onto the balcony, trying to clear his head. First Freya had missed an important appointment, for personal reasons, but she hadn't said what, and now she was nowhere to be found. It had crossed his mind that maybe she'd simply left. Spread her wings and flown away, without even telling him she was going.

But something about that just didn't feel right. He knew her better than that; she knew *him*. She wouldn't do anything like what Roshinda had done, she wouldn't just leave, at least not without talking to him. And not without a very good reason. Unless she was really upset by something he'd done…like share the whole truth about what had happened with Roshinda and then inadvertently pile on the pressure for her to stay, and be something she wasn't.

'Lucas!' Liv called him back inside. She was holding something in her hands, a piece of tourist tat. A fridge magnet with the words 'Miami Vice' on it. 'Look what I just found on the fridge,' she said, holding it up. 'There's only one reason Freya would have put a Miami Vice magnet there.'

Hurrying to the house phone, she made a call. He listened to the hushed voice, then heard what sounded like a gasp. When she came back, Liv was pale.

'I phoned Mum's house and Freya was there. I spoke to her,' she said, raking a hand through messy hair. 'She said she came to the house and saw us both together in the window. I tried to tell her we weren't doing anything… But she's just so…' Liv made an *ugh* sound and turned to get her keys. 'I'll go and get her.'

'No,' he said, feeling his heart rate spike. 'I'll go.'

Driving to Weesp, still with no answer from Freya's switched-off phone, Lucas considered that the old him might have given in and acknowledged that she was as infuriatingly independent as they came. Deep down he knew he needed more from her, after what he had already been through. But half the time Freya didn't think she needed him. Not only that, she didn't even *trust* him… Why else would she have disappeared when she saw whatever it was she *thought* she saw him and Liv doing through the window?

She'd run to her mother's house, though, which

meant she was talking to her again, at least. Gritting his teeth, the city roads turned into countryside, and the trams became sheep, and he pulled up eventually just out of view of the house with the green shutters and thatched roof. He sat there a while, considering how he'd been at this crossroads before, and done nothing.

He'd made the mistake of not going after a woman he'd cared for once. After a while he'd come to realise it had been the right decision, but he wasn't letting this one get away so easily. Because this one he truly loved.

Freya felt terrible already for overreacting and hotfooting it all the way here, but her old defence mechanisms had kicked in hard after seeing Lucas and Liv so close together in the window. She hadn't told her mother what she thought she'd seen—it had taken her this long to get this far. Plus Liv had been adamant on the phone.

'He's crazy about you, Freya, and if you think I would do something like that to you, you're crazy too. I'm not Beatrice, and Lucas is not Johnny!'

Freya knew that was true. Regret and shame were making her feel queasy. 'What's happened?' her mother said, patting the sofa beside her.

Her mother had let her in, dressed in purple PJs, and Freya felt bad for keeping her up with her jet-lag, but she really hadn't seemed to mind. 'Is this about your heart surgeon? Liv mentioned him, by the way.'

Freya let out a deep sigh and sat down. 'I've just messed up,' she admitted, looking around the room at the easel, the piano covered in photos of her mum and Stijn's travels, the satisfied-looking black cat now draped on another chair in the window. 'I thought I caught him cheating on me but…well, it's not like I've given us a real chance to even be together. And I know I was imagining it.'

Her mother crossed her legs in her robe, pulling them up on the couch. 'Well, no one could blame you, after what happened with Beatrice. Let me see him. You can tell a lot about a man by his eyes, you know. Does he have trustworthy eyes?'

'I don't know, you tell me.' Half amused, Freya pulled up the photo on her phone that she'd taken at his parents' windmill. Zooming in on his handsome face, a pang in her stomach almost brought her to tears. She'd been avoiding his calls for the last hour, letting old habits creep back in without giving him the benefit of the doubt. She knew she'd overreacted, leaving so fast, running on impulse. Seeing them in the window together had been the ultimate trigger.

Back in the bar that time, Beatrice and Johnny had sprung apart when they'd seen her heading over with their drinks, but not before she'd spotted the look on her friend's face. Pain. Desire. Guilt. That had been weeks before she'd even caught them on the couch, making out in front of the window. It had made her feel sick for months, years even, knowing she'd failed to read the signs. She hadn't thought about that in a long time, not until she'd remembered seeing Liv's hand move over Lucas's in the cafeteria…and then seeing them touching in the window at the house. What were they even doing there together?

Her mother was still studying the photo on her phone, her brow furrowed.

'I know that woman, that's Mira. She's in my life drawing class. I bought her an elf when I went to Iceland. We have coffee sometimes, after class.'

'Are you serious? You know Lucas's mother?' Freya shook her head, studying the photo—which had led her here, in a way. Her mother put an arm around her and pulled her in, and to her surprise she leaned in for comfort. 'If he's anything like his mother, he's wonderful.'

Lucas had trustworthy eyes, too, she thought now; she'd known that the second she'd met him. Thousands of people put their trust in him every year, and *he* had put his trust in her, even knowing she might just run away, like his ex had. Like she had just done.

'I'm an idiot, aren't I?' she said with a groan, just as the doorbell made them both jump.

Lucas was dressed in a summer cotton shirt with tiny pineapples for buttons, dark blue jeans and bright green laces in his trainers. The picture of summer in Amsterdam, standing in her mother's doorway.

She watched him shake Elise's hand, and heard her mother mumble something about elves and Iceland, and drinks in the fridge, and then she excused herself. It was all a blur. Freya's heart was a hammer.

'I don't know what to say,' Lucas said, stepping towards her when they were alone. They met in the middle of the living room and the cat leapt from the chair and started curling round their legs.

'I'm sorry,' she said, reaching for him. 'I didn't mean to treat you like I don't trust you, or Liv. I just got…'

'Scared?'

He took her hands and then her face, fixing her with vivid blue, searching eyes, and she almost melted. 'You got scared that you might like me more than you planned to like someone here. Scared that you might want to stay in one place and pin *yourself* down for a

while, so you made up another story that would allow
you to leave again.'

Freya was so stunned she could barely answer.

'Am I right?' he said, holding her at arm's length.

'You are,' she conceded, in awe of how well he knew
her. Most men would have left her to her own devices by
now, deemed her a waste of time, yet here Lucas was,
because he saw past her emotional blocks and crashed
through all her walls, and he still wanted to be with her.

'Freya, you happen to be the most frustrating,
difficult—' he lowered his head to hers '—intoxicating,
infuriating...'

She smiled under his lips as he kissed her. 'You're
so many things but that's exactly why I love you. I
wasn't about to let you run away from me. I will never
do that,' he vowed.

He loved her? A new lease of life seemed to open itself up in front of her suddenly. 'But, Lucas, what were
you and Liv doing? I went to your place to find out
about the surgery on Anne Marie, and to tell you why
I couldn't make it this afternoon. My mum just showed
up from the airport!'

'I know, I figured that out, it's OK. You had no
choice, we were fine, it went well. I'm going to be a
godfather to that baby. And I'm going to be a damn
good one.'

'That's amazing news, I'm so happy for you.' Freya
wrapped her arms around him. She had no doubt he'd
be an incredible godfather, and maybe even father too.

What was she thinking? She was getting way ahead
of herself—which was most unlike her—but, still, she
could suddenly see it all in her mind's eye. She could
picture the kids running about that huge house, with

the dog, maybe more than one dog, like Anouk used to have.

He curled one big hand through her hair and kissed her again. This time she really did melt into him, so much so that she almost forgot she was in her mother's house. 'We can stay the night here, there's a spare room,' she started to say, but he was already leading her back to the door, back to the car. 'Where are we going?'

'You want to know what me and Liv were doing?' he said. 'You're going to have to come back to Amsterdam.'

'I can't believe you did all this.' Freya was standing in the kitchen with her hands over her mouth. He'd had to blindfold her, coming back to the house, but as soon as she'd seen the new mosaic floor tiles and newly fitted top-of-the-range appliances in the kitchen she had squealed in excitement.

'I love it all,' she was saying, trailing a balloon around with her across the new blue rug in the hallway and back again. 'How did you find time to do all this today without me knowing?'

He encircled his arms around her, breathing in her lily scent. 'Well, you were supposed to be at work on the late shift, but your mum ended up helping us too by keeping you busy, without her even knowing.'

Lucas had planned it all, and he'd hired a twelve-man team he knew would do the best job in the heritage house. The designer stove top, copper piping through the sink, the new wooden table big enough for dinner parties…he'd had them in all afternoon, working hard and fast to get the surprise ready in time. Liv had been only too happy to help.

'Did you do all this just so I wouldn't sell it? I mean, it's beautiful,' she said, running a hand along the polished old-school windmill tiles again. She smiled. 'Even these have scrubbed up well.'

'I did all this,' he said, sweeping her hair aside to kiss her neck, 'to give you the best chance of selling… but, yes, secretly I was hoping you'd want to live in it.'

Freya laughed, crossing with him to the window. 'I think Shadow and I will be very happy here,' she told him. His arms snaked around her waist as they took in the moon shining on the canal below. 'I can't thank you enough, Lucas.'

'It was your sister, too. I don't think she wants you to move very far away again either. She was talking about moving back here herself. You know, Freya, there are a lot of people who think this city is much better when you're in it.'

Freya leaned back into his chest and sighed in what he thought, for the first time, might be contentment. She'd taken Liv aside when they'd got back and he'd watched them hug it out. Liv hadn't been upset. He had a feeling Liv knew that Freya had a habit of creating reasons to push people away; maybe she'd even been expecting Freya to do it. Maybe he'd been expecting it too.

He was glad he'd gone after her anyway. He wouldn't have done that for anyone else…he never had before. Then again, he'd never met a woman like Freya before either.

'I love you, too, Lucas,' she said suddenly, as if she was reading his thoughts about her.

He froze behind her, wondering if his ears had deceived him. She turned in his arms then, looked up at him, slightly worried that he hadn't responded. 'Did you hear me?' she said, pressing her hands to his heart over his shirt.

'I heard you.' He felt a smile take over his entire face before he lifted her up and carried her to the new table. 'I think I'd better pin you here for a while, in case you change your mind,' he said, but she was already unbuttoning his shirt, pinning him to her with her own legs wrapped around him.

He made easy work of removing her top, smiling as he felt her warm hands trail up and down his back as he stood between her legs at the edge of the table.

'I was thinking, I've never been to Vietnam before. I'd like to come travelling with you…as long as Fred is being cared for, and I'm not gone too long at any one time. Because I can't keep putting my life on hold for ever. I'd rather live it with you.'

'We'll make it work,' she said, kissing him excitedly. 'I'd love nothing more, you and me in Vietnam for a while. As long as we can come home together afterwards.'

'Here is home, is it now?' he said teasingly. 'I never thought I'd see you willing to put your wings away.'

Freya grinned. 'I'm not putting them anywhere. But it's nice to know I'll aways have a safe place to land. Even nicer to know you might come places with me.'

Lucas just smiled and kissed her. He had so many ideas for places he wanted to take Freya Grey. But for now he would start in this kitchen.

EPILOGUE

One year later...

'I KNEW IT! I knew those tarot cards were right!' Liv was clapping her hands in front of the laptop so loudly that Freya had to turn the volume down on their video call. 'The cards showed a wedding was coming up, remember? I knew it would be yours! Congrats, you two, I always knew you were sickeningly perfect together!'

Lucas snaked one arm around Freya and she held her hand towards the screen again so Liv could get a close-up look at her ring. Liv peered closer in wonder at the sparkling diamond and Freya felt tears spring to her eyes again as the ocean lapped the sand gently outside the open door.

Lucas had proposed to her the night before on the moonlit deck of their luxury beach villa on a private beach in Koh Lanta. 'I was waiting for Thailand,' he said, dropping a kiss on the top of her head and making her heart swell. 'I would have proposed earlier this year, when we were in Vietnam, but the ring wasn't ready. It had to be just right, and we had to be in the right place.'

'It was worth the wait, but I would have said yes anywhere,' she told him, nestling into his shoulder against the headboard. 'Even in that rickety shack, that night the storm trapped us inside.'

Lucas grinned, no doubt remembering that passionate night on his first medical mission to Vietnam, when the howling winds and rain had ravaged the camp. 'How could I forget what you did when—?'

'Ew, guys, I'm still here!' Liv called Shadow over, and Freya sniggered. She'd almost forgotten they were on a video call. Liv was housesitting at Anouk's while they were on holiday. She loved looking after Shadow as much as Fred and Mira did.

Lucas's parents took the dog every other week. Shadow had helped give Fred a new reason to get up and go for long walks, instead of feeling down about not being able to drive. He was stable for now in the family home, and Freya loved their Sunday lunches in Weesp, when she and Lucas would join them, and Elise and Steijn, to swap travel stories and remind Fred of all the meals he still loved.

'How's the new job going?' Freya asked her half-sister. Liv had left the UK and her ex firmly behind and had taken an accounting job for a PR firm in Amsterdam. Conveniently she'd also taken a studio apartment just around the corner.

'Better than my cooking,' Liv said now. 'Mum's coming here this afternoon with Mira and I promised to make a cake from some Icelandic recipe, but it's a bit…er…'

She walked their video call to the kitchen and Freya felt a pang of homesickness suddenly as she saw the beautiful space Lucas had redone, with Liv's help, just over a year ago. Who'd have thought back then that Anouk's house would come to feel so much like home to her, or that she would be engaged to the most handsome heart surgeon in the Netherlands…even the entire world?

They'd been on a medical mission and several holidays since she'd extended her contract, so she had the best of both worlds now. Roots and wings. She'd never been so happy…except when Liv used every pan in their kitchen to create another disaster.

Liv panned over to her cake. It was a flat blob of brown in the bottom of a cake mould. Lucas let out a snort and Liv sighed comically, before dropping it on the floor for Shadow to eat. The dog wolfed it up hungrily while they all laughed. 'Make sure he gets every crumb,' Lucas ordered.

Since Lucas had sold the houseboat and moved in, he'd become chief homemaker, much to Freya's amusement. He took huge pride in keeping things in order, and their dinner parties were highly anticipated amongst their friends and families.

Sometimes she swore she could feel Anouk's warm presence looking over them all fondly as they cooked and drank wine, and played games, and filled the place with laughter, just like she'd wanted. What would she make of their engagement? Freya wondered. Would she burst into tears of delight, like her mother had this morning?

When they'd hung up the call to Liv, they walked barefoot hand in hand along the empty beach as the moon beamed down on pure white sands. When they stopped to put their feet in the ocean she looked at the trail of footprints they were leaving behind on the shore. His were so much bigger than hers, but together, side by side, they left a path of perfection.

'One day there will be another set of footprints to go with those,' he said, wrapping his arms around her from behind as the breeze whipped up her hair. 'They'll be tiny, and they'll go everywhere we go.'

'A boy or a girl?' she wondered out loud. She'd often thought about the children they might have. It used to feel like an impossibility, but now the thought filled her with excitement.

'A girl, then a boy.'

Freya turned in his arms, smiling. 'Oh, really? You have it all planned out, do you?'

'Either way, I promised Ruben a playmate for Oscar. You wouldn't want to let a friend down, would you?'

'No, sir,' she said, smiling at the thought of Lucas's godson, whom he adored more than life itself.

'I can't do this alone,' Lucas said. 'I'm going to need your help getting started.' He tightened his hands on her waist and urged her closer by her hips in her bikini and sarong. 'We can start right now if you like.'

She laughed, looping her arms around his shoulders. 'You wouldn't want me pregnant on our wedding day, would you, Dr Van de Berg? What would people say?'

Lucas chuckled softly, and his lips curved into the kind of smile that still sent butterflies flocking to her insides and made her feel blessed to be alive. 'I think they'd say you were radiant, magnificent, *ongelooflijk*.'

'Well, I'm not making any promises when it comes to the sex…'

'Damn, is that how it's going to be?'

'I meant the sex of the baby.' She laughed, urging him further into the shallows. 'I think we already have the other kind of sex sorted, don't you?'

'I think there's always room for improvement,' he

teased, matching her licentious grin. With that, he picked her up in his strong arms and carried her into the water.

* * * * *

MILLS & BOON

Coming next month

ISLAND FLING WITH THE SURGEON
Ann McIntosh

"I'm going in," Zach said, after he'd arranged the cooler and towels to his specifications and adjusted the umbrella for maximum shade. When he pulled off his shirt, Gen bit back a groan of pleasure, seeing his bare torso in all its glory for the first time. "Are you coming?"

"Sure," Gen said, her heart going into overdrive as she stood up and unzipped her cover-up, aware of Zach standing just a step or two away, waiting for her.

Oh, she hoped he felt the same way looking at her as she did at the sight of those magnificent pecs and his firm, ridged abdomen.

She didn't look at him as she shrugged the sleeveless dress off her arms and stepped out of it, before bending to pick it up and fold it carefully.

Then, with the long strides she'd learned during her pageant days, she walked past him toward the surf.

He wasn't beside her as she ran the last few steps into the water before doing a shallow dive beneath an incoming wave.

When she came up and turned back toward the beach, wiping the salt water from her face, he was still standing where she'd left him. When their gazes collided, despite the distance between them a shiver of longing ran up her spine.

Then he was in motion, not running but following

her with decisive, intentional strides. He didn't dive into the water, but kept wading until he was standing just inches from where she was bobbing in the water.

"You're trying to drive me bonkers, aren't you?"

It was little better than a growl, and her nipples tightened at his tone, while her core turned molten and needy.

"Is it working?" she asked, holding his gaze, trying to figure out if the gleam there was anger, annoyance or something else entirely.

"Yes," he snapped. "But this…" He waved his hand between them. "This is supposed to be make-believe."

She shrugged lightly. "It doesn't have to be. I'm horribly attracted to you, so if you want to change the rules, we can negotiate."

"Consider this my opening bid," he said, pulling her close, placing his hands on either side of her face and kissing her as though he'd never stop.

Continue reading
ISLAND FLING WITH THE SURGEON
Ann McIntosh

Available next month
www.millsandboon.co.uk

COMING SOON!

We really hope you enjoyed reading this book.
If you're looking for more romance, be sure to
head to the shops when new books are
available on

Thursday 22nd
July

To see which titles are coming soon, please visit
millsandboon.co.uk/nextmonth

MILLS & BOON

LET'S TALK

Romance

For exclusive extracts, competitions
and special offers, find us online:

facebook.com/millsandboon

@MillsandBoon

@MillsandBoonUK

Get in touch on 01413 063232

For all the latest titles coming soon, visit
millsandboon.co.uk/nextmonth